Praise for

Inappropriation

"A witty, energetic send-up of the current pieties surrounding racial and sexual identity. . . . It goes without saying that *Inappropriation* is irreverent, but this is a loving, sisterly sort of ridicule, spoofing the absurdities of the very young and very woke." —*Wall Street Journal*

"*Inappropriation* skewers just about every societal and literary convention you can think of, making it one of the most subversive coming-of-age stories out there. . . . Go along for the ride with Ziggy, it'll be worth the fiery journey." —*Nylon*

"A lively, satirical coming-of-age tale." —*People*

"[Freiman] has the same thick, buttermilky compassion for her readers as she does for her characters, sour and full of saggy lumps. She burlesques them—and you—but only because she identifies. . . . Darkly funny. . . . Nimble and pert, parkouring disrespectfully across the suburban mall of the English language." —*BookForum*

"Intelligent and has its finger on the zeitgeist of the Instagram and Tumblr generation." —*New York Times Book Review*

"A laugh-out-loud satirical debut. . . . A mash-up of *Mean Girls* meets Kathy Acker, with a dose of *Seinfeld*." —*The Australian*

"Stellar. . . . Freiman perfectly depicts the timeless awkwardness of growing up with the more modern awkwa
on social media, and thus growing
This is a very strong first novel from

—

T0182256

"A bold and heady coming-of-age tale with a biting sense of humor."

—*Library Journal*

"Lexi Freiman is a savage writer, hilarious and brilliant, and in *Inappropriation*, she has reframed the traditional coming-of-age story, tackling it with irreverence and acid wit. This is a daring book, thrillingly of our moment."   —Emma Cline, author of *The Girls*

"*Inappropriation* is sly and risky, but also sweet, a wickedly funny machine built to make us laugh and think. The comic novel has a bold new voice in Lexi Freiman, and she could not have come along at a better time."   —Sam Lipsyte, author of *The Fun Parts: Stories* and *The Ask*

"*Inappropriation* reads like a modern-day *Gulliver's Travels*, exploring the psyche of a generation searching for a better world in all the wrong places. Wry and funny and unabashedly provocative, Lexi Freiman is a gimlet-eyed satirist of the cultural morasses and political impasses of our times."   —Alexandra Kleeman, author of *Intimations*

"*Inappropriation*'s crackling, electric prose is an uncomfortable joyride. You'll laugh out loud and squirm and wince, but you sure won't put it down. This novel is an original treasure—sentence by sentence, there is just no book like it."   —Alissa Nutting, author of *Made for Love*

"*Inappropriation* unpacks and skewers our confused age in the guise of a winning and authentic coming-of-age story. Only read Lexi Freiman's assured and enormously enjoyable debut novel if you want to discover an incisive new voice full of dark, merciless wit."

—Steve Toltz, author of *Quicksand* and *A Fraction of the Whole*

Inappropriation

Inappropriation

LEXI FREIMAN

An Imprint of HarperCollinsPublishers

INAPPROPRIATION. Copyright © 2018 by Lexi Freiman. All rights reserved. No part of this book may be used or reproduced in any manner whatsoever without written permission except in the case of brief quotations embodied in critical articles and reviews. For information, address HarperCollins Publishers, 195 Broadway, New York, NY 10007.

HarperCollins books may be purchased for educational, business, or sales promotional use. For information, please email the Special Markets Department at SPsales@harpercollins.com.

A hardcover edition of this book was published in 2018 by Ecco, an imprint of HarperCollins Publishers.

FIRST ECCO PAPERBACK EDITION PUBLISHED 2019.

Designed by Michelle Crowe
Emojis in text by Carboxylase/Shutterstock, Inc.

The Library of Congress has catalogued a previous edition as follows:

Names: Freiman, Lexi, author.
Title: Inappropriation : a novel / Lexi Freiman.
Description: First edition. | New York : Ecco, [2018]
Identifiers: LCCN 2017042690 (print) | LCCN 2017057307 (ebook) | ISBN 9780062699756 (ebook) | ISBN 9780062699732 (hardcover)
Subjects: LCSH: Self-realization in women—Fiction. | Identity (Psychology)—Fiction. | BISAC: FICTION / Literary. | FICTION / Coming of Age. | FICTION / Satire. | GSAFD: Humorous fiction. | Satire.
Classification: LCC PR9619.4.F785 (ebook) | LCC PR9619.4.F785 I53 2018 (print) | DDC 823/.92—dc23
LC record available at https://lccn.loc.gov/2017042690

ISBN 978-0-06-269974-9 (pbk.)

19 20 21 22 23   10 9 8 7 6 5 4 3 2 1

For Mum and Dad

PART ONE

Chapter 1

Celebrities sent their daughters to the girls' school. It was the only one with harbor views and an Olympic-sized swimming pool, and the foreign movie stars filming on Sydney's white beaches favored it for their itinerant young. Ziggy's first day at Kandara Girls happened to coincide with the American Heartthrob Hysteria Event. The diminutive superstar had come to watch his daughter in the musical adaptation of *Little Women*. He had snuck in through the auditorium's rear entrance, witnessed by two Kandara seniors who immediately alerted half of the high school. By curtain call, over one hundred girls had massed outside the auditorium's emergency exit. Ziggy slunk around this giddy hive; in their rapture, the girls kept making sudden, intimate eye contact with her. This urgent inclusiveness was how she had always imagined the apocalypse, and Ziggy gorged herself—meeting gazes with smiles and whimpers of excitement. But when the elfin actor finally emerged, furtively from the fire door, Ziggy's peers just stood there, gawking in eerie paralysis. Ziggy also felt immobilized by the grave sense of significance. The actor slid down his shades and nodded politely for the girls to clear a path. In a miracle of restraint and decorum, the sea of pink tartan slowly parted.

The girls followed the action hero from a short distance, right through the grounds and out to his street-parked BMW. Ziggy was conveyed by the silent swarm, shuffling in ecstatic fugue behind the iconic actor. She felt pulled by primal, subterranean forces and also pressure to keep quiet about it. As their ghostly march gained momentum, Ziggy saw the sweat beginning to bead on the man's forearms. He made it to his car, slipped quickly into the driver's seat, and activated central locking. Now safe, he glanced up and gave the girls a magnanimous wave. Which was when Ziggy's cohort abandoned their saintly discretion.

Two girls split off from their pack and rushed toward the vehicle. They smashed up against the car, screaming *We love you!* and pounding on the glass. Ziggy trembled, lust and dread monstering inside her, as three more girls flew off after them, saddling the BMW's hood then waving maniacally at the windshield. The third surging of girls thrust Ziggy along on its squealing tide as they ambushed the car's rear windows. Pressed against the trunk, Ziggy found herself beside two others, making kissy faces at the man's impossibly thick swoosh of hair. On all sides, the windows darkened with gaping mouths; the eminent American frozen in eye-popping horror, until a meaner sound cut above the shrieks. The PE teacher came bolting toward them like a brick in a tennis skirt, her whistle slicing right through the girls' bewitchment. Ziggy drew back with the rest of her peers, and freed the little man from his parking spot. The episode had both thrilled and horrified her, sensing for the first time that her body was part of a much grosser entity. She didn't even know the celebrity's name.

SET IN A VERDANT POUF of hillside, Kandara shines Pavlova white against the dirty, eucalyptus green. In the 1920s, lisping alcoholic Francophile Lady Flora Tivoli had purchased the convent on the cliff for her sortie into female education. Whimsically sloshed, she'd noted how the chapel holed into the cliffside and named her school Kandara, the Sanskrit word for *concavity*. One lawn planes to the harbor's staired descent, and the other runs right to the sea cliff's ragged drop, announcing the nation's coast like a hangnail. Kandara girls wear bright rose-and-emerald colored tunics; the boys leering from bus windows catcall them "watermelons." The girls don't mind. Watermelons are pretty and summery and sweet and everybody fucking loves them.

Ziggy Klein transferred to Kandara from a coed school because her psychotherapist mother preaches female empowerment and is the boss of Ziggy's dad. But the girls' school is no longer run by nuns pushing a subtle, domestic insurgency through classes in watercolor and embroidery. In the 1980s, the school board removed the sisters and built a three-story gymnasium, installing acres of Astroturf on which the girls could scrum out their teenage ire. And just in time: the limping feminism of the late 1970s had been rebooted in the form of female shoulder pads, and the young women of tomorrow required team sports and war cries for their emancipation; which would all be fine, if Ziggy's mum thought women should be allowed to wear sneakers. Ruth Klein says second-wave feminism made women butch and third-wave made them self-loathing and now the Feminine must be reclaimed along with the murky "art of seduction." But Ziggy thinks the rugby players at her new school look very empowered. Watching the senior A team from the oval's outer reaches, Ziggy observes a new species of hypermuscular Anglo-Saxonette. Even the cradling motion that precedes each ball toss has a casual, unmaternal deftness that Ziggy finds hard to square with the femininity sermonized by her mother. The rugby players move with an embodied ease that makes them seem more solid than the other girls. To Ziggy, the Senior As have the sharp presence of cartoon characters: there is no mystery, no inner weakness—none of the attributes she equates with that dreaded term "feminine vulnerability." She can't imagine these girls slunk under the hairy pits of proprietary males.

From downfield, a burst of tan legs and pom-poms now comes pinwheeling toward them. Watching the cheerleaders' sequined tennis skirts dance in the sun, Ziggy sees her mother's feminism on full display. Ruth says girls are allowed to wear princess dresses and the color pink and eventually lipstick and Wonderbras and high heels. Beauty is a woman's essence, and anything required to accentuate its outer manifestation is her birthright. The cheerleaders ooze a different kind of confidence. Ziggy watches one of them huff toward the rugby players then fling a pom-pom onto the field.

"Oi, Edwina!" she yells at the largest girl. "Quit looking up our skirts!"

Edwina chucks the pom-pom back. "You wish, skank."

Ziggy feels disappointed. On Kandara's same-sex campus, it seems a gendered ecosystem has emerged. The rugby players are just proxy men while the real girls are cheerleaders. That afternoon, Ziggy opts out of team sports altogether—citing her eczema as evidence of a grass allergy. There aren't many

Jews at Kandara, so the administration doesn't challenge the stereotype.

Ziggy quickly learns that the social stratification of her new school is far more complex and sinister than she first imagined. At the bacterial bottom of this food chain are the big-boned unpretty—hunchbacked by the shame of it; girls with lazy eyes and facial hair; all the moley, birthmarked, bowlegged, lisping, erratically sobbing, suspected lesbian and cat-molesting creatures unfit for boyfriends. And the impoverished scholarship students. This motley group receives the avoidant pity of unsalvageable spinsters; Ziggy assumes she slots in here. Above these girls sit the brilliant Asians, who are presumed virgins and suffer a constant stream of pens and erasers to their ponytails, especially on test days. Ziggy hopes their weekends are rich with friendship and adventure. Then come the cool, homework-averse Asians, who hide behind heavy makeup and an air of disaffection. They are both sexy and cute in a perfect ratio that Ziggy's own slight form fails to achieve. She covets their straight noses and smooth, hairless arms. Compared to her Jewish school, Kandara has an abundance of Asians and a softly pervasive racism. But these boyfriended ones are driven around in the usual blur of steel and smoothie cups—granting them vassal status within Kandara's social kingdom.

Just above them are the boarders, who dress in men's jeans, boat shoes, and blazers. Their administrated orphanhood has robbed these girls of aesthetic style and glamorous biography. They all play sport. It is assumed the boarders come from happy households with cheery, alcoholic parents who buy them horses, hoping they'll return one day to Dubbo or Mudgee as country doctors and attorneys. The boarders are uncosmopolitan: culturally homogenous, socially regressive, and operating outside the centralized sexual economy. But Ziggy was wrong to doubt the rugby players' wider female appeal; they are only macho for the purpose of intraschool sports. Because these girls get subhumanly smashed at weekly barn dances—returning to the city with grass-stained pant seats and tales of tampons finger-banged to emergency rooms—they still occupy the outer suburbs of Kandara's sprawling metropolis. Now Ziggy notices their girly anachronism: those bright ribbons they wear in their ponytails have a priss made for frisking on blue moonlit beds of hay.

Next come that broad caste of attractive, urban high-achiever who arrive at school with hickeys or blow-job lockjaw or just the vacant look of sexual daydream, replaying the luscious hurt of rabbit sex with a random boy. Some of these girls are Asian, many play sport and dress like wealthy farmers, but as long as they don't live on campus, even these pseudo-boarders are included in grade ten's sexually active, civic majority.

And perched at the top of an inhospitable, icy peak are the Cates. One of whom is called Fliss. The Cates are old money and old mansions and ancient values, and these things have serious cachet in a young country. They fraternize with older boys and have access to a society with social pages—an old-school virality that gives their blond auras a golden glow. Cate Lansell-Jones and Kate Fairfax kindly include Felicity Kunchai-Wells in their holy trinity because her pretty, "perfectly symmetrical" face has been gracing kids' clothing catalogs since Mrs. Kunchai-Wells could wrangle her from a stroller, and because "Eurasians are seriously the new Kate Moss." Fliss is nicer than the Cates—she never bullies her peers or laughs at their pimples. To her friends, Fliss's moral protest seems to register only as adorable squeaky sounds, which they just find cute and so pet her like a handbag dog. The Cates attribute Fliss's sweetness to her Thai heritage. Every summer Cate's family holidays in Phuket, and she says Thais are the nicest fucking people in the world, considering how many of them seriously have to be prostitutes.

Cate Lansell-Jones is the most popular girl in their year. Buxom, doll-faced; her farts are the whispered whips of shuttle-cocks. Everyone knows Cate popped her cherry in a pink canopy bed with a boyfriend who loves her. Her buxom, doll-faced mother brought them French toast in the morning, while Cate and Toby announced their sleepover on social media. Everyone knows Susan Lansell-Jones ("Suze," to the girls) parted Cate's pink curtains to let the sun warm the sheepskin for their toes.

Kate Fairfax is also a pre-PC Disney princess from a time when girls aspired to rescue-by-prince narratives and the companionship of songbirds. Kate keeps her lovebirds, Ansel and El-gort, in a cage in the year-ten common room—terrorizing the whole grade with shushes when her blankie bedtimes their little hanging prison. She is taller and leaner than Cate, with a severe cheekboned beauty that people say could probably model, or at least host a travel show. Kate has no known aspirations but walks with the catwalk swagger of a girl universally envied.

The Cates have their own lexicon to communicate complex cultural ideas. There is *yaysian* for anything Asian that is too threateningly adorable: "Those polka-dot pore strips are yay-sian." And *sannies*, an abbreviation of *sanitary pad*, which applies to dumpy girls who refuse to go swimming or wear leggings for athletics. But most of the Cates' intellectual energy is directed toward the sexification of the school uniform. Kandara girls have to wear straw sun hats and knee-high socks with shapeless tunics, and ever since year seven, the Cates have been refining workable alternatives. You can raise the hem on your skirt and pull your socks above the knee so that they resemble hookers' or Fuck Me boots. Shirts can be unbuttoned down to the laced cups of a black bra—made more alluring by a plunging gold cross (options include a sexy goth choker-cross or one that grazes the cleavage). Earrings are outlawed but clear plastic studs are permitted to keep holes open, and these can be worn in subtle shades of pink to match French manicures and the elastic bands between braces. Layering your hair undermines the eel-slick, sexless regulation ponytails; fringes hood eyes; and bold edges build architecture into cheekbones. And everyone, including the Asians, should obviously straighten their hair.

Much of the Cates' pedagogy exists in visual form online. Ziggy spends a lot of time on Kate Fairfax's Instagram. This is a place of white doves, frangipani flowers, and yoga platitudes. It is selfie-heavy and dense with Ansel and Elgort. Kate strives to project a sense of ethereal ecstasy—of birds in flight, feathers opalescent under golden sunrays; the maxim "happy girls are pretty girls." Instagram seems specifically designed for a crisp, WASP aesthetic. Ziggy can't imagine what she could share. The way a radiant sunset catches the down on her side-face? An after-school snack of whitefish salad? Still, she doubts that any of the Randalls boys actually come to this white, fluffy place to jerk off. Kate's daily struggle for the perfect pictorial story has to be lost on these boys. Or at least severely misinterpreted. Like decorating a house with delicate bunting before the demolition party. How do the Cates really feel after they spend two hours on makeup then let a boy jizz in their hair?

Despite Ziggy's misgivings, it is clear that these girls have achieved societal domination. Their feminine propaganda campaign is powerful on social media, but they also have a keen understanding of follow-through in the physical realm. Their digital efforts appear to aim toward a social event carved into the calendar and the collective heart of all Kandara girls. The year-ten formal is the Cates' Nuremberg Rally and a chance for all their virtual brainwashing to manifest in resplendent chiffon and blow-dry. Daily, Ziggy overhears her peers planning outfits and pre-drinks parties around an event slated for eleven months' time. The Cates have designed themselves an edifying evening, but so have all the lesser creatures of their universe. There are, it appears, alternate ways to shine at the year-ten formal. If you are a C-minus average Asian, you can bring your boyfriend with the Vietnamese gang tattoos and have him do wheelies in the valet parking lot. If you are a boarder, you can sew your own cocktail dress and attend as a group of Stepford Wives plastered on gin and tonics. In the first week of her Kandara education, it is clear to Ziggy that the formal is a kind of coming-out ceremony for all the girls—popular, pariah, and everything in between.

Except for Ziggy, who is what adults generously call "small" for fifteen. The zaftig fellow Jews at her old school called her a Holocaust survivor. In her final yearbook, getting sentimental, they cushioned it to "cute." But Ziggy knows "cute" is worthless without sexual appeal, and the doughy puff of her cheeks, her buggy eyes, and slim, unsensual lips all confirm its absence. Ziggy has a defiant center-part, which people love to draw attention to: fingering the symmetrical sheets of her blow-dry and saying, "Peace, Man." *Peace, Man,* she says back, giving them the sign then flipping it when they are no longer looking. Ziggy has internalized Peaceman. He shuffles around the dense museum of her inner life, dodging abstract statuary. His is the anemic voice she hears leave her mouth whenever Ruth forces her to talk about feelings—"I'm *fine*," whines the craven avatar—buying time until the sob in Ziggy's throat dissolves. Peaceman is probably just trying to protect Ziggy from her mother's obvious biological weakness.

At her old school, Ziggy had been somewhat of a pariah. The classic story of a charismatic leader sullied by minor corruption. Ziggy had at one time been the most popular girl in grade six—a talented illustrator of horse bodies and eyeballs, she had ascended to class captain using her natural charm and some light bullying. At the height of her power, she had even acquired an albino boy-minion, happy to collect her canteen sandwiches and clear the center of a coveted lunch bench. Then, away on a long weekend skiing trip, Ziggy had designated Rachel Katz the new leader of their group (because her brother had behavioral problems and was probably headed to public school, poor Rachel), which had created a safe space for mutiny. Returning from the ski fields, Ziggy was deposed and began her descent into a three-year social purgatory. During this time, there had been bright moments of near-acceptance; her Bat Mitzvah disco was one such unexpected triumph (thanks in large part to the Maypole dance devised by her mother). But Ziggy never again felt the snug fit of a loving clique walking to either side of her. Never had an inbox full of messages or two girls fight over the bus seat next to hers. Instead, Ziggy has withdrawn into imaginative games, elaborate and historical, closer in tone to punishing tests of survival. The mise-en-scène is clearly borrowed from her maternal grandmother. What gets Ziggy's adrenal glands going is undeniably the Holocaust.

Her favorite game involves an onion, a bottle of vinegar, and a sympathetic Nazi. Before her family were sent to Bergen-

Belsen, Ziggy's grandmother spent much of the war hiding in her uncle's barn just outside of Budapest. She has told Ziggy about the games she played, imagining at every hour of the day what Zsa Zsa Gabor might be doing as a new American émigré. Her grandmother could also recall the morning she and her older cousin, Andrea, were questioned in the street by two Nazis, and how Andrea had entertained them with a long, intricate story about her pet, Spinoza, a wild hare found by their town's philosopher hermit who drunkenly conveyed the creature to their household, ironically declaring it the Easter bunny. Ziggy's grandmother relayed this story often and with verve, channeling the famed charisma of precocious Andrea. She claimed the Nazis had been charmed by the clever young Jewess, and momentarily restored to their former humanity. Ziggy has never questioned the veracity of her grandmother's anecdote. Maybe because she likes it too much. The story hints at something opaque she senses about men and women, narrative and empathy. It dissolves the dense sick Ziggy feels at the mention of the word *Holocaust*, drilling a hole through the gray haze of skeletons and bone ash to a specific moment, bizarre and human that—thanks to the chutzpah of a very special little girl—seems to reverse the irreversible.

Nearly every afternoon, Ziggy takes her unappetizing victuals into the bathroom closet and pretends she is an SS officer's secret captive—forced to distract the Nazi with interesting personal anecdotes until the Allies invade. Usually she repeats the harrowing things overheard in her living room, where Ziggy's mother runs her women's workshops. Every kind of female suffering is represented here, but mostly Ziggy appropriates the sexual abuse stories. When she makes the SS officer weep, he tosses Ziggy a few fingers of onion skin; when he laughs she gets a small capful of vinegar. It is enlargening to feel other people's feelings. Or maybe it shrinks the world. Either way, Ziggy is good at it. She can describe a stranger's pain without crying, and under extreme duress. She can joke about incest with a Schick razor pressed to her throat. Which is kind of how she meets Tessa and Lex.

THE FRIDAY AFTER THEY BURY the celebrity vehicle under their skirts, the grade ten culprits are issued a two-tiered punishment. First they are made to handwrite formal apologies, and then they are all marched down to the ghoulish green stalls of sick bay, where the school nurse is waiting to jab them with HPV. It is obvious to Ziggy that the vaccination will be administered too late for most of year ten, as sexually active members of a high-risk demographic. Ziggy overhears the Cates in line ahead of her discussing the ethics of compulsory immunization. Their argument consists mainly of the fear that a dose of active virus might give them genital warts.

"Toby's only slept with one other girl, and she's in the Dutch royal family, so, like, seriously, he doesn't have diseases."

The other girls agree with Cate that none of their boyfriends could possibly be carrying the STD. In a fury of indignation, Kate Fairfax even calls her father, and for fifteen minutes there is a chaotic hiatus while nurses run between the rooms, holding out cordless phones and giving moral critique with their eyebrows. Then Kate's father is back in the palm of her hand, cooing apologies from the phone speaker. He has failed to abort the proceedings. The head nurse reenters and summons the first girl. The mass immunization will go on as planned.

Ziggy doesn't mind getting vaccinated. It makes her feel that sex might actually be imminent. That the teachers have somehow missed the fact of her prepubescent body, that they believe teenage boys are eager to give her STDs. Ziggy hasn't yet had her period, and she is both frightened by and covetous of menstruation. At her old school, Ziggy watched the other girls swaddling their swollen bellies like tiny, light-sensitive marsupial pets, moaning and pill-popping and flopping theatrically about. She thinks periods are disgusting. Ziggy knows the hot, animal whiff of her mother's sanitary products breathing in the bathroom bin. There is something both deathly and too alive in that fleshy stench.

The summer before starting at Kandara, Ziggy had spent a long afternoon with frumpy and morose Miriam Rosenburg, or "the Blob," as she was affectionately called. With the internet down, the two social outcasts found themselves in a strange, slightly hysterical boredom on the living room floor. Then, as if to embrace their outlier status more fully, the pair decided that witchcraft might be fun, and set off through the house— collecting organic matter for a gnarly brew. They'd scraped up Ziggy's father's nail clippings, plucked parental pubic hair from the bathtub, and then, in a frenzy of revulsion, Ziggy filched the pruned frankfurter of her mother's used tampon. The girls took their bounty out to the garden, and incanting some half-remembered mumbo jumbo from a movie about black magic and aerobic sex in tartan skirts, they blazed the pyre. Watching the flames, Ziggy had felt a violent euphoria—as if she had destroyed periods or at least severely punished them. Ziggy hates menses because hers hasn't yet come. Because that elusive spotting in her underwear somehow confirms that she will never fit in with the other girls.

Slumped on the nurse's waiting bench, Ziggy is roused from her neo-pagan reverie by the vicious trills of furtive bitching. It is Tessa, the pale, pudgy girl whose red bun perches on her head in chopstick-fixed eccentricity. Ziggy remembers Tessa from the American celebrity's car. How she smooched the glass then grinned dementedly at Ziggy. She has also seen Tessa smashing around the school corridors with a very gorgeous, brown-skinned girl called Lex. Just that morning she'd watched them ram into the swimming captain then brazenly stare the bigger girl down. Peering around discreetly, Ziggy sees Tessa and Lex behind her, huddling in sultry animus against the popular clique. Tessa draws out a complicated metaphor that places the Cates comatose in the ICU. Something about the relentless tube-feeding of consumer culture that is then metabolized and shat back out into the original feeding tubes. Ziggy is pretty sure catheters don't work this way, but she likes the gist, how gisty Tessa is.

"They want to be the *Real Housewives of Sydney* because of an algorithm," says Tessa.

"And because their mothers actually are the *Real Housewives of Sydney*," adds Lex.

"One day they'll wake up from their mothers' wish fulfillment and murder their own children."

The two girls continue their character assassinations, claiming Kate's blond highlights and golden tan and every staged snapshot of sun-filtered joy are attempts to seem in love with life and at one with nature.

"Kate thinks she's some kind of Eastern Suburbs sex-yogi," says Tessa. "But she's a Northern Beaches westie, and drinking Breezers on a paddle board is not the same as meditation."

Despite her geographical confusion, Tessa's psycho-spiritual commentary sounds like the kind Ziggy was raised on. But better. In the voice of her own generation. With scrumptious anecdotes about Kate Fairfax falling off the back of a speedboat.

Ziggy would diagnose the Cates as delusional and repressed—something she knows all about from her mother's therapy groups. The Cates have just convinced themselves they like to sunbake all day on boat decks for blond boys with no hair on their arms. To Ziggy, the whole enterprise sounds vaguely anti-Semitic. She twists around in her seat.

"I think Freud would say they only have sex to come boast about it at school."

Tessa makes a polite chin-tilt of interest. "You mean the reality principle?"

Ziggy isn't sure. Her mother often mixes Freud with her old guru from the Indian sex cult. She nods noncommittally. "Or the blond boy fetish could just be their own narcissism or even the incest taboo if the Cates secretly want to do it with their brothers?"

Lex giggles, but Tessa looks unconvinced. "Have you read Freud?"

Ziggy scrambles. "Yes, but personally, I'm on the fence about civilization. I mean, I don't think progress necessarily causes discontent. All my mum got from being a hippie was a love of ponchos."

Now both girls laugh and lean toward her in sweet, intimate congress. Ziggy has been comic at the expense of her mother's dignity, and though she feels her conscience pinch, the exploitation proves fruitful. The girls want to know more. So Ziggy tells them about the commune—the group therapy and maroon jumpsuits and how, when the whole thing imploded, all the Northern Europeans ended up on the east Australian coast, dealing ecstasy to backpackers. When she starts describing the sexual awakening workshops, Tessa interrupts with a concern. "Do you think the sex was all consensual?"

"I think so," says Ziggy. "There were lots of Germans, so everything was pretty well controlled."

The two girls exchange a glance. "You're Jewish, right?" asks Tessa.

Ziggy nods uneasily. "Why?"

"Just checking that you can make that kind of generalization." Her eyes flit again to Lex. "We're not really into excluding people."

"I wasn't trying to exclude the Germans," Ziggy bumbles, "I think control is good if used for the right reasons."

Tessa squints at her sternly. "Have you read 'A Cyborg Manifesto'?"

Ziggy has only really read Anne Frank and the Brontës. Science fiction seems kind of babyish. She shakes her head. Tessa holds out her arm. The skin is a waxy pink that makes it look slightly swollen. Then, with disorienting shock, Ziggy realizes the arm is a prosthetic. Her heart squeezes, but she senses sympathy is the wrong response.

"She's a cyborg," Lex says plainly.

"I'll send you a link to the essay," says Tessa. "It talks about how we're all transhuman because of our dependence on technology, which is good because it means you don't have to totally submit to the patriarchy. Cyborgs are part machine, part organism, so they don't have dads."

"She was basically writing about iPhones in 1984," Lex adds, her voice sparkly.

"Who was?"

"Donna Haraway," says Tessa. "She's cool. She really hates hot girls."

Ziggy's skin tingles. *Donna Haraway*. Even her name is like something speeding off into a distant future.

"Cyborgs identify as 'women of color,'" Tessa continues. "Because 'women of color' is the only category that doesn't exclude any of the excluded."

Ziggy sees a flash of agitation in Lex's eyes, but the actual woman of color quickly recovers. "You need to identify all the exclusion," she explains, "before you can create a system that's fair to everybody."

"So who gets to be a cyborg?" asks Ziggy.

"If you are oppressed and excluded," says Tessa, "you can identify as a cyborg."

Ziggy nods toward the three girls sitting opposite, their shirts unbuttoned down to their abdomens. She knows the psychological term for this. "What if you internalize the patriarchy?"

Tessa gives Ziggy a bright, commending smile. "The Cates are *not* women of color."

"They'd have to give up their privilege," says Lex. "And experience way more suffering."

Ziggy likes the sound of this. "You can just give your privilege up?"

"Men can't," Tessa says curtly. "But women can if they really try."

Ziggy wonders if this means amputating an arm or if low self-esteem is good enough. Tessa appears to register her confusion. "All women have been oppressed," she says. "So they're generally better at empathy."

This sounds a lot like Ziggy's mother. She considers telling the girls about the constellation therapy Ruth does on Wednesdays—where a group of women role-play one another's childhoods and then, standing very still while breathing deeply from their diaphragms, tap into diverse cultural and historical suffering. Ziggy has watched a line of women designated "the

Germans" fall weeping at the feet of an opposing line of "the Jews."

Ziggy's name is called. She rises slowly and walks toward the nurse standing in the open doorway, waving her gloved hands with sinister finesse. When Ziggy glances back between them, the two girls smile at her. Tessa gives an energetic thumbs-up with her prosthetic; Lex keeps appraising with those hot, woody eyes.

From her mother's therapy practice, Ziggy knows that trauma can change a person's DNA; there have been numerous epigenetic studies on mice and Holocaust survivors. She wonders if this is what the girls are saying: that it might be possible to traumatize yourself into a more sympathetic, morally superior class of identity. And if, every afternoon in the bathroom closet, Ziggy is already doing it.

TESSA SENDS THE LINK that night and Ziggy reads "A Cyborg Manifesto," learning all about the non-exclusionary, uncategorizable category of the "cyborg." Tessa explains that Australians are ill equipped to be cyborgs because they love borders, that a new country lacks the cyborgian self-confidence required for dissolving boundaries. But Ziggy thinks Haraway talks about affinities, not identities. And cyborgs seem to encompass everyone from drag queens in wigs to dogs with homing chips under their coats. Still, she really likes the gist.

Ziggy falls quite naturally into sitting with Tessa and Lex at lunch, where she learns many interesting concepts. Like "the void." Tessa ascribes it to any girl posing for a bathroom selfie or applying lip tint before the reflective glass of her phone. When Ziggy asks for clarification, Tessa's eyes stare off in decadent angst, like two pale gems polished by eternal malaise. Her gaze is cynical and Egyptianized (Tessa's grandmother had lived fabulously in pre-independence Cairo, and though the woman was presumably just another blobby-faced Anglo, Tessa wears a thick black line beneath each eye in homage to her eccentric matriarch) as she explains that the void is something you discover as a twelve-year-old who spent their summer holidays in the cancer ward. She brandishes her prosthesis, and thrillingly, Ziggy looks. Tessa says she first experienced the void in her hospital bed, reading an age-inappropriate giftbook that included the more uplifting parts of Sartre. *Seinfeld* had come next—on the recommendation of a kindly nurse, who said it was a show about nothingness.

Tessa grins at Ziggy. "George Costanza is pure death drive."

Ziggy smiles uneasily. Once again she has only an abstract sense of what Tessa is talking about. The cyborg says she watched all nine seasons of *Seinfeld* in recovery, swallowing lukewarm Jell-O while the neurotic Jewish bachelor maintained a glib existential stasis that Tessa found deeply soothing. She made her peace with nothingness. Returning to school, Tessa felt pleasantly numb and no longer cared that the other girls were prettier, thinner, and had both of their arms. They were clearly frightened of existence, and every moment of their lives was an aestheticized dodging of the void. All the sunshine and swimming and organic lunches were a vain attempt to seem at home in the world, as if this could save them from the ultimate fact of nothingness. Then Tessa had read "A Cyborg Manifesto" and discovered a female theorist who hated the popular girls too.

Listening to this, Ziggy thinks of her father. Jeff has recently discovered swimming and mateship and his capacity for building muscle. This past weekend Ziggy had been woken by loud bellows, and run downstairs to find four buff, shirtless men yelling at the rugby match on TV. Her father has always been a towering grayish blur—chest cowed by his ectomorphic hunch. But that morning Jeff Klein was radiant. He had pectorals, biceps. They were golden and glowing against the faded ethnic weave that covered the couch. Jeff's new swimming buddies perched around him. One of them—a vast, sunburned shouldermass—had offered her a beer shandy. At nine o'clock in the morning. Australia was slaughtering New Zealand in South Africa or some combination of those three; whichever it was, the rugby was early and the beers were very inappropriate.

Until now Ziggy had mostly dismissed her father's new hobby as a thin branch on the wintry tree of his obscurely dull existence—accountant at a large corporation who did five A.M. ocean swims to counteract the drudgery. But lately he had started flying to remote islands up the east coast, where crocodiles nested in ocean lagoons and jellyfish netted the shorelines like lacy sheets. And now these men. Smooth, tan rectangles like luxury leather suitcases, performing friendly headlocks then spanking one another's bottoms. That morning, Ziggy saw how her father's distant, depressive aura had sloughed off like lizard skin. Jeff Klein was saying "Yessss!" to the television. All week, he'd been adding winky faces to his texts. An emoji of a turd throwing dollar bills down the toilet. As far as Ziggy can tell, her father is still careful with money, but he has now added a disturbing sass. And designer Fitbits. If a wristwatch counts down the minutes till death, a Fitbit accrues steps like shares in immortality, and Jeff suddenly has one in silver and one in rose gold. The evidence is accumulating rapidly against him. Like the pretty girls at school, Jeff Klein is clearly dodging something deeper.

Or it might be something in plain sight, purple and extroverted. With her maroon frizz and bosomy blouses over sensual tights, Ruth Klein presents as a bolshy, Jewish kinesthetic. According to Ziggy's mother, if you aren't baring your soul, the conversation doesn't count; and Ruth unburdens herself everywhere—clothing store cash registers and cafés and always with an aggressive casualness that makes Ziggy think of public breastfeeding. Her mother runs group workshops specializing in the Sacred Feminine. Women meet daily in her living room to weep and dance and anoint one another's foreheads with body paint and bindis. Ruth subscribes to a belief system she picked up at an Indian ashram in the early nineties. She'd told Ziggy that Shunyata's teachings focused on drawing distinctions between the genders in quest of a satisfying sexual union and pathway to God. Throughout history, Man had used Woman as a measure of his own difference—assigning her the baser physical virtues while raising himself to loftier spiritual and intellectual planes. Ruth doesn't believe in gender equality. Because Woman is not Man. She is better. Woman is *being*, *eternity*, and *life* itself. She is the Source, the elemental substance that Man sought to separate himself from, to feel himself as a distinct presence, an ego or personality closer to his narcissistic notion of a Supreme Being. Man has denied Woman her totality, calling the highest, most impenetrable matter "God," which Ruth believes is just more of Woman.

Manipulating the guru's theology into something Ruth calls "the Magnetic Poles," her workshops acquaint women with their feminine natures then encourage them to take the final step—dissolving back into existence by merging (in the Kleins' swimming pool) with the Masculine. Ziggy's mother thinks sex should be a cosmic dance between the genders. Full of mystery and risk. "A woman discovers herself inside a seduction, which is a negotiation; it's very deep and very powerful." On her sass-ier days: "And anyway, agency is just an illusion."

The constellation therapy is used to decipher which par-ents have damaged the women's sense of self and then forgive them for it. Ruth has also added an artistic component where the women achieve further release through the decorating of symbolic pillows. There are fetus-shaped inner-child pillows for cradling; phallus pillows for kicking; and labial pillows for apologizing to then adorning with rhinestones. Ziggy under-stands why her father might prefer to spend his time submerged in freezing water.

Ruth is committed to her guru's philosophy, though in the last two decades some of the ideas have badly dated. Shunyata (or Shuni as her disciples referred to her) compared priests and monks to fascists, calling them all obsessive-compulsive perverts. She made gay jokes about beloved celebrity philan-thropists. Shuni wore a skullcap, reflector aviators, and a pointy-shouldered silver sports jacket like some sort of intergalactic matriarchal messiah. Toward the end, things had gone awry at the ashram—Shuni, allegedly high on nitrous, performing dentistry on her devotees and making everyone wear maroon. Ruth had already left by the time Shuni spent the treasury on a vast collection of high-end Jet Skis. When accused, the guru merely giggled that her corruption was part of "the big cosmic joke."

Ziggy's mother has publicly distanced her own therapeutic work from Shunyata's, while conserving the guru's contentious disdain for gender politics. Ruth's convictions around the gender binary have hung in there like her allegiance to the color purple. She believes that women are relational, intuitive, nurturing, and emotional; and to increase estrogen levels, they should wear flowing garments and submerge themselves in warm water. She says second-wave feminism went too far: producing ballbreakers like her own mother and denying the inherent softer qualities of Woman, qualities that third-wavers then also dismissed as "binary" in the quest to make everybody feel included.

The Magnetic Poles also prescribes testosterone-building behaviors for men. Your husband should be man enough to decide where you are going for dinner, to book concert tickets and weekends away, to insist you wear the sexy, sheer nightie and then shag you in it. And afterward, your man should be man enough to lie there, look deep into your eyes, and see exactly what your heart desires for breakfast. Despite his recent macho awakening, it seems to Ziggy that her father is still failing Ruth's tests. Jeff never makes any demands. Ziggy has not once seen him stand in meaningful eye contact with his wife, insisting she put on a nice dress because he can tell she feels like brunch at the Four Seasons. Ziggy's dad sort of drifts along behind Ruth—collecting receipts, extinguishing small fires. Ziggy has overheard fights, accusations of *you never pinch my bum*. Ruth says it isn't masculine to read twenty Yelp reviews before choosing a restaurant. *Just pick one!* she yells at Ziggy's father. *Just tell me what we are doing and I'll do it!* He rarely does. Ziggy's mother makes all the decisions. She chose their unusual, open-plan house with its triangular atrium, painting the walls in reds and dark salmons, giving it the meaty smother of a womb. Jeff enjoys his minimal homelife in the small office off the main bedroom, playing his old Bowie records and eating elaborate gourmet snacks. Ruth occasionally sees clients up in this mezzanine, its shelves crammed with books like *Pan and the Nightmare* and *Meeting the Madwoman*; below these is a crimson sofa where her private clients sit and weep. Sinking into its cushions, Ziggy

can feel the cumulative sadness like a cool mist. Her brother re-
fuses to sit on this piece of furniture, calling it "the Sofa of a
Thousand Tears."

AFTER SCHOOL TESSA TAKES ZIGGY on a tour of Kandara's car
pool queue. White women who collect their progeny in sheer
yoga-wear, chauffeuring boys' school drive-bys with the Top
40 up, windows down. Women addicted to Instagramming their
barista-crush's latte art; mums who gym themselves manic then
endorphin-buy more yoga pants and Apple accessories. Mothers
who, every afternoon at three, quit torturing housemaids to go
suck the life from their daughters and the compliments from their
sons all the way up until bedtime, when they turn (abusively) to
their catatonic husbands for further emotional sustenance. For
some unexplained reason, Tessa calls these women the Israelites.
Ziggy studies the bronzed Pilates arms elbowing out of open
windows, blond-streaked ponytails bouncing to bass-y dance
tracks. As if the promised land is an Ibiza nightclub with drive-
thru spray-tan. Ziggy wants to better understand Tessa's
metaphor. To know if it is anti-Semitic or if being a WASP
might, in fact, come naturally to a Jew? Exiting through the
white curlicued gates of their Anglican girls' school, Ziggy
wonders aloud how bumper stickers for boys' school rowing
teams chime with Exodus. Tessa's explanation is simple.

"They're slaves to the patriarchy."

Ziggy is relieved that the central enemy is not the Jews. "So
Egyptians are the oppressors?"

Tessa balks. "Do you see any Egyptians around here?"

Ziggy points a nervy finger at the cyborg's eyeliner.

"Men are the oppressors, Ziggy. Men." Tessa sighs in exasperation. "Moses made the Israelites wander the desert for forty years

so that they would forget their bondage. Which explains the amnesia between third-wave and postfeminism. Basically, Haraway and the Cates." She eyes Ziggy sharply. "But the car pool queue has just internalized their own oppression. Like the Israelis."

"You mean the Israelites," Ziggy mutters.

"I mean the Israelis who oppress the Palestinians."

Mortified, Ziggy tries to distance herself from Tessa's metaphor. "At the Wailing Wall I wished for a two-state solution."

Tessa nods approvingly, turning her animosity back to the line of idling, enslaved mothers. But a burning hub of activity has surfaced on Ziggy's upper lip. When her parents took them to Israel last summer, Ziggy didn't wish for a two-state solution. She had cast her mind back as far as the airport duty-free and then wished for a pair of Gucci sunglasses. Now Tessa has made her feel both guilty and persecuted. A feeling that, she supposes, is very Israeli.

Tessa concludes their tour with a final generalization. "Kandara girls are just like their mums. They go to uni to meet their future husbands, who are just like their dads."

Ziggy knows this isn't strictly true—the school brochure boasted an impressive list of successful women who had graduated from Kandara. High Court judges, esteemed scientists, and many members of parliament. Even their prime minister spent three terms writing history papers while admiring that magnificent view. It is difficult to know how much of Tessa's contempt for rich, white women is Haraway and how much of it is inspired by Tessa's own mother. Being a cyborg, Tessa doesn't identify as "woman-born." A convenience, as Mrs. McBride is the cruel overlord of five Filipino housemaids and afternoon drunk driver of two Mercedes Benzes. Or what Tessa calls "a patriarchal capitalist who happens to have a vagina."

Despite this militant infidelity to her own Israelite, the one part of "A Cyborg Manifesto" that appears to be missing is the Marxism. It seems neither Tessa nor Lex have any desire to give up money—Lex needs three laptops to produce her own rap albums, and Tessa needs multiple extracurricular performance classes plus summer workshops at film acting academies in London and L.A. But mostly, actual feminist socialism implies that nobody gets to be famous and special and morally superior to anybody else. Class privilege is what results from aspirations like theirs, so Ziggy's friends have not abolished it.

UNLIKE ZIGGY'S JEWISH SCHOOL—fortressed by ten-foot walls crowned with shards of glass, added after the Second Intifada—Kandara's pretty picket fences don't interfere with its spectacular vista. The pearly pages of the opera house, that handsome span of bridge, the tight clump of skyscrapers like blue bills squeezed in a fist. The school's website has a live feed of the panorama from the oval, and at any time of day or night you can see the whole city as Kandara students see it—in darling miniature like a sweeping diorama. This expansive view might have emboldened the girls, inspiring second-wave levels of feminist ambition, had it not included Randalls Boys.

The pillared monstrosity of the boys' school assembly hall dominates the hill opposite Kandara. Ziggy often sees her peers staring blissfully over the harbor, sunning their cheeks in little boy gaze. And when they aren't near a window, there is always Snapchat. Ziggy can feel boy specters gawking in the hallways, the bathrooms, on the sectional sofa of the year-ten common room. Boys tingle under the skin, as hyperactive and inscrutable as her eczema.

But Tessa and Lex have found a way to transcend Kandara's

oppressive social system or, as Tessa calls it, "upper-middle-class hetero-patriarchal whiteness." They have a method, a practice. And it is not feminist activism. Her friends have no plan to liberate their tenth-grade sisters, and their strategy seems, at least superficially, pretty counterintuitive. Ziggy's friends spend their afternoons hanging out at the mall.

That first delirious afternoon, Ziggy trails Tessa and Lex around Bondi Junction's six-story shopping complex, steeling herself for malicious male bullying: snickers of "pancake chest" or a barely kinder "mozzie bites." Leaning over the fifth-floor railing, wedged between her friends, the atrium below looks as dense and interesting as an aquarium. Even the sterile gleam of white tile and halogen is warmer today, their three bodies pressed together, the air bunching in humid like tinsel. It is amazing to Ziggy that intimacy has found her, so fast and in such cool clothes. Then Tessa turns her head, slow and mechanical, deliberate as an actress. Her eyes twinkle. "He's watching us."

Ziggy's friends take off, bolting down the concourse toward a bedding store and veering left at the last moment into King of Knives. Ziggy jogs after them, glancing around anxiously for the offending onlooker. But she sees only stroller-mothers and the shuffling elderly. No droves of malevolent schoolboys, not even a leering continental salami vendor. Inside King of Knives, Ziggy finds her friends panting behind a Leatherman display case. They smile at her with a beguiling, almost sexual, thrill.

"Was it the janitor?" Ziggy tries.

Tessa gives her a pitying look. "Why, because he's African?"

"No!" Ziggy's face scorches. "Because he's the only *man* in here."

"It was a *white* man," Lex informs her. "A tall white man in a suit."

The pair withdraw from their post with exaggerated trepidation, peering anxiously in every direction—even up at the ceiling. Tessa wipes her brow and Lex places a hand to her heaving chest. Ziggy can tell they are acting, but this only makes her love them more.

Next, they take her downstairs to the train terminal, where the three of them board the Illawarra line to Central Station. This is the grittiest place they know: the low, interminable tunnel of the Eddy Avenue underpass. Ziggy has always found this thoroughfare bright and cheerful—with its rush of suited commuters and Dreamtime mural in polished mosaic. But her friends are gifted fabricators. They swerve between the pedestrian traffic—endowing all men with lechery and forcing ambiguous eye contact with the dodgy-looking anarchist punk crayoning beside his kelpies. Again, after Tessa gives the signal (this time: "He's got a stiffy!"), the two girls run screaming down the tunnel. Ziggy dashes after them, trembling with sympathetic terror.

Intuitively, Ziggy understands their game. The potent mix of punishment and make-believe is familiar from her own culture. There is fasting for forgiveness on Yom Kippur, Passover's salted parsley as a proxy for bitter tears, and then there is locking oneself in a darkened closet with an eccentric SS officer. Like Ziggy's Judaism, her friends' feminism employs complicated rituals to inflict mild trauma and so dodge the worst afflictions of their forebears. When the girls break for bubble tea in Chinatown, Tessa describes their extracurricular activity as "Method acting."

"It's hard to get catcalled at an all girls' school," she explains. "Especially when *lesbian* is the main insult."

"Plus," Lex adds casually, "if we don't do these dares, we won't be famous in America."

And this is where their culture eclipses Ziggy's. She would prefer a system with tangible rewards but as far as she can tell, Jewish heaven involves sitting at the kids' table in a room full of priestly elders for an eternal Friday night dinner. Whereas Ziggy's friends have skipped over all practical plans for feminist liberation, and jumped straight to the promised land. America is their reward for self-inflicted female trauma. America had a civil rights movement; it is older, more mature, and the comedians know how to talk about issues on late night television. America calls to Tessa and Lex from multiple media platforms; inciting them to be braver, freer, more traumatized, individualistic, and opinionated than everybody else. Specifically, America wants Lex to be a famous rapper and Tessa a famous actress.

"I've been banned from school recitals," Lex boasts.

Tessa enumerates the many ways Kandara has failed to nurture Lex's talent. That forcing her to have vocal lessons with Mr. Tellyson—a rumored pederast from Randalls with his Gumnut Baby ties and perfect posture—was a form of ethnic cleansing. Lex doesn't need the school's help, Tessa tells Ziggy. Their friend has TuneSmith and a YouTube channel and a celebrity rapper she Snapchats.

"When school's finished, I'm moving to Brooklyn," Lex explains.

"Is that where you're from?"

"I'm from Rose Bay. But thanks for the compliment."

Tessa's vocational path is slightly more confounding. She wants to star in movies like those gritty French ones with the real sex scenes. Ziggy knows the type. She has stumbled on them late at night, flicking between the public television stations. Where women are graphically raped to make a point about misogyny. Lots of bruised legs hoisted against concrete pylons. Smeared makeup, pubic hair, cellulite. And then, in the loveless marriages and relentless banality, Tessa sees a special European nothingness that feels deeply familiar. As an existential Australian with an Egyptian grandmother and one arm, Tessa feels uniquely positioned to share this profound sense of emptiness with American audiences. Obviously, most sex is just filling the void, but Tessa will still need real-life experience to repeat it convincingly on camera. When Ziggy asks her friends what they do on weekends, Tessa answers, "Method acting."

Ziggy isn't sure what exactly she'll be famous *for*, but right now, it doesn't matter. She loves the cold kick in her chest as she dodges her Nazi's casual face-slaps or the swinging briefcase of a predacious male commuter. Running from imaginary attackers, her head gets still and clear and Ziggy feels invulnerable. Tessa and Lex have dismissed her white privilege and welcomed her into the diverse cyborgian tribe. Whether it is because of her prepubescent body, her light eczema, or her hooknose, Ziggy cannot say. It seems unlikely Tessa would include Jews in the "women of color" category because, despite the Holocaust, they allegedly control Hollywood. Regardless, Ziggy feels accepted. Whenever bus drivers ask an alighting Tessa how she lost her arm, the peppy cyborg tells them "shark attack," then nudges Ziggy. "But my friend gouged out its eyes." Her inclusion in Tessa's trauma makes Ziggy feel like family.

Chapter 2

Hitler Youth arrive one night while Ziggy is brushing her teeth. They think she can probably go a bit faster. When she finishes in under twenty seconds, Ziggy feels euphoric, and Hitler Youth urge her to set records in the areas of hair-washing, body-drying, and eyebrow-tweezering. So she sets records, then smashes them. Now Hitler Youth switch tactics. They tell her she is quick and coordinated like a boy. *That's sexist,* Ziggy thinks back. Hitler Youth don't care about sexist. *Look in the mirror,* they tell her. Ziggy does and sees her little torso, once blankly familiar, now ribbed and rangily boy. Hitler Youth lurk in the dreggy depths of Ziggy's mind—a scratchy illustration of some blond lederhosen'd boys she saw once in a Holocaust book for children. Their mouths flap like crude puppets, but their words are piercingly clear.

Ziggy can remember watching *The Sound of Music* as a kid with her grandmother. How they sang mightily along until they got to Rolf and Liesl's duet. Whenever the imminent Nazi appeared on-screen, Ziggy's grandmother got quiet and blinky. The air seemed to condense, holding its breath with Ziggy's. It made the love scene more excruciating, thinking her grandmother somehow knew and disapproved of the tingling feeling Ziggy was having between her legs, and over a Nazi. And now, in one dreadful evening, an entire squad of Rolfs have occupied her imagination.

The next morning they are there again as Ziggy walks to school. She can see their brown lederhosen through the dense lantana, and hear their German singsong among the varied birdcall. At lunch, these Nazis-of-the-mind tell her to eat every last chip crumb then turn the packet inside out and lick off all the grease. They tell her she is waifish and gangly. It almost seems they want to help her. *Drink this liter of soy milk,* they say as she stands before the common room's refrigerator. *Estrogen will grow your breasts and,* they counter, *give you cancer.* At the bathroom mirrors—surrounded by lip-balming, stomach-sucking girls—Hitler Youth tell Ziggy she might be smart but it comes out sharp and mannish through her small, square mouth; that her oblong-shaped head makes her seem drably cerebral; that she lacks sensuality and could never pull off that sultry staring face that endows the other girls with a mysterious feminine aura. Ziggy's vagina is bald, they remind her—prim and sexless as a little pink peace sign. An excess of flesh with a single, urinary function. *Shower in the dark until further notice,* demand Hitler Youth. *Or better yet, don't shower at all.* In a drought-prone country, the Nazis argue, Ziggy should stick to the quick rinse-off and the number-twos-only flush.

Ziggy's house sits on an over-irrigated hill beside the topiaried fortress of the Polish embassy. Year-round, buff young men snap their shears at the thick juniper hedges that lend the consulate grounds a woodsy, European creep. When she gets home from school that day, Hitler Youth instruct Ziggy to stand in her room, curtains open, and remove her top for the embassy gardeners. When nobody looks up, Hitler Youth explain that this is because she has the body of an eleven-year-old boy. Her little brother's little brother. Twelve-year-old Jacob, who has just started at Randalls Boys and spends most of his extracurricular life online, making jokes in Latin. Ziggy has seen him browsing Hentai sites and Katy Perry videos, which she believes makes her brother internet-sexual. Ziggy would prefer a mild, Millennial kink like this to the sickening thrill she gets crawling into the bathroom cupboard or now, staring dejected at the gardeners, when Hitler Youth tell her to hoist a leg on the windowsill and look up her own skirt. But from this angle, Ziggy's green school bloomers have a disturbingly gonad-like bulge. She tries to flatten it with her fingers and then presses down forcefully with her whole palm. The pleasure kneads into disgust and quickly Ziggy is ripping at the leg holes, tearing off her panties and attacking the rogue fabric with her craft scissors. When she is finished, Ziggy crouches between the angry green pieces of her underwear like a hunted animal. If this were one of Ruth's workshops, Ziggy's shredded garment would be an emotional victory—her feelings finally expressed, her voice restored. But Hitler Youth are unmoved by catharsis. They think Ziggy's violent episode suggests high testosterone and the possibility of introverted testicles. She knows that these can sometimes drop late, random as asteroids. Ziggy hates being vulnerable but not enough to want balls. She lies on her back and experiences a very Jewish sense of alienation: on her bedroom floor Ziggy is an insignificant speck in an uncaring universe, specifically chosen to feel bad about it.

OVER THE NEXT FEW DAYS Ziggy notices a new algorithm at work in the margins of her social media accounts. Virtual forces are conspiring to send her every imaginable herbal, pharmaceutical, and surgical remedy to restore a man's erection. Harvard scientists and Hollywood plastic surgeons offer pills and implants to help her stay hard. The ads appear with strange specificity and omniscient timing. When Hitler Youth tell Ziggy her pelvic bone looks protuberant in her jeans, a picture of men's Levi's pops up minutes later in her sidebar. She tries not to be superstitious. How could Hitler Youth have permeated her internet presence? Plus, there is something slightly oblique about the messaging. It seems to think Ziggy is also balding, suffers from acne, and wants to lose ten kilograms, as if the data mined belongs to some other deeply insecure male.

It would be easy to blame Ziggy's gender anxiety on puberty—her body's hard, bendy quality like a plastic action figure without the special powers. She could blame it on porn and the cyborgian pleasure of watching an anonymous penis have sex with female bodies, how her own childish shape seems an inconceivable substitute. She could call it a physical fixation with Lex and the girl's ability to do a split between two adjacent school desks, her own inflexibility somehow confirming that Ziggy will remain always a virgin. But Hitler Youth's presence is also, undoubtedly, the fault of Ziggy's mother.

Ruth's ideology is one thing, and then there is her behavior. Despite her high spiritual aspirations, Ziggy's mother is still attached to the objectification of her physical form. She has the poise of a ballerina in an Italian movie star's body; her face is broad and fine-boned, and to Ziggy it seems always set in the self-conscious poses of cinematic close-ups. Her mother is beautiful and knows it; Ziggy often catches her making cat eyes in the mirror. On long car rides, when Jeff admires the landscape, Ruth seems to shrivel in the front seat, as if in a losing contest with Nature itself. Her mother is jealous of trees, and it makes Ziggy frightened of womanhood. She has heard Ruth practicing vulnerability on Jeff: explaining that she feels sexually rejected when he takes too many photos of a sunset. Her voice gets heavy with grievance and to Ziggy it sounds like she is trying to bludgeon Jeff with her pain.

A disturbing recent development is that Ruth seems to be encouraging Jeff to objectify her in a more classically misogynistic way. Ruth's blouses have lately gotten very booby, her tights sheerer and with added witchy lace. Ruth has inherited dozens of her own mother's shoes—all narrow, high-heeled instruments of physical torture—which are now constantly catching on the fringing of her designer paganwear. Spying through the door crack this last summer, Ziggy watched her mother straddle Jeff then start gyrating over his crotch in her very threadbare tie-dye tights. Ruth slapped her own ass, then grabbed Jeff's hand and slapped herself again, harder. Ziggy stood frozen on the landing like a spooked Kabuki mask. This wasn't the kind of gentle femininity the women practiced in her swimming pool. Ruth performed the dissociated jaguar moves of a stripper; the dance bore no resemblance to the alleged sublimity of the heterosexual union. Ziggy believes her mother's hypocrisy is driving Jeff from loving father-husband to fun-loving, emoji-mad, patriarchal triathlete. And Ruth is definitely making Ziggy feel sexist. Hitler Youth claim that the Sacred Feminine is just what voluptuous women tell each other to feel better about sagging.

THAT SATURDAY, when her mother's annual menarche workshop commences in their living room, Ziggy is thrilled to have other plans. Ruth runs this particular piece of work for teenage girls and their mums. In a circle, both generations take turns telling the stories of their first period. The sagas mostly go like this: the mothers saw blood on their underwear and thought they were dying; the daughters saw the same, asked the internet, and understood they'd gotten their periods. In previous years, Ziggy has watched these sessions from behind a small citadel of goatskin jembes at the back of her living room, finding the teenage participants particularly insane. The way they declared their female pride, hugged their mothers, and made meaningful eye contact with total strangers. After the sharing session, everyone was instructed to draw their periods in crayons on large sheets of art paper. Ziggy had watched the scrolls fill up with thick reams of crimson and female faces contorted into Munch-like screams. Then Ruth talked about estrogen and progesterone and how women should monitor their cycles, making sure to wear long skirts and play with puppies at certain times of the month. This, she claimed, was vital to maintaining a healthy balance with the Masculine (who should play contact sports and kill spiders). Ruth told the women about the sacred geometry of their anatomies—how the womb is an inverse vestibular organ that makes you susceptible to interior decoration and baking, but is also the deep hearth of your feminine power. Ziggy recently learned the correct pejorative for her mother: Ruth is a biological essentialist.

But today Ziggy does not have to hear any of it. Lex has invited her and Tessa over to listen to her new songs. Ziggy knows that Lex was adopted from Bangladesh by two elderly white people who love and spoil her but also call her native country a "heartless place." Lex has made the most of their well-meaning ignorance by abusing her curfew, their liquor cabinet, and a border collie named Conrad, whom she walks every afternoon to a boat shed where the two of them Dutch-oven until sundown. Tessa says Mr. Cameron wears a hearing aid so Ziggy is looking forward to saying the eff word in front of someone else's parent.

When the intergenerational menstruaters return from morning tea, Ziggy flees to the front door. On her way out, she glances over the railing and sees a large woman just joining their group, apologizing as she tiptoes around the circle. The woman wears a pale pink smock and a pair of cherry-red hair clips set inches apart at the top of her head, dividing the jet-black hair into two slick sheets. This too-close placement of hair accessory makes most grown-ups look insane, but the woman's formidable brow, sensitive sunken eyeballs, and serious mouth lend the style a surprising gravitas and sense of dignity. Ziggy didn't know transgender women could get their periods. In fact, this and a lifetime of accumulated catcalling trauma, is her whole understanding of trans-exclusionary radical feminism. She decides to stay and watch for a minute.

Ruth begins the next session by asking the latecomer, Rowena, to share her menstruation origin story. The transgender woman explains that since starting her hormone treatment, she has experienced period-like symptoms. "Everything but the blood."

Ziggy watches the other women with interest. Their faces express a challenged but respectful listening; a few nod in obvious discomfort. When Rowena finishes, a very rotund woman with diverting tribal jewelry raises her hand. She wears a designer silk sack and a single feathered earring, giving her that Native American elder look.

"Pardon my ignorance," the spherical woman says. "But how can you get period-like symptoms without ovaries?"

Rowena is magnanimous. "Beats me," she says. "But I get nausea, headaches, mood swings, cramping, and explosive diarrhea."

The circle tsk-tsks and hums like a giant microwave oven. Rowena appears to have suffered to their liking. Now the day can continue with more vagina-sketching and estrogen-building and conclude unceremoniously with the eating of bland pasta salads in the kitchen. Ziggy doesn't understand why her mother has allowed a transgender woman to participate in Period Day, but she is sure that Ruth is faking it. Ziggy slips out the door, feeling abnormally angry with her mother.

When she gets to Lex's house, Ziggy takes the stair lift up the steeply landscaped garden to the Camerons' front door. Lex greets her, instructing Ziggy to turn back around and admire the view.

"Wow," says Ziggy.

"It's not the ocean," Lex says meanly. She points to the tawny wriggle on the horizon. "It's *America*."

Ziggy laughs but Lex stays entranced. A trick of refracted light, the Fata Morgana, is the cause of this mirage. But Ziggy doesn't tell her friend. Lex gazes at the hazy strip, intoning the word *America* with such mystical power, it seems possible that they really can see it.

Ziggy follows Lex inside to where Tessa is waiting in a nest of pillows on the bed. Lex leaps onto the mattress with a feline agility that makes Ziggy anxious to be comparing her friend to a wildcat. Ziggy clambers up awkwardly after her. Lex places the laptop on her chest and starts to play the song. Ziggy watches her friend's breasts rise and fall like the bass is booming from her curves. Hitler Youth observe that Ziggy's male mind is mired in racist, misogynist tropes about tribal beats and fertility figures.

Not only is Ziggy being classically racist, they say, she is obviously attracted to her girlfriend. But Lex's lyrics draw Ziggy quickly back into the room. They all riff on something called "eye-rape." How men eye-rape Lex in the street; on public transport; escalators at the mall; and how she is going to ass-rape them back with stiletto Louboutins then whip their balls into waffles with the chain straps of Chanel handbags.

Lex mouths the words with ferocious puff and Tessa bobs her head fiercely. Ziggy assumes you are only allowed to laugh on the inside. That anything else might detract from the menace, that Lex's threats are not a joke.

When it finishes, Tessa stares up blissfully at the ceiling. "So. Fucking. Good."

Ziggy nods.

"Do you get it?" says Lex, eyeing Ziggy suspiciously.

"It's about catcalling."

Lex's look darkens. "Does that even happen to you?"

Ziggy shrugs casually, while her whole body burns up. Under the blankets her little scraggly legs are a sudden aberration.

"Catcalling is like cavemen psychically clubbing women then dragging them into the bushes," explains Tessa.

"Totally," says Ziggy. "I get it." And she does. She has seen the grabby look in their eyes as road workers enjoy a passing woman. Walking with her mother, she often feels the whistles sail out like nets.

"My songs are all about white patriarchy," Lex clarifies.

"And how it's turning black people gay," adds Tessa.

Now Ziggy is lost. "Black people are turning gay?"

"In America." Lex speaks with authority. "The prison-industrial complex is making it nearly impossible for black people to stay straight."

"They put black men in jail so their wives are forced to be lesbians, while all the men inside turn gay." Tessa gives Lex a look of manic sympathy. "It's black genocide."

Ziggy has heard about black male genocide and mass incarceration, but the gay part is new. With marriage equality and all the medical options for same-sex conception, she isn't sure how being gay has any bearing on the survival of the black race. Still, she keeps quiet, thinking she must be missing something.

"Notice how many trans people of color there are?" says Tessa. "That's because the patriarchy failed black men. It's actually easier to be a straight woman."

"And now rich white men have started retiring as women," says Lex, fanning her fingers in mock coquetry. "But the kind who get manicures so they don't have to lift anything."

Tessa shakes her head. "So. Fucking. Fucked."

It all sounds terrible. Especially that last part about old white men vying for a piece of the action, trying to get out of building shelves and opening lids. Ziggy thinks she understands what her friends are talking about. "So transgender people have just internalized the patriarchy?"

Tessa draws back with theatrical exasperation. "Of course not!" she says. "Transgender people are a disenfranchised minority, so they can't be patriarchal. They're women of color."

Ziggy sees Lex shift restlessly between her pillows. "At least, transgender people would never eye-rape a woman," she says. "Because they know how it feels."

Ziggy nods along, the dread of complicity squeezing her skull. She has spent years honing her understanding of how the Holocaust felt, making a comprehensive punishment of her extracurricular life. But porn or popular culture or her mother's confounding therapies have deprived her of a clear sexual orientation, making Ziggy less accustomed to being eye-raped than to eye-raping. She sometimes stares too long at a spectacular specimen of passing cleavage and has lost entire afternoons to the Victoria's Secret Instagram.

Luckily, her friends now abandon the patriarchy lesson to critique their peers' social media. Cate's formal fashion Tumblr is a favorite pastime. Today she touts Kenyan beading paired with furry Eskimo boots and midriff-baring cholis. The look is completed with a white denim miniskirt or cheek-riding khaki shorts, securing the girl within her colonialist demographic. Tessa explains that the Cates' sartorial ambitions are best understood as cultural appropriation. They pose as mystical voluptuaries, slipping on an exotic aura over their white Anglo-Saxon privilege. Ziggy notices how Tessa places the word *exotic* inside quotation marks as if it were a pseudo-word, bereft of meaning outside the racist imagination. Ziggy makes a mental note to erase it from her vocabulary. She scans Cate's Tumblr for further incriminations. A still life of two Bacardi Breezers beside a bowl of licorice allsorts seems promising. Something about the candy's pastel colors hemmed in black makes her think of golliwogs and minstrel shows. "That's kind of racist," she says timidly, pointing out the offending lollies.

"How is it racist?" Lex's voice is spiky.

"Just, like, the colors."

"Black?"

Ziggy nods ruefully.

"Licorice is black, Ziggy."

"I know, but with the Breezers?"

"What are you saying?"

Ziggy has no idea. Something about Caribbean rum and

blackface. She has gone too far. "What about gender?" she says, trying to divert them. "Can you appropriate genders?"

"Of course," says Tessa. "Gender is a construction."

At last, Ziggy feels she understands what her friends are talking about. She points to a photo of Cate sucking on an Icy Pole. "There! She's *deliberately* acting like a slut."

"Feminists don't call girls sluts," admonishes Lex.

Tessa clicks her tongue disparagingly then ducks away under the bed. She rummages inside her schoolbag and pops up a moment later, grinning and clutching a grubby DVD case. She raises it ceremoniously aloft. Ziggy misses the title but catches the ancient Blockbuster sticker fraying across the front: *Foreign. Rated R.*

"You need to see this." Tessa extends the case to Ziggy. *Irréversible.*

Ziggy has heard the girls talk before about the French movie with the infamous eleven-minute rape scene. This is the kind of film Tessa aspires to be in. Something grisly and instructional. Something to make women want to rise up and kill.

"My sister studied international relations in the early 2000s," says Tessa. "She wrote an essay about female objectification and secular dress codes in contemporary France."

Ziggy takes the DVD carefully into her hands. The case is scratched and indented, a beloved relic. Lex eyes her testily.

"Lisa's so right-wing," says Tessa, "she thinks all women should wear burkas."

Ziggy's heart plummets. "So why do you want *me* to watch the movie?"

"To see how it feels," says Tessa.

"How what feels?"

"Female objectification."

Ziggy nods stoically through her humiliation.

Tessa's voice is kind but firm. "If you're going to be attracted to women, you need to watch the rape scene and see how it feels to be on the receiving end."

Tessa's presumption is a shock but also, almost, a compliment. Harboring a secret as epic as sexuality makes Ziggy feel both prized and inept, like benign aristocracy. Ziggy isn't sure she is gay, but she isn't against the idea. Already, she wears the weight of Jewishness like her grandmother's ancient mink—a heavy mix of chutzpah and crippling self-consciousness. So it feels natural to slide on the mantle of queerness. Tessa is differently abled, Lex is an actual woman of color, and now, perhaps, Ziggy has her thing too.

SHE WOULD LIKE TO GO straight home and watch the DVD, do some online research, and finally Google the word *cisgender*. But on the bus heading home, Ziggy gets a call from her dad.

"Have the menstruaters vacated our house?"

"I'm still out."

"Oh yeah? The game's finished so I'm just killing time near the stadium . . ." Ziggy hears a request in her father's voice that she wants to deny.

"Why don't you go swimming in the ocean?"

There is a pause. "Right. Well. Tell your mum I'll just get dinner with these guys then?"

"Why don't you tell her yourself?"

A richer silence. "All right, I'll text her."

"Send her some emojis."

"Okay, Ziggy."

Her father hangs up and then, as usual, rings back fifteen seconds later. This one is a butt dial, and Ziggy yells into the speaker with her usual frustration, "Dad! Hang up the phone!" Ziggy waits, listening to the muffled swish of his pants and some faint Muzak. It sounds like her father is in a shopping center. Which is strange. Jeff buys everything online and his gifts are all "experiences," like white-water rafting trips through the remote ranges of Tasmania or river surfing tours in harshest alpine New Zealand. In the last argument Ziggy overheard, Ruth told him to just give her ticket to Damo or Gamo or whomever has the biggest biceps for rowing the Milford Sound. Ziggy's mother says a male shared near-death experience is a gay orgasm for straight little boys still terrified of women.

It becomes quickly clear from the murmur of female voices and the amplifying pop track that Ziggy's dad is now not only walking through a mall, he is walking deeper into the throbbing endorphin chamber of a women's clothing store. Ziggy hears a familiar high ding—the celestial C of a newly vacated fitting room. The sound is one she recognizes from last summer, when her grandmother insisted they buy sports bras in anticipation of the breast-swell that never came. The memory of waiting in line and the sound of those dings—as the humiliation of entering a tiny room to get topless with a septuagenarian D-cup drew closer—has implanted itself in Ziggy's brain.

When she gets off the bus, Ziggy goes straight to Victoria's Secret. It is unlikely that her father is at this particular store in this particular mall, but not impossible. She scans the shop then runs up to the fitting rooms on the second floor. Implausible notions ping through her mind. Jeff has struck up an affair with some sun-browned C-cup he met swimming on the Gold Coast; Jeff is buying his wife a present to atone for the affair. Ziggy pumps adrenaline into several flimsy theories, peering under each stall for a pair of men's leather loafers shuffling around two lurid, stiletto flip-flops. Of course, her father isn't up here. But it doesn't matter. Tessa and Lex hover in her mental periphery, and each dramatic head-swivel and ominous narrowing of eyes is a theatrical offering to them. Her father's deviance nicely maligns Ziggy's sense of security in a white, patriarchal world, and she marches around the lingerie store in a light, pleasurable panic. Finally, she returns to the changing rooms for a forensic investigation of the floor debris, discovering a feminine wasteland of plastic hangers, discarded knickers, toxic scrunchies, and wide nettings of hair. As Ziggy rises to her feet, a shop assistant in a feathered corset bats her turquoise lashes and smiles like a giant, kindly peacock.

"Have you lost your mum?" she says sweetly, and holds out a hand.

Ziggy recoils and moves quickly to the exit. Everything around her—the cornucopian displays of padded bras and panties, the wall-sized TV screens where supermodels stomp raptor-like down catwalks—makes Ziggy feel mocked. The whole store seems designed to bully you into dressing like an emu in a push-up bra. It is a store for Israelites, for the internally patriarchied. Ziggy doesn't believe Jeff was just buying his wife some undies. Everything she knows about her parents contradicts this possibility. Ruth may have stripped for Jeff but it was out of dingy yoga pants into the fullness of her untamed bush. Ziggy's mother is always schooling her father in the isms of capitalist pornography. Every ad is sexist and ageist and designed to make men want to have sex with little girls. Ruth sees a vaguely homosexual misogyny in the depictions of lithe females with invisible genitalia. "All the single and sexually neglected mothers have produced a surplus of vaginally phobic men," she has heard Ruth lecture. "To the enmeshed male, anything untidier than Barbie feels like the jaws of death." Ziggy makes a final survey of the shop floor then concedes defeat. If her father was ever here, he has already fled Victoria's Secret with his diabolical bounty.

Outside, the white glare of the mall is shrill and mingy. On Saturdays, the lower levels swarm with schoolkids and elderly people. Despite their shared habitat, the two demographics take great pains to ignore each other's existence. In fact, Ziggy often feels like the only member of her generation who knows an old person and has to be seen with them in public. Ruth encourages Ziggy to treat afternoons with her grandmother as an opportunity to practice mindfulness. *Old people live in the past,* Ruth tells her. *Young people in the future. If you can meet your grandmother in the present, you might actually have a nice time.* But to be present with Twinkles is to risk dying of embarrassment. You must keep her moving at all times or else hidden away in a restaurant booth. Ziggy's grandmother is a tiny, richly painted Hungarian who dresses exclusively in shiny animal print. Her real name is Eva, but because 70 percent of her body is always covered in sequins, the sobriquet has erased her birth name from the collective memory.

It is no surprise then to see Twinkles wading through a sale bin outside Zara. Regardless, the sight of her grandmother triggers a fierce coursing of cortisol.

"Pippekeh!"

Ziggy waves discreetly. Already she knows what is coming. If Twinkles isn't actively shopping, the tireless mall rat will want to sit in a crêperie booth and get orgasmy on chocolate.

"We get *palacsinta*!"

Her grandmother ushers Ziggy to the food court, where they

order crepes. When her pickup buzzer vibrates, Twinkles's hand makes an ecstatic convulsion and she lets out a little squeal. Her grandmother has told Ziggy before that chocolate is what awaits an unmarried woman after seventy. Ziggy might have room for sympathy beside her revulsion if it weren't for the fact that her grandmother always has a boyfriend.

At their table, Ziggy watches Twinkles carve along the crepe's rubbery folds, Nutella oozing out fecally. She wants to get home to focus on the feelings of disgust for both her father and the French rape scene and move swiftly in to the next phase of cyborgism. But her grandmother talks a lot between mouthfuls.

"You know they now thinking God live in the large intestine?"

Most of her life, Twinkles was a gastroenterologist and indomitable prankster, playing colonoscopy footage nightly at the dinner table. Ruth has never really recovered. She doesn't cook for the family, and an ongoing battle over food rages between Ziggy's parents. Ruth is always telling Jeff that foodie culture is shallow pseudo-classist crap for hedonists. Which seems to hurt his feelings. Whenever Ruth's cooking amounts to something she calls a "deconstructed salad," Jeff gets a forsaken look, grumbling that salad is already a deconstruction.

"It true, my darlink," her grandmother continues. "They saying we all connected through the same bacteria. The mummies pass the fart."

There is always a stack of *Gastroenterology Today* on Twinkles's coffee table, and Ziggy has been avoiding eye contact with the magazine's gruesome cover photos for most of her childhood. She assumes this bit of gut trivia is sourced from its pages. Ziggy glances around the food court to see if anyone under age fifty is within earshot. "Pass the fart?"

"In her womb the baby get it mother bacteria, which stay in the stomach for the rest of it life. That mean you fart smell like you mummy's. And that—"

"Okay."

"—Mummy fart like mine."

Ziggy nudges her plate away.

"And it not just mummies. We get the germ from everyone. Our gut is full of other people. Some bacteria make us happy, some angry. Explain why so much irritable bowel syndrome."

"What has this got to do with God?"

"The stomach like a universe."

Ziggy decides to ignore her grandmother's metaphysical nonsense, and there is a brief, restabilizing silence. Then Twinkles presses a hand to her gut and releases a long hissy burp.

"It all contraction and expansion," the gastroenterologist extrapolates. "This how the rabbis knew about the Big Bang—they understood digestion."

"But the rabbis didn't talk about the Big Bang."

"They did, Pippi! 'God empty himself into a vacuum then exploded into light.'"

Ziggy draws a little frowny face in her chocolate sauce. "Rabbis are sexist."

"Why?"

"How they won't shake your hand in case you have your period."

"Because a woman body is the source of life."

Ziggy rolls her eyes. Twinkles could be gang-raped by a group of rabbis and call it a clever teaching moment.

The doctor continues. "When a woman menstruate, it dangerous—the forces of life and death in conversation. Same with kosher—that why you can't eat the meat in the bottom. Too much life force."

Ziggy thinks of Lex and blushes.

"Why you mad with the rabbis, Chibby?" Her grandmother sits up suddenly, her face a beaming powdered moon. "Did you get you period?"

Ziggy regurgitates a ball of crepe. She can do these things around her grandmother—the woman is more interested in the behavior of the human digestive system than its emotional corollary.

Twinkles speaks with medical seriousness. "What happen?"

"Bad bit."

Ziggy considers the possibilities of others in her stomach. How close that sounds to the unbounded inclusivity of cyborg theory. But Twinkles is only accidentally progressive. Really, she's so far back in the past, she's still stuck on Genesis. Her grandmother is always molesting science with God.

"So if a Jew eats baklava, will they get Muslims in their stomach?"

"Pippi, now you being facetious."

"It's a serious question. And why does God hate gluten so much?"

Twinkles flicks her wrist dismissively, harassing the long sleeve of silver bracelets, and Ziggy catches sight of the faded number underneath. Twinkles often checks her granddaughter's arms for tattoos. It seems nothing could be worse than inked Rumi or butterflies on her skin. But Ziggy doesn't subscribe to the idea that Jewish bodies are sacred. It isn't just because her new friends are cyborgs; Ziggy has a long-standing feud with her own skin cells. She doesn't believe that the vast inventory of

Jewish dermatologica, including her eczema, is just Hashem's loving calligraphy.

"I don't get what's so good about being Jewish."

Twinkles shrugs. "Nothing particularly good."

"We don't even have a heaven."

"Not all about rewards, Pippi. It also about how to live. The chosen people have a big responsibility."

"That chosen thing is gross."

Twinkles returns to rigorously devouring her crepe. Ziggy focuses on moving the food around her plate, carving out white space, squishing the carnage into compact pieces; her grandmother cannot tolerate waste. The woman spent much of her childhood starving and has subsequently developed a designer shoe fetish. Ziggy's grandmother has filled three wardrobes and a garage with stylish footwear, and at seventy-nine, she can still walk elegantly in a four-inch heel. Shop assistants applaud her and assure Ziggy her granny is super-cool.

Twinkles leans in bosomy over the tabletop. "Disgusting," she spits, eyeing something just beyond Ziggy's head. Twisting around, Ziggy spots the large woman in a gold velour tracksuit flipping through the *Telegraph* while her pudgy toddler licks a dripping Bubble O' Bill. The popular confectionary features a ball of gum gripped in the pink ice cream cheeks of Cowboy Bill, on which is printed *Go for Your Guns*. A bullet hole winks through his Stetson.

"Right before dinner?" Twinkles gasps.

Ziggy sees the hypocrisy dangling from her grandmother's fork but chooses to keep quiet. She knows this is less about bad parenting than the right-wing newspaper. Populism is a scary idea to a Holocaust survivor, and her grandmother has no respect for the poor and uneducated. To Twinkles, empathy is not innate but rather a learned behavior. Something they teach you in literature studies, Ziggy assumes. At her old school they read a lot of books about oppressed Jews, and at her new school it is all oppressed women. Ziggy wonders what they read in the Western Suburbs, aside from the *Daily Telegraph*.

"Ice cream on a cold day?" Twinkles continues, incredulous. "What then you look forward to when the weather warm?" She is taking the Bubble O' Bill snack very hard.

"Maybe on hot days the kid gets heroin."

Her grandmother chuckles, but Ziggy can tell she has slid into a dark mood. The only thing to pull her out will be talk of boyfriends.

"Can I see your dating profile?"

Twinkles whips out her gigantic, glittery slab of phone. "Which one?" she says, poking her nails at the screen with focused precision, as if conjuring web pages through the magic of sparkly acrylic.

Ziggy scoots in beside her grandmother for a closer view of the SeventiesMatch home page. Attractive white people in billowing white linen smile their obviously early sexagenarian smiles. In the sidebar the real septuagenarians grin humbly in an endless column of sagging gray faces. Twinkles clicks on her own thumbnail and is admitted into her profile. She swipes to her paramours. Or the men who have sent her rose emojis at three dollars each and been granted a single line of conversation. Twinkles's written English is inferior to her spoken, and Ziggy races hungrily down the dialogue boxes, glimpsing responses like

I already give you my password

and

no thank you too many wrinkle.

A stirring mix of pity and hilarity rouses Ziggy to pilot her grandmother's phone.

"Delete this guy," Ziggy says, clicking on someone called *Islam69* with a head shot of George Clooney. "Where's the nice one with the sailboat?"

"He died."

"Really?"

"Probably."

"Probably?"

"He had an operation, and I haven't hear from him since. So probably die. He was eighty-seven."

Ziggy pictures a spotty gray head, tearful behind an oxygen mask. "Why don't you call him?"

"If he alive, he call me. Otherwise, I'm not interested."

Her grandmother can be brutal like this. Despite her dread of scarcity, Twinkles has very little patience for men. If they stooped too much or wet their pants or lost their driver's licenses, she dumped them. *I like brave men,* she has told Ziggy numerous times. *Brave and strong and straight as a stick.* Ziggy hopes she was referring to their posture.

Returning to her seat, Ziggy decides to wrap things up and get home to her gender studies. "I have a geography test tomorrow," she lies.

"Which countries?"

"Europe."

"Easy," says Twinkles. "All our family there."

Her grandmother gazes a little forlornly across the food court. Twinkles has always hated Australia. After her husband died back in Hungary, she visited many consulates. America didn't want communists, even ones that looked like Zsa Zsa Gabor with PhDs; unfortunately the Australian consulate was much more welcoming. Not because they liked foreigners, but because of the natural slur to Australian speech and upward lilt at the ends of their sentences, which to monotonic Hungarian ears sounded friendly. Twinkles had taken a pamphlet, salivating over the cover image of a huge snowy mountain sweeping down to a turquoise sea. *Australia*. They said they could probably fit a few more white people. But when Twinkles got there, the avid skier/sunbaker discovered there were no magnificent mountains, the snow was mostly man-made, the ocean full of sharks. Also, they'd made her retake her medical exams, a policy designed to hold immigrants back. And then there were the men. Swaggering and laconic, they were not lovers of women. As Ruth described it, they had the primal reflexes for Twinkles's animal print and purring, and short-term, the language barrier created a false sense of mystery and mutual illusion. But Twinkles had found no real romance here.

"Well, thanks for the crepes."

Twinkles leans forward, breasts pooling like skeined milk in her décolletage. She speaks softly, one eye winked, nodding at Ziggy's chest. "They come, my sweetheart. Then you'll wish you still as free as a child."

Ziggy's face flames as she leaps up. "Going now."

"Study hard, little pillangó."

Even halfway across the food court, Ziggy can hear the wet gnashing of her grandmother's enormous plastic teeth.

WHEN ZIGGY GETS HOME, the women are gone. She hurries upstairs to the home PC, and there on the Sofa of a Thousand Tears, Ziggy sees a small, ribbon-tied pink box. Printed all along the sides are tiny Victoria's Secret logos. Ziggy sits at the computer and tries to understand her parents' sex life. Just from a hazy distance. Whether Jeff's new machismo is enabling Ruth's gaudy sexuality, whether her lap dance has inspired him to go out and dress her like a slutty butterfly. At least there is no mistress. The only other explanation is that the underwear is a gift for their svelte Slovenian cleaning lady with the flat hair and three young children. Sometimes the perfect symmetry with which she arranged objects in their house moved Ziggy to tears. Simple things like the alignment of computer speakers perpendicular to the mouse gave the whole room a quiet beauty that nearly overwhelmed her. Ziggy had had a passing paranoia that the Slovenian's elegant arrangements of her mother's chaotic decor were visual love letters to Jeff. But even now this seems extremely unlikely, and Ziggy decides to abandon the gift box with all of its mysterious significance.

Finally, she sits down at the computer to watch *Irréversible*. The narrative is presented in reverse chronological order, obscuring causality and lulling Ziggy into a disengaged stupor. Until the rape scene. Watching the eleven-minute torture in the Mètro underpass, she feels a wincing sick, spiked with hot jolts of pleasure. Ziggy knows that the film is art house and must have a larger social conscience, but her body is still aroused. *Sadistic misogynist*, Hitler Youth clarify. The Nazis explain that Ziggy is just like all the men around Monica Bellucci who objectify her, the camera making everyone who enjoys her curvy ass complicit in her rape. Which means Ziggy is failing Tessa's test: if she wants to be gay and still squish up under the covers, Ziggy must experience female objectification from the victim's perspective. She focuses on the sinking in her stomach—the deeper sensation she has while watching the brutal scene—and now it starts to work. Ziggy feels a churning nausea, as if the cogs are spinning backward—reversing the psychic damage of her internalized misogyny.

So now that that is underway, Ziggy feels ready to learn more about her new culture. She dives into some rudimentary online reading—from Dictionary.com to Wikipedia to *Teen Vogue*'s advice column. Ziggy learns the categories, studies their criteria, then wades deeper into the memey esoterica of queer social media, where she discovers many more variations. You can have a vagina, dress like a woman, and still identify as agender. You can call yourself a heteroromantic homosexual, meaning you have crushes on the opposite gender but only have sex with your own. You can be a homoromantic pansexual, denoting, Ziggy thinks, a boy who prefers cuddling boys but will happily have sex with everyone. There are demisexuals, who only sleep with people they have a strong emotional connection with. Some of the labels seem a little premature. Heteroromantic asexual just sounds like a twelve-year-old girl who still plays with Ken and Barbie.

Tessa has talked of a site where men go to share their fears and dreams in a rich patois, dense with meanings, harrowing with misogyny. A place that seeks to critique, intimidate, and silence. A place where excluded white men go to exclude. "Stay away from Reddit," Tessa has warned. "It's like online dating for date rapists." Ziggy has mostly heeded her friend's advice. But sometimes Jake leaves the home page open on the family PC, and scanning the website's side panel, Ziggy has noticed other more tolerant subreddits. Typing in a few key words, she quickly finds a message board for queer women of color. Most of the users are American—she can tell from the way they spell *people of color* and *marginalized*. Ziggy is excited to ask them about their high schools and how much they resemble *Gossip Girl*. Apparently not very much.

Still, it's cool talking to authentic Americans,

she posts, and is assailed by a chorus of lowercase admonishments.

authenticity = problematic

authenticity < humanity

sorry,

writes Ziggy.

i meant "real"??

plz ↑. this = a fetish-free space.

Chastised, Ziggy stops posting and watches for a while. She is amazed by the subreddit's aggressive commitment to empathy and their bullish imperatives to respect each other's feelings. It makes her think of having to wear knee- and elbow pads as a kid in the sandbox. How cumbersome and overcautious it all seemed until they'd discovered the joy of jumping off the side and smashing into one another.

Eventually Ziggy starts to chat with people about her tormenting inner voices. How Hitler Youth tell her she is flat-chested and worthless. Ziggy is surprised to hear a similar thing happened to theyRus. And natty19. Apparently, boys who want to look like girls are often force-fed by Nazis-of-the-mind. But along with niggling taunts, Ziggy's queer allies also have strong inner convictions. The transmen actually feel male. Even the fluid people have more than just a cruel Aryan chorus. Ziggy only has the mental bullies, and no real sense of herself as anything. But her new queer allies are supportive, even, of uncertainty. *You do you*, they encourage her. Ziggy didn't expect to have a self to do so soon. She has been deferring it for an imagined future time when she won't have to compete for emotional primacy with her mother.

does any1 else have problems w/ vulnerability?

she asks the subreddit. The response is emotionally overwhelming—everyone here is scared for their lives. Which only adds to Ziggy's confusion. She wanted to know if they also found it hard to share their feelings.

Ziggy chats all night, but by dawn, the only category she can commit to with any confidence is bisexual genderqueerness. A kind of placeholder. Anything more specific seems to require rejecting all gender norms or embracing them wholeheartedly. If she is genderqueer, Ziggy doesn't need to take hormones or wear a baseball cap or even call herself a *he*. She doesn't need to get her period. Bisexual genderqueerness is wonderfully diffuse, dissolving all boundaries. In fact, the only uncyborgian thing about queer culture is that every category gets its own flag. Ziggy logs off as the consulate lawnmowers fire up. Outside her window the red and white Polish eagle whips against a blazing blue. It is a beautiful day to start her new life as Kandara's sole bisexual genderqueer secular Jewish person.

Chapter 3

That morning when Ziggy gets to school, she encounters four stoner girls in the common room, playing cards. Lex buys her weed from the one with the knotty hair who is presumably aspiring to dreadlocks. Ziggy takes a seat on the sectional sofa behind them and listens to their game. One of the girls is losing badly and keeps threatening to withdraw. The other three berate her bad sportsmanship and eventually move on to her character at large. What is striking to Ziggy is not the stifling animosity within which these girls can sit and play a card game—their bodies so close that knees and ankles touch—but the way they keep diffusing it with song. Each time one girl starts humming, the other three— even the besieged loser—join her in a sweet, soprano harmony that sets the aggression back to zero. *"Let's get together and feel all right. . . ."* Listening to them, Ziggy has the first feminist thought of her life. Men could never do this.

"Ugh, is there anything whiter than Bob Marley?" Tessa has crept up behind Ziggy and sits haughty at her back, on the other side of the sectional. "Did you hear what happened to the prime minister this morning?"

For a moment Ziggy is confused. Was their PM heard singing Bob Marley? Would that make her too white or not white enough or else prove something about her disloyalty to the coal miners?

"What happened?" she asks Tessa.

"The leader of the opposition pinched her bum."

Ziggy feels somehow responsible. "I'm sorry."

"Why are *you* sorry?"

Ziggy isn't sure. "As an ally to women," she tries.

Tessa nods vaguely then looks suddenly incensed by the cardplayers. She faces them. "If you're going to sing reggae, can you please not do it like Anglican choir girls?"

IN FIRST PERIOD, their English instructor informs Ziggy's class of the prime minister's vile sexual assault and the country's larger problem with misogyny.

"Australian men might call you 'mate,' but they are not your friend." Dr. LeStrange runs a frantic hand through the flop of her undercut. Her hairstyle, paired with loose, tailored pants and boxy dress shirts, gives their teacher the look of an indolent teenage boy conceding to smart-casual. It is widely rumored that Dr. LeStrange is a former student of Kandara who won History prizes and played cello solos and slowly wallflowered herself lesbian. Ziggy understands why she might be triggered by the sexual harassment of a childless woman who wears ill-fitting pantsuits, holds the highest office, and has a husband who identifies as a heterosexual male hairdresser. But starting a mature feminist dialogue with a class of Kandara's most patri-archally internalized is bound to be disheartening.

"Why would anyone even *want* to pinch her bum?" is the opening insult from Cate.

"Her suits are so *baggy*," Kate agrees, crinkling her button nose in distaste.

Dr. LeStrange's teaching methods are unconventional. In-stead of giving the girls a feminist lecturing, she marches them all down to the drama department; tells them to don long, debilitating rehearsal skirts; and makes them act out scenes from *A Doll's House*. Ziggy sees the therapeutic value of this approach. Their teacher is trying to get the girls to tap into historical pain. Perhaps her syllabus is designed to be a year-long constellation.

In the empty assembly hall, they are divided into pairs and allocated a small section of stage. Ziggy is partnered with Lex, but her excitement dies fast. Instead of rehearsing, Lex sits in a greenroom beanbag and Snapchats the rapper, angling her phone over a swathe of upper inner thigh where her skirt meets her panty line. On her leg, Lex has sketched an arrow pointing upward beside the acronym *YOLO*. Each time she receives a message, she squeals and slaps her thighs together. Ziggy can imagine how celebrity-gaze might feel thrilling, sending the skin into rapturous tingles. But she is annoyed with her friend. It seems an insensitive day to send half-naked photos to power-ful men.

"Did you tell him about the prime minister?" Ziggy asks.

Lex laughs. "We don't talk about stuff like that." She shoves the phone under Ziggy's face. "With the kitten ears or with-out?"

Ziggy feels a heavy wave of exhaustion. The filter makes

Lex's eyes sparkle and her cheeks a rosy pink. "With," says Ziggy, wondering if Lex's rapper has ever seen her face without graphic augmentation.

Surprisingly, when it is their turn to perform, Lex rouses to emotionally tortured life. Ziggy's friend gives a moving performance of Nora the oppressed housewife. Ziggy is less successful. As the destitute female friend, she stumbles over her lines in a droning monotone. It is embarrassing to say words like *delightful* and *darlings* and *pooh!* in front of the other girls. She thinks it sounds draggy. Ziggy may not be quite ready to come out today.

Tessa also embodies the play's florid language, delivering anguished *good gracious*es with passionate flourishes of her arm. She has also been cast as Nora and paired with Cate, who is playing Torvald, her paternalistic husband. Though, it is quickly obvious that Cate is not engaging with the text.

"Ms. Lansell-Jones," says Dr. LeStrange. "Is there a reason your performance is so uncharismatic?"

Cate scowls at their teacher. "Maybe it's because you're making me play the man?"

Dr. LeStrange chuckles, and the whole class enjoys a unifying giggle at Cate's surprising misandry. But the eponymous clique leader looks afflicted. She jostles her leaden rehearsal skirt.

"*A Doll's House* is dated," she announces. "Like, maybe it's still relevant to women in Afghanistan, but my mum would just be like, *Um, get real.*"

"My mum wouldn't eat so many lollies," comes Fliss's simpering solidarity.

"Yeah," says Cate. "Nora can't be *that* ambitious."

"If you think about it," says Kate Fairfax, chewing seductively on a hot-pink highlighter pen, "Nora is basically a bored housewife who can't be trusted with her husband's credit card."

Dr. LeStrange snaps her playbook together. Her small, quick eyes blink rapidly in frustration. "What you girls are talking about is *post*feminism. Which is what happens to a movement when everybody in it dies or a new generation doesn't bother to learn the achievements of the one before."

"If you want to *liberate* us," Cate says with theatrical disdain, "let us take off these stinky old skirts."

The sartorial mutineer receives a raucous round of cheers. Dr. LeStrange hangs her head in despair. She speaks in a voice utterly drained of idealism:

"Who has heard the term 'feminist intersectionality'?"

Silence, then Kate's giddy attempt: "Is that where you dissect a feminist?"

Laughter echoes through the empty auditorium, but their teacher remains impressively sober. "It's where you analyze feminism to see where class, race, gender, and sexuality complicate it for different identities."

"Sounds complicated," says Kate, snorting.

"And what's the point of it?" whines Cate.

"The point, Ms. Lansell-Jones, is to expose how our privilege implicates us in other people's oppression."

"This is an English class," says Cate. "Can you please speak English?"

Dr. LeStrange glares at her smiling challenger. "We use intersectionality to see how our experience of being female is different from other women's."

"Ohhh," says Cate, slapping her hands to her thighs in mock-bumpkin epiphany. "Like when it's obvious you have nothing in common with a nineteenth-century Norwegian housewife?"

Kate gleefully waves her playbook. "Feminist dissectionality actually proves that *A Doll's House* isn't relevant to anyone born this century!"

"Unless," says Cate, "you're like a Muslim girl from Punchbowl."

Dr. LeStrange glances between the two girls with trenchant disgust. "And do you know what it's called when you don't want to hear other people's stories?"

"Busy?"

"White. Patriarchal. Narcissism."

Cate eyes their teacher testily. "Are you calling me a narcissist, Dr. L?"

"Your *actions* are narcissistic," the woman says carefully. "And the patriarchy, obviously, is not your fault."

The Cates glower at their teacher. They will surely send a petition around to have her fired or at least ban her from turning Advanced English into Gender Studies. The bell sounds and the girls fling off their rehearsal skirts and then flee to the doors. Ziggy hears Kate whisper to Cate: "She probably just has a crush on you."

Walking back to class, Tessa has commentary.

"The Cates think female empowerment means finding the right cut of jeans for your body type."

Lex shudders in agreement. "Or a formal dress that looks like something Cate Blanchett wore to the Oscars."

"Or just going to the formal." As the words leave her mouth, Ziggy knows they are wrong. The air curdles. Her friends withdraw.

"Everybody goes to the formal," Tessa says brusquely. "You just have to come up with a personalized outfit and a complementary date."

"But I don't know any boys."

"You could take a girl, Ziggy." Tessa's tone is magnanimous. "Or even Alexa or a Google Assistant. It doesn't matter. You just have to be true to yourself."

The sentiment is right, but Ziggy doesn't fully believe her.

"Who are you taking?" Ziggy asks Lex.

Her friend is again swiping at her phone. "Him." Lex points to her screen, where a close-up of the rapper's crotch shows his erection faintly contoured through his jeans. "He'll come if his girlfriend dumps him, which the internet says she will."

Tessa smiles a little condescendingly at Lex. It is obvious she has other plans for both of them.

"And what about you?" Ziggy asks Tessa.

"There's a guy I like at Randalls," she replies. "We did a play together last year."

Ziggy pictures a slim boy in a black turtleneck, performing a perfect sun salute.

"He has cerebral palsy," Lex informs Ziggy.

"Is that why you're taking him?"

"We have a lot in common," Tessa snipes. "But I haven't asked him yet. There's still ten months to go, and I also like this guy from acting class."

"Who's legally blind." Lex is smirking.

"*And* he has a friend who might be good for you." Tessa tilts her chin up in clement benevolence. "He's half indigenous and does poetry slams."

Ziggy wonders what her friends have in mind for her. A water polo player? A newt? Dr. LeStrange? It is enough to worry about her own gender and sexual identity without having to find an appropriate dance partner. Her friends' world is not as isolated as she had hoped. All day she worries about this special person, animal, or object that must accompany her to the formal. It seems your date must be your complementary opposite. An advertisement for everything unique and wonderful about you but in the opposing gender. Ziggy has encountered such ideas before: binaries in service to an ultimate, sacred synthesis. The ancient notion of twin halves completing a perfect whole and dissolving into Oneness with all of existence. The formal is a postfeminist event whose ideology overlaps with that preached weekdays in her living room.

WHEN ZIGGY GETS HOME, there is a circle of scraggly, gray-haired women dancing around the sofa. Some are banging jembes, others are shaking rice-filled gourds, a few wave gnarly sticks strung with bells. African tribal beats blare from the sound system. Ruth stands on the chaise lounge, knees bent, arms extended, swinging her hips in a skirt that jangles like a festive horse saddle. Ziggy watches from the top of the stairs. As the percussion swells, her mother cries out to the women:

"Let the music take you back to your primal animal-self! What is it? A tiger? A buffalo? A baboon?"

The women stomp their feet louder.

"Where does it *live* in your body? Find its hooves, its claws, its huge, powerful thighs. *Dance* your animal!"

Some women experiment with pawing motions and jerking turkey heads; others bull-charge the beanbags; a few get down on all fours, slinking like big lascivious cats. The music builds and the women grunt and roar and shriek. A dumpy lady in solar system tights sprints outside and dive-bombs the pool. She thrashes around in the shallows then does a few swift side-rolls. Ziggy's guess is crocodile.

Afternoons when the women occupy her house, Ziggy usually shuts herself in the bathroom closet with an onion and a bottle of vinegar. Thus far, Ziggy's Nazi fantasia has been inspired by her father's metrosexual jacket collection and her grandmother's formative years. When she thinks of the Holocaust, Ziggy imagines gay leathermen leering over malnourished girls in paper-bag shoes. But today she wants to be a better person. Someone who has consensual sex, even when they are only masturbating. In her fantasies, Ziggy usually plays both parts—victim and abuser—which makes her feel that there is a split in her psyche. A self-contained sadomasochism or what Ziggy has recently diagnosed as her internalized misogyny. The cure she prescribes is heteroromantic bisexuality. If Ziggy can project her sexual desires onto a connected, loving Nazi couple, she can eliminate the objectification and violence.

The obvious choice for this experiment is Rolf, with his rosy cheeks and heel-clicking passion for the Führer, and bright-eyed, amply bosomed Liesl, soaring over the gazebo benches in a graceful split. Ziggy starts as Rolf—her shoulders stiffen, closing in around a soft, silk-lined sports jacket. She pictures Liesl's face over the monogrammed breast pocket—her cupid lips, button nose, fluttering eyelids—and moves in slowly, so slowly that she loses interest just before her lips make contact. Disheartened, she tries again, dipping Liesl's back in a dramatic swoon over the tennis bags and laying her down on a stack of towels. This time, something about the way the sleeve is twisted rouses her and Ziggy pins the jacket to the closet wall. She presses hard against Liesl, pulling on her ponytail. *Stop*, Ziggy hears herself say to someone. She drops the jacket and buries her face in a hanging chambray shirt. Hitler Youth zap vicious thought-Tasers at Ziggy's limbic system. *Patriarchal sadist. Misogynist softcock.* How can they accuse her of being both virile *and* castrated? It feels so unfair, and yet strangely familiar. The kind of insult Ziggy has been overhearing in her house for months. She slumps back between a pair of designer jackboots. And then the bathroom door opens.

Ziggy hears loud footfalls thudding into the room. Heavy, with a soft thwappy underside like a large fish dying against a deck. Rowena's gargantuan ballet slippers. Ziggy makes the quick, thrilling decision to stay and watch through the door-jamb, to see what shapes fill Rowena's underwear—what exotic, hybrid organ might hang or petal there. But the woman moves straight to the sink. She has spotted Ruth's self-portrait. The explicit nude that hangs over the vanity; two thick, parted thighs framing a series of concentric ovals in dirty pinks; an icon glowering, openmouthed, over every morning shave. Rowena shakes her head and giggles, and Ziggy feels vindicated. She wants to be on the outside, mocking the smug anatomical superiority of her cisgender mother. The urge is very strong. Ziggy grabs a tote bag full of old toys and backs out of the closet.

"Sorry," she says, fussing with the bag. "I was just getting these."

Rowena seems pleasantly surprised to see her. She observes the bag's opening: a silent orgy of reaching Barbie doll arms and snarling dinosaur beaks. Ziggy worries Rowena thinks she is going to play with them.

"We're writing origin stories at school."

Rowena cocks her head. "In English?"

"Science."

"Wow, that's liberal."

Ziggy's school is vaguely protestant and scientifically rationalist, and their principal never honors the traditional custodians of the land. But she can't quit now. "Our teacher thinks the Rainbow Serpent could have been a T. rex."

Rowena grins. "And which landscape feature did T. rex create?" She is being droll. Which is nice. Adults are never droll with Ziggy. It makes her feel like Rowena has missed the whole drama of Ziggy's flat chest.

"Probably Rose Bay."

Rowena laughs. "And Pyrmont. And Darling Harbour."

There is a warm, smiling hiatus before Rowena glances up again at the painting. Ziggy studies her face. The blue eye liner has sweat into Rowena's sockets, forming dark, marsupial rings. Her features are coarser up close—the bulbous nose, square jaw, jutting brow. A huge Adam's apple bobs anxiously above a fine, silver chain. Rowena sighs and raises a hand to her chest—a movement so delicate, it seems to refine her larger features. She is more feminine than anyone Ziggy has ever seen.

Rowena nods at the painting. "It's very expressionistic."

Ziggy looks up and is irked anew by the vagina's dramatic chiaroscuro.

"My mother thinks her vagina is a magical netherworld."

"Well, it kind of is."

"My point is that she thinks you can have a primeval vagina that men are then supposed to find sexy in Victoria's Secret."

"Ah yes, the sacred and the profane . . ."

"Are men really equipped to handle those kinds of contradictions?"

"Definitely not."

Ziggy's heart leaps; she has an ally. "And don't you find the Magnetic Poles too binary?"

"Personally, I quite like binaries." Rowena smiles, adjusting a hair clip.

Ziggy feels disoriented and then very hot in the face. She sits on the edge of the tub. "Sorry, I'm sure sometimes they're helpful."

"But I absolutely agree there's got to be some room for ambiguity."

"What kind of ambiguity?"

"All kinds." Rowena faces the mirror and now properly attacks her hair. "Of course men aren't always a certain way and neither are women, but when they want to trigger one another romantically and sexually, the Magnetic Poles can be useful."

Rowena forms a perfect center-part with her fingernail and Ziggy instinctively checks her own reflection. She didn't straighten her hair this morning and the curls are returning in kinky chunks. "But how do the Poles work for gay people?" Her voice sounds frantic. "Or genderqueers?"

"Dualities usually arise naturally between most couples."

Ziggy still thinks Ruth means to wipe out all queer, nonconforming people like her. She nods, disappointed but deferential.

Rowena speaks gently. "Do you identify as genderqueer?"

"I don't know. Sometimes I hear voices telling me I'm a boy."

"Do you feel like a boy?"

"No."

"Then you've probably just got a strong self-critic."

"It doesn't feel like me. The voice is German."

"That sounds very critical."

An ache bobs at the back of Ziggy's throat. "It says I'm not female enough."

"Well that's different from feeling male. Sounds like this German voice is very immature."

Ziggy nods, relieved. "I think it's adolescent."

"Don't worry about the labels. There's no need to rush yourself."

"Yeah," says Ziggy, fortified by their shared defiance. "I'm definitely not ready to commit to a flag yet."

"Forget the flags. Unless you're marching for something." Rowena smiles. "I take a more Taoist approach to gender, you know: 'Am I me dreaming I'm a butterfly or am I a butterfly dreaming I'm me?' I'd just try to stay open—sometimes mansplaining actually feels like foreplay."

Ziggy feels lightheaded. Everything seems permissible in Rowena's presence. Ruth's shrill opposites hang in tranquil lunar orbit all around her. As Ziggy meets her gaze in the mirror, Rowena's eyes are suddenly deep and syrupy with solicitude. She nods at Ziggy's head.

"I think there's a very rowdy mob in there trying to shout you down."

A sob hops up Ziggy's throat. She holds it in, her whole body tight and steamy as a wonton.

"Don't let them do it."

Ziggy nods gratefully. She would like to ask how the Magnetic Poles apply if you're not a boy but you don't have breasts or high estrogen levels, if you enjoy rough imaginary sex with women and also get aroused by Aryan men in jackboots. But she is still choking down her feelings. Rowena walks to the door, daintily waves, then glides back out to the other women.

Chapter 4

Between classes, Kandara's hallways hemorrhage girls, and Lex, Tessa, and Ziggy make a game of bucking the current. They smash shoulders and shout and shoot furious stares at the big-boned country girls. Their school's busy tributaries are transformed into the gropey red streets of a coal mining town, while the three friends embody their fiercest cosmopolitan stereotypes.

"What are you looking at!" Lex barks at an approaching wall of boarders, flushed and sweaty from rowing practice.

"I'm-a walk-en hee-ya!" Ziggy yells. Her accent adenoidally Jewish.

"Very *Seinfeld*," Tessa congratulates her. "Or, like, early Woody Allen."

The larger girls dodge her aggressive elbows, and Ziggy sails along on the amazement of being a physical threat. Which is confusing. Ziggy and her friends are supposed to be the victims.

In their acting game, they are the ones being eye-raped and cat-called and sneakily felt up.

Now Prue Fielder—the most box-jawed and perpetually sunburned of the seniors' rowing squad—flings an arm out like a boom gate, blocking their path.

"What the eff is wrong with you, Cameron?" she bellows at Lex. Ziggy observes that Prue's thighs are thicker than her own torso.

Lex steps right up to the rower's broad, muscular chest. "What, Fielder, are you going to sexually assault me with your canoe paddle?"

The epic girl-span shakes her blockish head. "You seriously need help."

"And you need to go back to England and return that loaf of bread."

Prue gives Lex a long, sickened look, cinching it with an "ugh." Then she turns and walks away.

Ziggy and Tessa beam triumphant at either side of their ruthless friend. Lex hates the country girls. She knows their parents' politics. If it were up to them, the nation's borders would be closed, the mines open, the sprinklers on, the clocks set back to 1955. These are the people who would prefer that brown girls stayed in brown countries, that advertising had remained in neat, preordered catalogs and not clogging up their inboxes. All the spam pouring into their nice, spacious nation is muddling everything up. Algorithms and Asians are taking their jobs; their golden girls can no longer get into the best university courses. Too many Chinese. Too many desperate, striving people with no interest in after-school sports. People with no feel for leisure. Unbalanced people. UnAustralians.

"The cyborg revolution is coming," announces Tessa. "And

Prue Fielder is going to be up shit creek. Which is probably an actual creek somewhere out near Wagga."

As Prue is swallowed back up in the girl-crush, Lex turns to Tessa, her eyes poppy with scandal. "She just checked out my ass."

"Conservatives are always secretly gay," Tessa sneers, and the two of them keep charging down the hall.

Ziggy hangs back. Like the cheerleaders and the Cates, her friends also seek intra-school objectification via the more masculine girls, which for Ziggy is both homophobic and self-loathing. But mostly, a risk. She doesn't want to end up on the wrong side of the male gaze. Tessa and Lex's game extends to every sphere of life, making Ziggy's role feel very unstable. Her friends objectify themselves in the underpass and at the mall, colliding with the sporty girls in campus thoroughfares, and also, she now notices, on social media. Instagram is where they go to get catcalled alone in their bedrooms. Ziggy scrolls through hours of smoochy lips and deep cleavage. Tessa posts a lot of vampy bed-hair shots; Lex prefers a classic bath towel. Ziggy doesn't get it: If you are constantly inviting boys to look down your top, how can it be eye-rape? Hitler Youth congratulate her for applying the standard argument used in rape culture. *Welcome to the club,* they tell her. Ashamed and fearing further scrutiny, Ziggy temporarily disables her account.

That week, e-vites go around for Cate's Valentine's Day party at her harbor-front mansion, and Lex gets one. Ziggy is shocked to learn that Cate doesn't despise Lex as much as Lex reviles her. The girls are old family friends, and Lex's exotic skin color and extreme beauty have inspired a mythical fascination among the Randalls boys. Tessa tells Ziggy that they call her Rihanna and beg Cate to bring her to all social gatherings. In fact, Lex always gets invited to Cate's parties. Occasionally Tessa and

Lex even attend, though mostly for anthropological reasons. Tessa tells Ziggy that the debauchery is so excessive, it promotes egalitarianism across the social strata. One year, the very zaftig and deodorant-averse Patricia Katsatouris gave a hand job to Randalls's head prefect. Or that's what she said. The boys get blackout drunk and conveniently forget their conquests.

Hearing this, Ziggy senses a political opportunity. "It's like the white settlers with the Aboriginals."

Lex looks offended. "The Aboriginals were prettier than Patricia Katsatouris."

Tessa pats their diminutive, in-earnest friend. "It's okay, Lex," Tessa placates her. "Jews are just very metaphorical."

Ziggy isn't sure how to take this. "You mean the Old Testament?"

"Yes, and how God gave you a 'promised land.'"

Israel is too complicated for first period so Ziggy lets this go. She knows Zionism is a dirty word but still feels, in some deep preverbal place, that Jerusalem is not just a metaphor.

After lunch, Ziggy is informed that the three of them will be attending Cate's party. This time the purpose of their social outing is not to imbibe the low-level female trauma and make nuisances of themselves. Engagement rumors for the rapper are rife, and Lex might need to find an alternative formal date. Tessa thinks her friend could get lucky with Randalls's first African American exchange student—if he deigns to show up. Tessa has her eye on a brilliant scholarship student rumored to be autistic. Nobody mentions finding a date for Ziggy, which comes as a great relief.

ARRIVING THAT SATURDAY at Cate's gated mansion, the girls are buzzed through two electric fences and into an elevator.

Descending to the pool deck, Ziggy avoids the reflective glass. Her friends are, like all the other girls, wearing short skirts and crop tops. Ziggy has tied her hair back in a ponytail and borrowed one of her brother's dark navy dress shirts. She feels like an awkward Bar Mitzvah boy but hopes the overall ambiguity will be socially intimidating.

The doors open on a pulsing hive of bodies, pink under gel lamps—everything bouncing, even the palm trees. Ziggy weaves through jungling limbs, along the gooey lick of pool. She senses there are girls here getting fingered. Her friends stop at the deep end. The black exchange student is nowhere in sight, and Tessa's potential paramour also appears to have skipped the event or else been less popular than she thought. Then three pink-shirted, loafer-heeled blond boys sidle up and engage the girls in adult conversation.

How's your night going? Been a good night? Having a good one?

Ziggy can feel them tamping down on darker instincts with their hollow stock phrases. She doesn't appreciate how close they are standing to her friends, and one of the boys is grinning at Lex with a rapaciousness that could be considered sexual harassment. Ziggy feels protective and jealous and alarmed by the sensual way her friends are leaning into their hips. Ziggy is cut off from their quorum; she occupies a cool, lonely space tinged with despair. What she would like to call "the void" to Tessa, but her friend is busy responding to these little CEO disguise kits.

"It's going good," says Tessa. "How amazing is the view?"

"I can see my swimming pool," says one of the boys.

"Me too," says another.

The deeply tanned boy in salmon-colored shorts points to a cluster of tall ships. "There's my granddad's yacht."

Thankfully, Ziggy's friends aren't very skilled at small talk. When Lex remarks that big boats are compensation for small penises, Tessa stewards the conversation toward the depressingly elaborate snacks prepared by Suze Lansell-Jones, and gossip about attractive male movie stars. After she assigns sex addiction and domestic abuse to all their favorite action heroes, the boys start to agitate. They quickly turn on one of their own, mocking his Cartier watch.

"Well," the boy rebuts, "your parents' beach house is in *Wollongong*."

"What's wrong with Wollongong?"

"A holiday house needs to be in the actual bush, not just the outer suburbs."

"Whatever mate, your dad drives a Porsche *SUV*!"

Now the connoisseur of vacation homes gets very red and relays a nasty little story about the boy with the Wollongong beach house—how he got his Islander nanny arrested at Fratelli Fresh when he slipped a bottle of artichokes into her handbag. "Because they looked *elegant*!" he screeches.

The boys start to scuffle—a series of light slaps and one long, painful-looking ear-pull. It is a relief that they would rather bicker over status symbols than seduce Ziggy's friends. Sabotage may not even be necessary—men seem quite capable of undoing themselves.

Ziggy places a puny arm over each of her friends and guides them away from the boy-skirmish. She can feel their shoulders relaxing, softening into the clammy undersides of her arms. They like being led this way. Ziggy walks them to the far end of the pool; from here she plans to start a scathing social commentary, mocking the heteronormative bluster all around them. But before she can begin, a boisterous drinking game materializes on the other side of the water. Two thick, squarish boys are swilling beer and thrusting their pelvises at the girls with vicious specificity.

"Rugger buggers," scoffs Tessa, eyeing them nervously.

"Roid ragers," Lex concurs.

"Or just medium-high testosterone levels," says Ziggy, casually damning the whole gender.

The song is "Roxanne," and each time Sting says her name, the boys take a swig. Watching them hump and stumble under the reddish light, Ziggy remembers the lyrics.

"He's talking about a prostitute," she informs her friends, then watches them scowl harder. At her feet, Ziggy notices a discarded plate of sushi rolls. She picks off a California roll and holds it up in front of Lex.

"Dare me?" Ziggy asks her.

Lex's eyes go soft and dreamy. Ziggy feels her chest broaden, the muscles get tight. Taking aim, a cool current runs up her arm, like she is partially machine. The sushi roll shoots over the pool, splats into the bigger boy's face, then plops off onto his loafer. He spins around and sees her.

"Little fag!"

The boy hurls a pool noodle that falls short, belly-flopping into the water. Tessa and Lex hoot in triumph. Elated, Ziggy swipes up the noodle and thrusts it out in front of her, aiming it like a sword.

"She's got a dick!" someone yells, and Ziggy freezes. She drops the noodle and edges back toward her friends.

"They're just jealous," she says, then clarifies: "That I've got better aim."

But her friends are transfixed by a sudden massing of male bodies around the sushi roll victim. The boys are scrumming together—slapping one another's backs, gulping their mixed drinks and plotting.

"Uh-oh." Lex seems to know what's coming. She holds her hand out to Ziggy. "Give me your phone."

The boys split off into two packs. The twin lines make a barbarous dash around either end of the pool, whooping and growling toward her. Ziggy watches limply as their foisty chests close in; their rough hands grip her shoulders (almost tenderly—treating her like a girl, which she almost takes personally) and raise her up over their heads. For a moment the elevation feels like victory, and then Ziggy is being shunted toward the blue. Her screams are drowned in the primordial bellow of the Randalls school song. The boys pause at the edge, count *one, two* . . . then toss her into the water.

Ziggy sinks to the bottom then hovers over the pool filter, shame gnawing at her flesh while the air thins and her head starts to twinkle away. Watching herself, Ziggy feels dense and placid as a toad. She feels herself doubled, partnered, and shoots to the surface like synchronized swimmers. But breaking water, the sensation is gone. All along the pool's edge hangs a wall of laughing faces. Some girls eye her pityingly, others smirk— relieved that someone else is the worst, most pathetic cretin of the evening. Paddling to the side, her face feels naked as roadkill, her brain is the tingling smash of glass. As she climbs the pool stairs, Jake's shirt suctions to her chest and Ziggy aches all over. The next moments are a shivering blur of being passed from Tessa to Lex to Suze Lansell-Jones bearing a large bath towel. Ziggy is surprised that her friends seem animated, electric almost, at the event of her harassment. They dash around Cate's bedroom, fetching Ziggy dry clothes and thick socks and ornate scrunchies. Suze has let them in here without her daughter's permission, and Ziggy can feel the errant joy radiating from their bodies. But the room is pristinely curated and reveals no information they didn't already have from Instagram.

"She's even emptied her rubbish bin," groans Tessa.

They find nothing aside from a small plastic case that could be evidence Cate wears a night retainer. When Ziggy is dressed and verbal again, the three girls abandon Cate's bedroom. Ascending back to street level in the Lansell-Jones elevator, Ziggy feels her friends' sympathy cloak warmly around her. The two girls are still buzzing. None of them met a potential formal date, but Ziggy was traumatized, which seems to be just as good. Tessa and Lex eye her expectantly, eager for her emotional condition and whatever she might want to do next.

"We could go back to mine for a Jacuzzi?" she offers, realizing this is exactly where she wants their evening to end: snuggled together in warm, bubbling water.

Her friends are surprisingly enthusiastic. Despite the absence of danger or men, they seem excited to join Ziggy in isolated and luxurious self-soothing.

At her house, Ziggy lends her navy one-piece to Tessa, while Lex gets the bikini. As they drop their modesty sarongs, Ziggy watches her kiddie costumes bloom new curves like exotic sea sponges. She stands at the pool fence, swaddled in a giant beach towel.

Lex steps straight in and glides to the wall, leans back against it, head tipped skyward. But Tessa toes in anxiously, her eyes cutting between the pool gate and the deep blue of the Polish topiary. Then she performs a full-body shiver, squeals, and plunges into the water.

"He's there!" Tessa cries, midair. "Watching from the bushes!"

"Where?" whispers Lex. She turns to face the wall then presses flush against it. Tessa does the same.

"Now I've lost him," says Tessa, resting her chin catlike on the edge. "We'll have to keep watch."

Ziggy assumes sentinel on the side adjacent to Lex. A strange, menacing silence enfolds them as Ziggy's friends slide in closer to the spa jets. She recalls the rumor of a faucet-humping girl who wound up in the ICU with an air-bubble aneurism. A pounding amazement fills her head as Ziggy realizes what Tessa and Lex are doing.

"Now he's watching us from the house," says Lex. "On his wide-screen."

Tessa peers around anxiously. "There's surveillance everywhere."

"He's got ten security cameras filming us from different angles—" Lex's breath catches. "And he's just *watching* us from his massage chair at the fireplace."

Ziggy has seen photos of the rapper's palatial estate. She is familiar by now with the layout and appliances. What surprises her about Lex's fantasy is that Tessa is playing along.

"'YOLO,' he says, and then starts to rub his penis." The cyborg is very slightly shuddering.

Ziggy's friends stare off into the dark, eyes glazed with a strained inward focus. Together, they continue to narrate in a tone that moves between outrage and arousal. Ziggy presses into the wall too, but she is fighting hard against the hot shiver building inside her. She doesn't want to be aroused. She doesn't want to be thinking of a black man thinking of two young girls masturbating in a Jacuzzi. It feels like a trap—a test that she is going to fail. Ziggy tries to make it unsexual; first she conjures the taste of chocolate and then she tries to imagine what the Latin electives at school think of when they masturbate, and finally she just stares down through the bubbles to the hazy white of her submerged thigh. Ziggy orgasms and it feels intensely autoerotic.

Once her friends leave, Ziggy researches the word *autoerotic*. After reading three articles about auto-asphyxiation deaths and then watching a walrus jerk off in captivity, she decides it could be a sad and lonely path. But it seems too early to tell if Ziggy prefers masturbation to sex with other people, considering her lack of experience or options. Checking her emails, Ziggy sees that at ten P.M., Hitler Youth sent her an ad for nunchakus; which was probably the exact moment she was hurling the noodle at her loutish rivals. Ziggy understands that if she identifies as a transgender male, Tessa will include her in the women of color category; whereas if she only likes girls, it seems Ziggy is just another predacious lesbian. But she feels less like a boy than an alien. Cartoon lizard might be closer. Even "genderqueer" is probably too queer for someone who just wishes they had pubic hair. If anybody asks, Ziggy thinks it's now safest to call herself a gender-neutral autoerotic secular Jewish person, happy to live in the diaspora.

DAYS LATER TESSA CALLS a moratorium on their games. She has new information about trauma, gleaned from a new girl in her extracurricular acting class. Tessa does jazz ballet and acting at a dance academy in the Inner West, where she has access to public school girls. The new girl, Charmaine, has had small but meaty roles in three feature films, and last year—handing her the gold statue for Most Outstanding Newcomer—Cate Blanchett whispered to Charmaine that she thought the younger actress was "just fabulous." At the ceremony's after party, Charmaine flirted with Cate's husband until she realized he was just a caterer, so she ran off with his cigarettes, which she smoked on the balcony with Cate's real husband, who gave her his email.

Charmaine says Tessa is wrong about Method acting, and you don't make your suffering up; you have to dredge up past suffering. She says real Method acting is like being black. You can't just slip it on like a costume or paint it over your face. It must already live inside you and be hauled up in a process called "affective memory." Charmaine says difficult childhoods are good, trauma is better. Emotional suppression is for people who only want to do Oscar Wilde plays or wish you a happy Australia Day. And she would know: Charmaine is indigenous.

Tessa drags Lex and Ziggy along to a Saturday afternoon dance recital, where it becomes quickly obvious that she is infatuated with the Aboriginal actor-singer-dancer. After the show, the three of them huddle in the foyer, watching as the other girls dash around in leotards, swigging from champagne flutes. Ziggy is entranced by these government-schooled girls; she has seen them at Central Station—rolling their own cigarettes while wearing sports bras as tops or standing in loud, abrasive clusters, fingering their belly piercings on public transport. Once she witnessed a pack of them stationed at opposite ends of an escalator, forcing two private school girls to ride up and down for a full Sisyphean ten minutes.

In hushed tones by the foyer exit, Tessa relays a few of Charmaine's recent celebrity encounters—an epic bender on the yacht of a nineties pop icon, a gropey limo ride with a drunken soapie star—claiming that, actually, she and Charmaine share a similar trauma. That they really "get" each other. Lex listens with a raised eyebrow; Ziggy doesn't like the sound of it either.

As if friendship were a prize for mutual suffering. But when they are finally introduced that night, Charmaine is really nice.

"So you're all Kandara girls?" she asks them.

Lex and Ziggy nod uneasily. But Charmaine seems genuinely interested. She even has gossip about the tiny celebrity whose daughter goes to their school.

"A makeup artist told me that her wardrobe lady had a suit delivered to the guy's house and saw him standing on his balcony beside another man in matching dressing gowns."

The three friends gasp.

"Which shouldn't be surprising," she continues. "Seeing as he belongs to that alien cult."

"What alien cult?" Ziggy feels herself leaning too close to the affable prodigy.

"You know, the cult that says humans are descended from birdlike aliens?"

"Don't the members all fly around in private jets?" Evoking class consciousness, Lex is clearly showing off.

"Yep," says Charmaine. "To remind them of their origins."

"I heard it was to deter them from violence and homosexuality."

Charmaine meets Lex's sass with more amenability. "Yep, they're all closeted celebs with fake girlfriends."

At this revelation, Lex's face visibly falls, taking personally the news of an outed male celebrity. She can tell Lex doesn't like Charmaine, but Ziggy feels a deep, psychic attraction. She has never met anyone so special. During the Jackson 5 medley, when the beat died and the other girls dropped to the floor, Charmaine rose like a thin, brown stamen from the tight bud of red leotards to serenade her pet rat floating high in the nosebleeds. From the dark, musty hind of the auditorium, Ziggy and

Lex watched Charmaine quiver onstage with flamelike intensity. When Charmaine's voice soared, Ziggy felt Lex's shoulders scrunch up. Charmaine's alto had the harsh, clarifying quality of strong cleaning product. On Ziggy's friend it had both a startling and slightly toxic effect.

When Charmaine abandons them in the foyer, the trio return to Ziggy's house. Tessa disemminates a steady stream of anecdotes, including Charmaine's first acid trip, which ended in a hotel pool passed out on Heath Ledger's old surfboard. Lex glowers. Ziggy isn't disturbed by Tessa's infidelity and finds she can nourish herself on mere proximity to celebrities. Knowing someone who knows someone almost famous, she can feel the electric emanations buzzing off her own skin. Then Tessa tells them Charmaine once did a karaoke duet with Iggy Azalea, and Lex gets mean.

"Can you please explain how your prosthetic arm is just like Aboriginal genocide?"

"My trauma isn't about my arm," Tessa says with calm condescension. "It's about alcohol."

"Well, Charmaine's is still worse."

"How?"

"Her trauma is historical."

"So's mine!" yells Tessa. "Everyone on my mother's side has been alcoholic since the convicts."

"Yeah, but nobody committed genocide on your culture then fucked you up with booze."

"What do you think the Potato Famine was?"

"The Irish drank *before* the Potato Famine!"

"Fine," says Tessa. "I don't need your approval. The fact is, I have trauma, and you saying 'The Irish drank anyway' or 'Now you live in Rose Bay' isn't going to take that away from me."

"Fine," says Lex. "Keep your Potato Famine trauma."

"I will," says Tessa. She eyes her friend doggedly. "And actually, I need some help with it."

"Help?"

"I need to get stoned."

Lex snorts. "I thought you didn't like 'that out-of-control feeling'?"

"Which is why I need to experience it. If I can't drink, I need to get stoned." Tessa rolls her shoulders back courageously. "Would you please roll me a joint?"

Ziggy doesn't understand this. She speaks tenderly. "But Tess, what does getting stoned have to do with the Potato Famine?"

"I need to know how my ancestors felt."

"When they were drunk?"

"When they were drunk because they were being persecuted."

Lex isn't buying it. "But I thought real Method acting meant you could only access old suffering, not create any new ones?"

"Yes, but when your trauma is hundreds of years old, you need to supplement Charmaine's method with the intensive Leonardo DiCaprio version."

Lex rolls her eyes epically. Ziggy thinks Tessa could probably just cast her mind back to yesterday afternoon, when her alcoholic mother was no doubt drunk and abusing the housemaids. But she doesn't want to rattle Tessa, her friend seems anxious enough. Then Ziggy sees the tremble in Tessa's hand, and feels herself caving. For the first time since they met, the invulnerable cyborg looks genuinely terrified.

"We can smoke in here," Ziggy offers.

Tessa beams gratitude. "Thanks, Ziggy." She looks at Lex, her eyes rounding with secret significance. "It will be good for all of us to enter a different reality."

"All right," says Lex. "But seriously, no panic attacks."

"I promise," says Tessa. "That would be inflicting emotional labor, and I've already spent this month's allowance."

Ziggy is dumbfounded. All this time, she could have been charging her mother a fee.

IT IS EARLY SATURDAY EVENING. While they wait for Jeff and Ruth to leave for dinner, the three friends make their preparations. The mood is now buoyant, all aggravation dispersed into jittery mania. Tessa downloads several hours' worth of sexually explicit music videos; they fill the fruit bowl with oranges in case one of them OD's. Ziggy imagines getting stoned will be like alcohol but with a dry mouth, less energy, and the strong possibility of a panic attack. Her grip on reality already feels infirm. She is a closeted autoerotic gender-neutral secular Jew who will most likely be taking herself to the formal. Unlike her friends, the only thing that doesn't scare Ziggy about their endeavor is the risk of getting caught by her parents. Ziggy's mother would let the girls shoot heroin into their eyeballs if it pushed them closer to selfhood. Still, there is some satisfaction in following the protocol for teenage delinquency. Only when they hear Jeff's car growl out of the driveway does Lex start to roll the joint.

Packing the weed, folding the filter, licking the paper shut—Ziggy experiences her friend as possessing a powerful, adult mystique. When Lex lights up, seeing her lips purse against the filter feels somehow intimate. A private behavior on new display. Like watching her kiss someone. Lex pulls hard on the joint then passes it to Ziggy. The lit tip jewels at the ends of her fingers and Ziggy takes it, feeling Lex's wetness all around the filter. Ziggy inhales and the smoke comes fast, stuffing her throat like cotton. She coughs once, waits, and is pummeled by a rogue swell of coughing. Tears surge at her eyes. Ziggy can't tell if she is breathing. She rasps at them, but her friends are suddenly distracted by something on Lex's phone. Tessa appears utterly relaxed. Ziggy takes a glass of water and gulps from it rapidly. Now her throat feels too cold and disturbingly deep. Hitler Youth think Ziggy is probably headed for a heart attack; but while checking her pulse, Ziggy realizes she isn't coughing anymore. Moments are eclipsing themselves. Time has a thick, alien consistency that swallows her thoughts. Sensory boundaries are dissolving. It is even possible that Hitler Youth are now talking out loud. Saying things like "masturbation" and "pussypenis." For this reason, Ziggy would like to go downstairs and start blasting music videos on the home entertainment system. Luckily her friends show great enthusiasm for leaving the bedroom.

By now, Lex and Tessa are acquainted with Ruth's home decor. They have accepted that certain rocks can come inside, placed on the hides of certain beasts whose bones might sit adjacent on side tables covered with tapestries depicting those same beasts running free, tapestries woven by women with real relationships to the natural world around them. That all of these things might be resonant, even meaningful, to Ziggy's mother, her friends have accepted without political argument. Maybe it is too subtle with homewares. Like the aura bestowed by a celebrity eau de toilette. Tessa's Nicki Minaj-shaped perfume bottle seems to be an equivalent cultural appropriation.

But then there is the living room's fifteen-foot mural. Ruth's bizarre feature wall depicts goddesses hanging from hot-air balloons, Buddhas cross-legged in tree crotches, and Frida Kahlo riding a stallion, bareback, into the setting sun. In the past, Ziggy's friends have simply laughed at the mural and then sped off to her bedroom. But tonight, confronted with the wall, Tessa breaks away from their orderly little line.

"Why are all the women white?" she baits Ziggy.

"They're Greek goddesses," Ziggy replies, though this isn't strictly true. There are Hindus and Native Americans and Russian folkloric witches with names like types of fungi. Ziggy doesn't know how to defend her mother's feminism. "Can we please just go down to the TV?"

Tessa marches to the wall. With her newly indigenized gaze, she studies a patch of savannah, sprigged with meerkats. "If this is Africa, the women should be black."

"It's definitely Africa," says Lex. "Look at the lion cubs."

"Aw, Simba!"

Lex shakes her head at Tessa. "Not every lion is the Lion King."

Fearing conflict, Ziggy moves away from her friends to the far end of the wall, to the green base of Mount Everest where Frida Kahlo rides her sable horse. At school they have just studied the Mexican artist. Ziggy was most fascinated by the bus accident, particularly when their teacher refused to share the gruesome details. Ziggy had pressed her: Wasn't it necessary to know what the artist's injuries were? Especially because she did self-portraits? Ziggy had pictured Frida's crotch with a protruding metal appendage not unlike the actual instrument of wounding. Something about her monobrow and downy mustache made it seem possible that she had replaced her broken parts with a mechanical penis. It annoyed Ziggy that their teacher was more interested in the artist's colorful head scarves. Ms. Schlager was always talking about Frida's self-consciousness, something about the male gaze and how she used it to paint herself into existence. According to their teacher, the artist's "subjective ob-

jectivity" was evidenced by her bold stare and eccentric tribal
jewelry. But not her facial hair or her protuberant brow and how
they might relate to her private parts. Looking at the mural now,
Frida's "subjective objectivity" seems as ambiguous as Ziggy's.
Maybe they both lack a talent for self-objectification. Unlike
Tessa and Lex. Ziggy turns back around and sees her friends
huddled together beneath Mount Kilimanjaro, taking some sort
of internet personality test.

"I'm blue, Thursday, banana, Paris."

"I'm green, Friday, kiwi, Rome."

In a brave attempt to be known Ziggy declaims: "I'm purple!
Tuesday! Mango! Cuba!"

Both girls give her a glare of intense irritation.

"Cuba is not a capital city," says Lex.

"Then I'm Rio!"

"You can't just choose one," Tessa snaps. "You have to take
the test."

"Can't you just tell me what I am?" pleads Ziggy. "Do I seem
more like a week*end* or a week*day*?"

Lex shakes her head, eyes fixed to her phone. "No idea."

Ziggy storms off into the kitchen. Her friends don't follow
her. She can tell they are now playing with a celebrity face-
swapping app. Tessa is doing an American accent and Lex is just
making duck faces and flicking her hair. Ziggy feels alone in a
way that makes her think of vacuum cleaners in deep space—
something she knows she's misunderstood from physics. Tessa
and Lex claim they don't ultimately want to be objectified, yet
they strive to be famous people—the most unattainable objects
of all.

After an indefinite period of time in which Ziggy may have
eaten three sobering oranges, her friends wander downstairs to

the TV. Now Tessa wants to watch music videos. Observing black female dancers in booty shorts brandish chainsaws, Ziggy tries very hard to understand the feminist message.

"They're reclaiming the ass," Tessa explains. "White women got to reclaim words like *cunt* and *slut*, but black women have to literally reclaim their butts."

Ziggy watches Lex cringe but remain peaceably mute, staring at the television, where a line of perfect brown butts bounces in formation. Ziggy doesn't think the chainsaws are undermining the attractiveness of their asses. In fact, the fleshy gorgeousness of these asses seems to be reclaiming the chainsaw. Ziggy isn't sure it is possible to reclaim the female ass. She slides the words around in her brain—*subjective objectivity*—but now she can't remember what they mean. The forgetting makes her anxious, and Ziggy checks the microwave clock to see how many more hours she must be stoned. It is only nine thirty, which means many. Ziggy knows her mother would say *just be in the moment*, but the moment is suddenly squeezing her skull. It pounds through her ears and presses on her lungs. Ziggy needs Time to keep marching forward, quickly and away from this terrible feeling. Maybe if she can tie her shoelaces in under three seconds.

Sure, say Hitler Youth. *Knock yourself out.*

So she does, and she was right. Hitler Youth are very goal-oriented. Ziggy has completely forgotten why she was panicking.

That's because you have Israeli amnesia.

Ziggy considers retying her laces. Eating another orange. Then she looks at the clock and sees that only one minute has passed.

"Guys." Her voice is distant, subaquatic. "I think I'm having a heart attack."

Her friends crack up. Their mouths gape meanly, lips curling with cruel delight. The whole room seems to buckle and skid into the television. But the dancers keep grinding. Ziggy turns frantically to the window, looks out at the calming jade of the pool, and remembers Rowena. Perched on the edge, tracing her long pink toenails through the water.

"I'm just going to get something!" Ziggy says too loudly, then starts for the staircase.

Tessa and Lex share a look. They probably think she is going to go masturbate. But Ziggy forges on up the steps. The only thing that can save her now is the soothing two-tone of Rowena's voice. As she'd hoped, her mother's ancient, leather-bound address book is there on the bedside table. Ziggy finds the number and dials.

"Hello?" Rowena sounds impatient. Ziggy considers hanging up. "Tim, is that you? I'm just leaving the parking lot."

"No, um, it's Ziggy. Ruth Klein's daughter."

"Ziggy!" Rowena's exuberance emanates from the phone speaker and all through Ziggy's brain. She relaxes and, to confirm it, checks her pulse.

"Are you there, love?"

"Sorry," says Ziggy, her mind suddenly blank. "I can't remember why I called you."

"That's okay! I'm very happy to hear from you!"

Rowena's kindness has a calming effect on Ziggy's nervous system. She feels she can be totally honest. "I was just worried I'd given myself brain damage."

"Oh my god, what happened?"

"I smoked too much pot."

There is a pause. A little giggle. "Ziggy, you definitely don't have brain damage. Pot just makes you paranoid."

Now Ziggy remembers the anodyne Tessa devised in the event of a panic attack. "Paranoia is just an overactive death drive," she recites, hopefully.

"Sure," says Rowena. "Or life force on steroids."

Ziggy likes this. It makes her feel better about needing to do the soap twice each time she washes her hands. Now she can hear Rowena humming. The tune is familiar, but Ziggy can't place it. The melody runs like warm lights along her ear canal.

"I'm going to have to get off in a minute. . . ." Rowena says, a smile creeping into her voice. "I've got to get dressed for my show."

"Which show?"

"My drag show."

Ziggy imagines a small, glittery room full of Rowenas, and her mind dilates with happiness. She urgently needs to be there. "Can I come?"

"Now? Sure . . . if you think that would be cool with your mum?"

Cool with your mum. Ziggy doesn't care what is cool with her mum. And she has an acute desire to be in Rowena's presence. To behold her onstage.

"I'm with some friends," says Ziggy. "Can they come too?"

"Of course! Ooh, here's Timmy." There is a muffled squeezing sound, like the phone is being hugged to death. "Ziggy, love?"

"Yes?"

"The show's at Dong Dong and I go on in an hour!"

Ziggy hangs up and runs straight to the door. She looks down through the railing at her friends, catatonic on the couch below. There's no easy way to say this, so she barks it loudly over the landing. "We're going to Dong Dong!"

"The drag place?" Tessa asks.

Lex looks confused. "Why are we going to Dong Dong?" She rises slowly to her feet, hunching over as though the ceiling might be suddenly very low. "Is it because you're a *purple mango*?"

Tessa sputters. Ziggy can't tell if Lex is making a gay joke. Whether this means her friends don't want her to be male or gay or if gay jokes are just part of the package. But right now, Ziggy can't access the requisite humiliation or anger. She just needs to be near Rowena. Right now, it feels like the only way she might not have another panic attack and die is to see Rowena standing on a tall stage under the silver spangle of a disco ball. Her mind has pared to a slim arrow aimed solely at Dong Dong.

"Come to Dong Dong," Ziggy says. "Or America thinks you're frigid."

In ten minutes, they are on a bus.

THE GIRLS GET OUT at the five-fingered intersection with the big gay pub throbbing on the corner. Rainbow flags flutter out windows; disco balls throw spears of light from pharmacy doors. Boys in shredded denim shorts with lurid abdominals streak through the pedestrian traffic. Just beyond the jet spume of a public fountain, several Aboriginal men sit on the skimpy strip of grass. They drink from brown paper bags, squinting at the preened fuss tearing past.

Dong Dong is in the lane behind this hub of activity. Its pink neon sign peeks through the chimneys, and when passing it on school excursions, Ziggy's peers always fling the bus windows open, hurling their laughter like eggs. The sign is a vestige of the storefront's former incarnation as a karaoke bar. Driving past, Cate Lansell-Jones will inevitably shake her head and drone "Yaysian." Then she'll smile at Fliss Kunchai-Wells and

Fliss will smile back as Cate says, "Not you, Fliss," dropping her head onto Fliss's shoulder before Fliss tips her own head onto Cate's head and they both close their eyes and purr. All the other girls usually chant "dong" until a teacher starts screaming.

But Lex says the neighborhood is gritty and very New York. The converted factories have fire escapes, the old apartment blocks have stoops, and outside the tobacco stores meth-heads sit fizzing on empty milk crates. This, says Lex, is how Australia would look if it was actually cosmopolitan. Inside every building Ziggy pictures junkies scrunched along stairwells, rats gnawing chicken bones, syringes tinseling up the corners. She acknowledges her insomniac *CSI* phase may account for some of the stereotyping.

The three friends slip into Dong Dong's snaking line. They have dressed up. The girls figured they'd have to dupe a doorman, so made a hasty sacking of Ruth's wardrobe. Their loot amounted to a lot of tie-dye and much distressed lace. Also, ethnic patterns on skirts with wool pom-poms and bells. Tessa and Lex look like menopausal neopagans. Ziggy found a pair of crushed velvet tights and a dark purple pleather vest, shooting for leatherman but landing somewhere closer to pirate.

"Evening, ladies," says the doorman in an adenoidal singsong. He sports a thin mustache and orange-tinted aviators. Ziggy recalls the reflector aviators she'd wanted so badly the previous summer. She had tried them on in the store with Miriam Rosenburg, enjoying how the Blob recoiled from her own reflection in Ziggy's lenses. The glasses bestowed a sense of power that Ziggy felt might push her more confidently through puberty. A place to hide while exposing the flaws of others. Later that summer, Ziggy had slipped her request into the Wailing Wall. Secretly, she felt a prayer for cool sunglasses was not completely ignoble. With a little boost in self-esteem, she might be the person to cure cancer, discover alternative energy sources, usher in the matriarchy.

"Where did you get those?" she asks the doorman.

He smiles and leans toward her. "Actually, they're just bargain bin at Price Attack."

Ziggy nods, watching her own face reflected back in the grungy sepia. "They're so cool."

"Thanks, darl," says the doorman. "Just the three of you?"

"Yes." Ziggy's friends inch closer. In the mirrored lenses, she sees the two of them press in on either side of her, merging into one enormous head with a wide melon slice of grin. The doorman raises the rope. Ziggy is a natural.

Inside, Dong Dong looks like an old postcard she once saw of an AusLink dining car that gave her recurring nightmares about living in the Outback. The ceiling is lowly chandeliered, and the pleather booths are covered in clear plastic. Ziggy knows the aesthetic is retro but can't separate the feeling of despair from the kitschy fun part. Which might mean she isn't actually gay.

But she loves it here. The crowd is a mix of twinks, leathermen, and drag queens. The latter perch at the bar; everyone else writhes on the dance floor. The girls sit to the side of a low stage, where a microphone stand braces against the thrusting tide of short shorts. The pot is wearing off and Ziggy is feeling serene. Her friends also seem happy to be at the drag bar, watching the explicit dancing from inside their giddy huddle. After a few minutes, the curtains billow portentously, the dance music dies, and the room hushes. A familiar piano solo begins just as the curtains part—revealing a towering queen in a skirted yellow leotard with the translucent ruff of a frilled-neck lizard.

Tessa nudges Lex. "It's that scene from *Priscilla, Queen of the Desert*," she says, smugly.

The lizard flicks her tongue and hisses at the crowd. She lip-syncs listlessly to the first verse of "I Will Survive," stops, then taps the microphone. "Testing, testing," she says flatly. "So, frilled-neck lizard. Scientific name: Chlamydiosaurus."

The audience laughs and a queen in a sequined muumuu drones: "Everybody, run."

"Shut up, Luke," says the lizard. "No need to fear Chlamydiosaurus anymore. There's a pill for me."

Ziggy likes this droll MC—how mean she is, how stingy with her smiles.

"By now I've got everything," she says, sighing loudly into the mic. "Clap, chlamydia, crabs, warts, herpes, that new strain of late-stage autism you get from swallowing. I'm a bitch, but they call me Frank."

People boo lovingly.

"Frankie Frankenfurterstein. It's German for *transgender*."

Ziggy hears herself gasp in delight.

"You know, I got the surgery," Frankie continues. "But my boyfriend doesn't like it. Says my pussy smells too much like pussy, not enough like MacBook."

Someone throws a coaster and misses.

"So I tell him: the internet is *made* of pussy! You've got Happy Cat, Anxiety Cat, Existential Cat. At least my pussy is a meme." Frankie peeks in under her own skirt. "Not-Fucked-Enough Cat."

Another coaster flies stage-ward and grazes the MC's thigh.

"All right, all right," she says. "I will survive. Hey, hey." Frankie lifts a leg as if to fart, blows a raspberry into the mic, and struts offstage. The crowd cheers. Ziggy is astonished. That someone who wears false eyelashes and six-inch heels can also make fun of being female.

"I want to be a drag queen," she blurts to her friends.

"Why?" says Tessa. "That was sexist."

"And ablest," adds Lex.

"And transphobic."

But how can it be transphobic if the person is transgender? Ziggy shakes her head in exasperation. "I think she was joking."

"Doesn't matter," says Tessa. "She's a white man, and they aren't allowed to make jokes about oppressed people."

"But she's a woman."

"We don't know that for sure."

"She said she's transitioned."

"That might've just been a joke."

Ziggy's shoulders feel heavy; her whole body is burning up.

Tessa leans in and lowers her voice. "Gay men love divas, but they can be really mean to normal women."

"And when the divas get cellulite," says Lex, "they can be mean to the divas, too."

Ziggy had no idea her friends were so critical of gay men. "So they're basically misogynists?"

Lex resists the pejorative. "Well, they control the beauty industry."

"Which means they are benefitting from white patriarchy," says Tessa. "And profiting off black female bodies."

"But I thought gay men were women of color?" says Ziggy.

Tessa chortles. "They *were*," she says. "In, like, the eighties."

When "A Cyborg Manifesto" was written. Ziggy didn't realize Haraway's text was in need of a new edition.

"Now they're basically just white men again," says Lex.

"What about the black ones?"

Tessa gives Ziggy a scalding look. "What do *you* think, Ziggy?"

Ziggy has no idea. She sinks back in her seat and tries to understand what is happening. Who she is allowed to be. Ziggy objectifies women like a gay man but wants to penetrate them like a straight one. She likes the phallic pounding of a jet stream and the pelvic spaciousness of tailored pants. The only category she can hold in her mind without immediate counterargument is "patriarchal vaporstream."

The music starts again and the three friends turn back to the darkened stage. A tall female silhouette stands still in the center. Ziggy recognizes the song. "Life on Mars." What Rowena was humming on the phone. As the lights come up, Tessa gasps. "A cyborg!"

Rowena wears a tight silver bodysuit and a helmet with one huge googly eyeball jiggling on a wire. Her pelvic mound is as smooth as Barbie's. It might just be a coincidence that Rowena is singing a David Bowie song, but it feels significant. Ruth says Ziggy's name comes from the Latin, *Ignatius*, and means, "unknown," but her father says she's Ziggy Stardust. Jeff claims Bowie changed his life and taught him it was okay to have a softer, feminine side. Which must be why Ruth started emasculating him in the first place. (Ziggy's shameful origin story: sixteen years ago, a manly woman and a girly man had stripper sex in a chair, producing Ziggy So-Flat-the-Walls-Are-Jealous Klein.) Ziggy has never really understood David Bowie—the petrified red hair, cosmic eye shadow, and enigmatic snaggletooth—but there is some comfort in encountering him here, now, in the form of Rowena. Ziggy listens to the words. He seems to be saying the world is savage and stupid and maybe it would be best to just start over again on another planet.

To forget this place, all our parents, penises, and vaginas. Ziggy wonders if Tessa is right and Rowena really does identify as a cyborg.

When the song ends, Rowena bows and then dedicates her performance to "Ziggy Klein and the Seekers." She winks at the three of them and strides offstage.

Surprisingly, Ziggy's friends are excited to meet Rowena. She explains that Rowena is Ruth's client and nice but mostly just weird and funny to talk to. When she appears at their table in her customary pink tunic with pearly hair clips, a warm rush of affinity floods Ziggy's body. Rowena is proof that white people with pronounced Adam's apples aren't always the enemy. Her friends smile up mutely at the woman's sweetly expectant face. Ziggy knows what to say. From Tessa's dance recital she learned that after the performance there is a certain line the audience is expected to deliver.

"We really enjoyed your work," she says earnestly.

Tessa's voice burns in Ziggy's ear. "You only say *werk* to people of color."

"I thought transgender women were people of color?"

"Ziggy, there are people of color and then there are *people of color.*"

Ziggy can feel herself getting angry. "I said *work* anyway."

Tessa turns back to Lex, and the two of them presumably collude against Ziggy. But she is more focused on Rowena. The cyborg eye has made transhumanist feminism clearer in her mind. Ziggy wants to know if the eye is a bygone penis or something more abstract like "man's dominance over nature." From her queer subreddit, Ziggy knows you aren't supposed to ask these sorts of questions, but "A Cyborg Manifesto" might be her way in.

Rowena takes a seat beside her and Ziggy leans in close so the others can't hear. "Have you heard of Donna Haraway?"

"Did she do 'Hot Stuff'?"

"No, 'A Cyborg Manifesto.'"

Now a teenage boy comes shooting toward them from inside a tight weave of queens, as if birthed. He hurries to Rowena's side, frowning and smiling at the same time. He is slight and angular under baggy white pajamas, giving him the long-suffering look of a prisoner of war.

"This is my son," Rowena says proudly. "Supporting his mother's filthy habit."

The boy smiles—his doe-sweet features shying, black eyes urgent with intelligence. He puts out a hand. "I'm Tim."

Ziggy blushes horribly but extends her hand; Tim has left no room for irony. "I'm Ziggy," she mumbles. Up close, his clothes have a more deliberate and textured, South Asian look. His lank brown hair parts down the middle. *Peaceman.*

"Is that short for Sigmund?" says Tim. His face waits innocently for an answer as Ziggy grapples with the implications. It seems Tim thinks she's a boy.

"Like Freud?"

"Yes," says Tim. "But not because you're Jewish. Or because your mother is a therapist. I just can't think of what else Ziggy could be short for."

"It isn't short for anything."

"So just Ziggy? Not that that isn't enough."

"Just Ziggy. Ziggy Klein." She feels strangely calm in the presence of Tim's nervous logorrhea.

"Which is 'small' in German," he observes. "Not that you're necessarily German. Or small. I know lots of Jews have German names."

From Tim's left hand, a yo-yo suddenly springs to the floor, then leaps back up like a lizard tongue. The world remains oblivious and unchanged, but Ziggy finds the moment extraordinary, as if an alternate reality had shot through clear scrim.

"Ziggy was just telling us about 'A Cyborg Manifesto,'" says Rowena, her eyebrows jauntily encouraging.

"It's an essay about transhumans," Tessa interjects, brandishing her bionic arm. "Like me."

"Wow-ee," Rowena says, gawking.

"Mum," Tim admonishes.

"Your googly eye is transhuman," Tessa informs Rowena, a little condescendingly.

"Well, that's good," says Rowena. "Trannies are meant to be uncanny."

Ziggy catches a dark look flit between Tessa and Lex. They have taken issue with the word *tranny*. Ziggy's anger is momentarily paralyzing. She sits back in her chair, breathing deep and slow, then experiences a small neuronal miracle. Donna Haraway's elegant prose floats to the surface of her mind. Ziggy speaks in the baritone of some imagined adult woman in a tweed blazer. "'Blasphemy protects one from the moral majority within.'"

Tessa is testy. "And?"

"And so you guys need to learn how to take a joke."

Rowena giggles, but Ziggy's friends are quiet. They think she is siding with the drag queens. Tessa and Lex inch back in their seats, then return to their phones. Ziggy can tell they are again swapping their faces with celebrities'. Tessa probably merged with the Kardashians, Lex moving between various dead East Coast rappers. Haraway's ideas of collectivism have never appealed to Ziggy's friends. She has brought them to a cyborg stronghold, yet there they sit, speaking only to each other.

Rowena gives Ziggy's shoulder a squeeze. "I'm afraid we've got to head out."

"It's my fault," says Tim. "I have to make *lokma* for two depressed friends." He sighs, hunching over with chronic-looking sympathy. "One depressed friend. One friend with seasonal affective disorder."

Ziggy has never heard of this and also, she didn't think Sydney winter counted as a season. "That's really nice of you."

Tim makes a curt nod (either shy or distracted, Ziggy can't tell) as he whips out his phone and starts furiously typing. She watches the charm on his bracelet tap against the screen—a star and crescent moon. Ziggy's phone pings. Friendship request from Timothy Sadik-Bowen.

"My mother is Turkish; my father is my mother," Tim says, his face suddenly radiant with mischief. "*Salaam alaikum.*"

Ziggy thinks she hears *shalom aleichem*. So do her friends. When Rowena and Tim are out of earshot, Lex nudges Ziggy. "He's perfect for you!"

Tessa and Lex appear to have made a full recovery, their faces shining at her from across the table. But Ziggy doesn't understand their enthusiasm. Is Tim perfect for her because they are complementary opposites or because they are both male-presenting lesbians? If her friends think she might like boys now, is it because she is a straight girl or a gay male? Ziggy is too embarrassed to ask. There is something she likes about Tim, which she senses has little to do with his maleness. Not that penises have ever occurred to her as exciting objects of desire. Sexual fantasies of men have always involved an objectless sense of pressure applied to the vulva. But never a penis. To Ziggy, the penis has the personality of a smiling axolotl, detached from the menacing human man it belongs to. Confusingly, Tim is all axolotl: no violent thrust, no sexual menace. He doesn't seem male to her.

But now Tessa scoots over and squeezes Ziggy's arm with strange, goading sorority.

"He'd be so cute in a tuxedo."

And suddenly, however she identifies, Ziggy likes boys.

Chapter 5

Ziggy's mother had loved another man at the ashram. Ruth talked too vividly about the effete, artistic boy whose diplomat father had moved the family around, gifting young Edward a mysteriously international accent and a talent for making bad friends. After high school, Edward had lived for a spell in the rambling townhouse of a British rock icon's idle son and his supermodel girlfriend. Paying his rent in haikus, Edward slunk around with the supermodel's group of supermodel friends: long, loopy nights on barbiturates and bright, speeding days launched by morning enemas. One evening, Edward met an older man recently returned from Shunyata's ashram. "The master says Gandhi was a fascist," the man told him. Edward was intrigued. The man said that the guru preferred Westerners to Indians because they had more to lose. Indians were still striving for cars and mortgages, but white people were ready to give theirs up; they were ready to abandon their empty existences. So was Edward—sunk in the cold bosom of a bar lounge, the twiggy girls mumbling beside him, eyes rolling back in their chiseled skulls. A few days later, the icon's idle son got very drunk and forced Edward to wrap himself in furs and recite florid poetry from World War I. Gentle, waifish Edward obliged his cruel landlord, and even fed the pet python when it became obvious that everyone else was either passed out or too vegetarian. Then he packed up his designer kaftans and his haikus and bought a one-way ticket to Bombay. Ziggy never knew how to interpret her mother's evocations of the London townhouse scene. It seemed she mostly used Edward's origin story to clarify that wealthy, young attractive people were spiritually bereft and boring. And that one of them had chosen her over a houseful of supermodels.

Meeting at the ashram, Ruth and Edward fell instantly in love and began a scandalously monogamous relationship. One of Shuni's strategies for exacerbating the male-female polarity was to make the men chase the women around the complex and into the neighboring fields. Edward chased Ruth and cut his long wispy hair and stopped wearing necklaces. He was still sensitive, but their love had seemingly conquered gender; that is, until the day they strayed too far beyond the ashram's walls. The couple found themselves in a village, obliviously smooching and groping each other, when a pack of angry local men appeared before them. Edward bolted and—thinking Ruth was just behind him—kept running, almost all the way back to the ashram. But Ruth stayed and talked to the men, who, quite reasonably, asked her not to walk around their village kissing and cupping the cheeks of her lover's bottom. When she returned to the ashram, Edward was mortified. Worse than this, his cowardice had made it so Ruth no longer found him attractive. His personal growth now seemed purely cosmetic. Soon after the incident Ruth decided the ashram was an artificial paradigm and that it was now time for her to take Shuni's teachings back into the gritty real world. One week later Ruth returned to Sydney's leafy harborside suburbs.

The week she arrived, Ruth met Jeff at a Jewish mixer. Twinkles had made her daughter attend the event as reparations for five years with a guru who claimed Hitler was a saint. Ruth had spent the evening explaining the cult and Shuni's sense of humor to Jeff, who also had Holocaust-surviving parents—still clinging to private tennis courts in South Africa. He adored a good Jewish joke. Humor had kept their flame robust through a joyful courtship. The couple loved their pranks. Meeting Twinkles, the good Jewish accountant passed around photos of his Cape Town relatives, swapping his mother's image for a woman with severe acromegaly, and his father's for a dwarf. Twinkles was polite, exclaiming that Jeff's mother's gigantic forehead made her seem very intelligent. His father must have also been a huge mensch. For their honeymoon, the couple went to Cairo, meeting Jeff's teenage sister at the airport. They dressed in thobes and dark sunglasses, approaching the petite South African from behind, then grabbing and dragging her out through the arrivals lounge, whispering in pidgin Arabic. That was in the year 2000. Ziggy had often heard her parents regale their friends with this thoughtless act of Islamophobia. It was hard to know who had encouraged whom and what had come first, the cultural insensitivity or the romance. At least child-rearing or professional life or both had dissuaded them from this unsavory pastime. Ruth's terminal disappointment had probably choked off Jeff's rebellious spirit. Until recently it seemed her father's whole personality had withdrawn mollusk-like into the hard shell of adult behavior. Ziggy supposes it is sad her parents no longer do anything fun together.

Jeff's new friends are a confusing blend of homosexual body-vanity and hetero-tribal male-bonding, but they have certainly brought him back to life. Despite this, Ziggy's mother continues to insult him; only now it is for being too macho. For their wedding anniversary, Jeff buys them tickets to cage-dive with the great whites off the South Australian coast, and Ruth calls him a male chauvinist. When he gives her ticket to Damo, Jeff is accused of literalism. Ruth calls her husband "avoidant" when he checks his phone at the table, says it is a "failure of empathy" if he goes for a jog after dinner. Tonight, having achieved a genial family meal, Ruth suggests they all watch television together. Ziggy wonders what her mother is up to. And what the four of them could possibly agree to watch. They squish up in eerie intimacy on the sofa, Jeff flicking through the channels. The Kleins do not have cable, which means their options are six. These are quickly exhausted and so they agree to wait for the nine o'clock news. In the meantime, there is a car commercial. Wild horses run beside a haunchy bronze SUV. Ziggy's heart runs with them, and she feels herself tearing up. Ruth, of course, catches her.

"Remember when Ziggy loved horses?" she says nostalgically to the group.

Jeff nods and Jacob sits up straighter, sensing an opportunity for teasing.

"Whenever we went on long car rides," Ruth continues, "she had to wave at every single one and say 'I love you, my darling.'"

Jacob howls and Ziggy makes her eyes very narrow and piercing like they might break her brother's skin.

"You were such a sweet, sensitive little girl." The grief in her mother's voice makes Ziggy feel like a part of her has died. It seems unfair that Ziggy has to be a sensitive little girl when her brother just gets to be a boy who's good at sharing his feelings. Ziggy's ongoing failure of vulnerability has forced Ruth to nourish herself on Jake's emotional intelligence. When it comes to emotions, Ziggy's brother possesses a fluid, otherworldly ease that can probably be traced back to the moment at age six when, naked at play with the utensils in a kitchen drawer, he got the tip of his penis stuck in the garlic crusher. Ziggy had watched Jake flap his arms at hummingbird speed, dancing in frantic circles as he thrust the offending instrument away from his body, trying to distance himself from the pain. Ruth quickly extracted the utensil and Jake's genitals were entirely unharmed, but the shock sent him weeping into his mother's arms, and from that day forward Ziggy's brother was always emotionally transparent in front of their mum and dad. Jake can discuss his feelings in a soft voice, quavering above a trip wire of tears with the unself-conscious candor of a menopausal psychotherapist. Ziggy has tried to emulate her brother, but even articulating certain words—*vulnerable, tender, depth*—makes her face burn and her throat constrict in terror. She isn't sure what her own origin story is. Since Ziggy can remember, Ruth has told her to open up, and Ziggy has panicked, shut down, and deferred to the soft-voiced man fussing at her rib cage who desperately wants to avoid conflict.

Mercifully, everyone's attention now shifts back to the television. Jeff has found a show about Muslim gold diggers in the far Western Suburbs. Ziggy feels uneasy being one of four affluent Eastern Suburbs Jews watching such a program. But her mother's immediate critique seems safely class-based. Ziggy is even surprised to agree with some of it. There is a part of her that knows exactly how much cleavage is too much, that grown women should never wear tiaras. Predictably, the Kleins' spontaneous group activity soon deteriorates. Jeff unwisely remarks on the awesome derriere of the youngest gold-digging sister, and Ruth scolds him.

"*Callipygous* means 'shelf-like,' Jeff."

Ziggy's father bristles. "Not true, Ruth. It simply means beautiful, shapely buttocks."

"Still, you shouldn't be commenting on their bodies."

"*You* just did."

"As a woman I'm allowed to."

Ziggy groans. "Mum, I think you need to read Judith Butler."

"Who's that again?" Her mother already sounds irritated.

"A legendary feminist thinker," says Ziggy. "If you think women are the ocean, you should probably read Judith Butler."

"Well, I'm glad Judith Butler has been sitting in a library finding a grand theory for all of us out here in the real world." Ruth gestures broadly to their large, open-plan entertainment area. "I work with women, Ziggy. I'm on the ground, doing the fieldwork."

"And?"

"And nothing. Woman is the Source," Ruth says bluntly. "It's like the ocean saying it would rather be a bottle of soda water."

"That's so ancient it's like indigenous. Appropriator."

Ruth blows a dismissive raspberry. "Woman is the highest incarnation."

"Well, that's great for Jake."

"I'm fine being male—"

"Gender is just a construction," Ziggy intones over him. "You should all read Butler's book."

Ruth tucks a smooth, shapely calf under her bottom, eyeing Ziggy with aggressive interest. "What about transgender women? Is their gender just a construction? Are they also making it all up?"

Ziggy hadn't considered this. Panic goiters in her throat. She couldn't argue even if she had read Judith Butler. Ruth shifts, thrusting a large pillow knob between them.

"You tell me if gender still feels like a construction when you've hit puberty, or maybe after you give birth to your first child? In the meantime, you can stop offending those of us who've actually had these experiences."

The absence of these experiences mists coolly through Ziggy's chest and crotch. Ruth never fails to make her daughter feel somewhat missing. She nudges Jeff roughly. "And your father knows when I'm joking."

"Does he?"

Ruth stares at Jeff, her eyes shining with challenge. "Do you?"

"Of course." He leans in and pecks the crown of his wife's head. Ziggy can see the white skull through her frizz, and wonders if these glimpses of frailty are how he still loves her. Jeff grins at Ziggy. "But I *am* going for a jog now."

Jake and Ruth laugh but Ziggy stares hard at the floor. If she cries in front of them, she risks dissolving into Ruth's flesh and living forever as a damp spot between her mother's breasts. Ziggy rises stoically and then makes a stompily indignant exit.

In her bedroom she remembers the offending adjective, *callipygous*. A whimsical word that makes her think of little twig-legged, potbellied birds. But Google has bad news. The word describes a protruding bottom so extreme, it resembles a shelf or other flat surface good for resting jugs. To Ziggy's great disappointment, her mother was right and her father was most definitely objectifying the gold diggers.

FROM HIS SOCIAL MEDIA PROFILES, Ziggy learns that Tim is a practicing Sufi. He posts Rumi quotes, clips of Whirling Dervishes, and Michael Jackson music videos, and in every selfie he wears the same sexless white pajamas. Tim talks a lot about queer and Turkish cuisine. He posts his cis-mother's traditional recipes and long discourses on the origins of various food with headings like "When It's Racist to Call a Dessert Too Sweet." Less frequently he posts frivolous recipes for heavily sprinkled cupcakes. Ziggy is slightly terrified of Tim but would still like to chat. When he posts an extensive piece about the history of something very syrupy called *revani*, Ziggy sees her opportunity. Tim claims that the semolina cake was brought to Turkey by Sephardic Jews who migrated there after their expulsion in the late 1400s. Despite this, in Israel *revani* is consumed with yogurt, which is a Mesopotamian invention, thus originating in Turkey. The question seems to be: which came first, the revani or the yogurt? As if this might prove something about a people's claim to Jerusalem. At least, this is how it sounds to Ziggy. Tim's friends quickly weigh into the discussion. Someone claims the dessert actually hails from Egypt. Someone else gets granular and lists off the geographic origins of all the ingredients. Ziggy types, erases, then retypes her comment below an impassioned post about who gets to claim the almond. Finally she sends it.

isn't "authenticity" < humanity?

Tim loves her comment with a big red heart emoji. His written reply is less affirming.

Ziggy, I agree that many cultures contain aspects of others but also acknowledge that some cultures have received little or no attribution for their culinary traditions. As a half-Anglo, half-Turkish Australian with one transgender parent and one corporate solicitor, I always try to give voice to the less-privileged parts of myself. Look out for the rainbow-sprinkled *revani* I will be posting here tomorrow!

Then his friends chime in.

Exactly—I'd really rather not hear about the Israeli occupation of the honey cake.

And hate to break it to people, but the Pumpkin Pie is not actually American.

As a person of German heritage, I would NEVER Instagram a hamburger.

Western food porn is diabolical. They've already poisoned the rest of the world with their calories!

Ziggy thinks anxiously of her favorite Jewish food: pickled herring. She is now certain that her ancestors appropriated it from the Scandinavians. The conversation on Tim's wall moves into a general evisceration of meatloaf. Ziggy's beloved *fashit*—the dense, meaty log her grandmother makes—is suddenly strange to her. For the first time, she hears the *shit* part of the word and feels ashamed. Ziggy clicks away from Tim and his Anti-Western authenticity police and onto Reddit. The tone on her queer subreddit is not dissimilar, but at least she feels secure about her inclusion in the all-inclusive sphere. Opening the Reddit home page, she can see which of the popular threads her brother has already viewed. An article about the trolling of a female scholar who claims Rome was ethnically diverse leads Ziggy down a rabbit hole of gnarly links. Is it hate speech to say a movie with an all-female cast is unfunny? Or only if you also call the women fat and unrapeable? Does affirmative action mean you have to like the movie, too? The lines between egalitarianism and fascism seem blurred. It is obvious when a politician misuses their power, but if an anonymous school-boy mocks a respected feminist thinker, should Twitter shut him down? Is a white penis always power? Ziggy finds she is drawn to the articles defending free speech. Reading them, her brain feels hot and sour like spoiled fruit, fermenting with in-dignation. Imagining Tessa and Lex know what she is doing, Ziggy revolts—reading all the way to the outer edges of the far-right news and arriving back again at Reddit. To a group called the Red Pill.

Ziggy reads their threads with morbid fascination. The men are biological essentialists and claim to have seen reality for what it truly is: an impending matriarchy. They prey on women and speak in a language of alpha and beta males. There is no admitting weakness: any woman who doesn't want to sleep with you is just a bitch or an abuse survivor. "Anyone notice how suddenly all girls have been raped?" is one of the threads Ziggy follows until she feels her soul has been lanced out with a cold syringe. But a lot of the threads sound like one-liners. Everyone is encouraged to take a joke. Especially the Asian men. Ziggy finds conspiracies about estrogen poisoning (it's in all plastic bottles and body washes) and others about testosterone treat-ments that will fix erectile dysfunction, depression, obesity, and a general fear of failure. One man advises the others to tell their physicians they are lesbians transitioning to males:

They'll give a 13-year-old girl higher dosages than any of u impotent fat fucks.

On the Red Pill there is incessant talk of the blue pill, or Viagra, and a delicate dance often ensues around saying you need it when needing it is tantamount to an admission of weakness. Still, women can nearly always be blamed for killing boners. Some of these ideas are almost familiar to Ziggy—things she may have heard from her mother's mouth or Hitler Youth's running commentary in her head. She reads a long post about why overbearing mothers are responsible for most genocidal maniacs and mass shooters. There is a post that features GIFs of men in skinny jeans walking beside women holding car keys. The passion and detail with which they denigrate the female enemy makes the Red Pill feel oddly like a fan page. These men write emotionally supportive listicles and pine together for female sex robots. Ziggy tries for a moment to empathize with them. Or rather, an image comes to mind that makes her feel almost sympathetic to their cause. She recalls the two Kandara seniors she watched last week in the library. The way they occupied the whole study station, stretching languorously across the table in their oversized jerseys, loose hair flicked carelessly to the side, affecting a kind of unself-conscious lounging that oozed sensuality. They knew their sexual power and played with it under their beguiling, baggy sweatshirts. Something about this had made Ziggy fume. The word *whore* skulked in her mouth like bad breath.

Ziggy leaves the Red Pill, and closing tabs she comes upon Tim's Facebook wall. She watches a newly posted video of the Mevlevi Order's mystical dance practice. Initially she is captivated by the soothing constancy of the men's twirling movement; and then, watching these wide, white triangles spin, Ziggy sees beyond the abstraction of geometric shapes to what they really are: men in skirts, arms raised and slightly rounded as if embracing an invisible groom. Tim might be even less datable than she thought. Even if their gender-ambiguity is somehow complementary, Hitler Youth think Tim's boner is probably just for the sublime. Disoriented, Ziggy logs out.

But she doesn't tell her friends that Tim is most likely in a romantic relationship with God. Ziggy upholds the fantasy that he might be her formal soul mate. She tells the girls that like her, Tim isn't really religious, only spiritual. Like all her mother's friends who think that God is just higher particle vibrations and somehow proven by string theory. From his Instagram, Ziggy learns that Tim is vegetarian and doesn't believe in soap or coffee. Like Ziggy, he enjoys conspiracy theories (*has anyone noticed that conditioner never really washes out??*), and unlike Ziggy, he tends to overshare—posting erotic dreams of psychedelic fish and female world leaders. Which makes her suspect Tim might be gay. As a prospective Kandara formal date, this doesn't necessarily preclude him if Ziggy is genderqueer. Which she isn't. But she keeps the possibility open for her friends. They are being so much nicer to her.

EVERY WEEKEND, TESSA GOES to the casting calls posted on her dance school's bulletin board. Now that she has alcoholism trauma, Tessa smells whisky on everyone's breath, especially the casting agents. The fatigued women she describes sound fairly benign to Ziggy—slouched behind tripods while their toddlers whine from playpens, catching Pokémon in the auditionees' hair. But Tessa says the boozing is frightening and endemic. Australia, Tessa claims, has a big drinking problem.

It makes everyone lazy and provincial and unlikely to ever succeed in America. Ziggy thought the low-grade ambition was because of things like democratic socialism, good weather, and antiauthoritarian convict genes, but Tessa paints a more negative picture. Most vehemently, she complains about an alarming lack of diversity in TV and film. Being a woman of color in the cyborgian sense doesn't, apparently, translate to the Australian screen. Tessa says all the roles are for wispy Northern Beaches nubiles who can surf or skateboard as convincingly troubled tomboys. Where are the real Australian stories, Tessa wants to know. The stories about drunken teens and rape culture? No one wants to see a pretty Pymble girl lying unconscious in a dumpster. Which is why Tessa is writing herself a date-rape coming-of-age TV pilot.

At least she starts it. And then, a few days into the autumn semester, Tessa sees an unusual audition notice pinned to the board. It is printed on the letterhead of an American casting agency, the only one with a Sydney office. This slick, windowless structure stands impenetrable as a luxury storm shelter on the corner of a busy city block. Ziggy is familiar with the building. Soapie stars are often seen exiting with immaculate blow-dries, emotional support animals in tow. But this time the role being cast isn't for someone blond and athletic. The description is uncannily specific: fifteen, female, pale, redhead, can cry on command. Tessa emails a head shot and biography and gets an audition the following afternoon.

When Ziggy calls her that night, Tessa is ecstatic. She tells Ziggy all about the TV show. It isn't gritty; there won't be any cellulite or pubic hair. The part is small—a guest role in an ongoing crime series—but Tessa's character gets shot in the leg on a speedboat and has to hyperventilate then bleed to death. As she tells Ziggy about the audition, Tessa talks in a deeper, more adult voice that makes Ziggy feel simpering and small. Tessa says the American casting agent asked her to close her eyes and recall the feeling of waking up from surgery and realizing that her arm was gone. Then he got her to immediately lie down on the carpet and read lines from the script. Tessa says she cried uncontrollably for ten minutes and now has a callback. Something tells Ziggy that what the casting agent made Tessa do is the closest she's come to real Method acting. She also thinks her friend is probably going to get the part, which gives Ziggy a losing feeling. America has made its choice, and the chosen person is Tessa.

That Saturday morning Jeff is gone. Swimming in Thailand. A last-minute decision to join his mates at an annual ocean race. Ruth insists he mentioned it multiple times that week and Ziggy obviously just wasn't listening. Regardless, there is something suspicious about her father's spontaneity. The last time they went overseas, Jeff spent nine months planning their trip with a travel agent; it seemed every time they left the house he would drop the words *Athens* and *Istanbul*, just to see if there was a cabdriver or waiter or friendly bystander who had tips about the cuisine or transport facilities. He bought three guidebooks and bribed Jake and Ziggy with quizzes for weeks before they left. And once they were there, Jeff made them savor every bite of *gozleme* and *saganaki* and keep a constant tally of their favorite meals and moments. When they forgot their guidebook trivia, Jeff gave them long lectures as monotonous as the winding alleyways of the cities' ancient quarters. One afternoon during a rainstorm, the Kleins had sat inside a café, drinking mint tea and smoking hookah. Gazing into the downpour, Jeff had produced the first visual metaphor of his adult life. He said the pelting water resembled tiny falling clock hands, like Time had lost its meaning, like History was an illusion. *Eternity*, he'd clarified with a mystified sigh. Their father's metaphor has been a major teasing point for years. But whenever it is invoked, Jeff's eyes glaze over and it is clear he has returned to that perfectly curated moment of cultural transcendence. Flying to Thailand for a swim seems an aggressive impulsivity that makes Ziggy think her father has a terminal disease or a girlfriend.

But that Sunday night, Jeff emails his family a video. Ruth calls the kids up to the home PC, and the three of them huddle in over the screen. In the orange glow of a tiki bar, three large male figures stumble onto a small stage. Damo is wearing a tiara and poufy blond wig; Gus swishes a long black plait threaded with daisies; and most offensive is Ziggy's father with his dark sunglasses and gigantic rainbow Afro. They begin yowling into a pair of microphones. The song: "Golden Years."

"What is this?" Jake says, horrified.

"My guess is karaoke," Ruth says, unnervingly calm.

"Then why is Dad cross-dressing?"

Ruth chuckles. "That's not cross-dressing, Ziggy. It's just dress-ups."

"They're wearing ladies' wigs."

"Yes . . . well . . . Thailand's a funny place."

Jake appears to be on Ziggy's side. "They look like the lesbian Village People."

"Dad is like some kind of psychedelic Diana Ross."

"Come on, you two," says Ruth. "Your father's very PC; it's just a bit of fun."

But Ziggy disagrees. Her father is not very PC, and also she knows what this is: they have just studied it in Latin. The Romans were even more afraid of women than the Greeks—

luscious Aphrodite was reimagined as icy seaweed sculpture, Venus; Dionysus lost his long, feminine tresses and his female mysticism and was rebranded Bacchus, drunken sexual deviant. But the Roman nobility loved cross-dressing. They were misogynists who could only handle femininity when displayed on other men. What Ruth herself would call "pathological male narcissism."

"It's offensive to women."

Ruth eyes Ziggy strangely. "Do *you* feel offended?"

Ziggy sees her mother's trap; she is not going to be offended on behalf of cisgender women. "It's offensive to transgender women."

"And birthday party clowns," adds Jake.

"That's transphobic," says Ziggy. Ruth giggles, and Ziggy shoots backward like an inking squid in her desk chair. "You hate transgender people, don't you."

Her mother slaps the table. "Of course not!" she yells. "This whole transgender thing is nothing compared to second-wave feminism! That's what really broke things apart!"

"So what?!" Ziggy cries.

"So transgender women are generally pretty happy to perform gender roles! They are deeply in touch with the Feminine and balance out the polarity very nicely. It's these fluid people who are the real existential threat."

"You're talking like a Nazi."

"*You're* talking like a Nazi."

"What gender roles are you even referring to?" Ziggy spits. "You never cook dinner!"

"I nurture in other ways!"

"If you're so good at balancing the polarity, why is Dad always out?"

Ziggy's chest locks up; bracing itself for her mother's tyrannical hurt. But Ruth appears unharmed, reframing the issue. "Would you like it if I bought more after-school snacks?"

Her mother's sudden act of nurture has skewed things so that Ziggy wants to cry. "No, that's okay," she mumbles. "They're all delicious."

And now, humiliatingly, her brother takes the emotional lead.

"Actually," he says, "can you please stop buying those little pasta salads? They make me feel sad."

"Of course I can," says Ruth, squeezing his shoulder.

"Dried fruit with macaroni is really depressing."

Elated that her mother chose to de-escalate, Ziggy wheels back over and joins in. "Where do they even make those miserable little salads? A shelter for suicidal chefs?"

Then with touching diplomacy, the three of them workshop snack alternatives. Ziggy has seen some tasty-looking yogurt cups at school. Jake says dark chocolate is good for both acne and the heart. "It's like red wine for kids."

Their mother agrees to everything. Making the karaoke video and the status of her marriage feel alarmingly dire.

ON MONDAY MORNING ZIGGY FINDS Tessa at the lockers, conspicuously reading through a script. "Oh, hi, Ziggy," she says. "I got the part."

Immediately, Ziggy's friend is occupied with rehearsals and costume fittings and American accent coaching sessions. And when she isn't busy with the show, Tessa is talking about it—the bitchy wardrobe lady, the violent seizures she has to practice nightly in front of the mirror. She now speaks mostly in an American accent. It is important, Tessa explains, to use a "neutral transatlantic" accent so that people don't typecast you. At school, she rolls her *r*'s and pushes her voice out flat and honky through her nose. Lunchtimes are spent on the oval, listening to Tessa's schedule. Terms like *boom operator* and *Netflix debut* jangle the air with a new unreality. Across the harbor, the city skyline now seems skeletal; the buildings spread out in a neat little line. Ziggy feels responsible for all this smallness—every racist politician and inarticulate movie star and the lack of diversity in TV and film.

By the end of that week, Lex has homework to do at lunchtime. Ziggy spends a miserable hour alone with Tessa, but after school at the lockers, Lex is there, urgently whispering over Ziggy's shoulder. "Follow me." She hurries off after Lex, down the hill to Kandara's lower gates. From here, Lex explains, they can bypass the school bus stop and Tessa by taking the cliffs out to the public interchange. There is a glorious first burst of closeness as they flee the grounds, but beyond the school's purview, Lex advances a cool three paces ahead. Ziggy tries to cling to the larger compliment of two-ness.

Taking the cliffs means walking single file along a cracked concrete path with sharp, rusted handrails. Ziggy has never liked it here. This liminal place where the ocean flows into the harbor is called the Gap—an epic gorge between the east and northern shorelines, notorious for jumpers. At the far end of the path stands a mean-spirited, monolithic high-rise. It is a singular structure—unnecessarily tall in an area of squat, freestanding homes. In a way, Ziggy admires it. It is also the building that houses her grandmother. Twinkles lives on the eighth floor in an apartment cluttered with tchotchkes and photos of distant Hungarian relations. From her kitchen window she has seen five suicides. Boys, she's told Ziggy. All boys.

Ziggy tries not to look over the edge. The ocean is wild here and the waves hurl themselves violently against the rocks. But Lex gazes out across the water, her whole being drooling toward America. Behind her friend, Ziggy feels like an afterthought—a literal drag on Lex's aspirations. Without Tessa, their bodies seem to want more distance; their private thoughts sit inside a thicker silence; and each utterance is tagged with an asterisk that hovers over them, undermining the friendship.

Or maybe Lex is just afraid of Ziggy. An inexperienced feminist, clearly attracted to girls. Her anxiety makes Ziggy compulsively chatty. She starts to relay a story—a rape-culture cautionary tale she remembers from her old school. Ziggy tells Lex about the warm September evening when three unpopular eighth graders arrived, uninvited, to a Bar Mitzvah reception at their city's famous revolving restaurant. Inside, the Sydney Swans were signing football jerseys beside a world-renowned string quartet; an *Australia's Got Talent* runner-up sang "Hava Nagila" while the Bar Mitzvah boy crowd-surfed; and then, just before dinner, a spectacular fireworks display filled the sky with many dazzling renderings of the words *Joshy-boy*. But the three disliked thirteen-year-olds missed all of this; the doorman had denied them entry. In their floor-length gowns and diamante drop earrings, the dejected trio wandered out into the night and caught a bus to Bondi Beach. Here they planned to drink beers with some English backpackers and slide down the skateboard ramp on their bums. But when they got there, the backpackers were Polish and the beer was vodka and they found themselves roughly escorted down onto the sand. The girls claimed to have been unattracted to the backpackers. Their faces were red and they all had receding hairlines, but it was easier to pretend to the men and themselves and one another that they were having a good time. Pretending made it so, in a way. The Polish backpackers left the three girls fingered and sandy on the freezing wet shore and then hobbled back up to their dorm room. Traumatized on Monday morning, one girl blabbed to a classmate, and by lunchtime the whole grade knew about their sexual escapade. Everyone said they had AIDS for the rest of the school year.

Lex cringes. "Polish people don't have AIDS."

"At my old school everyone who was ever bad to the Jews had AIDS."

"Some people actually *do* have AIDS," says Lex. "Because white people brought it back to Africa."

Ziggy freezes. She can't tell if her friend is accusing her of racism or homosexuality.

"Are you saying gay people gave Africa AIDS?"

"I'm saying the West owes the East reparations."

"I know it does," Ziggy apologizes. "And Polish people are no exception."

"I'm sorry," Lex says coolly. "But I just don't feel any sympathy toward the girls in your story. They sound like idiots."

"They were," says Ziggy, straining for emotional neutrality. "And massive attention-seekers."

She watches Lex drift unperturbed into some kind of superstitious crack-leaping game. A painfully disinterested silence accompanies them all the way back to the main road.

At the traffic lights, Ziggy spots two of the Cates on the front porch of a new home decor shop. Cate sits on a hanging cabana chair while Kate takes photos of her from the door. Today, Ziggy is grateful for the Cates. For the contrast they provide. Ziggy may be offensive, but at least she is not one of the popular girls.

"Look," she says to Lex. "Kate is Cate's selfie stick."

Lex snaps to snickering attention, but the shoot is unfortunately finishing. Cate bounds out of the swinging chair, and Kate runs after her. They are racing toward a blue BMW idling in the bus zone. Some insipid dance track bleats out the windows. Ziggy can see the shadowy figure of a large boy in the front passenger seat. From the driver's side, a Rolexed wrist breaches the roof, flicking aggressively toward the girls.

"Come on Katie!" the driver calls sharply. "I'm not getting booked so you can buy the perfect wind chime!"

The two girls reach the car and hurl themselves inside. They are greeted with amplifying beats as the throbbing vehicle revs off up the road. Ziggy's friend stares gravely after it, intoning the words "Lance Fairfax." Then she shudders and gives Ziggy the dating history of Kate's notorious brother. Lance has dumped girls for underarm stubble, oversized areolas, spider veins, cellulite. He is quick to tell a girl she smells fishy. Lex and Tessa have watched Lance's latest girlfriend swan around the mall with the sudden benevolence of a beauty queen, and pitied her. Even at peak arrogance, when the girlfriend was most giggly and hair-swishy and immaculately preened, a fart had to be imminent, and with it, her banishment from the kingdom of Lance's heart.

"He sounds terrifying," says Ziggy.

"Toxic," amends Lex.

"Do you think he farts?"

"Of course he farts. Men are allowed to fart. They're just not allowed to express their feelings."

"Yep," agrees Ziggy, then wavers. "But feelings seem maybe harder to hold in?"

"I don't think so," Lex says brusquely. "Anyway, WASPs are born that way. It's easy for them to ignore their emotions."

Ziggy thinks of the last time Jake cried—yesterday, in the laundry room with Ruth, telling her about some school bully, and helping her fold the linens. "Do you think if men cried more it would be harder for them to dehumanize women?"

"Maybe." Lex looks pensively into the traffic. "Or maybe it's just genetic. If more women did science we might actually hear about a cover-up."

Ziggy decides to leave the conversation there. Women are bad at science, men lack the empathy gene. She's had enough argument for one day.

Now Suze Lansell-Jones shuffles out onto the porch. She stares sadly into the distance, then slumps back onto the cabana chair. Dark circles drag at her eyes and her mouth tightens to a trembling blue nub.

"Suze looks a bit rough," says Lex.

"Maybe we should go."

"Nah, let's say hi."

Ziggy doesn't understand this. She can't tell if Lex's sympathy is just nostalgia for a simpler time when Lex and the Cates were still girls and everyone sat around poolside eating watermelon. Or if it is something more strategic. Ziggy cranes her neck to get a better view of the shop. Everything inside appears to be cream-colored. There are chandeliering seashell mobiles and bosomy milk-glass goblets and white "feminist"-printed pillows with frilly fringes of antique lace.

"It's like a cream pie in there," says Ziggy, then clarifies: "The one from porn."

Lex screws her face up in disgust. "Suze's shop looks like a vagina leaking semen?"

Ziggy shrugs dejectedly. If she is gay, jokes like these might require a less intimate audience.

When they reach the porch, Suze leaps up from the seat almost into Lex's arms. She hugs the girl for a long time.

"Come in, come in, let me get you a coconut water!"

"That's okay. We've got heaps of homework."

Suze seems to startle at the word *we've*. She peers down over Lex's shoulder.

"Oh, hello, there. Iggy, isn't it?"

"Ziggy."

"Yes, Ziggy." Suze gives her an irked once-over. "Can I get you something to eat?"

"No, thanks."

"I've got some lovely organic chocolate from Peru?"

"That's okay." Ziggy botches a smile and tugs at Lex's tunic.

"Well, come in anyway and take a quickie little look."

Inside the store, Ziggy picks up a creamy leather pouch that houses a large, smooth beach pebble. *What does it mean?* she wonders, but doesn't ask Suze—who is aggressively tailgating the girls around the displays. Ziggy fondles the cream feathers of a dream catcher hanging over a cascade of jasmine in a cream pot on a cream tablecloth with cream pom-poms baubled between cream-colored cockles. The only other shade is the gray of distressed patches of whitewashed wood. The space feels inhumanly sanitized. Like an airplane restroom. She taps Lex's shoulder. "I think Suze is on painkillers."

Lex flinches at her comment. Or maybe it is Ziggy's fingers. Ziggy lets a wide space stretch out between them as they complete their circumnavigation.

When they reach the counter, Lex smiles at Suze and says the shop is awesome, that she'll totally tell her mum to come and take a look. Ziggy has never heard her friend be so polite to an adult. The Israelite beams, slouching over the counter with desperate casualness. Ziggy can't help but notice her golden cleavage gleaming under the halogens. Hitler Youth remind Ziggy that despite all her feminist efforts, she still sees big boobs and mental weakness everywhere.

"Thanks for stopping by, babes."

The girls nod and hurry out the door. Or Ziggy does. Lex glides out whimsically. Walking to the bus stop, she begins to recall fond memories of the Lansell-Jones house. She speaks wistfully of their vast cream-colored sofa with all the pretty throw pillows. How Suze brought them *prosciutto melone* while they watched reruns of *Gossip Girl*. How there were always mangoes in the fruit bowl, Belgian waffle cones for the salted-caramel ice cream, a baby animal to play with.

"Poor Suze," Lex says, glancing back. Then, the kicker: "Sometimes Cate can be kind of entertaining."

TESSA'S NORMATIVE TRANSFORMATION IS even more pronounced. She now has a website with many glossy, duck-faced head shots. Her prosthetic is never on display anymore; her tops are all long-sleeved. Tessa's school tunic is shorter, and she seems to have forgotten her harrowing first day of filming. For the scene where she fell in a miniskirt and bled to death from an upper-inner-thigh wound, makeup had fashioned Tessa a blood-gushing prosthesis. She had told Ziggy and Lex that the silicone wound had a puckered, vaginal quality, and that between takes the boom operator had made wet, fappy sounds for the gaffer. Tessa said she'd felt sexually harassed and found it hard to keep pretending to hyperventilate: she worried that her performance had been compromised. Which sounded like Tessa's harassment fantasy had finally come true. Here was her moment to be a feminist and stand up to two misogynist male techies so that no young actress would ever have to face the same humiliation. "This isn't America, Ziggy," was Tessa's response. "It's not like I can get a settlement from a boom operator." She had so internalized patriarchal capitalism that experience was worthless without compensation.

And now, days before her episode's online premiere, Tessa seems uncharacteristically positive and aesthetically in love with life. She updates her Instagram hourly with photos of herself standing under a rainbow in a parking station or drinking

my last green machine till you know what!

There are even nostalgic posts of group shots with cast and crew.

<3 these guys sooo fucking much!!!

Ziggy's friend is no longer nourished on emptiness, terror, and the threat of misogyny. Tessa now appears to be identifying only as an actress. When Ziggy mentions the boom operator, Tessa says it wasn't that fucking bad.

But when the episode streams its first night on the internet, it is obvious to everyone that Tessa's performance was severely compromised. Her eyes are too poppy and while screaming, her face makes strange, vaguely erotic contortions. Ziggy's friend overacts in an addled panic never before witnessed in any of their imaginary games. It is painful to watch and then distressing to scroll through social media, as the insults accumulate. Lex texts, not altogether joking, that they might need to spend the night on suicide watch. Ziggy waits for a despairing missive from Tessa as people start augmenting the image of her prosthetic wound with tampons and sanitary pads. Ziggy wants to defend her friend, but knows that chivalry will only incite the online equivalent of being dumped, fully clothed, in a swimming pool. Then a genuine expression of concern comes, unexpectedly, from Ziggy's brother. Jake taps on her door.

"Your friend's leg is on Matt Sullivan's revenge porn page."

"Who is Matt Sullivan and what is a revenge porn page?"

"What's important here is that your friend is about to become a meme."

Ziggy opens the door and glares at her brother. She doesn't believe he has Tessa's best interests at heart. "What do you care?" she asks him.

"If you want to beat them to the punch, I can help you."

"Help me do what?"

"Make her into a meme. A good one."

"You want to help me make Tessa into a feminist meme?"

"She seems like a nice person." Jake is sincere; Ziggy is moved to be almost friendly.

"How would we do it?" she asks him.

"I have the technology; just tell me what kind of meme you want."

Ziggy considers this. If the meme's purpose is to reclaim the prosthetic pussy on Tessa's thigh, it is obvious which kind she needs.

"Cats," she tells her brother.

Jake grins and swings the door wide for his sister. They hurry together into his room.

Once Existential Cat is staring ponderously into Tessa's gash, thought-bubbling *why am I here?* and *what is the void?* Ziggy selects Grumpy Cat's face for the all-important position over Tessa's crotch.

"You need one more," Jake instructs. "For the trifecta."

There is one more cat meme Ziggy has always felt drawn to, in an uncomfortable way that compels her now to choose it. Kitlers are cats that look, by virtue of their coloring, like cat Hitlers. "If we make Tessa's face into a Kitler, isn't it kind of like she is taking control of her own image?"

Jake frowns. "I don't know if feminists will get the joke."

"Hey."

"Plus I don't find Nazis funny."

Now Ziggy sees her mistake. As a feminist, Tessa can't be likened to a Nazi. That meme must go to her vagina. Ziggy makes Jake put the Kitler over Tessa's crotch, while Existentialist Cat gazes into the gaping leg hole and Grumpy Cat is repositioned over Tessa's face. Which still makes her friend seem too humorless, so she has Jake swap Grumpy out for Happy Cat. Ziggy is satisfied, but if the meme is to be an authentic reclamation, it must be approved by Tessa herself. Ziggy sends the image to her friend.

After thirty excruciating minutes Ziggy decides that Tessa's silence just means she is out celebrating with her family. That she has missed not only Ziggy's text but also, hopefully, the wider public ridicule. But Ziggy is anxious. She is too afraid to show Lex her meme. Lately everything Ziggy does is suspiciously lesbian. Finally she logs off and tries to get some sleep.

Arriving that morning at the year-ten common room, Ziggy sees a steely Tessa flinging loose script pages from the depths of her locker. Lex and Ziggy gather around the rising sea of white. Tessa doesn't make eye contact with Ziggy, but she also doesn't mention the meme. Overnight, the actress has made some profound career decisions. She doesn't want to be just another fair-haired Australian sex object rising through the skeezy ranks of *Home and Away*. Tessa declaims into the deep echo chamber of her locker that a *serious* actress studies at the National Institute of Dramatic Art—three years at NIDA under the tutelage of avant-garde Austrian directors and cranky, ancient Brits who have seen it all, including Olivier in blackface. Ziggy glances at Lex, but her friend's face is masterfully inscrutable. Tessa continues: she will take classes at NIDA this winter break—clowning with legendary Parisian buffoons, mask workshops with blind Italian sculptors, inner animal with Russian celebrity hypnotists. She will learn how to waltz for Chekhov and sing for Brecht and develop her nascent talent for heightened language. She claims to be rereading *Lear* and "loving it."

Lex rolls her eyes. "And what about Charmaine?"

"What about her?"

"Is she a *serious* actress?"

Ziggy has never heard Lex side with Charmaine so assumes this is a black thing and that Tessa is done for.

"Of course," Tessa says carefully. "It's just harder for her to land character roles because she gets type-cast."

"What's so good about character roles?"

"It's what Australians do best."

"Why?"

"Because we're trained."

Lex snorts. "Or because you invaded this country and have no real *character* of your own?"

Ziggy's arm hairs go static with schadenfreude. Lex is clearly using Tessa's anti-Australian polemic against her. Hopefully, being Jewish gets her off the hook for Aboriginal genocide, though Ziggy knows almost nothing about Australian history. Each year, her Jewish history teachers promised to get to it, but only ever played *Gallipoli* then returned to the Third Reich. Ziggy tries anyway. "You mean how the prime ministers refused to say sorry?"

Lex remains glaring at an oddly reticent Tessa. "And how they keep the borders closed because they're so insecure about themselves."

Now Ziggy understands: Australians make good character actors because they suppress their shameful history then unconsciously repeat it at offshore detention centers.

"It's like they have no sense of self," she ventures.

Lex is more specific: "It's like they're sociopaths."

Tessa nods, contritely. Ziggy can see she is being magnanimous. The aspiring sociopath looks at Lex and makes a small national sacrifice. "You mean like Mel?"

"Yes," Lex snaps. "And Russell."

"And Geoffrey?" Tessa offers kindly.

"Obviously Nicole," Ziggy adds, enjoying the game.

But Tessa's calm accountability seems to be aggravating Lex. It appears she wants blood. "And Heath," she snarls.

This is blasphemous; as unpatriotic as calling the Joker a bad performance, and Tessa won't have it.

"Hey," she says. "Leave him out of this."

Ziggy makes a meager attempt at diffusion: "I think Nicole's most realistic role was that psychotic weatherwoman."

Lex ignores her. She glowers at the thespian. "So you're saying trauma is actually bad for acting?"

"It depends on your craft," Tessa says with aggressive pomposity. "Feelings can be a hindrance to language-based plays."

"Language-based plays?" Lex over-articulates with theatrical disgust. "You got objectified for wearing a miniskirt on TV and now you only want to do theater?"

Tessa is suddenly trembling. "I got objectified and trolled!"

"Every girl—except Ziggy—who steps outside in a skirt gets fucking trolled!"

"Well I'm a better actress than that!"

"Than what? Oppressed people?"

Tears gleam at Tessa's eyeballs, but for Lex, even this is not enough.

"You're a racist!" she yells, and then charges off down the hall. Tessa begins to bawl into the crook of her bionic arm. Ziggy feels a sharp tweak of sympathy.

"I'm sorry you got trolled," says Ziggy. "Was it bad?"

Tessa looks up, slowly, as if into a harsh light.

"*You* trolled me."

"I was trying to make you a feminist meme!"

"I'm a *serious* actress!" Tessa screams, her face a dangerous purple. "*She* is a whore and *you* are a predator! You two can go fuck each other!"

It still wouldn't be consensual, thinks Ziggy. *LOL*, think a delighted Hitler Youth.

Chapter 6

Now that their friendship group has shrunk to two, Ziggy feels completely unsafe in her gender and sexual ambiguity. Even with the dwindling specter of Tim. Lex has increasing issues with homosexuals, and now even transgender women can be too white to be women of color. Ziggy doesn't dare ask if Tessa showed her the pussy reclamation meme. The neutral cargo pants and T-shirts Ziggy had been wearing are now swapped for short A-line skirts and shoulder-baring peasant tops. She rattles around inside booby blouses; the fabrics jut and sink, impervious to her shape. To appease her friend, Ziggy walks around on weekends feeling squarish and wrong and angry with women. The shameless flaunting of curves now seems grotesque and manipulative. Of course Lex gets catcalled. Forty percent of her ass is always peeking out of her shorts. Rowena, at least, enjoys the attention. She seems like the only woman Ziggy knows who isn't a whining, menstruating biological contradiction.

Everywhere she goes, Ziggy is terrorized by boobs. Or by her own misogyny. It is impossible to wrench the two things apart. She dreads school and going to the mall. And at home, on her queer PoC subreddit, Ziggy now feels like an imposter. No one else talks about their own uncontrollable leering. The subreddit no longer seems like a viable support group; if Ziggy actually bared her soul, she would trigger someone else's anxiety; if she asked for emotional help, she might have to pay a tariff. Reading a post about transgender incarceration, Ziggy is reminded of Tessa's grand theory, but she is too nervous to share it. The atmosphere tonight is unusually anarchic. Then someone posts a political manifesto, which at first seems vaguely cyborgian.

> abolish all prisons + ban the police!
>
> open up the borders + confiscate all guns!

But the focus quickly narrows.

> free palestine + fuck israeli pinkwashing!
>
> stop US intervention that makes it unsafe for trans PoC 2 live anywhere but these transphobic united states!!

This last one seems contradictory. Ziggy Googles it, and learns that in Gaza, homosexuality is punishable by death. Does this mean you can't fly a rainbow flag beside a Palestinian one? And wouldn't US intervention be welcome in gay Gaza, to free these Palestinians from their own murderous rule of law? But these are not questions Ziggy feels she can ask the queer subreddit. She considers messaging Tim, but imagining his response makes her feel more alienated. It was bad enough that the Israelis stole the honey cake. Ziggy wouldn't call him a beta, but she finds Tim's moral relativism annoying—always apologizing and rewriting and editing himself out of any actual point of view. Ziggy logs back in to Reddit, but this time to the Red Pill. Just for a little calming irreverence. Just for the lols.

AFTER WINTER BREAK, Tessa is cast in the Randalls-Kandara coproduction of *Down with Demon Drink!*, a musical adaptation of the nineteenth-century temperance melodrama. She plays the lead, Edward Middleton, who leaves his family destitute to become a drunken vagrant. Apparently, Tessa is mixing well with the other thespians and singing her aphoristic ditties in an off-key but lively falsetto. These are the reports from rehearsals, as Tessa is no longer speaking to Ziggy or Lex. Patricia Katsatouris, who plays "the maniac," says their erstwhile friend is in her element: performing a male part is very Shakespearean.

Ziggy remembers fondly the one play she did at her old school. Yoni Kessler, their sixteen-year-old theater prodigy, had convinced the drama teacher to let him direct a 1970s Woody Allen play called *Death*. Ziggy was Mob Member Four, one of twelve tasked with hunting down the psychopath. She spent many hours of rehearsal in trust exercises—falling back into the outstretched arms of her fellow vigilantes—and got very good at saying "Unique New York" backward and forward in rapid succession. Ziggy knows there will be first-rate entertainment in the rehearsal room of *Down with Demon Drink!* She would love to scale the walls of Randalls's drama department— angling a camera down against the grimy basement windows to film their warm-up games and what is sure to be a sexless and ungainly dance choreography. But Lex would rather stay home on Google Earth. The virtual stalking of the rapper's Hidden Hills estate seems to be the last extracurricular activity left to their compromised friendship. Lex zooms in on the network of swimming pool caves and the outdoor screening room with its faux-stone fireplace. They try to tilt in behind the blurred sheets of waterfalls for a glimpse of the man himself, or his women, or even his pool cleaners, but the technology doesn't allow it. Still, Lex would rather be virtually in America than physically anywhere else.

Then surprisingly, when *Down with Demon Drink!* opens, Lex suggests she and Ziggy attend a performance. Hate-watching Tessa's play could be fun. Returning to school after dark, Ziggy waits on the oval for Lex to arrive. The school buildings glow a deep, milky blue that softens their imperious facades. The cool air makes her whole being feel washed and new. Ziggy imagines the oval is a dark dune on planet Mars. She wanders in aimless circles, enjoying how the crisp air tickles her hairy little legs.

Ziggy and Lex sit at the back of the auditorium bleachers, snorting each time Tessa exclaims in her atonal singing voice. But as the play goes on, Ziggy starts to warm toward Edward Middleton, the tipsy, wayward landowner. When Tessa appears in the spotlight for her solo, Ziggy is unexpectedly moved. Their friend has tapped into some ancient, Gaelic suffering.

"Poor little Potato Famine survivor," Lex whispers. Ziggy chuckles, and the thin line of feeling between her and Tessa snaps.

Afterward Lex has venomous commentary. She says the play is dated; casting a girl in a male role doesn't change the fact that they are telling some dead white man's story and putting all the Asian kids in whiteface. As they pour out of the auditorium, Lex eyes the joyful hordes with enmity. "It's like the amateur theater society of Narrandera."

Ziggy tries to sympathize with Lex's hatred of rural communities, and mimics her friend's contemptuous march all the way out to the foyer. Lex wants to wait here, hoping to catch a glimpse of Tessa's alleged boyfriend. It takes only a brief scan of the room to spot him. As reported, Eamon Gameau is a pasty waif with the rosy, bee-stung lips of a Classical pervert.

"That boy is gay," Lex pronounces.

Ziggy feels herself recoil. "Then why would he want to date Tessa?"

"I don't know, Ziggy. Why would Tim want to date you? Because everybody's 'fluid' or whatever."

Ziggy doesn't like the way Lex has said "fluid," but she is too embarrassed to admit that Tim almost definitely does not want to date her. She watches Eamon. He wears a purple T-shirt with the words EVERY DAY IS CONSENT DAY printed in huge white Helvetica across the front. As Tessa leans across him to accept somebody's roses, Eamon taps her bum. Lex grabs Ziggy's wrist.

"Did you see that?"

Ziggy shrugs. "The slap?"

"Gay men are always slapping girls' bums! They think they're exempt from sexual harassment in the workplace."

"But it's the theater. . . ."

"It doesn't matter!"

"And she's his girlfriend."

Lex juts her chin out testily. "So you're on Eamon's side?"

Ziggy shakes her head, defeated.

"The theater is so confused," Lex says. "The men are all gay and the gays are all misogynists and the women let everyone publicly molest them."

Ziggy's friend is becoming a reactionary. But at least she is squeezing Ziggy's arm.

Now someone in the courtyard calls out to Tessa and she blows an air kiss then starts bounding toward them down the stairs. Ziggy can see that Tessa is headed in their direction and she panics, suddenly ashamed to be there.

"Let's go," she whispers to Lex.

But before they can move, Tessa trips and tumbles onto the carpet. The moment goes slow because Tessa makes an opera of falling, bunching the air in around her like an epic load of laundry. Eamon dashes over, dropping theatrically to his knees; a second later Tessa's face pops up over his shoulder, a smug pleasure blinking through the shock. Ziggy knows she should feel sorry for Tessa (the prosthetic arm compromises her balance), but the fall is infuriating. Tessa seemed to relish the chance to crash to that dramatic burgundy carpet, reaching heteronormatively for her boyfriend's strong, sinewy neck. Now Lex laughs loudly, drawing attention to the two of them. As Tessa sees her, Ziggy loses control of her face. The muscles twitch between real and faked animosity, forming a clownish smirk that trembles with bad acting. Tessa returns the insult, looking melodramatically away.

Dragging along on Lex's forearm as they exit up the drive, Ziggy has a strange yearning for the crowd back at the auditorium. When they reach the gates, she glances back at the warm lights across the deep field, and for the first time since starting at Kandara, Ziggy feels pulled in the wrong direction.

THE TWO FRIENDS RETREAT TO ZIGGY'S house and Google Earth. Like an old couple, they get comfortable in house socks and oversized T-shirts and lay some snacks out in a line on Ziggy's bed. Minutes later Jacob is hovering in Ziggy's doorway. He crosses one foot over the other, leaning into the doorframe with gentlemanly poise.

"Pardon me," Jacob says. "But is this a Google Earth surveillance session?"

Lex addresses Ziggy. "Was your brother adopted from the nineteenth century?"

"Jacob, leave."

"Please, ladies, allow me to show you some of the more current technologies."

"Stop talking like that."

But Ziggy and Lex are stuck outside the rapper's arbored patio. They follow Jacob into his room, where he brings up a series of web pages. First, there is the Lily—a drone that can track your slalom down a mountain. Next, the Phantom 3—to be air-sticked into active volcanoes. These seem a little extreme, and also, they cost thousands of dollars. Jacob plays the girls Keynotes. Lex drifts back to her phone. On Jacob's desk, Ziggy sees a small square camera with a plastic strap.

"What's that one?"

"A GoPro," says Jacob. "It's no good for stalking celebrities."

It seems her brother can only fathom these devices as tools for spying on famous people or else conquering untouched natural wonders. Which, she supposes, is kind of the same thing.

"Let me try it," Lex says, poking Ziggy's brother in the back.

Jacob swiftly hands it over, blushing as their fingers touch. Then he passes Lex an iPhone strapped to an extendible rod. "You can see what you're seeing on this."

Which sounds strange to Ziggy—can't Lex see what she's seeing with her eyes? But watching the footage live on the little screen, Ziggy learns that the camera sees things differently. The focus narrows back to a fixed, still point—that being Lex's head. Moving outward from here, objects shrink and flatten out, forming a more compact, manageable panorama.

Lex hops up on Jacob's bed and does a few jumps. She gets good air. Ziggy spends a long, envious minute watching Lex enjoy her own athletic body. She tenses her thighs as she bounces, her mouth curling into an indulgent grin. Ziggy has never experienced the thrill of athletic aptitude but imagines it is a sense of physical power close to godliness. She can see how the camera might enhance this effect.

But quickly, Lex is bored. "Yeah, this kind of sucks." She yanks the GoPro off her head. "How far does the Phantom Three fly?"

"Five hundred meters high and two miles across."

"That isn't going to get us into the pool caves." Lex's voice is accusing. "What about the Lily?"

"You'll need military-style drones to get to America."

The doorbell rings and Jacob snatches back his camera then makes a decorous little bow.

"Ladies, I'm afraid I must now attend to my own war plans."

His friends have arrived for a Wii tournament.

BY MIDNIGHT, LEX'S BOREDOM IS nearing dangerous new levels. She checks her phone incessantly for Snapchats, Instagram-stalks all the rapper's ex-girlfriends, Google image-searches herself, then someone with the same name, then someone with slightly different spelling. Ziggy knows they can do better than this, but she must avoid old pastimes like Method acting and the straddling of spa jets. They can't watch music videos together, even ironically. Ziggy is too scared to get stoned with Lex. Hitler Youth might make her say the word *queef*. The last thing Ziggy can think to offer her friend is the boys downstairs.

Leading Lex out to the third-floor landing, Ziggy begins to

paint a picture of her brother's new private school friends. How last time the boys stayed over, she watched them make chocolate sundaes while discussing the pitfalls of masturbation. Lucien, the pretty blond one, had relayed the tragic fate of his older brother—a Randalls alum who'd squandered his law school dreams to take a girl behind the tennis courts and squeeze her perfect C-cup breasts. The other boys had chimed in with a brief history of great white men who believed ejaculation would bring them to ruin. Lucien's brother had warned him that morning sex could turn even the most ambitious boy into a useless junkie. The other three agreed that you should never spill your seed the day of a very big test.

Listening to Ziggy's story, Lex's legs get noodly; she rocks against the bannister, heaving her bosom over the railing, eyeing the little boys below. The three seventh graders are perched on cushion stacks, consoles poised, cross-legged and coolly glaring like child princes. Ziggy had expected Lex would want to fling boogers onto their heads or maybe let a mysterious drip slowly drive their evening insane. But Lex wants to know more about them. The blond one, she thinks, looks at least fourteen. Ziggy can feel their evening turn, the air needle, the atoms get screwy. She concedes the blond one has a certain charisma. Even from their bird's-eye view. His patrician features are finessing and his sheer cheekbones are starting to fuzz. The sounds of warfare rise up in loud complicated blasts. Lex is getting giggly. Ziggy feels herself leaning boyward too.

The girls have no plan. They don't even have mutual honesty, only a tacit agreement to wander downstairs and mope seductively around. At the top of the steps, Ziggy has a sudden urge to go back for the GoPro. She slips into Jacob's room and swipes the camera off his desk. She isn't sure why. But strapping it on feels good in front of Lex. Something rebalances between them. Lex lets Ziggy walk ahead.

Downstairs, Ziggy sees that Jacob has dozed off, which only increases the heady feeling of inconsequence. The girls slink around the kitchen, and the boys pretend not to notice them. Ziggy pulls two beers from the fridge and passes one to Lex. The gesture feels mimicked but fluent; Ziggy's body is somehow not her own.

Lucien turns to face her, smiling sweetly. "Can I have one?"

Ziggy cracks the beer like she has watched her father and his menfolk do many times before. She raises the bottle and takes a gulp. Almost instantly a calm, white space floods her mind. She grins at Lucien, swipes another longneck from the fridge door, and tosses it to him. He catches it and takes a moment to study the label.

"This was a good year," he says, nodding at the bottle.

"A good year for beer?" Lex giggles.

Lucien looks up, his face feral with hurt. But Lex smiles back, warm and encouraging.

"2015," he says shyly. "I heard that somewhere."

Lex doesn't tease him, which must mean she's flirting. Now Ziggy notices the taste of her beer. It is stewy and metallic, like licking a Brillo pad, like some kind of punishment. The pasty redhead and lanky brace-face are murmuring for beverages. Ziggy removes two more bottles and holds them out. Then as the boys inch forward, she yanks the beers back. They eye her helplessly.

"You can only have one," she says, "if you play our drinking game."

Lex grins her approval, and the two beerless boys slump back into their cushions. But Lucien is more tactical.

"Of course we'll play," he says, rousing the other two to resentful obedience. "What are the rules?"

Ziggy thinks fast. "We ask the questions. If we don't like your answer, you have to take a sip."

"Easy," says Lucien. "Can Rupert and Oliver please have their drinks now?"

Ziggy hands over the beers. Lex scoots in beside Lucien and he puffs up, almost manly, as he sips from his bottle. Annoyed, Ziggy begins her interrogation with him.

"First question," she says. "What do you prefer—blondes or brunettes?"

"Brunettes . . ." Lucien says carefully. "But it also depends on their personality."

His friends giggle and Lucien grins unctuously. Lex seems impressed.

"Wrong," says Ziggy. "That's like saying you only like small dogs if they don't bark too much."

Lucien shrugs and takes a big swig. It seems he doesn't mind being wrong or intoxicated while his knees are touching Lex.

"The next one is also for Lucien," Ziggy announces. "What's better—short skirts or short shorts?"

"Is this another trick question?"

"Answer."

"Culottes," says Lucien, already sipping. Lex watches him and laughs, enjoying his hijinks. Ziggy resents the dynamic emerging within their group. Perhaps it is the camera on her head. Or the fact she isn't pretty. But the boys have not warmed to her. Still, Ziggy remains in charge. She knows a drinking game should involve sex and humiliation, and that Lucien is top of her brother's Latin class.

"Or do you prefer togas?" she suggests.

"Togas?"

"Boys in togas."

Lucien laughs, his face tight with contempt.

"I had to ask due to your love of Romans."

But Lex defends her admirer. "Just because you like classical antiquity doesn't mean you're gay."

Ziggy pretends this doesn't hurt her. She nods, conceding. "Even if, statistically, it probably does."

"Exactly," says Lucien, confused.

Now Ziggy opens the game up to the other boys, but their answers are less damning than adorable. When orthodontically challenged Oliver admits to a crush on Audrey Hepburn, he receives affectionate coddling from Lex. "That's so cute," she says, poking him.

"My sister is an Audrey Hepburn historian," he says proudly.

"What's that?" Ziggy sneers. "Someone who studies neckerchiefs?"

Nobody laughs, so Ziggy's questions get overtly embarrassing. But now it is too late—the boys are having fun. For Lex they unfurl, pink and willing like well-walked dog tongues, giddily confessing that yes, they all picture their female teachers naked, and yes, they all jerk off every day, even mornings when their newsfeeds are crammed with murder and climate change. Ziggy sneaks looks at Lex, who is eyeing Lucien in her low-lidded, burning way. Ziggy feels herself shrinking, dissolving back into the room's gorging red. The boys are charming her friend. Ziggy had not expected the thirteen-year-olds to be so responsive. Or emotionally mature. Though there is one way in which Ziggy knows they are as kiddish as she is. For all their bluster, these little boys are incapable of anatomical follow-through. Ziggy turns the camera on her friend.

"Hey Lex, do you think the boys should show us how they do it?"

The laughter is unanimous and nullifying. For a moment. And then Lex leans back queenly into the couch cushions. "That could be interesting . . ."

The boys go quiet. Rupert pretends to be focused on the abandoned game, his avatar bowling into a tree then butting repeatedly against its trunk. The air is suddenly hot and surging. A molecular consensus of low vibrations. All of them pulled along, equally.

But more precisely, it starts with Ziggy.

"Let's move up into the living room."

Away from her brother. The boys rise and drag their blobby, socked feet to the stairs. Lex follows languidly behind. She seems soft and loose in her body, happy to let Ziggy lead them astray. In the living room, they make a circle. The girls sit on their haunches; Jacob's friends lounge with bent legs, clearly trying to disguise their fly-tenting boners.

It seems to happen organically. With both dreamy slowness and mechanical inevitability. Ziggy aims the GoPro at Lex and repeats the question. Her friend titters, eyes downcast and illegible, which the boys interpret as an unambiguous command. With only a brief preamble of giggling, the seventh graders begin worming their hands in under their waistbands. It takes a moment for Ziggy to comprehend that the boys are actually tugging. It is a dull shock that fuzzies the air. From somewhere far back inside herself, Ziggy observes the scene, reduced and quiet, as if projected on a screen. Lex's face is set in a neutral mask, minutely grimacing, but the boys have fierce purpose. There is a reddish aim in their eyes as they strain toward Lex, then Ziggy, then back again to Lex. Their mouths are twitching;

their lids flutter. They seem to hold the girls there, caught in the fever of their gaze. Ziggy knows the feeling in the room has turned too animal, but she feels safe with the camera on her head.

There is a soft wheeze from Lucien and then all three boys are shuddering into their laps. The bleachy uppercut of semen knocks Ziggy off-balance, and the whole room seems to dunk underwater. But, folding over their crotches, the boys look as frail as seahorses. Lex makes a little yelp but Ziggy ignores it, feeling suddenly sorry for exposing these fragile internet-sexuals to the harsh physical realm. Then she glances at her friend; Lex is violently rubbing her left eye. She stops and looks up at Ziggy, the eye red and puffy and seeping.

"They got me," she growls. "They got me in my fucking eye!"

The next hour is a furious blur of Lex panicked and raging in Ziggy's bedroom. Her eye swells and pinkens horribly. Google thinks she'll need antibiotics. Every ten minutes, the little boys knock on Ziggy's door, eager and terrified to know how Lex is doing. The girls yell them away. Mostly Lex wants to blame Ziggy. Apparently, Lex didn't want to watch a circle jerk. The boys are thirteen. They could both go to fucking jail. Ziggy apologizes over and over. She doesn't dare try the line: *I thought it would be funny.*

The inflammation slowly subsides, but Lex remains irate. What Ziggy made them endure is a type of sexual harassment. She's a bully. Ziggy pleads that she is only an aspiring filmmaker.

"Tessa showed me the meme you made." Lex's mouth crimps with disgust. "It was creepy."

This insult is familiar from the Red Pill. A word women use to make men want to shrivel up and die. Ziggy's creative instincts are off, and worse: Ziggy herself is a biological aberration.

After another hour of verbal abuse and many cold compresses, Lex finally relents, falling into an agitated sleep.

But the circle jerk keeps Ziggy up most of the night. She worries about Lex, then Jake, and then her thoughts are moving with a kind of violent, game-play dissociation. She sees her shirtless father and his bare-chested friends wrestling on the couch while eating drippy mangoes; reels of sidebar comments from porn-cams; a slut-shaming session on Reddit where a celebrity Instagram account was decimated by a group of anonymously impotent men. There are circle jerks happening all around her, and Ziggy feels implicated in each of them. With her flat chest and ambiguous sexual identity, Ziggy must have seemed to Lex like the little boys' ringleader.

Chapter 7

After Lex's eye-rape, Ziggy understands that she must now identify as a straight, cisgender female at the pretty popular end of the spectrum. In tight, rib cage–revealing dresses and heavy makeup, Ziggy finds she can dissociate from her body and transport her sense of self to that distant future time when she is famous and nobody can make her share her feelings. In borrowed crop tops, belly exposed to universal ridicule, Ziggy escapes to her mental fantasy of an impenetrable identity, fortressed by celebrity aura and framed by illustrious facades. In this soothing reverie, Ziggy's body is nothing but a dim glow inside the gilded jaws of the Dolby Theatre or floating in the dark, elegant sea of tuxedos on the Cannes red carpet. Sometimes she can feel the musty esteem of a tweed blazer and the airy blithe of an undercut, but her own image is mostly void.

Lex appears to have forgiven Ziggy for the circle jerk but has moved into a very demanding phase of their friendship. She is suddenly desperate to go to nightclubs and for the two of them to stand around at Bondi Junction, licking ice blocks in jacket weather while pretending not to be molecularly aware of the adjacent Randalls seniors. Ziggy finds that a thin outer layer of irony can get her through these afternoons with minimal discomfort. While Lex preens her confectionary with the sensual indifference of a jungle cat, Ziggy views their surrounds with a critical eye, silently commentating. She likes to watch the Randalls boys drink protein shakes at the juice counter, their voices dropping and egos inflating with every sip. After thirty minutes Ziggy's friend is usually finished waiting for a frightened teenage boy to morph into an adult movie star and approach her with compliments. Unfortunately, Lex's nightclub aspiration is a lot more focused.

There is a club the Kandara seniors patronize on Sunday nights, seemingly for the Monday morning glamor of a faded wrist stamp. Embassy is all underage girls and bald Eurotrash valet parking their Maseratis. Inside, a real estate mogul might buy you a Fresh Pussy then show you photos of his teenage daughter from a rival school. You can hear sex and vomiting in the bathrooms and see cocaine frosting along the edges of Amex cards. The bouncers are known to sniff out the girls Uber'd in from the southwest of Sydney. Fake handbags induce hyena laughter and a Rolexed wrist-flick that means, *Go back to the Western Suburbs.*

Embassy is in the harborside suburb of Double Bay, where the houses sit on wide, bright smiles of marble staircase and all the SUVs haul speedboats. Jeff says this is because Double Bay is below sea level, and thirty years ago there was a flood. Yachts came jaunting up driveways and stingrays coasted over deck chairs. Nothing so nightmarish had ever befallen the high-functioning conservative Coalition voters of Double Bay, and so they had landscaped their gardens and added second and third stories to their homes. Ruth says Jeff's fable is social satire, and: "Don't blame Mother Nature for the nouveau riche."

On Double Bay's main shopping street, wedged between the sparsely stocked and darkly carpeted designer boutiques, sits the sinister black cube of Embassy nightclub. The tinted-glass monolith has made a violent impression on Ziggy's imagination. Figures shift slyly in the doorway, and Ziggy pictures a cabaret of sexual perversion behind its smoky glass. She knows that management is lax on IDs and gives out memberships to attractive young girls in the form of a heavy steel key. The owner is a young millionaire and alumnus of Randalls, notorious for his orgy parties and his coke dick. He has many friends in the music industry.

Which is why, this year, the club is hosting the ARIA's after party. Normally, the Australian music awards are a joke—Lex says the local industry is a bunch of *Australia's Got Talent* contestants supporting real stars until they get big enough to host a travel show. But this ARIA's is different. This year, her American rapper is the international guest of honor.

Lex's plan to infiltrate the ARIA's after party unfolds over an anxious, unusually intimate week between the two friends. Ziggy listens and asks no challenging questions as Lex enlists her in the scheme. She maintains a generous faith in Lex's ability to laminate fake press passes and transform their birth years from 2001 to 1998. When Lex requests they get dressed that night in her parents' spacious en suite, Ziggy is flushed with new hope. It seems possible that their friendship might have made a full recovery from the traumatic circle jerk.

In the bathroom that night, Lex lays out the heteronormative ensembles Ziggy is allowed to wear to Embassy. The miniskirt she settles on makes Ziggy feel pornographically exposed. Her mother's sordid painting scowls overhead, making Ziggy feel both desirous and terrified of pubic hair. Thankfully, Lex hasn't noticed it or else doesn't have an eye for abstraction. She is busy emptying an entire duffel bag full of makeup: things she has purchased or stolen from multiple department stores. Her excuse for shoplifting is a Marxist-feminist phase that Tessa dragged them through briefly last year—Tessa harping on about female beautification as labor and how they had already earned the cosmetics through some invisible economic exchange process. When Ziggy asks why their Marxist phase ended, Lex says, "Because Tessa got a credit card."

When they are ready, the girls study themselves in the mirror. Behind their reflections, Ziggy spies the Barbies spilling from their bag in the open closet. Then Lex sees them. She spins around and grabs one, rips out its arm, and starts tap-dancing the doll across the toilet seat.

"We are all women of color!" chirps the Tessa doll. "I have a great aunt who was born in *Egypt*!"

Ziggy giggles nervously.

"Even my new boyfriend is a woman of color!" Lex continues. "Because he's gay! Because he has braces!"

Ziggy's skin goes cold. Lex's rant feels pointed, sucking all remaining affinity into its icy orbit. Ziggy doesn't want to go to Embassy. The rapper has been ignoring Lex's Snapchats for weeks, and there is no way their evening is going to end in triumph. The rapper will not be returning to Sydney to escort Lex to her formal, Ziggy will not be meeting the middle-aged property developer of her dreams, and neither one of them is going to enjoy standing around awkwardly in a room full of seniors who know they are tenth graders. Ziggy snatches back the Barbie, refits her arm, and returns her to the closet. Hovering there, wanting desperately to stay hidden in the cupboard's cozy dark, Ziggy remembers a story. It won't dissuade Lex from her impending romantic humiliation, but Ziggy decides to tell her friend anyway about the four year-seven girls who sexually harassed the famous American swimmer.

After the London Olympics, the four unathletic victims of puppy fat had fallen in love with the gargantuan, bucktoothed goofball who slashed all the world records and had his own leisurewear label. Every lunchtime, they "borrowed" the mobile phone of Natalya (their grade's richest Russian émigré) to call the Mission Bay Aquatic Center, where they were put straight through to their Olympian paramour. The American thought it was hilarious. These four teenage girls (they were twelve at the time but bumped their ages to fifteen) calling him to talk about his day, his girlfriend, her boobs, whether he liked to suck them? The American wanted to know if kangaroos jumped through their streets and koalas hung off the telephone poles? The girls humored him—saying they rode their native fauna to school. The American guffawed and then admitted to being a breast man. And an ass man. Or really mostly a breast man. Six months later, the Olympian told them he was coming to Sydney for a swim meet, and the girls made their arrangements. Rachel Rubenstein's father got them into the Sydney International Aquatic Centre as volunteer towel girls. The four of them had to walk around with plastic baskets, collecting used towels and laying out clean ones. That day, when the American strode out to his diving block, Rachel R. was there to greet him. She placed a fresh towel on his chair and batted her thick Jewessy lashes and pouted her hot-pink twelve-year-old lips.

Then she told him who she was. The American came third-last. Afterward he avoided the girls, slinking quickly into the green-room, where towel bearers were not allowed to go.

Unsurprisingly, Lex does not seem moved by Ziggy's story. "I didn't know the Jews also controlled swimming."

Ziggy is speechless. She sits on the tub's rim with her chin in her hands, despair thinning to apathy. "Jews can't even swim," she lies.

Lex nods distractedly, molesting her side part in the mirror. "Can you blow-dry my hair?"

Ziggy cannot. But she knows who would relish this almost as much as childbirth. Ruth loves blow-drying Ziggy's curls. It has always been a kind of unspoken bonding activity enjoyed in the enforced silence of the dryer's blast. Ziggy summons her mother from the top of the stairs. The woman is there in less than ten seconds.

While Ruth homogenizes Lex's hair, the two women yell loudly about makeup. Ziggy's mother has helpful hints about eye shadow. How to make the lids look fuller, how to achieve the "smoky effect." Of course Lex would like the smoky effect. Ruth completes the blow-dry and then pulls up the Instagram of Italy's first lady.

"She's got great technique," admires Ruth.

Lex sighs dreamily and Ziggy's mother gets to work, the two women slipping into a silent, trancelike state. In the first lady's eyes, Ziggy sees a self-conscious blankness. The same not-being-thereness that she sees in all her peers' faces. The trade-off for male attention seems to be a woman's entire inner life. Ziggy is disturbed to find the smoky effect sexy; it makes Lex's eyes look dewy and bruised, abused but somehow alluring.

When Ruth finishes, she steps back and catcalls Lex with a soft parachuting whistle.

"Thanks, Mrs. Klein."

Once the preparations are over and the two girls are standing in the doorway—painted, straightened, accessorized, and armed with convincing fake IDs, Ruth tells them they look beautiful. Lex's smoky eyes go opiate. Ziggy wants to weep. Hitler Youth seem pleased with the total mess they have made of Ziggy's gender identity. Tonight she feels like a drag queen who has misplaced her sense of humor.

THE CLUB'S LINE IS a fat snake of dark, scintillating glamor and Ziggy gets stuck on the pavement just staring at it.

"Should we buy some glitter glue from the chemist?"

Lex wrangles her cleavage, tugging her bra down like the hand of a grabby child. "Trust me," she says. "The men will just think we're interns. Which is a good thing."

They slink into line. Pale important faces glow above a black sea of warbling sequins. And up ahead, celebrities are cutting in. Ziggy can tell by their casual clothes and giant sunglasses. She keeps her head down as she shuffles along beside Lex; avoiding eye contact even as they reach the bouncers, Lex flashes their lanyards, and the men say *enjoy your night* and wave them in. And they are in. Ziggy floats up the stairs in a daze. Like rats circling toward the club's warm, inner chamber, Lex and Ziggy breach door after door stationed with gigantic muscle men squeezed into shiny suits, smiling narcotically at Lex's ass. The final door opens onto an enormous glass room. The city lights glint off naked forearms and pale bouffants, and the whole room is slicked with silver. Out the windows, Ziggy sees the stately white wedding cakes of Double Bay's residential zone. These palatial homes—whose orange windows glow with the sanctity of birthday candles—seem virtual from this vantage. Ziggy is surprised to feel a sense of event, of being on the precipice of her own adult life. It is like her mother said Shuni said: to bear conscious witness, you need a very expansive view.

The bar is in the center of the room: a white marble block rising from the black carpet with the cool luminescence of an iceberg. Behind it gleams a mini metropolis of bottles backlit by warm amber—a city paused in eternal happy hour. A dark hedge of suits encircles the bar. Ziggy sees only a sprinkling of girls—their e-cigarettes blinking furtive green signals across the marble.

Lex and Ziggy line up for drinks. In seconds, a man with a tremendous silver mane comes shining out of the dark.

"How's your night going, girls?"

Ziggy has been briefed. Anyone in here could know the rapper, or at least have access to the VIP room. She smiles and tells the man she is well, and thank you for asking. Lex is more strategic. She wants a drink. The man worms back into the dense, Armani underbrush and returns a moment later with two cloudy shot glasses.

"Fresh Pussy." He grins and passes the girls their beverages.

Now Ziggy notices the man's shirt is unbuttoned halfway down his chest. His face is square and handsome in the biscuity way of middle-aged celebrity men. Lex is looking at him strangely.

"You're that judge," she says.

The man flashes the fluorescent tube of his orthodontia. *Australia's Got Talent,*" he confirms.

"No, it doesn't," says Lex.

The judge loves this. Which surprises the girls. They are used to offending boys and alienating themselves within the opening seconds of interaction. But the judge seems intrigued. He is doing something focused with his eyes: narrowing them, squeezing Lex into a more appealing package.

"Sexy. Bitchy. Badass. I love it."

Lex smiles at the talent scout and Ziggy is reminded of the Magnetic Poles. How women are meant to be receptive and relational; how men must forge through the space-time continuum with aggressive, linear force. Lex leans plantlike toward the judge as if trying to increase the surface area of her skin, and Ziggy has the impulse to call her friend a prostitute. Instead, she sips compulsively on her Fresh Pussy, staring into the froth as Lex and John discuss the music industry. The talent scout is amused by Lex's critique of his reality franchise. He wants to see her YouTube channel. He wants to take her out on his yacht. Then the scout glances between the friends with a rakish smile and places his feet in a wide, martial arts stance of readiness.

"Righto," he says. "Let's get you two to the VIP room."

John whisks them across the dance floor to the megalith of a giant Māori man, perched on what must be a very tiny stool. The man looks them up and down, inspects John's VIP pass, then cracks a door open with one gigantic hand. They slip through into a room that is a miniature version of the club outside. There are a few plush, velvet booths and a smaller luminescent bar in the corner. The obvious difference is that in here there are almost no men.

While Lex and John chatter, Ziggy studies the room, and Hitler Youth confirm that even with her padded bra and the pencil lines Lex called "contouring," she has the smallest boobs here. And Ruth didn't straighten her hair properly. It is still frizzy underneath so that it puffs out like a triangle. The way John's gaze flinches from her makes Ziggy feel like an angry troll doll. But she doesn't like him either. The violent squash game his eyes play with Lex and something over her shoulder; his name-dropping of Britpop stars and sentimental paraphrasing of John Lennon. He doesn't seem to care that neither girl knows what he is talking about. It is probably time to exchange emails and get away from the talent scout. Ziggy tries to tug Lex toward the bathroom, but her friend says she doesn't need to go. A breach of their friendship contract, but Ziggy manages to remain aloof. Next she suggests they go find the rapper.

"I already texted him," says Lex.

"And?"

"The reception's bad in here."

"So let's go outside."

John folds his arms and grins; his chin squishing back into many supercilious layers. "He's in the *secret* VIP room."

"Isn't that where we are?"

"This is the VIP room," says John. "There's also a secret VIP room."

Lex hooks an arm over John's and the judge brushes a long, wet look up the canvas of her body. Ziggy tries not to watch them, fixing her eyes instead on an e-cigarette blipping redly at the far side of the room.

"Righto," says John, and walks them to a set of elevators in the passageway. At the doors, another monstrous man dominates a twiggy stool. He checks John's lanyard, grunts something, and then admits the three of them into the elevator. It is wide and industrial and asynchronous with the stark glamor of the club—a freight elevator that takes them down via an ugly concrete parking garage where a guilty-looking coat check stomps out her joint before stepping inside. The doors close and the elevator drops lower.

The secret VIP room is blizzardy with cigarette smoke. The air stings Ziggy's eyes, and in seconds, she has lost Lex and John. She finds a booth, then slides in to rub her eyes and sulk. The girls gyrating around her table appear to be in a deep trance of vanity. Their need for attention seems primal, biological, and gross.

Then a cigarette appears under Ziggy's nose. "You want?"

"No, thanks," she says.

"You sure?"

Ziggy looks across the slim white stick, proffered by a dark male hand, extended from the sleeve of a yellow sweatshirt printed with the words: NO WORRIES, MATE. Ziggy blinks up. The rapper smiles back at her.

"Actually, okay."

He lights the cigarette then turns back to the woman grinding at his side. Ziggy is shaking. She tries to focus on the simple act of inhalation. Then she starts looking around for Lex. She spots her friend on the other side of the room and tries to make subtle flicking gestures with the cigarette, but she fumbles and it slips, taking a white spin to the floor. Ziggy feels a sting beneath her foot; the cigarette has dropped into her shoe. She tries to kick it out, but the burning stick lodges deeper into the tight space between leather and heel. Ziggy reaches down to unbuckle the straps, but female legs press in all around her, crowding out her hands. Now the rapper is watching. Ziggy smiles and feels a tear pop through her eyelashes. The pain is incredible. She keeps smiling as tears stream down her face. The rapper cocks his head.

"You okay?"

"I'm fine!" says Ziggy, then thinks: *I'm going to die*. Her brow blisters sweat and her vision blotches and she gets violently dizzy. "It's hot in here," she thinks she says.

The rapper nods. "Way too hot."

Ziggy focuses on the swoosh of his left eyebrow and her mind starts to clear. The pain is easing; the butt must be out.

The rapper leans in across the table. "But you know the stores?"

"The shops?"

"The *shops* are way too cold," he says. "The shops are icy. I had to put on a cardigan. Australians don't understand air conditioning."

The rapper seems to be engaging Ziggy in conversation. She takes a deep breath and tries to think why her countrymen wouldn't understand air conditioning. If there is any truth to the allegation. Whether or not it matters. Her mind comes up blank. Perhaps this proves his point. "I guess people mostly just use fans."

"In the US we use air conditioners. Or ACs. That's what we call them. ACs."

"*A* for *air* and *C* for *conditioner*?"

"Exactly. You're the first Australian I've talked to who understands what that word means. Australians just don't *get* air conditioning."

She thinks Tessa would describe what is happening between her and the rapper as "nothingness." Ziggy finds it relaxing. Perhaps the extreme pain she felt moments earlier has flushed her with endorphins. She feels no insult nor any eagerness to defend her nation's ignorance; what she says next is simply the first thing that pops into her head: "But ACs are bad for the environment."

"That's true," the rapper says, pondering. "But you can get energy-efficient ones. And you can use them in moderation. That's what I'm talking about: Australians turn them up too strong. It's unnecessary."

"I think people know the shops are cold so they just bring jackets."

"That's crazy."

"We have fans at home."

"Good for you."

"Thanks." Ziggy thinks she might be getting bored. "I should probably find my friend." She looks back across the room and sees Lex, her face burning murderously out of the crowd.

"Good luck with the air conditioning," Ziggy says, jumping up and hobbling back into the crush of bodies. As she moves toward Lex and John, Ziggy decides that whatever unwarranted hostility awaits her, she cannot leave her friend alone with the talent scout. A middle-aged man in skinny jeans who calls her "badass."

When Ziggy reaches them, Lex is still eyeing her ferociously. For a second the anger feels flattering. Like they are lovers in a play.

"Why didn't you invite me over?"

Ziggy doesn't know. She thinks it might have been the shock. But there is an obvious and easy remedy. "We can just go back!"

Lex links an arm through John's. "Go home, Ziggy."

The bodies beside Ziggy twinkle away; her heart lobs hard against her ribs. Through the hurt runs a thin silver pulse of self-righteousness. Ziggy doesn't mean to injure Lex. The lie that comes to mind is a white one—a mere finessing of the emotional facts. The lie you tell when a white person has been racist but you can't prove exactly how.

Ziggy leans close to Lex's ear. "John said your ass was cal-lipygous."

"What?"

"It means 'like a shelf.'"

"So what?"

"So it's racist!"

"Why?"

Ziggy isn't sure why. Perhaps it's just misogynist. But maybe it can be both. "Because it's making black people into furniture."

Lex laughs and the boundary between them—the wall Ziggy's kindness has crashed and died into all these difficult weeks—feels suddenly dissolved. The air swarms in sweet and warm as Ziggy watches the laughing bounce of Lex's tongue. Then her mouth claps shut and her breath gets chesty as she appears to gather some huge inner energy.

"It's you!" she yells. "*You* are the sleazy, white, dude!"

Stunned, Ziggy flusters. "You guys told me to be gay!"

"We told you to be a feminist not a dyke!"

"You're not allowed to say the d-word!" Ziggy cries, then startles, delighted at her accidental proof. "And neither am I!"

Lex backs off through the crowd. In the freight elevator Ziggy stares up stupefied as the numbers glow white; each ding sinking through her, deepening the knowledge that with every floor she is moving further into a new life without Lex.

ALL WEEKEND, ZIGGY'S NEW REALITY waits in a fog at her forehead, ready to assail her with shock and pain. She analyzes the intentions of her now former friends. How they had been trying, not to nurture a latent queerness, but rather to shape her into an empowered straight woman. How they had treated her like a test subject, ripe for DNA modification via traumatic misogyny; making her watch a gruesome rape scene like a pair of Christian psychiatrists hoping to reverse her homosexuality. And even if this is excessive and they weren't actually trying to make her straight, Ziggy's friends still have a suspicious tendency to blame things on gay people. Poring over every conversation only leaves her more confused. But most disturbingly, Ziggy still wants to be friends. All weekend, she misses them. Ziggy drags herself around the house, tearing up at the sight of a table lamp she once watched Lex switch on, a yogurt snack cup Tessa said probably tasted like cum. Her grief is insidious and doubled. As if only now realizing that Tessa is also gone.

On Monday morning, Lex avoids Ziggy—pivoting swiftly whenever she starts to approach. It hurts but Ziggy lets herself hope this is just a game. That Lex will get bored or lonely and be texting her by lunchtime. But when the bell goes, Lex follows the Cates from the common room out to the harbor-facing hillside. Ziggy spies from the balcony as the four girls make a sparse picnic of their eating disorders. From modern, modular lunch pails, they lay out macrobiotic snacks origami'd in pastel-colored crepe paper—like mealtime at a Japanese space station—while sipping mineral water infused with spring and sucking heart-shaped mints someone's dad brought back from Dubai. Ziggy can imagine their conversation is a similar suffusion of cis-feminine heterosexual Styrofoam. Lex's new allegiance is so stunning and mean, it makes Ziggy weirdly euphoric. Her mind spins like Ruth's rolodex, like pages flipping and tearing off into the wind. Her incomprehension reaches the sweet spot where a cataclysm feels like liberation. But this moment is just the calm before the obsession.

All week, Ziggy puzzles over what happened that night.

How she tried to save her friend from racist misogyny and was attacked then dumped for a group of white patriarchal girl-pimps. Ziggy doesn't even know what Lex was trying to do with the talent scout; no selfies with the rapper have appeared on Instagram nor can Ziggy find photographic evidence of brunch mimosas with the judge. Still, she thinks Lex is an opportunist who isn't even trying to reclaim her ass from popular culture. Tessa would understand this, possibly better than Ziggy does herself; something tells Ziggy that *callipygous* might have been the most manipulative move of the evening.

As the days pass, it becomes undeniable that a new era has dawned, and Ziggy edges toward despair. Strangely, what makes her saddest about losing Lex is recalling the last thing they watched together: a short clip of a woman who could fart on cue with her vagina. Lex had laughed hysterically, but Ziggy barely chuckled, feeling somehow responsible for the woman's indignity. When she thinks of it now, Ziggy feels a deathly shame. If it must be over, she wants their friendship to tower in Lex's mind, to cast a deep blue shadow across her heart. Ziggy wishes, more than anything, that they had watched something better. With Lex and the Cates assembled hillside on their yoga mats, the school buildings look sallow, the grass is sickly pale; even patches of sunlight seem blanched and flat. The whole world is somehow gone. Ziggy wonders if this is how it feels to have a political awakening.

THE FOLLOWING WEEK, THE PRIME minister is deposed by a man. The morning it happens, Dr. LeStrange comes to class with red pinny eyes and sweat-streaked temples, and her accent is suddenly British. She lets the girls tear through *A Doll's House* in their most vacant monotones while she stands at the window, glaring across the bay. Then she speaks right over someone's *goodness gracious.*

"The problem with the literary canon," Dr. LeStrange says to her own reflection, "is that it's mostly men."

The silence is brutally courteous. The teacher continues.

"When we read men's books, we are listening to them—hearing their stories, feeling their pain—and in a sense, allowing ourselves to become them. Listening is an act of empathy, but it is also a form of self-annihilation."

Cate chuckles. "Does that mean all women are transgender?"

Dr. LeStrange smiles defiantly. "In a way, Cate, yes it does."

"Gross."

"It is not gross, Ms. Lansell-Jones. What's gross is that house of parliament." Their teacher turns her fury back on the invisible enemy outside the window. "Those men are boars who don't even speak proper English."

This spawns a light effusion of giggles. A small tension release that Dr. LeStrange mistakes for a swelling tide of feminist dissidence. She gives a triumphant smirk then slouches aggressively from her hips, in impersonation of a sleazy lout. "Who bloody cares, mate? Let's just leave the object right out of the clause!"

Her performance is too energetic. The girls draw back as though their teacher has just strapped on a dildo. But Dr. LeStrange continues, hand cocky at her hip.

"And what about the idiom *sweet as?* Sweet as *what?* It doesn't matter! You get the *idea*, and that's apparently good enough. That's *sweet as!*"

From Cate comes a dripping "Good one."

The light dies in their teacher's eyes. "Lansell-Jones. Out."

"Pardon?"

"Get out of my classroom."

Cate glances around, incredulous.

"Out!" yells Dr. LeStrange, charging back around the desk to her chair. She raises *A Doll's House*. "Page thirty-four."

"My parents are paying for me to be here."

The teacher slams down her book, and the front row of ponytails whip back widely over their chairs. Dr. LeStrange leans across her desk, clutching the front corners and glowering at the girls as if into a slew of bad weather.

"Either you're with us or against us, Lansell-Jones," she says bitterly. "A vagina does not a feminist make."

Cate flinches. "Can you please not swear in front of the class?"

The teacher laughs sharply and again the ponytails make a sudden swing.

"I told you to leave my classroom."

Cate rises slowly, her rosy cheeks bruising a mad purple. Their teacher returns a slightly crazed smile.

"Feminism isn't over, Cate. Just because you're rich. Or white. Or straight."

Cate swoons back as if struck. Her face blanches and she shoots out a trembling arm—pointing viciously at their teacher. "Sorry I'm not a *lesbian*!" she screams, then bursts into violently self-pitying tears.

Kate jumps up and rushes to her friend. "What you said to Cate was, like, racist, Dr. L," she cries in a voice cracking with emotion.

"She hates us!" Cate whimpers between hiccupy sobs. "She hates us!"

Dr. LeStrange looks down and calmly leafs through her playbook. Cate watches their teacher in breathless fury, makes a sudden diabolical screech then pushes past her desk and runs howling from the room. Her friends dash after her, leaving the rest of the girls in resentful silence—stung by the insinuation of privilege. Ziggy also feels admonished, and worse, left out. Of both feminism and the patriarchy. The lesson ends in a mood of fractured dissonance. Ziggy can see their teacher's mistake. Invoking feminist intersectionality among a group of mostly white private school girls will only send them running back into the subjugating arms of the patriarchy. Ziggy sneaks a glance at Tessa, who has a constellation of hickeys cloudy across her neck. Not even their prime minister's ousting can rouse these girls. There was never going to be a revolution.

WHEN SHE GETS HOME, Jacob's GoPro is sitting, unsupervised, on the kitchen counter. Ziggy slips the camera on and walks around the room. She likes how it feels, this small sturdy weight at her forehead, driving her around. She takes a running jump from the stairs onto the couch, then trots out into the yard and up to the barbecue deck. From here she takes a slow plunge onto the grass—feeling, mid-fall, only faint regret at her imagined suicide. Ziggy lies on her back for a long time, staring up, soothed by the regal green of the Polish topiary. Then she hears a fart. Deep in the hedge she spies two shirtless gardeners, their slick muscles pulsing through the leaves. Ziggy crawls toward them on her stomach. When they see her, the gardeners pose, peace-signing and flexing their muscles. Ziggy doesn't smile back. At her forehead, she feels a cool intransigence. She keeps filming; even when the gardeners get obviously bored, when their cheeks slacken in hostility and the first rude finger flashes through the green. Then she films their huffy pivot and the four tight buttocks charging back into the bushes.

Returning the GoPro to the counter, Ziggy notices that the table is set for five. As usual, there is only a large bowl of salad on offer, but it is uncharacteristically sprinkled with bacon bits.

"Who's coming for dinner?" she asks Ruth as her mother sets two beer coasters on the table.

"Damien." Ruth's voice is suspiciously neutral.

"Damo?"

"Mhm."

"Pass."

"No, you won't." Ruth eyes her daughter sternly. "Today is a sad day for the women of Australia, and I want you at the table."

Ziggy finds her mother's gendered insinuation offensive. But the thought of trolling her father and his swimming buddy is surprisingly appealing. Ziggy puts a beer coaster beside her own placemat. "Can I have a Coopers?"

Dinner is boring. Nobody mentions that morning's political coup or anything aside from Damo's recent open-ocean swim in South Africa.

"The Cadiz Freedom Swim," he tells them proudly. "It's the race from Robben Island to Cape Town."

Jacob looks impressed. "Where Nelson Mandela was imprisoned."

"Yes indeedy," says Damo. "And it's surrounded by great white sharks."

Jacob's eyes bulge. "The water must be freezing!"

"Yep. Thirteen degrees the day I swam."

Everybody gasps. Except Ziggy. She finds the story unexceptional.

"What's the point of it?" she sneers.

Damo smiles good-naturedly. "The point?"

"Are you raising money for something?"

"Sort of," he says. "But it's also just symbolic."

"Symbolic?"

Jacob leaps to Damo's defense. "It's called the Freedom Swim, and he just told you about Robben Island and Mandela."

Ziggy glowers at the swimmer's vast, bronze forearms. "So you're pretending to be Mandela swimming to freedom?"

Jeff gives Ziggy his warning glare. But the human porpoise maintains his sense of humor. "Well, nobody's in blackface if that's what you're worried about." The three men chuckle.

"That's not what I'm worried about," says Ziggy; though, it is, symbolically, exactly what concerns her. How a few hours of swimming alongside a speedboat stocked with protein bars and energy drinks is not the same as eighteen years of imprisonment on an island. Ziggy places her fork down. "Can I be excused?"

Ruth pokes her daughter gently. "I think Ziggy is taking the day's events a little hard."

"Oh, it's terrible," says Damo, slapping a massive hand over his left pectoral. "She was a great leader. Very strong. And terrible timing for a coup." He stabs his fork through an artichoke heart. "When we've got an opposition leader who denounces abortion and wants to give gay people electroshock therapy."

Now Ziggy observes Damo more closely. His eyebrows are definitely plucked. She remembers the offensive karaoke costumes and her heart quickens. If her father's friends really are crossdressers, what does that make Jeff? A homoromantic heterosexual misogynist? And what if Ziggy's dad is actually gay? A catalog of soft evidence assails her. There is the time Jeff said the rash on his neck was a neoprene allergy; that nude swim across the northern beaches; the mankinis he claims are just "part of the scene." And then there is her email spam. The internet probably thinks Ziggy's penis isn't working because her father's doesn't. Or not for Ruth. Ziggy stands and clears her salad bowl.

Upstairs on the home PC, she studies her junk folder. Protein supplements. Bra and panty sets. Now her father's gift takes on a sinister new meaning. Victoria's Secret is the kind of lingerie you buy your fake girlfriend as a closeted celebrity in an alien cult. Ruth's striptease is similarly imbued with a sense of hetero-romantic desperation; which makes her staunch defense of Jeff's cross-dressing even sadder. Admittedly, Ziggy can also think of a few reasons why her father might not be gay. Jeff objectified the callipygous Muslim gold digger (though this might have just been gay diva-worship); Ziggy has often caught him ogling waitresses; and then there is the hetero-sexist bedtime story he used to tell her brother: "Jake and the Magic Blonde." Ziggy retires to her room, unsure whether to plunge headfirst into the speculative drama of having a gay parent, or else the more banal fact of parents who are no longer having sex. Either way, their physiological failure makes her hate them. They put her in this body. Her biology is their fault; everything from the bent nose to the rashy skin to the stubborn tenure of her child parts. Her queer friends would tell Ziggy to love herself, that she's being ablest or sexist or triggering their pain. So she doesn't ask them. Ziggy knows she isn't male or queer; the correct terminology remains elusive, but her unique identity must still, somewhere, exist. When she logs in, it feels significant that tonight the most popular post on Reddit reads, "Scientists find water on Mars."

PART TWO

Chapter 8

n the morning Jeff stands at the counter, furiously shoveling in his raisin bran. He points to the GoPro.

"That's Jacob's."

"I'm just borrowing it."

"Did you ask him?"

"I'll text him."

"He's at Model UN."

"So I'll text him," Ziggy says snidely. "It's only *Model* UN."

Ruth wanders out into the living room, nodding sleepily at Jeff's cereal bowl.

"His raisin d'être," she says in a dopey voice, touched with dejection. Ziggy watches her father devour his breakfast cereal with disturbing animus. He brings the bowl up to his face and power-scoops the remaining flakes. Ruth clears away last night's empty beer bottles. The breakfast scene conjures up the murky pathos of watching a dictatorship resign its power to the military. Ziggy's sympathy is reserved for the children.

From her bedroom, she watches Jeff jog across the driveway to his Audi. The wind is icy, but her father lowers the roof and places a green baseball cap on his head. Lime green. With an unfamiliar triangle logo like some arcane insignia. Ziggy pictures a long chandeliered dining hall with robed men and under-age boys. Which is homophobic and way too Hollywood. She checks herself; Jeff is only an accountant.

Ziggy sneaks out the front door without saying good-bye to her mother. At the front gates, she sees two primary-school boys approaching along the pavement. Ziggy waits for them to pass, watching as she pretends to aim the camera at a kooka-burra sitting fat and lordly on the fence post. When the boys are safely at the corner, she hears the words "Google Glass," then, "head injury." Knowing she has disturbed them, Ziggy steps confidently onto the street. The GoPro makes her feel tall and brainy and in a rush to get somewhere. On the bus, she ducks (unnecessarily) into a side-facing seat, and stares brazenly at the other passengers. Her head seems to swell, like Ziggy's whole body has jumped inside her skull, the organs pumping courage at her temples. She smiles at a gawking year-seven girl, and for the first time, Ziggy doesn't worry if she seems male or female or gay.

At the school gates, Ziggy connects her phone and watches the GoPro footage in real time. The fish-eye effect gives Kandara's grounds the neat, picture-book smallness of binocular-view from the wrong end. It makes her giddy, regaining that sense of omnipotence, like a little kid.

By the lockers, girls eye her suspiciously. Cate gives Ziggy a soft diagnosis of "attention seeker," while Kate's is more pointed: "pervert psychopath." Both girls seem on edge. Ziggy studies Kate's nostrils, magnified on her own phone. There, on the left: a cruddy pinch of cover-up, which means Kate has a zit. Girls are so vulnerable it's pathetic.

"Scared I'll film your third nostril?" Ziggy says, a little light-headed. Like she has just pulled her pants down in a dream. Like she has suddenly started masturbating but knows it's a dream so will probably just keep going. Then make herself fly. Or punch someone. An avataristic freedom.

Kate's face shocks white, with blue tinges of umbrage. "You post anything online and I'll sue."

With supernatural calm, Ziggy angles her camera directly on Kate. The girl scoots back, then scurries roach-like around the room's perimeter—pausing to shake her head, mouth *psycho*, and flip Ziggy the bird. Eventually she flusters.

"I'm going to Ms. Hawthorne!"

Ziggy films Kate's clumsy foal legs scamper out the door, then turns to a group of girls lounging on the sectional sofa. Penny Ward sits up straight and fluffs her hair. Lucy Abbott undoes a shirt button and starts applying lip gloss. Other girls are tracking Ziggy too. She perches on a chair and pretends to watch Kate's lovebirds. Now the whole room leans toward her. When she looks up, they return to their sham lounging, but Ziggy can see the tension in their muscles, a new alertness in their limbs. It seems some part of them wants to be watched, even preyed upon. It might be the same vanity Ziggy felt when her Jewish school got security guards. The confusing flattery of being a target.

THE AIR IN MS. HAWTHORNE'S OFFICE is stale and depressed, and Ziggy feels fatigued just looking at the soy sauce sachets stuffed into their plexiglass penholders. Kandara's principal is a stiff, coiled woman who tends to send crying girls away with a backslap and a Latin aphorism. In rare cases, compassion can be squeezed from her like a pellet of dried toothpaste.

"They bully me," Ziggy boldly lies.

"Who does?"

"The other girls."

"And how does the camera help?"

"It's like surveillance."

The principal makes a dismissive *hmph*, signaling her immunity to teenage nonsense. "That's not how the world works, Ziggy." Ms. Hawthorne looks down to smooth her skirt, seeming to find her thoughts in the gridded pattern. "You can't protect yourself through personal surveillance. That's impractical and antisocial. And it's not how Kandara girls behave. You don't need a camera. *Esto sol testis*: 'Let the sun be your witness.'"

The discussion appears to be over. Ziggy touches a hand to the GoPro. It feels both familiar and strange, like a brand-new haircut.

"You need to remove the camera," says the principal.

But Ziggy has the strong, inner conviction that actually she doesn't have to. She looks straight at Ms. Hawthorne and watches her bristle. The headmistress folds and unfolds her arms like they are too long or very slippery.

"Camera. Off."

Ziggy remains still. The GoPro's small weight against her brow is coolly fortifying. It makes her think of the third eye— what her mother calls the "higher conscience" or "conscious witness" or "witnessing consciousness." But Ms. Hawthorne is middle-aged and will be well defended against the counterculture. Better to frighten her headmistress with visions from the future.

"Have you read Donna Haraway?"

"I've heard of her."

"The essay on cyborgs?"

Ms. Hawthorne rattles her head like a snake charmer.

"Donna Haraway would call me trans."

"Transgender?"

"Transhuman."

The woman freezes; she appears to no longer be breathing. Then she uncrosses her legs and hunches toward Ziggy. Her voice is quiet and intense. "So you're saying you're transgender?"

Ziggy rides a heady crest of righteous indignation. "Donna Haraway says we're all augmented by technology, which makes us inorganic orphans beyond the gender binary."

Ziggy's principal is pleading. "So you're *not* transgender?"

"I'll send you a link to the essay."

Ms. Hawthorne nods slowly, taking in this information, or the frightening potential of its online residence. "Well," she says finally, "we're going to need a letter from a psychologist."

"Easy," says Ziggy, feeling, incredibly, that everything suddenly is.

The headmistress lurches gracelessly to her feet. She stands there a moment, perhaps searching for the Latin or else quietly conceding that there are some conversations she doesn't have the language for. Watching the woman, Ziggy's whole body feels light and inviolable. The thing on her head like a punch line drowning out all other noise.

"Thanks, Ms. Hawthorne." Ziggy surprises them both by jumping up and sticking out her hand. The principal gives it a limp shake.

As she strides out the door, Ziggy wants to laugh. She can keep the camera on. She can film her peers. Ziggy's shoulders have never felt wider, her thighs more powerful. She strides around the campus, filming the girls then panning out over that view, the awe mixing, for the first time, with a strong sense of the proprietary.

Ziggy calls Twinkles at lunch. She arranges to meet her grandmother after school at the mall, inside the Apple Store. Ziggy gets there early and finds the GoPros on a back wall beside the drones. Within seconds, a shop assistant is greeting her, offering a tutorial.

"I'm fine, thanks," says Ziggy.

"What sports are you into?" persists the sun-kissed outdoorsman.

"Sports?"

"What are you going to film?"

"No sports," says Ziggy. "It's for personal use."

The assistant chuckles; his voice is huskily exuberant as if he has been riding waves and whooping at Mother Nature all morning. "You don't have to be a pro to wear a GoPro!"

"I hate sport."

He eyes her warily. The assistant is clearly a pacifist surfer-type—intimate with sunrise and gratitude. "That's cool," he says, smiling. "So you want to film more naturey stuff?"

Naturey stuff. Ziggy would like to film the ocean swallow this man like a watermelon seed. She shrugs dismissively, then turns around to the startling vision of Twinkles, deeply entangled at an iPad station.

"Pippikeh!" Ziggy's grandmother yells over the noise coming through her headset. On the screen, Ziggy sees two bloody kickboxers facing off.

"You want one of that?" Twinkles points at the GoPro on Ziggy's head.

"This is Jake's," says Ziggy. "I want my own." She gives her grandmother a cloying smile.

Twinkles twirls herself free of the cables, then snatches the box and starts to turn it on a mysterious axis, appearing to read the instructions upside down. "This for bike riders? You riding the bike?"

Ziggy shakes her head, already weary of the endless interrogations. She is beginning to worry that the camera might be more trouble than it's worth.

"Then what for?" But Twinkles isn't asking Ziggy; she's asking the assistant who has turned away to assist someone else. Twinkles grabs his arm and holds it an unnecessarily long time. The kindly clerk smiles at the old woman and then at Ziggy.

"This your granny?"

"She's my grandmother, yes."

"That's cool."

"Very cool she call me to come shopping!" Twinkles is doing a little waltz around the assistant's sneakers. He laughs, and now Ziggy is doomed because her grandmother has a willing audience made of lean, golden man-meat.

"So what the difference between these ones?" Twinkles asks, pointing to the drones.

Now they get the drone lecture. How the Phantom Three can fly hundreds of meters high and across a distance of many kilometers. How the Parrot is less mobile but smaller and better for stealth.

Twinkles is enthralled. "Amazing!" she says. "What you use for? To spying on people?"

"Well, no," the assistant says, soberly. "They're good for filming places you can't get to by foot."

"They're for men who need to climb mountains," Ziggy says quietly to her grandmother. "Who cares."

"Australians," Twinkles snickers, slipping into a cheerful Eurocentric collusion.

Then, on the Parrot's box, Ziggy sees a photo of a boy wearing thick, wraparound sunglasses. They appear to be sold separately.

"What do those do?" Ziggy asks the assistant.

"The glasses let you watch what you're filming."

Twinkles giggles. "Like being in the cockpit?"

"Bingo."

Ziggy knows her grandmother has used the word *cockpit* to unsettle the man, but it appears not to have registered. For a moment, she pities the little blond bouffant in the cheetah-print leggings whose dentures have the unnatural glow of a sleeping MacBook.

"Can you use the glasses with a GoPro?" asks Ziggy.

"I guess so," he says, now hesitant. "It's all Bluetooth."

"What Bluetooth?"

The assistant speaks slowly. "It's a wireless technology that sends information across small distances, so between the camera and the glasses or the phone."

Ziggy can see her grandmother's face short-circuiting with further questions, but there is only one more thing Ziggy needs to know.

"So the glasses will let me watch what the GoPro is seeing as it's seeing it?"

"Bingo."

"Darlink, why you don't get one of these little helicopters? More fun, no?"

"They're two thousand dollars."

Though that's beside the point. Ziggy takes a moment alone with the GoPro. She studies the small black box—so compact and mysterious with its internal nanotechnology. She wants it. She wants to wear it every day.

"Can I try it with the glasses?"

Clearly, this is an annoying request, but the assistant is a good sport. He begins dismantling the Parrot's packaging.

"Which headband you use, Pippikem?" Her grandmother is pointing to a rack of plastic straps and harnesses. Ziggy flips through to something called the Chesty.

"That one's good for skiing," advises the assistant. "I think we have some Junior Chestys out the back."

Junior feels like a challenge. Ziggy rips the larger harness off its hook and holds it out in front of her chest. The crisscrossed straps give the Chesty an aura of sexual torture. "Can I try it on?"

"Sure," says the assistant, handing her the freed glasses. Ziggy fastens the GoPro to the Chesty's buckle, fits the glasses, and begins to walk around the store. What she sees makes her wince with delight. Ziggy's eyeline is level with everybody's breasts. Gliding down the aisles, the passing boobs seem harmless and fascinating as giant groupers. It isn't so much arousal she feels, more the thrill of secret access.

"There's also the standard FPV," says the assistant. "Or first-person view, for the head."

"Can I get both?" she asks her grandmother.

"Darlink, what this for? You going skiing? Why you can't just use Jake's?"

Ziggy pulls Twinkles away from the shop assistant. She lowers her voice. "It's hard to explain, but I need it for school."

"They make everyone pay two hundred dollars for a tiny camera?"

"No one else has one. That's why I need it."

Her grandmother looks affronted by Ziggy's obfuscations,

but the word *transhuman* will not be useful to a loopy sex-elf in sheepskin.

"You inspired me," Ziggy says, brightly. "With your colonoscopy videos."

Now Twinkles clutches her fur collar. "Pippi!" she rasps, appalled and titillated. "What you filming?"

"Just interesting stuff at school . . . the social dynamics."

Ziggy's grandmother clasps her hands together then breaks into a rapturous shimmy. "I knew you have the artistic eye! You used to draw those beautiful horses and the ladies with big breasts . . ."

Ziggy had forgotten her preadolescent coloring pencil phase. It is true that she spent many hours hunched over "fashion sketches" of women with gigantic boobs.

"I guess it's kind of like that," she grants.

"My Pippi have the eye."

Twinkles buys her the GoPro, the glasses, a flexible tripod, and the two straps.

"Early birthday present," she says with a wink, though Ziggy knows there will still be several enormous, chintzy kaftans on the actual day.

Ziggy removes her new camera from its cardboard casing and slips it on, then does the same with the glasses. She takes a slow panorama of the room and experiences a light, dizzying euphoria. Striding to the exit, they meet the assistant again at the doors.

"Looking good," he says, grinning sweetly at her grandmother.

Ziggy nods once and keeps walking, realizing now that the man is merely a beta.

WHEN SHE GETS HOME, the Wednesday group is in session. Ziggy has been noticing a sociodemographic shift in Ruth's clients. More blond highlights, less witchy capes. More swollen upper lips and less mobility of the eyebrows. There are Israelites in her house.

The constellation they are doing centers around a fitness granny in a steel-colored safari suit with a nuclear tan, slicked bouffant, and indoor sunglasses. She looks like a very glamorous moray eel. Like one of Twinkles's friends; women who sit on the United Israel Appeal board and order gigolos while holidaying in Surfers Paradise.

"Janet," says Ruth, "how's the anxiety?"

The powdered eel shakes her head aggressively. "I'm afraid I am still struggling to tolerate my own vitality."

Within minutes, Ziggy's mother has diagnosed Janet's inherited Holocaust trauma. "You're reacting as if there was still something to fight or flee," Ruth explains. "But the war ended before you were even born."

Now she orders all the blond women into a line of penitent Germans. Once they are assembled—straight-backed and unsmiling—Janet eyes them skeptically. Then, with great vitality, she again rattles her head.

"My mother is a narcissist," says Janet. "She gave me an eating disorder."

Ruth's voice is silky. "Sometimes when a child doesn't get the necessary parental mirroring—"

"I know all that stuff. It makes no difference. I'm still screaming at waitresses."

"Right," says Ruth, clapping her hands together with spurious pragmatism. "Let's talk to your mother." She nods at

Rowena, who rises and walks into the center of the circle. The towering woman faces the Germans, her arms slightly rounded in maternal receptivity.

"Mother," says Ruth, "how do you feel standing in front of these Germans?"

Rowena pauses, shuts her eyes, and appears to look inward. She places a hand on her chest. "I feel anxious," she says. "Like I'm not safe here."

"Good," says Ruth. "And does it feel safe here for your daughter?"

Rowena shakes her head. Ziggy can see that Janet is cringing.

"You've really tried to protect her, haven't you, Mother?"

Rowena nods. "I have."

"Let's tell her that." Ruth smiles at Rowena and makes a rotating motion with her hand, like she is twisting on a tap. Rowena turns to face Janet. The scowling elder lowers her insectoid sunglasses.

"I'm sorry," says Janet, squinting violently at Rowena. "But how am I supposed to believe that this person here knows how a ninety-five-year-old female Holocaust survivor feels?"

"That's an excellent question, Janet." Ziggy can tell Ruth is grinding her teeth. "And the answer is: you don't have to believe it. But you might want to consider the possibility that there are universal energies we can *all* tap into."

"And why would I want to do that? I don't want to know how my mother feels or how *he* thinks my mother feels, and I sure as shit don't want to know how that stupid-looking line of Germans feels. Especially when they're just depressed housewives from the Eastern Suburbs." Janet stands. "Sorry," she says. "And also: not sorry."

The women watch Janet charge across the room, up the

stairs, and out the front door. A petite redhead frantically pets the Shiba Inu scratching itself in her lap.

"Sybilla," Ruth snaps. "Please take Fennel outside."

The woman springs up, scolding her insolent fluffball all the way out to the yard.

Ziggy can't believe her luck. The GoPro has captured everything. She pans across the room: from her mother's flushed grimace to the scandalized Israelites to Rowena's calmly contemptuous glare. Then, for no discernible reason, Ruth looks up. She sees Ziggy peering down at them, the red light winking from her forehead.

"Jesus, Ziggy!"

Ruth calls an emergency tea break and comes bolting up the stairs. But Ziggy feels prepared, braced on the Sofa of a Thousand Tears to reject her mother's life philosophy. Now she is excited to come out. Ziggy has the upper hand: her transformation has nothing to do with the human body.

"Firstly, no borrowing Jacob's stuff without his permission, and secondly, no cameras when the women are here."

"It's mine and it isn't coming off."

"It's yours?"

Ziggy nods. A dull electricity buzzes through her. She gets Ruth squarely in the frame. "I'm trans."

"Gender?" Ruth's eye is twitching.

"Mostly human."

"Well, that's a relief!"

Ziggy's death stare lets her mother know this is not the time for levity. "Transhuman."

"What's transhuman?"

"Like cyborgs."

"Like robots?"

"I'll send you a link."

"A *link*? Is this an art project?"

"No, actually, it's a type of identity."

Ruth's face goes soft and rosy. She giggles. "Zigs, *what*?"

"I'm sorry that I don't subscribe to the Magnetic Poles theory." Ziggy glances down over the railing. She has a perfect aerial of a beige bob scrolling through her Instagram. "Gender is more existential for me," Ziggy says with heavy condescension. "As in, it doesn't exist."

Ruth nods at the camera. "I don't see what that has to do with gender."

"Because you're dated."

"Dated?"

"You're not even on Facebook, you think all women have to have vaginas—I could go on."

"You were watching that constellation!" Ruth whispers forcefully. "If I'm so dated, why would I let a transgender woman with size-sixteen shoes play a nonagenarian female Holocaust survivor?"

Ziggy shrugs. "Because you believe in magic?"

"I chose Rowena to play Janet's mother because she's a woman and because she *is* a survivor."

Ziggy waits for her mother to continue, but Ruth goes quiet, rubbing her forehead roughly, perhaps realizing she's said too much. Ruth looks down at her hands and pinches the skin around her wedding band. They have the same fingers, but Ruth's nails are painted, her skin is looser and pearly with cream.

"This might be hard for your generation to understand," says Ziggy, "but I refuse to submit to your biological categories."

"So you're not a girl?"

"Or a boy."

"Are you Jewish?"

Ziggy considers this. "I guess so."

"Are you white?"

"Obviously."

"But if it's all just imaginary, couldn't you also be black?"

"That's offensive."

"So you're a white Jewish transhuman?"

Ziggy knows she is being mocked. "Transhumans are orphans."

Her mother laughs sharply. "So who's paying your school fees now, Google?"

"GoPro is an independent company and you are not the boss of me."

Ruth's hurt pours amoeba-like into the camera lens. But even in her mother's pain, Ziggy still sees the smug puff of her beauty. She turns away, angling the camera down between the railings.

Ruth's voice is small. "Stop. Filming. The women."

Ziggy tilts the camera ceilingward. "I'll send you the link."

Ruth nods stoically then begins her woeful descent to the living room. When her mother is out of sight, Ziggy slinks back between the bars, points the camera down, and continues to film the women.

THAT NIGHT, ZIGGY SENDS the Haraway essay to her whole family. Subject heading: *FYI*. Jacob has tricky follow-up questions and ridicule; her father says she should enroll in a photography course then signs off with a gay sequence of emojis. Ruth doesn't respond at all. Ziggy assumes her mother thinks this is a phase and the less attention you give it, the quicker it will die. Which is fine with Ziggy. The less seriously Ruth takes her, the less likely it is Ziggy will be forced into psychotherapy. She knows her mother has too much pride to refer Ziggy to a psychiatrist. Ruth writes the school psychological evaluation note on her own letterhead, using terms like *aggressive super-ego* and *healthy id expression*.

Newly trans, Ziggy returns to her subreddit. She tells them that she has finally started wearing a strap-on and stopped straightening her hair.

as a jewish ally,

she clarifies. The subreddit are very supportive.

jew-fros welcome!

warning ziggy: now white ppl will try 2 touch ur hair.

She is moved by their inclusion. It feels too late now to explain that she is not *exactly* like them. And for the purposes of a unified front, it even feels unnecessary. Ziggy has read enough to know her struggle is similar to theirs. At least metaphorically. Which gives her new confidence to post comments on a wide range of issues. She even responds to a thread about abolishing incarceration—offering loose facts and a creative interpretation of Australia's own racial genocide.

theyre trying 2 end the aboriginal race,

Ziggy informs the Americans.

they send all the men 2 jail so theyre forced 2 turn gay and all the aboriginal wives have 2 become lesbians.

whats wrong with being gay or lesbian??

nothing but our opposition leader thinks all lgbtq
should be electrocuted . . .

#@$%*!!!

. . . so it seems like part of the plan 4 a whiter
australia.

Ziggy's queer friends are horrified but credulous. Australia,
they agree, has always seemed an intolerant place. They applaud Ziggy for being brave enough to call herself trans and
wear what sounds like a very pronounced codpiece.

Riffling through her wardrobe, Ziggy decides *trans* means
black hoodie paired with baggy shorts or tracksuit pants. She
feels anonymous and free in her new uniform—as though she
is part of some large technical crew setting up an important
scientific instrument like the Hadron Collider. Ziggy is not
dressing like any particular gender. She is dressing like she has
more important things to do than get dressed up.

THE NEXT DAY, ZIGGY GETS permission to wear the glasses
and the GoPro with its FPV strap at school. The Chesty, she
has to keep for weekends. The teachers are briefed on Ziggy's
apparatus, and an email goes around to all the girls, a kind of
press release on the sudden advent of transgenderism and the
enduring tolerance of Kandara's community. There are various
links to supplemental reading material—the Haraway essay as
well as Amazon pages for Philip K. Dick, *Transgender History*,
and several celebrity memoirs. That morning, Ziggy explains to
her English class that these texts are more of a gateway drug to
understanding her singular condition.

"I'm not saying I feel like a boy," she verifies, cautiously, for

Dr. LeStrange. "Or even a robot. The point is: my experience is unique and nobody can understand it."

Her teacher nods wearily. "Yes, I can't think of a single book from the perspective of a GoPro. But I'm sure the genre is imminent."

The rest of the class seem too annoyed to argue. Which Ziggy finds a little disappointing.

The only person who demands more information is Tessa, despite the fact that Ziggy's old friend appears to no longer identify as anything aside from a heterosexual nymphomaniac. After class, the former cyborg confronts Ziggy at her locker.

"Did you even read Haraway's essay?"

"Better than you, apparently." Ziggy's confidence continues to surprise her; she has never stood up to Tessa before. Admittedly, the camera gives her a few extra inches. "Haraway says you dissolve borders by sharing metaphorical affinities."

"You think you're dissolving borders by wearing a camera on your head?"

"You think you're dissolving borders by being a fag hag?"

"Feminists don't call people hags, dickhead."

"When will you learn to take a joke?"

"Maybe when I don't need a prosthetic but decide to start wearing one anyway."

But this is Ziggy's point. It's about staying open. And staying up-to-date.

"Feminism is redundant."

Tessa shakes her head. "You're mental."

"Ablest." Ziggy is smiling, but Tessa has started slowly backing away.

"Very dramatic," Ziggy teases.

"I am seriously *not* acting now." And even though her sliding feet resemble the somber glides of a Noh theater performer, Tessa's disgust looks disturbingly authentic.

SOME OF HER PEERS GIVE ZIGGY understanding smiles and winks of encouragement; others cower from the camera in shame. Several girls want to know why, if she's trans, Ziggy isn't switching to Randalls? So Ziggy informs them, again, that they have misunderstood; technically she could attend either Randalls or Kandara but just prefers to be around girls. Ziggy is stealthy with her filming, but her schoolmates still seem leery. A buzz follows her through the halls, and though she can't tell if it is fear, disgust, or pity, Ziggy finds she can coast along on a heady mix of all three. At recess she sometimes sits in a toilet stall and just records the audio, but her lunchtimes are solely reserved for stalking the Cates. Ziggy trails the four girls around as they sunbake all over campus. She makes a game of it—filming from behind drink fountains and trash cans as they expel year sevens from the tennis courts or stake out the oval's coveted far corner—the only lunch spot visible to vehicular traffic. During Tuesday detentions, Ziggy captures Cate and Kate yoga-stretching in a sliver of sunlight outside the hot young history teacher's classroom.

Every afternoon, observing the Cates also constitutes Ziggy's homework. She replays her footage, listening for veiled insults and gossip and language that could be construed as racist. It is painful to hear Lex laugh at Cate's jokes, but it is also motivating. Ziggy makes a folder on her desktop and fills it with clips. She isn't sure why, but collecting footage of the Cates feels necessary. She also just likes watching them. The way they use each other's bodies to lounge and pose, the physical symmetries they create, and their pure abstract girliness are all strangely pleasurable to her. Watching the Cates on her screen, Ziggy's head rings with shrill purpose, her whole body humming. It is, she imagines, the closest a computer might get to masturbation.

Ziggy's hobby only starts to feel political two weeks later, when the Cates announce their self-appointment to the formal committee and the evening's multiple locations and costs. The committee has chosen the Double Bay hotel where Michael Hutchence auto-asphyxiated, for the glamor and sense of event. There will be mocktails in the lounge, followed by a three-course dinner and thank-you speeches to the formal committee. The after party is at Embassy, which will be closed to anyone *not* wearing a fluorescent-yellow wristband. Alcohol will be served because Suze Lansell-Jones plays doubles with the club's owner and he agrees that girls just want to have fun—especially when the event is private and the local cops owe him favors. Lex will choose the music; the floral arrangements go to Kate; Fliss has already decided on the deconstructed Pavlova to be served just after Cate Lansell-Jones presents Tiffany bracelets to the four of them for organizing such a fucking great formal. Right now, the evening comes in at three hundred and fifty dollars per head. Girls should pay for their dates unless they bring their boyfriends, and then the boys—assuming they attend Randalls and aren't scholarship students from the Western Suburbs—should pay for them. Because they can only get the club on a Sunday night, Monday will be a holiday for all year-ten students.

It is clear to Ziggy that the formal committee is not representing the needs of their constituents. The Double Bay hotel is now dull and stuffy; most of them don't even know who Michael Hutchence was. A lot of students will go into debt paying for themselves and their formal dates—or worse, not be able to attend at all. Embassy is not a place many of them will feel comfortable—especially with the doorman judging their apparel as Cate has threatened he is paid to do. The Christians and girls with strict parents will have to forfeit the after party altogether. Gone is the lively tone and thrill of possibility that accompanied early talk of the formal. Everyone is now religiously following Cate's formal fashion Tumblr. Daily, a different girl arrives at school with a shopping bag spooling receipts, hoping to return an erroneous purchase after class. Ziggy, of course, will not be going to the formal. But she has an acute sense of the unfairness inflicted upon her peers. At certain unhinged moments she'll catch one of them scowling at a Cate or an otherwise disengaged student will challenge some female stereotype in class discussion. And then there are the anonymous frustrated screams that carry over hourly from the bathrooms. From her favorite stall one recess, Ziggy listens to the violin prodigy telling the stoner card players that she's heard some girls are refusing to pay their formal deposits.

"But then the price goes up for the rest of us," says the lead stoner.

"What bitches," says her lackey.

Ziggy peers through the door jamb. The card players look furious. One of them twists her blond dreadlock around a fat angry finger. "Not paying is undemocratic," she informs the brilliant instrumentalist.

"No," says the smarter girl. "The formal committee is undemocratic."

Then the door opens and the girls fall silent. A ninth grader shuffles past and into a stall, but the would-be mutiny is over. Ziggy feels a stinging disappointment as she watches her peers file out of the bathroom in a jumpy little line.

THAT WEEK, THE HIGH SCHOOL is treated to a student assembly performance. This usually involves an R and B song spine-chillingly belted by one of the Tongan scholarship students or a green group of year sevens break-dancing in sweats, stunting their socialization for the next six years. But today Ziggy opens the printed program to discover that Kate Fairfax will be doing a "contemporary chair dance" for the whole high school.

The girls pour into the auditorium, frenzied with ill will for their attractive and allegedly talented peer. Minutes later, the stage is plunged into bluish darkness as a deep bass thumps through the speakers, jiggling the Colonial brass pendant lights. Ziggy sees no pole, but in the center of the stage, she can make out the contours of a desk chair and Kate's body planked across it. As the lights slowly brighten, Kate makes a series of small flickery movements, like a corpse coming to life. The strings start, and she arches her back, drawing up from her sternum like a resuscitating zombie. She pauses, looking out at the audience with an aching expression that shifts swiftly to sex-eyes. Her legs make a sudden cartwheel and she straddles the chair.

There is something familiar about the song—a classical piece with insistent, plaintive strings—that distracts Ziggy from Kate's high kicks and mournful shimmies. Twinkles comes to mind, but Ziggy dismisses her, thinking it must be the sequined bodysuit that offers up Kate's pronounced pubic bone each time she backbends over her chair. Then someone else recognizes it. Two seats away, Emily Esposito—both the hairiest and most emotionally sensitive girl in their grade—whispers to Cyndi Yang that she knows the music. Ziggy leans closer.

"It's the theme song from *Schindler's List*."

Cyndi gasps, and at almost the same moment, Ziggy hears

the loud honk of Tessa's laugh three rows behind. Ziggy traces a trembling finger over the bump on her nose.

When Kate's final doleful pirouette is met with wild applause, Ziggy jerks up and out of her seat. She bounds over girl-laps, eliciting a wave of rustling skirts and titillated squealing as she wades out toward the exit. Ziggy bursts through the fire door, and the murmuring behind her thunders into primeval chaos. She tears across the courtyard, half expecting a procession of girls to manifest silent and adoring in her wake. Ziggy glances back and sees that she is alone. Her hands are shaking. You can't set a striptease to the theme from *Schindler's List*. You can't make the Holocaust sexy. Not even if you're a Jew. The only person who might be allowed to do this is a drag queen, and even then they would still need to be Jewish. Kate is neither Jewish nor in drag. But no one at Ziggy's school cares about anti-Semitism, her queer subreddit hates Zionists, and intersectionality doesn't seem to apply to white Jewish transhumans. The injustice of this is a vise on her skull that squeezes Ziggy small and feral. She kicks Kate's locker but the tinky sound only makes her feel feeble. And then, like some spooky genetic dispatch, Ziggy is reminded of the *Australian Jewish News*.

Neatly stacked beside the grisly covers of *Gastroenterology Today*, Ziggy has often flipped through her grandmother's other beloved publication. The *Australian Jewish News* is trifling with articles that defame anti-Semitic bus drivers or lionize local featherweight lifters of Jewish extraction. Always, some Jew has made a movie about his Holocaust-surviving grandparent; always, some Jewess has written a book about a grueling Soviet hunt for a family heirloom. The editors at the magazine represent a small, homogenous community that likes to celebrate one another and demonize anyone who says Jews are stingy or run banking. Ziggy storms into Ms. Hawthorne's waiting room and demands to see the principal. A student has been racist while acting like a stripper at a private girls' school petrified of bad press, and Ziggy knows exactly which anti-Semitic trope will get the administration's attention. When her secretary says the headmistress is busy, Ziggy threatens to take her grievance to the global Jewish media.

In five minutes, Kate and Ziggy are seated opposite each other in their principal's dour office. Ziggy feels an unfamiliar pleasure leaning back in her armchair. The hot, stodgy conviction that she has been deeply wronged.

Ms. Hawthorne wants first to hear her side, so Ziggy explains that she was offended by Kate's Holocaust-themed music for what was essentially a striptease. Then the headmistress asks Kate where the music came from.

"A classical chill-out mix," Kate says with shrugging innocence. "I didn't check the song names."

"Well, that seems like an honest mistake," says Ms. Hawthorne.

Ziggy looks incredulous. "You didn't recognize it from the movie?"

"I've never seen the movie."

This strikes Ziggy as part of the problem, but she can tell Kate's general ignorance is winning her sympathy. Ziggy tries to think of other ways in which the chair dance is offensive. Almost instantly, several class and racial issues come springing to mind.

"I'm sorry," says Ziggy, "but a wealthy private school girl should not be chair dancing at all."

"And why is that?" Ms. Hawthorne looks pale.

"Because chair dancing is what strippers and Janet Jackson do. And Kate doesn't fall into either of those demographics."

"You are insane," Kate seethes.

Ziggy ignores her and addresses their principal. "If the school administration doesn't want to be accused of cultural insensitivity, they should be more aware of these things."

Ms. Hawthorne stiffens in her chair and Kate turns to her, pleading. "I'm not allowed to use a piece of classical music?"

"Not if you are profiting off Jewish bodies," answers Ziggy.

"I wasn't making a profit."

"That's because you're not very good."

Kate whimpers in rage. The principal is sweating. Ziggy continues.

"And there isn't just insensitivity happening in our year group; there's also exclusivity."

Ms. Hawthorne squints, terrified, at Ziggy. "How do you mean?"

"Kate's lovebirds, for example, are not inclusive."

"Her lovebirds?"

"Kate keeps them in a cage near the main sofa," Ziggy explains. "She calls them our mascots and their names are Ansel and Elgort."

Ms. Hawthorne looks at the floor. She scans the carpet with a whimsical smile, as if imagining a whole new world of tiny people parading across the weave. They rise like a tide, sweeping her back so that she slumps diagonally against the seat rest in total, emotional submission. Kate also looks dazed and defeated. Ziggy watches both women with sudden tenderness, touched by their intimidation. Slowly, Ms. Hawthorne regains an upright posture in her chair.

"Okay, Ziggy," says the principal. "I think it's fair to say we may be a bit behind the curve here at Kandara. What would you say, Kate?"

Kate remains staring at her hands. She mumbles something.

"Speak up, dear."

"I didn't read the song names."

Ziggy still feels that Kate is missing the point. "I don't think our formal committee should be chaired by someone who hasn't even seen *Schindler's List*."

"What has that got to do with anything?" Kate is getting weepy.

"I shouldn't have to explain it to you."

The principal starts again to crumple, then thrusts herself heroically to the front edge of her seat. "Kate—I think it would be best if you went home tonight and watched the movie."

Kate nods at the floor. Ziggy strokes the GoPro lovingly.

"Well, this was productive," chirps the headmistress, rising quickly to her feet. "Kate is going to learn all about the Holocaust, and, Kate"—their principal gives a curt, disciplinary nod—"this afternoon please take the birdcage home with you."

Kate sinks blobby into her chair, blank-faced as a mollusk.

"And, Ziggy, perhaps you can be patient with us as we learn together what it means to be tolerant and inclusive as Kandara girls." The headmistress smiles, beseechingly. "Let's please try to keep the teaching moments confined to this campus."

Ziggy nods vaguely and collects her sun hat. She refits the GoPro glasses, rises, and steps back out into the day. From the second-floor balcony of the administrative offices, the harbor view looks even grander and more sweeping. Or perhaps this is the camera. The breeze slaps Ziggy's shirt flat across her chest and she stands there for a moment, enjoying the cool hard contours.

AFTER HER SUCCESS IN MS. HAWTHORNE'S OFFICE, Ziggy
has new fervor for her cause. She labels her surveillance folder
"Impeachment," and begins fantasizing about a formal run by
herself and Patricia Katsatouris, where everyone has to wear a
silly hat and take their first cousin. She starts stalking the Cates
through Bondi Junction, hiding behind potted plants and between the bamboo thicket of a beloved water feature. But the
girls seem inhibited in front of Lex. They never say "yaysian"
anymore, not even about Fliss's anthropomorphic phone case
with its sparkly eye-lashes and bejeweled red lips. Ziggy considers sending some raw footage to the queer subreddit; their
ears are more attuned than hers and she might be missing some
egregious syntax. But first, Ziggy decides to attend the school
swimming carnival. With all the half-naked female bodies—
many of which are not white or solarium-bronze—Ziggy
anticipates a rich occasion for racial bullying.

The Sydney International Aquatic Centre still has a mythical aura from thirteen years earlier when Australia hosted the
Olympics. Ziggy's parents still spoke wistfully about that historical time in the lives of Sydney-siders. The streets had been
electric with interlopers. The borders were opened (just not to
asylum-seekers) and Herculean supermen had poured in from
mostly Europe and America. The world had traveled all the
way to the isolated sporting nation, and Australia had shown
the hospitality of a teenage pariah newly legal and possessing a
limitless supply of fireworks. Their country had impressed. For
one magical fortnight, Australia had been famous.

To Ziggy, Kandara's largest sporting contest appears to be an
opportunity to prance around the Aquatic Centre in hot pants.
The students are divided into three subunits called "houses,"
each with its own corresponding color and clear-cut essential-

ism. Winchester is red, combative, bullish, and lesbian; Goodwin is blue, slothful, and perennially menstruating; Eldridge is green and peppy and seems to have a lot of bake sales. The war cries are similarly specialized. Eldridge sets its chants to Justin Bieber; Goodwin prefers a darker Miley Cyrus ballad; and the Winchester girls sync their lyrics to Drake, substituting "neighbor" for the *n*-word. Most of the day is spent on the bleachers, posting photos to social media.

Concealed by the tint of her wraparound glasses, Ziggy studies the strange shapes wet Lycra makes of the female pubis. Curly tufts cauliflower under damp fabric, and she notices small, dark stains on their sheeny mounds, where girls have laughed too hard or their reproductive cycles are seeping. Thanks to the camera, Ziggy doesn't have to wear a bathing suit and waddle around in flip-flops and a swim cap. She is sure the Cates would have seen her bony chest and pronounced cranium and called her a concentration camp survivor.

Instead of participating, Ziggy spends her day trailing the Cates around the Aquatic Centre, and recording their cruel observations. But by lunch, there is a disappointing lack of racial taunting. Or maybe they are just being cautious around Lex. Their new friend might not have fully internalized white patriarchy yet, and Ziggy is sure that overt racism would still move Lex to defect. For a few seconds she fantasizes about the two of them cochairing the formal committee and banning straight hair altogether. And then Ziggy watches Lex point out two scholarship students whose hot pants show camel toes. Tessa once told Ziggy that this effect occurs in cheaper pants where they scrimp on fabric at a crucial panel over the crotch. Another ploy of patriarchal capitalism—to associate the well-defined vulva with the poor and powerless. But Lex doesn't appear to be giving the feminist-Marxist reading. She whispers something to Cate, and the two of them laugh loudly at the underprivileged vaginas.

But Ziggy holds out for race and is rewarded. When Lex wanders down to the diving blocks for her heat, Ziggy sees the Cates sneak off under the bleachers. She hurries after them and hides behind a large blue trash can. From here, she films Kate haul herself up one of the bleacher's steel struts while Cate plays a rap song on her iPhone. Ziggy witnesses a pole dance of extraordinary cultural insensitivity. The flexy blonde twerks from eight feet in the air, spinning herself upside down, then twerking faster. Her friends are laughing. She crumps and twerks and bounces in a split, inches off the ground. It is obvious why the girls snuck away. If Lex saw their sordid cultural appropriation, she would be horrified. If there is one behavior Lex will not abide, it is white girls trying to be women of color. Kate's dance isn't the racist chorus Ziggy had hoped to capture, but she has definitely filmed something valuable.

Immediately, Ziggy Snapchats her footage to Lex and then locks herself inside a toilet stall. Ziggy waits here, imagining Lex's reaction; her fury cooling to hatred, the sudden panic and intense longing for her clumsy but caring former friend. But Lex doesn't respond to Ziggy's Snapchat. Instead, minutes later, Ziggy receives a Facebook notification. Lex Cameron has liked a photo from Kate Fairfax's album, "Babe Watch: Swimming Carnival Edition." Clicking through the leggy compositions, Ziggy's rage focuses to a cold white point in the center of her forehead. It is from here that she begins to correct Kate Fairfax's spelling. The careless pole dancer leaves comments like "amaze hot" and "babest," so Ziggy writes snarky grammar tutorials, closing with a smiley face or giant thumbs-up. Ziggy extends her critique to an older album titled "Best Friend Eva," where she finds a photo of Kate papering over a dilapidated brick wall with a giant photocopied selfie of Cate. "happy bday, boo," is the caption, and under it, over three hundred likes. Ziggy leaves her appraisal: a concise paragraph about the gentrification of Aboriginal neighborhoods and how street art appropriated by wealthy private school girls is a form of cultural whitewashing that erases minority voices. Seconds later, Ziggy is unfriended. She messages Lex.

> Hello?? Kate is appropriating black culture!

> So what?

Ziggy is baffled. Maybe Lex finds Kate's dance flattering? Maybe there is such a thing as cultural homage? Still, it seems too convenient.

> So? So ur black!

> I'm a PoC. Bangladesh is in Asia.

Ziggy's stomach drops. This whole time, Lex has never been black. She scrambles.

> So then who's allowed to twerk?

> Idk Ziggy? a Jew who wears a 📷 on her head??

> I wouldn't dare.

Whatever. Ur the fetishist.

KATE is the fetishist! and she's whiter than me! and u
HATE whiteness!??!

No Ziggy I hate fakeness and u are full of 💩 .

Lex's tolerance for the Cates is bewildering. She doesn't
even understand what Lex is doing with these girls. Or what,
for that matter, she was doing with Tessa. The answer might
be as simple as: there are no woke students at their private
Anglican girls' school. But maybe it is much more complicated, an elaborate personal narrative built from a complex
system of meanings that Ziggy has missed or no one has told
her about. Perhaps something she skimmed too fast on Wikipedia. The only thing Ziggy knows for certain is that Kate
Fairfax has done something deplorable and deserves to be exposed, reprimanded, and removed from office. In a final attempt
to stay afloat on the rough sea of political correctness, Ziggy
sends her video to the queer women of color subreddit. But not
before she has doctored it for the purposes of clarity. When
she gets home, Ziggy follows her brother's instructions, and in
the gray space around Kate's pole dance, she adds some black
back-up dancers. Just to be crystal clear that the over-entitled
white girl is stealing from black culture. The finished clip
makes her giggle and Ziggy worries she might have a tonal
issue. She posts it anyway.

wtf australia?

what r u, aussie miley cyrus??

But that's exactly Ziggy's point.

> i'm just highlighting how the dance is racist!
>
> we don't need u 2 highlight our oppression 4 us
>
> allyship doesn't mean powerpoints
>
> crocodile dundee 2 the rescue
>
> the white savior from down under

Ziggy can accept that she is not an individual, rather a symbol of systemic oppression deserving of online dehumanization. But the geographical slur really pisses her off.

> u know that down under thing is kind of offensive?

Now the moderator steps in.

> ziggy_lestrapon, u post any more videos & I will block u.

Ziggy doesn't understand their aggression.

> but the dancer is the transphobe from my school!!
>
> male gazing transphobes is still not ok
>
> yeh y is the camera right on her ass?

Ziggy considers this, perhaps too briefly.

because she's pretending 2b black!

Ziggy is blocked. She can't believe it. The video was only meant to be funny at Kate's expense, not anyone else's. But Jake was right: feminists have no sense of humor. For several minutes Ziggy sits, paralyzed by anger and confusion, playing the day's events over in her mind. She looks out her window, and the world appears staticky and unreal. The tall topiary sways in the breeze, imperiously offended. In her gut, Ziggy has the cool, wriggly sense of total wrongness in the world. Something the Germans must have a good word for, which they do not now deign to share. Instead, Hitler Youth return to compound Ziggy's despair, insisting that she is still a misogynist. Which reminds her: there is one more place to send the video. Unsurprisingly, the Red Pill loves Ziggy's work.

Finally an OP with balls,

admires mma_mutha_fucka.

And they love what she says about rich girls wanting to be strippers. That callipygous white women profit off black female bodies. That cis-women are scared of incarcerated men turning female because they think it undermines their biological function. This last one is received less enthusiastically, but the general consensus persists:

Women will always attempt 2 dominate men,

writes cuckoff.

Even when it's just men with boobs.

Now Ziggy opens up. She has never posted on the subreddit before and so begins by painting a dark picture of the coed private school where a boy called z-man fights the female fascism of a year-ten formal committee. Her post is long and detailed; she even backtracks to Lex's betrayal in the nightclub:

I wingman'd so hard i burned my foot on a cigarette
& had a long conversation about air conditioners.

The men are touchingly sympathetic.

Definition of Hypergamist: Female who dumps u 4 a
reality TV judge,

consoles mma_mutha_fucka.

The Red Pill are patriarchal but at least they are honest about it. Like her, they hate the hypocrisy of straight women, and within their ranks there is unanimous agreement that the Cates deserve to be knocked from their perch. If Ziggy can't depose them from the formal committee, surely she can date-rape them at the after party? First Ziggy laughs and then she considers the idea. Figuratively, as a figurative suggestion. Which is how all the comments feel on the Red Pill. Theirs is a language of Classical analogy and naturalist metaphor, a support group where the men inhabit useful archetypes. Ziggy likes the idea of being someone who would not literally date-rape the popular group but rather spike their drinks so that they wet themselves or have horrible diarrhea. Someone who uses lols as their weapon. Picturing herself as this person—the one who throws a sushi roll and is martyred in the swimming pool; the one who pours laxatives into the punch and vindicates an entire year group; the one who wears a camera on her head—feels even more intoxicating when she plays house music loud through her laptop speakers. The base throbs in her chest, vibrates from her forehead. Ziggy may lack the nuance for a smear campaign, but she is on the right side. She just needs the right tactics.

With this fire raging in her head, a trip downstairs for water becomes a menacing march. When Ziggy gets to the fridge, the phone rings. She answers, and a woman starts to talk very fast about internet service and updates and quickly Ziggy decides it is a scam. But the woman talks right over her, plowing through her script, and when Ziggy says *excuse me* and the woman just keeps talking—aggressively like it is a game and she is winning—Ziggy feels impotent and furious and then she hears herself call the lady a cunt. The woman pauses and then says thank you very much and have a nice day. The line goes dead. Ziggy moves numbly through the motions of pouring her drink. Then the phone rings again. A man asks to speak with Mrs. Klein.

"That's me," Ziggy lies.

The man pauses then reads briskly but politely from a long script that essentially says, if you call tech support a cunt, the internet provider has the right to terminate your account. Ziggy makes a brief attempt at outrage, then decides there are other internet providers and hangs up. But now the Kleins don't have Wi-Fi. In ten minutes, everyone is manic, yelling into the kitchen from their open bedroom doors.

Ziggy knows she is going to be blamed for this. There is some implacable adult principle where no matter what someone does to you—how violently they ambush you with data, in the cold, deathly drone of a machine—you are not allowed to call them certain swear words. Particularly not women, and not that word.

Ziggy hollers up into the atrium. "Tech support was being a cunt!"

Ruth's voice is razored. "You called tech support a cunt?"

"She was abusing her power!"

"What power?" Ruth leans over the railing. She shakes her head, making a smacking sound with her tongue like she is tasting something rotten. "You can't call anyone in a subordinate position 'cunt.' And tech support is always in a subordinate position."

"But she was being a cunt."

"Go to your room."

Ziggy is already going. Trudging up the stairs, letting the injustice boil her blood. Ruth grounds her daughter just as Ziggy reaches the bedroom door. Which is kind of like subordinating someone and then calling them a cunt.

But Ziggy is not a cunt. That would be her mother. Ziggy knows this is really about the camera and how she has hinted that she might not want to go to the formal. And Ziggy is right. An hour later, Ruth stands outside Ziggy's door, announcing an amendment to her punishment. She has informed Twinkles of the impending rite of passage. Tomorrow afternoon, her grandmother is taking Ziggy dress-shopping.

"She can buy me some camera accessories, but I won't be wearing a dress."

"You can explain that to her."

There is no explaining this to Twinkles. Which is exactly why Ruth has organized the outing. Female beauty is a second religion to Ziggy's grandmother, and she takes clothes shopping personally. When a mouse was found stitched into a skirt from her favorite retailer, Twinkles denied the sweatshop's tragic protest: "the fabric so soft the mice want to sleep there!" But Ziggy can play along. She will go gender-worshipping with Twinkles tomorrow, then discard the sartorial propaganda in a dumpster.

Lying in bed, Lex's admonishments spoil darkly through the room. Ziggy's estrangement from Lex seems weirdly retroactive, as if it were the true condition of their friendship. Their time together now has the gauzy unreality of a dream. The lamp that Lex once switched on has a powerful new presence, claiming secret knowledge of Ziggy's bygone friend. She switches it off and lies there, a grim resignation sinking through the topography of her duvet. Ziggy might be able to destroy the Cates and preserve the dignity of all grade ten, but Lex's antipathy runs far deeper than Ziggy can fix.

Chapter 9

I n the colossal white laundry room that is Zara, Ziggy is reminded of her former friend's quest to share nothingness
and misogyny with the English-speaking world. The shopping atmosphere here lacks the reverence of Ruth's high-end
boutiques. The desperation is more diffuse, the zombies arrive
already disappointed. With its epic posters of blithe, blank-
eyed dolls casting a cold cone of envy over everybody else, the
megastore is an unholy temple to gendernormativity.

Twinkles paws through the clothing racks, smacking her lips
together and unconsciously flicking her tongue. As they browse,
Ziggy's grandmother relays the fond memory of her own first
formal dance. The dress her mother sewed, the borrowed shoes
she waltzed in all night like Cinderella. The blue-eyed boy who
promised to take her to the Champs-Élysées and teach her how
to peel an artichoke.

"He wore the bow tie." Twinkles gives a luxurious little
chuckle.

Ziggy wonders what gruesome details her grandmother is imagining. An adolescent boy's probing tongue? Her laddering stockings as he chafed along her thigh? Ziggy shudders considering the pedophilic nature of memory. Now Twinkles is holding up a gigantic, blue kaftan printed with the sleek sixties ad graphic of a black woman smoking beneath a wide-brimmed hat.

"You wear with a belt," she explains, bunching the fabric of her own cotton manta ray at the waist. "This 'the look.'"

Ziggy flinches at the word. "What's a 'look'?"

"You know what a 'look' is, darlink. Fashion."

"What's 'fashion'?"

"Ziggy, come on. You know what these thing are. The kaftan is funky."

"Funky?"

"You want a definition of *funky*?"

"I thought funky was a bad smell."

"Funky is black people and soul music. *Cool*. Funky is *cool*. Don't you want to look cool?"

"You can't call black people funky."

"Why not? It a compliment!"

"It's a stereotype."

Her grandmother pouts, scolded.

"And," Ziggy continues, enjoying the lesson, "you can't wear black people on your body to make you look cool."

Twinkles seems repentant. "Okay, Pippi. Then how about this one with the parrots?"

Ziggy relents and enters the fitting room line. She watches the girls up ahead hunched over their phones, eyes scrolling behind the stringy hang of fried hair. A few notice her GoPro and begin a nervy fidgeting; others get a soft, self-conscious flicker in their eyes. Ziggy couldn't explain the joy of this to Twinkles. Her grandmother thinks the GoPro is some sort of rebellious fashion statement-cum-art project. The besequined Hungarian could never understand the politics of her grand-daughter's identity. Even to Ziggy, it is fleet and dispersed as a complicated meme.

On her small, anemic frame, the kaftan looks obscenely festive. Ziggy consoles herself with the promise that whatever happens, she isn't going to wear it to the formal. Then she permits Twinkles a peek through the door.

"It beautiful," she says. "Cool but no stereotypes. We buy it?"

Ziggy nods. At least it is over.

At the register, Twinkles snatches the kaftan from the checkout girl and holds it up to the light, inspecting the fabric with forensic attention. "We need a nudie slip," she announces to the apathetic shop assistant. The woman shrugs and then points to the sliding glass doors; at the opposite storefront with its feathered angels in crotchless panties.

As usual, Ziggy is disturbed by the Victoria's Secret window display. The busty mannequins with their spangled wings and frothing tutus; then inside, the same illogical bulges buttoned into corsets and projected onto wall-sized screens. She thinks of the celebrity cult's avian origin story with its fabricated girl-friends and feels fresh ire for her homoromantic father.

When she gets to the slips at an unglamorous back alcove of the store, Ziggy sees Rowena. In her bright floral overcoat she seems uninspired as she flips through a rack of utilitarian beige stockings. But instead of saying hello, Ziggy pulls her hood down. She doesn't want to introduce Twinkles, but also, Ziggy doesn't want to explain the thing on her head. She waits behind a stand of lacy sockettes until Rowena has moved on toward the second-floor escalators. Twinkles finds her here, peering up at the mezzanine.

"Who you staring at, Chibbykem?"

"One of Mum's clients."

Twinkles's arachnid eyelashes squint in Rowena's direction. "A transvestite."

"They don't call them that anymore."

"A transsexual."

"A transgender woman."

Her grandmother nods, corrected. "She very feminine."

"What does that mean?"

"You know what it mean."

"That she's wearing a dress?"

"No, Pippi. The way she move, the way she match her clothes. Maybe in the genes, I don't know. Television?"

"So there's a feminine gene?"

"Maybe . . . some gay have it too."

Ziggy can't tell if her grandmother is being homophobic. Sometimes Twinkles backs herself into a surprisingly liberal idea.

"Your mother let her sit with the women?"

Ziggy considers mentioning Ruth's casting for the Holocaust constellation, but decides against it. A more recent psychodrama session seems safer. "She played the Rainbow Serpent in one of Mum's Dreamtime role-plays."

Her grandmother cackles. "Make sense. The serpent a hermaphrodite."

"I thought it was a woman."

"The snake androgynous," Twinkles says authoritatively. "It precede creation. In the Book of Isaiah, Greek mythology, Norse, Hindu. Someone always fighting a snake to separate the land from sea, or the good from evil, knowledge from the un-known."

"Mum said the serpent was female."

"Your mother bad with detail."

Ziggy wonders if Ruth's mistake was intentional. More of her gender manipulation for facilitating a successful workshop. Then Ziggy hears her own name, in that voice, both jarring and gentle. Rowena is waving from up in the mezzanine. "*I'll* come to *you*!"

Ziggy feels her whole body contract. She wants to curl up under a rack of tote bags that say DANCE LIKE NOBODY'S WATCHING. Twinkles gazes up at Rowena, pursing her lips in excitement.

"Wait!" Ziggy cries. "I'll come to you!"

But Rowena hasn't heard her. Ziggy watches the rose-print overcoat vanish behind a mannequin, then reappear, coasting regally down the in-store escalator. Ziggy considers removing the GoPro. She doesn't want to go back into Donna Haraway and the cyborgs. She senses her interpretation might be insensitive. Trying to explain it in front of Twinkles is also bound to be explosive. But Rowena is swiftly upon them.

"Don't you look fabulous?" she says, scanning Twinkles's outfit. "You must be Ruth's mother?"

The small, twinkly woman stares up with wide eyes. "Hello, darlink."

"I'm shopping for a new costume," Rowena tells them shyly. "Tim got me a gig with his friends where everyone has to be nonbinary." She smiles at Twinkles. "That means I'm not allowed to wear fishnets unless I pair them with a fishing vest."

"Like the hermaphrodite."

Ziggy shrivels. But Rowena is, as always, gracious. "Yes, or intersex. Or just fashion."

Twinkles nods. "Whatever make you feel good, darlink."

The three of them share a brief moment of genial calm. Then Rowena's gaze drifts to the GoPro. "What's the camera for?"

"School," Ziggy generalizes. She catches Twinkles ogling Rowena's chest. "Look," Ziggy says to her grandmother, pulling a black bandanna off the rack. "This might go well with the kaftan."

"Darlink, black doesn't go with baby blue."

"But it goes with the GoPro."

Twinkles looks stricken. "You wearing the camera to your formal?"

"I can't keep up with the trends either," Rowena says kindly.

But Twinkles doesn't want sympathy. Her eyes darken and the fleshy bulb at the end of her nose goes alarmingly pink. She flicks the hem of Ziggy's hoodie. "You a beautiful girl and you waste it."

"Beauty is labor," Ziggy experiments. "And I'm not participating unless I get paid."

Her grandmother gasps. "You want to be a prostitute?"

Rowena giggles. "I think she just wants to spend her allowance on technology rather than makeup."

"I buy her that thing!" cries Twinkles. "I didn't think it mean she want to be a little boy."

"I don't think that's what she's saying."

"What you saying then?" Her grandmother's eyes bore into Ziggy; two dark mirrors shining with an epic, impersonal hatred. "You want to look *ugly?*"

"I'm just saying I don't want to wear animal print."

Twinkles tosses her head, batting her eyelashes in a lavishly sarcastic pantomime. "No funky, no cool, no animal print . . ."

Ziggy knows Twinkles grew up on thawed turnips, that some days they had to eat the pets for dinner—she understands that after a childhood like that, diamond rings and silk stockings might take on mythical proportions. But just because you ate putrid horse meat in World War II doesn't mean you get to spend the rest of your life shaming women who don't paint their nails.

"Animal print is sexist."

"How sexist?"

"It's internalizing the patriarchy."

"Pippi, that fascist."

"No, the gender binary is fascist!"

Twinkles looks hurt. "Now you being a very little girl."

Rowena is pretending to distract herself with hair accessories. Ziggy realizes she might be insulting both of them but she can't let her grandmother get away with "little girl."

"You really think dressing like a leopard makes you sexy?"

Twinkles's laughter has a blunt, butcherous quality. Spite quivers in her slabby cheeks. "All this nasty because you haven't yet get the breasts?"

Ziggy lets a coat hanger fall to the floor; but it's not quite violent enough. "At least I don't dress like a slut."

Twinkles gapes up at her granddaughter. To Ziggy she looks like a series of black holes contracting and expanding with the wheezing cosmos. The two of them face each other, panting; their trauma seems to conjoin them—like a single organ pulsing back and forth between their bodies. Then in her periphery Ziggy sees Rowena moving toward her, and she panics—tearing away from Twinkles and bolting for the exit. Shame propels Ziggy all the way across the shop floor and out into the mall.

It is painful to imagine Rowena standing there beside Twinkles, consoling the tiny, bewildered septuagenarian. But Ziggy can't go back. And she can't stop running. People eye her warily, angrily, as if they know what she has just called her grandmother. Probably they are only nervous about someone running indoors. Which makes Ziggy run faster. She takes the corners aggressively, making herself lungy and hazardous. When she sees a sign for the women's bathroom, Ziggy turns sharply then smashes through the swinging door.

Inside, she sits on a toilet seat, catching her breath, trying to figure out who is wrong and who is right and whether she looked irreparably bad in front of Rowena. Ziggy pictures Twinkles's face: the shining eyes and kohl tears sludging through her blush. Hitler Youth think Ziggy is not just a little boy; she is now a little bastard. Even they can see it isn't her grandmother's fault she's sought solace in the spiritual void of sparkly aesthetics and binary terrorism. If anyone has a legitimate narcissistic wound, it is a child Holocaust survivor. Twinkles is entitled to her never-ending mirror phase. But also, she is just very old and very precious and Ziggy can see that now, flashing on those bluish, barnacled fingers Twinkles is always pinching her with. Head in hands, sousing in shame, Ziggy apologizes to the phantom grandmother that sits merciful at her heart. Which will have to be enough. Returning to the scene of her crime is too terrifying. Ziggy knows she wouldn't be able to make it through the word *sorry* without crumbling into tears.

Stepping out of her stall, Ziggy now notices the bathroom. The walls are a gummy pink, and the mirrors are lined with frosted bulbs, giving the whole room a glossy, artificial glow. There are framed prints of pale sunsets, calm oceans, and insipid cloud formations. In one corner of the room stands, inexplicably, a giant gum-ball machine. Breathy through the speakers comes a feathery female voice above soft synthy beats. Being inside this bathroom is like stepping into the twee dystopia of Kate Fairfax's Instagram or Cate Lansell-Jones's lunch box or possibly her underpants. Ziggy feels coerced by the overidentified bathroom with its nauseating girl-palette and aggressive imperatives to Live, Laugh, and Love. Ziggy's sweet, doting grandmother is entitled to her perennial princess party; the Cates, however, are not. Ziggy makes a gagging face in the mirror, and storms out of the toxic restroom.

When she gets home, Ziggy goes straight onto the Red Pill.

So where can I get some roofies?

she asks, punctuating it with a *lol* in case a moderator is watching.

But the subreddit is very forthcoming. Ziggy is informed that benzodiazepines are not available without prescription and Rohypnol is banned in most Western countries. But there are many types of muscle relaxant that do the same thing. There is a black market for all of this, and also, self-taught medicine closet chemists willing to advise her on various homemade poisons. Ziggy plays along, thrilled and horrified to be toying, even figuratively, with these possibilities. She imagines the Cates slurring and frothing their way down to Embassy's sticky black carpet. Or the four girls stripped and incontinent on an empty football field. Waking with the harsh morning sun—panicked and disoriented, covered in mysterious grass stains, feeling for the first time in their perfect lives, the crushing sense of powerlessness. In that infinite, shivering instant the Cates would comprehend the full history of female oppression—from Eve to the internet meme who farts with her vagina—and maybe, at last, they might empathize.

Either way, Ziggy wouldn't even have to lay a finger on them. She could give them date-rape trauma without the actual date rape. Feminists probably won't like this, but the Red Pill are going to find it very funny. Ziggy already receives spam for all kinds of pharmaceuticals, and knows there are countless invisible forces vying to take her mother's credit card details. She *could* do this and for now that is enough. That night Ziggy pays the formal's $180 deposit.

THIS YEAR, HER PARENTS HAVE INVITED Ziggy and Jacob to their wedding anniversary dinner. Which can only mean imminent divorce. A reservation is made at the famous restaurant on the top floor of a skyscraper. Ascending in the elevator, Ziggy notices her brother is shaking his head at her Converse.

"What?" she snaps.

"If you're going to wear a GoPro, you could at least wear dress shoes."

Ziggy scans her brother's outfit: pastel pink shirt over crisp chinos. "Sorry I don't subscribe to Satan's clothing catalog."

Jacob smiles. "You dress like a homeless man from the future."

"Good. That's basically what I am."

The doors open on a dark, hushed dining room, and Jeff glares them all into penitent silence. Ziggy notices now, with creeping shame, that her parents have really dressed up. Jeff has even removed his Fitbit and replaced it with a gold chain bracelet. Ruth sports the usual witchy frayed layers but in funereal shades of eggplant.

When the Kleins have been seated, Jeff begins ordering feverishly off the menu. The food comes quickly, and Ziggy watches her father savor the subtle fusions with disturbing nakedness, eyes fluttering orgasmically each time the fork enters his mouth. Ruth doesn't like it either.

"Jeffrey, I think you've mistaken that entrée for the sublime."

But Jeff waves her off, forming a swift bond with the bald man in thick tortoiseshell frames who stands imperiously over their table, discoursing on the wines. *Delightful*, Jeff praises the man for his recommendation; *Goodness gracious*, he exclaims at the palatial architecture of a cheese soufflé. The ritual is embarrassing to Ziggy, to sit in dutiful reverence of these high-concept dishes. It reminds her of eating the symbolic items on the Seder plate, and straining for the transportive aftertastes of ancient sentiments. As if dinner is going to produce a religious miracle.

Ziggy's mother is clearly drunk, on to her third cocktail and unsubtly disparaging the other diners. She nudges Ziggy and with hot, berried breath points out a young couple swishing wine around their mouths while staring at the wall. Then she turns her discontent on Jeff.

"Let's be honest: the quality of this experience lacks depth."

"Sharing sublime food with the people you love?"

"The word *sublime* is for Renaissance art, not cheese."

Though she thinks her mother is being a gnarly jackal bitch, Ziggy agrees that the soufflé needs a different adjective from very old paintings.

"No one is asking you to call the cheese *sublime*, Ruth."

"Actually, Jeff, I think you are."

"Then you aren't receiving me."

Ziggy and Jacob shudder in unison.

Ruth sits up straight, an angry exclamation point in maroon. "Well, you certainly aren't sensing into my needs."

"You wanted me to book a restaurant!"

"That's not the only job of the masculine!"

"That's right—I'm paying for it too."

Jacob chuckles and Ziggy thumps him. "Not funny," she says.

"You're not."

"Not trying."

Jeff drops his fist lightly on the table. "Stop."

"Tell Beelzebub's webcam."

Jeff glances between his children with a look of deep alienation. He throws his napkin down on the table and pushes back his chair. "I'm using the men's."

"Can we please not call it that," Ziggy scolds him. "Why does everything have to be so gendered with you people?"

"Excuse me?" Jeff looks puzzled, then slightly hysterical. "What should I call the room with the word *men's* written on the door?"

"Jeff."

"I'm just asking what I'm permitted to say in front of our daughter?"

"She's not your *daughter*!" Jacob ribs. Ziggy kicks her brother's shin.

"I can't call the cheese *sublime*," whines Jeff. "And I can't call the room with the little male symbol on it *men's*, so what *can* I say?"

"Maybe the cheese should be *trans*cendent!"

Jacob gets another, harder kick.

"Stop it, both of you," says Ruth. "Come on, this is our wedding anniversary."

"We're probably not allowed that word either, right, Ziggy?" Her father is angry—she has never seen him so histrionic. "Are wedding anniversaries offensive too?"

"Yours is."

"And why's that?"

"Because you're gay."

Jeff thrusts his chin under and snorts. He thinks she's kidding. Ruth and Jake giggle too. For a moment, the space between the three of them looks warm and inviting. Ziggy could just slip in and join them all inside the big, hilarious joke. But the effort required to back down, to breathe evenly, is now far too great.

"Everyone knows gays are intolerant of trans people!" she shouts over them. "You resent us because we don't aspire to your regressive heteronormativity."

Ruth attempts a serious expression. "Ziggy, what are you talking about?"

"Gays have won their rights and left their trans comrades in the dust."

"Where do you think you live?" scoffs Jeff. "America? We don't have gay rights here."

"You would know."

"What are you now, homophobic?"

"I'm only homophobic if you're gay."

"Ziggy," Ruth says, smirking. "Why do you think Dad's gay?"

"You think I'm gay because I take care of my body?"

"No," Ziggy snaps. "I know about your friends."

"What about them?"

"That they like men!"

"They're all married to women!"

"Then what about Thailand?"

"We were swimming!"

"Except when you were cross-dressing!"

Ruth interprets for her husband. "I think she means the karaoke video."

"Your wigs were disgustingly culturally insensitive."

Jeff's jowls sag in bafflement. "To who?"

"To me!"

"What, that thing on your head is *cultural*?"

Ziggy puffs up over the table. "Yes, it is."

Her father takes a fork and sticks it behind his ear. "Okay," he says. "Then this is *my* culture and you need to respect *that*."

"Brilliant," Jacob applauds. Ziggy watches her brother take a fork and wedge it behind his own ear. "I call it transcutlery," he says.

The three of them chuckle again, Jeff and Jacob beaming smugly at Ziggy. She can feel a sharp pain rising in her chest. And a pressure on her shoulders, like someone is pushing them down. Ziggy picks up her own fork and points it at her father.

"You don't scare me," she says.

Jeff stiffens in his chair.

"Ziggy!" Ruth hisses. "Drop that fork!"

Ziggy lowers it. Her father looks hurt. "You just threatened me with a fork?"

"You were bullying me!" Ziggy's voice is breaking.

"I didn't mean to."

"I won't take it!"

"No one is trying to fight you, Ziggy!" Ruth leans toward her with wild, shaky tenderness.

"He thinks I'm weak!"

"No!" Her father is angry again. "I think you're frightening!"

"Good!"

Ruth's wisdom comes booming and slightly slurred. "What is this 'weak'?! There is nothing *weak* about yielding! It's stubbornness that's a sign of insecurity!" Ruth looks around and sees that she has confounded everyone into silence. She continues.

"Women are strong in their vulnerability, and their facility for yielding is a great inner strength!"

"That's nice," Ziggy snaps, the heat of her anger just holding her together. "But I'm transhuman. As in, *beyond*."

On the car ride home, Ziggy seethes, watching Jeff's head turn stiffly in the driver's seat; she sees intolerance in the back of his haircut, the crisp collar of his shirt. She doesn't know what it is, but Ziggy knows he's still hiding something.

As they turn into the driveway, the GoPro glasses find her father in the rearview mirror. Her mother was right. Whether he's gay or not, Jeff is a sensitive man. He stares ahead with a strange, swollen blankness; his face bereft as a peeled potato.

AT HOME, ZIGGY GOES STRAIGHT ONLINE. Her Red Pill friends love the clip she posts from her parents' anniversary dinner: the sea bass foam with its pubic-looking wild licorice garnish.

Beta dad loves gay food presentation.

Ziggy is beyond gender, but until the rest of the world joins her, the Red Pill's mythology is very useful. Posters share GIFs of Nemo strung up in a fishing net, swaying perilously over a gay dance floor. Ziggy gets *lol*s and fist bumps, but then, amidst the memetic fanfare, appears a frowning unicorn face from natty19.

What are you doing here?

Ziggy asks the queer interloper.

u transition & str8 away become a misogynist? shame.

Ziggy is being trolled.

> I never said my GoPro was a dick

> u said u wore a strap-on??

> The GoPro is agender

> so u identify as what?

> Trans

> You're transgender???

This is let_them_eat_balls.

> Transhuman

> u said u thought u were male,

natty19 presses.

Ziggy stays quiet. She has never felt male, but admitting it won't win her any friends here. The Red Pill doesn't like cisgender girls any more than the queer subreddit does.

> fyi,

natty19 continues.

> u don't wear a camera 2 feel like a man, u feel like a man then wear a camera.

Now the men are insulted.

Hey! Men don't need 2 wear GoPros,

writes ironman17.

Confused, cuckoff chimes in to condemn Ziggy too:

Run along now little beta.

Ziggy logs out. She steps away from her laptop and feels her-self crumpling forward onto the bed. She lands GoPro-first, bruising her forehead. Ziggy really didn't mean to make this about gender, or only metaphorically. An affinity to share with the vast cyborg nation. But again, she has managed to insult everybody and get banished from the culture. It once seemed her queer friends would accept a dolphin with TV antennae, but now even they have rejected her identity.

There is a knock at her door. It opens, and her parents move swiftly to either side of Ziggy's bed. Her head tingles with in-credulity. First her trans status is revoked, and then her parents announce their divorce? Ziggy wonders where this sits on the trauma scale.

But Ruth belly-flops onto the mattress, cupping her face on propped elbows. Jeff tucks his feet kiddishly under his bum. Ziggy edges back to the wall. The tone is too fraternal. Their tragic tableau lacks the air of quiet devastation.

"Your dad and I want to talk to you," says Ruth, taking Zig-gy's hand. "About what's happening inside your body."

Ziggy braces harder against the wall. They have already had this conversation. The puberty talk. Years ago: in this room, on this bed. Ziggy has never forgotten the horror of hearing her father say the words *vaginal discharge*.

"I don't want to talk about it," she says.

"But we do," says Jeff. "We want to know if you feel like a boy, and if there's something more you need to do about it."

The wall is suddenly icy against Ziggy's back. She feels caught. In a lie she didn't fully realize she was telling.

"I told you this isn't about gender," Ziggy says, the words cottony in her mouth. She looks at her mother and Ruth's face is so warm, so open and accepting—inviting her daughter to be whomever she is—that Ziggy relents. Peaceman shrugs his shoulders and chutes down the hot spout of her throat.

"Why are people so intolerant?" Ziggy bawls, looking between her parents' unconditionally loving faces. Her sadness is intoxicating. She takes a huge yawning gulp of it and the tears pump out like liquid exhalation. Even as her ribs start to sink with the dead air of insincerity, Ziggy hears herself whimpering in magnificent pain.

Ruth strokes Ziggy's back. "Which people?"

"These American people I met online."

"Did they tease you?" Her mother looks angry.

"I think they thought I was teasing them."

"What did the Americans say to you?" asks Jeff.

"That the camera wasn't trans."

"Well, I'm sure some other Americans will think the camera is trans," her father says kindly. "That's the good thing about the First Amendment."

"I don't care anymore," says Ziggy, wiping her nose with noble resignation. "I'm sick of fighting for my rights."

An opaque look passes between her parents. Then Ruth gets sphinxlike on her elbows. She speaks with diagnostic seriousness. "I think you and I need a mother-daughter weekend."

Daughter is still insensitive, but Ziggy doesn't really have a substitute.

"We can go up into the rain forest and get massages," her mother says in a seductive drawl.

Ziggy knows Ruth means Byron Bay. A mother-daughter weekend in the lush hinterland where all the broken men of ashram infamy came home to roost.

"I have exams."

"I'll write you another mental health note."

Ziggy tries to imagine what a trip to Byron Bay might be like with just her mother. Full-moon drumming and surprise acupuncture sessions. This happened once when Ziggy was studying for her Bat Mitzvah. Ruth said they were getting facials, and two hours later, Ziggy was dropped off at synagogue with religious stigmata.

But her mother is so excited.

"We can stay in Turiya's cabin and swim in the creek and you'll finally get to film something good!"

Which is the only reason Ziggy says yes.

Chapter 10

Ruth rents the two of them a cabin in the hills just outside of town. In Byron Bay, wearing the GoPro feels different. It might just be the weather but Ziggy is newly conscious of the strap, which is tight and hot around her head. The glasses are also somehow disorienting. She takes the camera off in her room and then forgets it when they leave the bungalow.

Their first excursion is to a tiny Israeli masseuse who works out of a converted garden shed humid with ferns and Japanese water features. The Israeli has a stout hourglass figure and she trots around the room, her black noodly hair swishing just above her coccyx; the more Ziggy watches her, the more she experiences the masseuse as a super-intelligent, sensual pony. The woman's tights are flesh-toned, and Ziggy can make out the contours of her labia. It isn't sexual attraction Ziggy feels, but awe, at this woman who seems to occupy a much higher spiritual plane.

Drilling her thumbs into Ruth's back, the masseuse apologizes for her plants who, she informs them, can no longer sing.

"That's a shame," says Ruth. "I thought Ziggy would get a real kick out of them."

The woman exhales with loud, huffing regret through her nostrils. "Sadly, I have to stop after ze water experiment."

"What water experiment?"

The masseuse turns to Ziggy as she explains the technology. "First we taught zem how to sing. We attached nodes to zeir leaves, and zese nodes were wired to a synzesizer. We teach zem to play Bach and some Neil Diamond. We really zought zey are enjoying zemselves." The Israeli sighs deeply into the space between Ruth's shoulder blades. "So zen we hooked zem up to zeir own irrigation system. We train zem for weeks, and finally zey started to feed zemselves. At first it was fantastic! Ze plants are singing for zeir food!" The masseuse claps her hands together and laughs, her mouth wide and childish with an eager crowding of teeth. Then she swoops on Ruth's back, making short hard chops with the side of her hand as if pantomiming a sushi chef. Her tone is suddenly grave. "One morning we come in and ze plants are all droopy, ze water is spilling over zeir pots. Zey look like alcoholics. I can't tell if it were a suicide or protest. To me, it feel very political." She wipes her brow and then walks with great forbearance around to Ruth's other side. "Zat's when I decide zat plants are like people. We zink we know zem, but we don't. So no more singing of ze plants."

"It's true," says Ruth, clearly fighting back a smile. "For all we know plants might be our enemies. In a way, climate change is *nature* trying to murder *us*."

The masseuse doesn't appear to find this amusing. She digs into Ruth's lower spine. "I can't even eat zem anymore."

"You're not eating plants?" Ruth is aghast. "That's ridiculous, Mitzi. All this misdirected anxiety about plants and animals. It's like nature is the new Palestinians."

The masseuse takes a moment to consider this. "You're right, you're right. People get too sensitive in Byron Bay." She gives her sweet, snaggletoothed smile. "I'll start again with ze lettuces. I just find it hard sometimes to eat zose big leafy greens."

While the women discuss various ethical eating habits, Ziggy thinks about the masseuse's story. She imagines the little vegetal cyborgs singing as their stems soaked and shriveled. The story, of course, feels personal. Technology failed to enhance their lives; worse, it caused the plants to commit suicide. Ziggy is suddenly aware of a dim pain at the nape of her neck and is glad to get a break from the GoPro.

While she massages Ziggy, the masseuse gossips with Ruth about a German man whom they both knew at the ashram. She calls him Shunya Gerhard and then explains that all the disciples were addressed with the Sanskrit word for *void* before each of their Christian appellations. Ziggy wonders if this is the good void that Tessa talked about, the one that comes with a neutral acceptance of people like Cate Lansell-Jones. Ziggy learns that Gerhard had been Shuni's personal tantra teacher and now holds sexual awakening workshops for women in his tree house. As she listens, certain details of Gerhard's biography afflict Ziggy with a confusing pleasure. *German aristocracy; fathered six children in Scandinavia.* When the masseuse elbows up onto Ziggy's shoulders, she pretends the deep needling is the German's powerful tantric hands. Her feet inexplicably tingle. Ziggy imagines the tantra master can make your ankles come.

In the car after the massage, she feels anxious. Ziggy doesn't understand her own arousal. How she could be turned on by the story of a womanizing German baby boomer who has probably had sex with her mum. But Ziggy has promised herself not to think about gender this weekend. She is feeling shaky and raw—always on the achy brink of tears. When Hitler Youth inform her that attraction to Gerhard means Ziggy must be a homosexual boy, she cries; just to make a neutralizing point about female hormones.

That night, Ziggy's mother takes her to a rooftop party in town. The masseuse greets them under a canopy of fairy lights. She kisses mother and daughter hot on the lips and then leads them to a large blond man picking pistachios from a bowl in his lap. When Gerhard looks up, Ziggy is surprised by his handsomeness. And horrified to feel the quick thrum of her heart. His fringe has a boyish flop (an enigmatic detail on a fifty-year-old man), and the corners of his mouth sag in what looks like long-term dissatisfaction.

"What's that thing on your head?" he asks her.

"I love Germans," giggles the masseuse. "So frank."

"What is it?" Gerhard's voice has the dull slap of a paddle.

"A GoPro," Ziggy seems to be apologizing.

"You shouldn't be filming here."

Ziggy could get angry. She could tell him that the camera is part of her body, and if he makes her remove it, he is stripping away her identity, denying her a basic human right. But she feels herself nodding and blushing and loosening the hot strap with her fingers.

He points at her lens. "Please. You are shitting in the space."

Ziggy whips the camera off over her head. The action is so swift, it takes her a moment to realize she has done it. Ruth makes a quiet little gasp.

"Would you like a glass of wine, sweetheart?"

Ziggy nods. Her heart pounds loudly in her ears.

Ruth and the masseuse leave for the bar, and Ziggy perches on a chair a few feet from Gerhard. He peels and eats three pistachios before addressing her. The third one he spits back into his hand.

"You like psychedelics?" Gerhard's voice drives hoarsely from his throat. Ziggy imagines he has a rough, forceful tongue. A mouth that has loofah'd the feet of a thousand febrile women.

"I've only tried pot."

"Never ayahuasca?"

"What's ayahuasca?"

"A plant. It interacts with human DNA so that you access the deepest parts of the universal unconscious." Gerhard throws back two pistachios in quick succession. "Last week I was Tutankhamen."

"Cool." Ziggy looks down and jabs her hand into the pistachio bowl at the same time Gerhard does. Their fingers touch.

"It's not recreational," he says bluntly. "It's medicinal."

Ziggy doesn't want to speak with all the nut shards moving around inside her mouth. "Sounds interesting," she mumbles. As Gerhard's eyes move over her face, Ziggy feels a bright burn like sudden sunshine.

"Then there's San Pedro," he continues. "That's the grandmother."

Gerhard brings his large hands up to her cheeks and frames her face. Ziggy stops breathing.

"Ayahuasca is the mother," he says, jiggling her cranium. "She takes your head and shoves it deep in the shit."

Ziggy's skull feels huge and unstable, like Gerhard might be holding it there. When he slides one muscular hand to the nape of her neck, Ziggy's head bobbles.

"But San Pedro," Gerhard goes on, "puts its arm over your shoulder and shows you the world."

Now he squints intensely into her eyes. Ziggy senses that she is supposed to cry or else orgasm, but she can only grin in a strangely pleasant state of paralysis. The German turns her shoulders toward the valley, and pinches her neck hard and slow as they stare together into the darkness. Ziggy wonders if this is it: clarity or enlightenment or whatever happens when the Magnetic Poles merge.

The masseuse is walking back toward them. Gerhard springs his hand from Ziggy's neck and the skin there goes cold. The tiny woman drags Gerhard up and tries to lure Ziggy with a curly, equestrian samba. When she sees Ruth's face brighten, a little pink with heat and wine, Ziggy obliges.

The dance floor is a stomping hive of leathery limbs and bulging harem pants. The DJ is playing some type of hardcore trance music that all the Aryan-looking men seem to be enjoying. The women punch and yip, and make sporadic primal grunting sounds. The roof scene reminds Ziggy of a movement class Ruth made them attend on Saturday mornings when her and Jacob were kids. Lots of scrappy middle-aged people rolling their torsos sensually; a few pretty-boy professional dancers pirouetting around, avoiding eye contact, and eventually collapsing into the pillowy arms of an Earth Mother; always some ancient person curled on the floor in fetal position like a dried crustacean. It was a frightening place for a child, a sea of unbounded adult emotion. Her mother would be prancing around the room, holding meaningful eye contact with various men and women, occasionally clasping their hands (afterward in the lobby, everyone was introduced as "aunty this" and "uncle that"). But Ziggy's dad stuck with her and Jacob. He was worried they might get trampled by the toady men with thrusting pot bellies and angry stamping stick legs. Or the obese woman who bowled herself across the room, fresh from a bout of tearful rocking in the corner. Jeff would kneel beside Ziggy and Jacob on the wood floor—she loved this dark, shellacked surface, like a pool you could walk on—and float his hands over their heads, bringing all the chaos of the room into sharp focus, distilled to the two wonderful, hairy snakes of his arms. He twirled and twisted his limbs above them, holding their attention so that they wouldn't wander off into the path of someone's violent catharsis. She isn't sure what to call her father's dance moves. Feminine or masculine or some sort of folkloric, serpentine hermaphrodite. Whatever it was, it had kept Jake and Ziggy alive.

Later in the evening, there are fireworks. Everyone clumps together, gaping up gleefully. After each explosion, a few of them say "ooh!" or "ahh!" or give a little cracker of applause. Ziggy is sick of fireworks and doesn't understand why adults find them so amazing. Staring up at the usual gaudy bouquets and predictable configurations, Ziggy rolls the word around in her mouth: *ayahuasca*. She likes the idea that you can be anything, even an ancient Egyptian. Ziggy pictures Gerhard in a loincloth, guiding her through the Red Sea's parted curtains and into a desert oasis. When he lays her down on a bed of palm fronds, Ziggy's face flushes and she glances around to make sure no one is watching. Now she sees that Gerhard is standing at the far end of the rooftop, actively ignoring the fireworks. Ziggy wanders indirectly toward him. She walks beside the railing, pretending to be transfixed by the dark field beyond.

"You found me," says the German.

Mortified, Ziggy blurts the first thing she can think of.

"I forgot to ask if you had any Egyptian DNA?"

"You've misunderstood." Gerhard clears his throat, rhetorically. "Ayahuasca disables the thought mechanisms that erect the barrier of time. So that everything that has ever happened is happening to you right now."

"Even the Holocaust?"

"Especially the Holocaust."

"That sounds bad."

"It is at first, and then you start to see all the concepts disintegrating. Nazi. Torture. You."

"And then what happens?"

"Nothing." Gerhard blinks out at the field. "What you understand when you take ayahuasca is that you don't understand anything. And that there is nothing to understand."

Ziggy feels deliciously light-headed. As if she is receiving a consensual lobotomy.

"And then," Gerhard continues, "the only thing left is Being."

"What exactly *is* that?"

"You already know what it is." His voice is cooler. "But you won't remember until you let go of all the social illusions."

"Which social illusions?"

"All of them. Nationality, race, gender, class . . ."

Ziggy presses the expression deep into her brain. *Social illusions.*

"Well," says Gerhard. "I have an early morning client. But you and your mother should come visit me if you have time. It's the tree house at the end of the creek." With that, the German tantra master bows his head and walks off across the rooftop, disappearing down the darkened stairwell.

All night, Ziggy replays the feeling of Gerhard's fingers

pinching her neck, how her neck felt delicate and feminine and orgasmic when he touched it. She pictures him standing above her—a broad shadow in uniform. Her mind's eye obscures the specifics of this uniform, but the woods are definitely Central European. She hears distant gunfire and a river panting through the trees; the German squeezing her tightly to his chest, pressing hard against her. *Against what?* ask Hitler Youth. *Ziggy-So-Flat-the-Berlin-Wall-Is-Jealous-Klein?* Her second glass of wine helps alleviate the Nazis.

IN THE MORNING, ZIGGY TAKES A BATH. Jets on and legs akimbo, Gerhard grips her thighs with his huge, rough hands. He wears a gold proscenium-shaped headpiece with a cobra flared out over his forehead. Gerhard is the Pharaoh and Ziggy is his Israelite and the entire kingdom watches as their leader positions his slave against the pyramid wall. He hoists her legs like the handles of a wheelbarrow, tilting up her pelvis. Ziggy likes how simple this feels, her body an object and yet still, somehow, hers. She pictures his eyes—widening as he takes her in, then narrowing with pleasure. His desire is bigger than hers, bigger than her. It starts as a spasm in her gut, coiling up in little ribbony twists, higher and higher . . . until a dense heat surges up the length of her body, like another body crashing through her own. Ziggy turns off the jets and lies back, feeling penetrated. And bloated. And suddenly crampy. She wraps herself in a robe and leans over the basin, but the steam makes her feel faint. Out in the living room, her mother is playing world music. Ziggy tries to sneak past to the bedroom, but Ruth sees her and does a huge, loony hip-swivel.

"Come and have a dance!"

"Barf."

"Come on, Ziggy."

Ruth raises her hands and twinkles her fingers. "Ziggy-wiggy . . ."

"Don't."

"Just move to the music."

"No."

"Just move a *little* bit." Ruth rotates her pelvis, huffing her nostrils wide like a water buffalo.

"You look weird," says Ziggy.

"So do you."

Ziggy tugs her robe around tighter.

"Feet," says Ruth, pointing at her daughter's toes.

Ziggy raises a foot, then plonks it down. And the other one. Every smidge of movement is a monumental, life-draining effort.

"That's it!" says Ruth. "Now your hips."

Ziggy sways with passive-aggressively infinitesimal momentum.

"Do you feel more open?"

"I feel dizzy."

"Sort of *porous*?"

Ziggy cringes at her mother's word.

"What's wrong with porous? You don't want to be porous? Fine." Ruth stomps her feet with sensual force. "Just listen to the beat. Feel the rhythm. Where does it live in your body?"

"Live?"

"Yes. Where do you feel the bass? In your feet? Your thighs? Your perineum?"

"Mum."

"In your chest?"

Ziggy feels her spirit leeching out at the sternum. She sags inward and doubles over.

"Great! In your chest! Or is that the breast of a wild bird? A big bird of prey?"

Ziggy just wants to lie on the floor. She begins dropping slowly to her knees.

"Ooh," says Ruth, her voice dippy with excitement. "What's happening now?"

Ziggy lunges onto the carpet. "I'm tired," she says, and curls up in a ball. "I'm an elderly pigeon dying of natural causes."

"Very funny."

"Sorry I'm not an eagle."

Ruth makes an angry little pivot on her hooves, then stamps over to the other side of the living room. Ziggy is suddenly nauseous. She rises to her knees, then swoons back in pain. It feels like someone is scraping out her guts with a chilled spoon. She clutches her belly, but the harder she clenches, the more it hurts. Ziggy lurches up from the floor and staggers courageously to the bedroom.

She lies on the mattress in agony. The sun comes shrieking through the window, burning into Ziggy's temples, and she cowers, whimpering into her hands. Then, in the hot-pink squish of her palms, Ziggy starts to apologize. First, again, to her grandmother. Then to her mother and even, a little bit, to Lex. The holy trinity of female bodies that Ziggy has offended. She begs them to stop the pain, offering all kinds of absurd promises. That she will wear a dress to the formal, that she will cease all fantasies of poisoning Lex and her friends. But the cramp intensifies, and now Ziggy's prayer gets religious. *Help,* she thinks into the ether, and then starts to recite the only Hebrew prayer she can remember: *Baruch ata Adonai Eloheinu melech haolam asher kidishanu bimitz-votav vitzivanoo lihadleek ner shel Shabat*. It is the prayer for the lighting of candles—something she learned at school, the one the women say.

But nothing happens. Ziggy rolls into a ball, wanting to die, wishing Gerhard would save or kill her. Feeling, confusingly, that those are sort of the same thing. She curls in tighter and brings her hands between her thighs. The skin feels wet. Ziggy sends in two exploratory fingers, looks down, and there it is. Red. For years, every time she wipes, Ziggy has pictured this bright smear, imagining the primal horror and strange satisfaction that might accompany the sight of blood seeping from an orifice. And she was right. There is shock. And a deep inward sense of being, somehow, magic. It makes her feel tender and strong in her body. She speaks softly through the pain. "I am bleeding," she tells Hitler Youth in a powerful sotto voce. "I am bleeding but I am not going to die."

Ziggy jumps up, forgetting the cramps, and runs out into the living room. Ruth appears to be dancing a rhino while making a cheese sandwich.

"Mum," Ziggy says, straining for casual. "I need a tampon."

Ruth drops her knife and leaps into action. "Pass me the car keys," she says, pointing at the bundle hanging from the door.

"It's okay," says Ziggy. "I'll come with you."

RUTH IS MANIACALLY CHATTY all the way to the general store. Ziggy sees the blood has left slim brown crescents under her fingernails, like the dark veins of prawn shit. What her grandmother might call "life force." Ziggy would love to shake a rabbi's hand right now, but the scrubby back road is not likely to produce one. Then as they pull up in the parking lot, Ziggy senses they are going to have a different kind of religious problem. It might be the glowing Jesus heart in the window or the small elderly woman embroidering a pillow at the counter, but Ziggy knows they will not be leaving with tampons.

Ruth spots the feminine hygiene section hidden away in the back corner: some dusty old maxi pads beside the adult diapers. Ziggy hobbles along behind her mother. Ruth is angry too: it is a deliberate imposition that they must now walk all the way back to the counter to ask about the tampons. So she doesn't.

"Hey!" Ruth calls to the lavender-haired lady fussing with her cross-stitch. "Do you guys stock tampons?"

The woman gives a short, mortified headshake.

"So sexist," Ziggy mutters under her breath, and pulls the maxis off their shelf.

"Christian women who hate their vaginas," Ruth extrapolates.

But for once, Ziggy thinks her mother might be right. She sees the logic: the Pope hates dildos and condoms, and then there is miraculous, bloodless Mary.

"If I don't die from period pain, I'm making that into a meme."

Ruth's face is incandescent. She clearly doesn't know what a meme is, but it's the sentiment that's important. Ziggy is on her team. They storm back up to the counter, maxis in hand.

"And some ibuprofen, please," Ruth says, unsmiling.

The woman jerks her wrist rudely as she hands the pill bottle over.

"We've all got one," says Ziggy. Which feels, emotionally, true.

IN BED THAT NIGHT, Ziggy thinks again about Gerhard. His aristocratic heritage. His Scandinavian progeny. How her mother and the masseuse had seemed so hungry to know more about him. Maybe Dr. LeStrange is right: that history has groomed women for listening and their own subjective annihilation. It makes sense of Ziggy's Nazi fantasies, the feeling she had watching *Irréversible*, and the fact that she can't stop thinking about the German despite his not even asking Ziggy why she wears a camera on her head. As she starts to drift off, Ziggy pictures Kate's Instagram—with all its carefully curated images and aphorisms—and thinks Kate must know, deep down, that the boys aren't really paying attention.

ZIGGY SPENDS THEIR FINAL DAY lounging on the back of a giant pool floatie shaped like a white swan. Ruth takes the pink flamingo. With a few ibuprofen in her stomach and the sun on her belly, Ziggy feels peaceful. It is a relief to finally have her period. In her bathing suit, she can see her nipples have soft new puff. It is strange to have only just noticed her emergent breasts, like two small stingrays rising slowly through sand. Hitler Youth offer predictable insults—they think her breasts are puny enough to be merely an allergic reaction. But Ziggy's period makes their main point moot, which has severely compromised their authority. They linger at the dim base of her brain, firing anemic flares.

Mother and daughter float all the way down the creek to a huge purple amethyst standing erect in the grass. Here, the water swells to a furry brown basin hemmed in by tall grass. This, Ziggy decides, must be the end of the creek. She peers around for a tree house. Despite the strong intuition she has that Gerhard wouldn't care if she lived or died, Ziggy would really like to see him again. She doesn't want to return to school an ordinary girl—primed for boyfriends and a life of disappointment and shame. Ziggy wants to come back stripped of all social illusions, and with a really weird sex story.

"Doesn't that German guy live here?" Ziggy asks her mother, rolling with great, lethargic indifference onto her back.

"I think so." Ruth squints through the trees. "Up on that hill."

"He invited us to come by," says Ziggy, hiding her blush in the swan's neck. "So I could film the tree house."

Her mother seems dubious. "You got the German to break his no-camera rule?"

Ziggy knows Ruth has issues with the Aryan race. Not so much from inherited Holocaust trauma but rather a sexual trauma that occurred twenty years ago on an Indian train, when a ponytailed German man sat opposite her and rubbed himself through the flap in his Thai fisherman pants.

"He said to come by," Ziggy persists. "But it would also be cool to just film from outside."

"He might be with a client."

"I can be discreet."

Ruth giggles, then starts paddling for the bank. She looks back brightly. "Come on then!"

Her mother's tone is irksomely sororal, and Ziggy is beginning to feel that all the forced intimacy of the mother-daughter weekend aims toward an acknowledgment that they are two women sharing one body. Ziggy slides her swan farther up the bank, away from Ruth's flamingo.

The air inside the rain forest is moist and ticklish. Sun rays splinter through the trees like giant quartz crystals. Ruth keeps pausing to admire the light.

"Film this, Zigs!"

Ziggy aims her camera at a mossy branch, panning along a strip of hoary patches like ancient psoriasis. Which is nice, but Ziggy is anxious to get to Gerhard's tree house, where she is sure there will be handcuffs and vibrators just lying around. When she thinks of his big meaty arms, her brain still tingles. That hand on her neck, jangling Ziggy into many fine silver bracelets.

The first thing she sees is the rope ladder. Her eyes scale the tree trunk to a lumpy wooden structure sunk in the Gum's crotch. Even Gerhard's tree house has a bulbous, bodily quality. Ziggy wants to get inside, where she imagines it is as dark and juicy as a mouth. She only wishes Ruth weren't coming with her.

At the foot of the tree, her mother makes a loud, spirited *coowee!* then winks at Ziggy with far too much of her face. "Just giving him some warning," she explains.

Ziggy watches the window—envisioning a naked woman with sex-eyes and electrocuted hair, facing out at them with dark, threatening nipples. The latch turns.

"*Wilkommen!*" Gerhard says and leans out over the ledge, almost smiling. "Please leave your shoes on the grass."

THE MAIN ROOM HAS FOUR enormous orange beanbags and a low wooden table. Gerhard sets out cold meats and cheeses. A very German meal, he explains. Ziggy imagines her mother would enjoy this life: limited food preparation and pillows for furniture. Before they sit, Gerhard gives his tour—walking them to the second room, announcing "sleeping quarters," then turning swiftly back to the kitchenette. Ziggy lingers. The bedroom has a deeper smell: damp towels and the oily fug of scalps, but also a musky something else that makes her body feel thick and slow. She scans a cluster of bottles on the bedside table. Tiny travel shampoos filled with blood-dark liquid. Maybe this is the ayahuasca. Or the San Pedro. Ziggy doesn't ask; if she is going to get any, it probably won't be in front of her mother.

Over dinner, Gerhard and Ruth discuss their work, swapping amusing anecdotes that violate patient confidentiality. Ziggy is far more interested in Gerhard's food presentation. On one side of the platter there is some pale ham layered in little lippy folds like a giant vulva. Just below this lay several stout gherkins. Which feels deliberate: as if Gerhard is catcalling her from his meat display. When their eyes meet, Ziggy's cheeks flush, and turning her head she feels an airy drag of radiance.

Soon the conversation moves to ayahuasca. Ruth leans in conspiratorially over the table.

"Don't tell your father I told you, but . . ."

Ziggy should have guessed her mother has tried it. She tells Ziggy and Gerhard about the white shaman who uses ayahuasca to take people deep into Dreamtime mythology. Ruth says she did it years ago in a conference room at a Holiday Inn near the airport. They'd spent the first forty minutes vomiting into plastic sand buckets while the shaman played a didgeridoo and blew smoke in their faces. Then Ruth began to feel euphoric, seeing small trails of light and patterns, and eventually, with the shaman's guidance, she could make out the gigantic black serpent curled around the perimeter of the room. Later, Ruth felt a stabbing sensation in her foot. The shaman inspected it and gave her a diagnosis: past-life snakebite. She took Ruth's foot in her hands and bit down on the heel. Then she sucked out the poison.

Ziggy is horrified. "Why did you let her do that?"

"It was the site of a trauma," says Ruth.

"A foot trauma?"

"Your grandmother's shoes."

Now Ruth tells Gerhard about her mother's shoe collection and how she'd made Ruth wear a tiny ill-fitting pair of Christian Diors to her own wedding. Ruth describes the violent hora she was made to dance with a group of drunken Hungarian guests of unknown origin, the subsequent trips to the podiatrist. Ziggy notices that Gerhard is barely listening. It is only when Ruth rolls a large strip of ham into a fat tube and slides the whole thing into her mouth, that he seems to reanimate. Together, they watch the meat bounce between Ruth's teeth, tossed by the pink creature of her tongue. The German frowns. Ziggy realizes her mother is chewing with an open mouth, and feels ashamed for both of them.

"I'd like to try it," Ziggy says to Gerhard, willing his gaze away from Ruth's mouth.

But her mother is the one who responds. "Try what?"

"Ayahuasca."

Ruth nods and then, still chewing, unfortunately speaks again. "It's great for working through family-of-origin issues."

The German makes a dispassionate tongue-click of concurrence. "It is," he says. "But also, you have to be ready."

"You don't think she's ready?"

"I don't."

Ziggy is shocked. "Why not?"

"The camera," Gerhard says flatly. "It's a mask."

Ziggy feels betrayed; she has so far kept the GoPro tucked away in her bag. "I wouldn't wear it while I took the drugs."

"It's not a drug."

"It's not a mask," Ziggy snaps. "You should read Donna Haraway."

"Should I." The German's voice shaves off icily. Ziggy isn't going to get the drugs. Not only is she not going to get the drugs, she isn't going to shapeshift or time-travel or partake of any other wild scenarios that might have brought his big, menacing body into tantra with her own. While her mother tries to steer them toward a lighthearted accounting of the local yoga schools, Ziggy sulks at the table. Then she excuses herself to the bathroom. The toilet is through Gerhard's bedroom: a skimpy stall without a sink. She closes the bedroom door behind her and sits on his bed. From the other room, she can hear snippets of hubristic therapist-speak. Phrases like "transitional object" and "teased at school." Ziggy pulls the GoPro from her backpack. It feels good to fit the camera on over her forehead, angle it around the room. *Shitting in the space.* Ziggy films herself raising a plastic bottle from the side table. She holds its little bloody belly up to the light.

Beside the full ones, there are a few empty bottles bunched together, and Ziggy takes one of these with her into the bathroom. She holds the tiny receptacle below her stream and fills it with bloody piss. When she is finished, Ziggy reenters the bedroom and switches her bottle for a red one. Doing this, she experiences a very pure thrill. It feels powerfully clear to her that if anyone should be poisoned, it is the male tantra master, not the Cates. Ziggy takes a final slow 360 of Gerhard's bedroom, removes her camera, and rejoins the adults outside.

Chapter 11

Returning to Kandara, Ziggy has a charitable new feeling for her peers. When she sees Penny Ward walking around with a booger fluttering in the breeze of her nostril, Ziggy makes a subtle flicking gesture instead of filming it. When the girls lie out for a leg-tanning session on the common room balcony, skirts hiked to asses like a production line of lime-flavored Paddle Pops, Ziggy stays inside, reading. Even when she catches the Cates practicing some sort of belly dance routine in the bathrooms, Ziggy walks directly to the stalls—gaze averted. The camera still gives her days meaning and focus, even if she is not trying to humiliate her peers. However, grade ten remains wary of Ziggy. Which is understandable. She has traumatized them. Ziggy is sorry for this and for insulting Tessa with her convoluted cyborg theory. The mother-daughter weekend has clarified some issues. How it feels to be defined by your body. How it feels to be catcalled by a sausage. For Ziggy, being female is a full-body blush when you want to disappear. In place of her scanty theories, Ziggy now feels like a physical fact—the words natty19 used to describe herself stretched out on a yoga mat in her favorite leotard. All Ziggy's misunderstandings seem glaring now: a prosthetic arm is not the same as a flat chest; an oppressed butt is different from an unoppressed one; a GoPro is not a phantom penis or even a religious head scarf—at least not for Ziggy. Longtime conflations like PMS and PTSD also expose the flaws in her thinking. She drafts apologies to Tessa, but it is impossible to explain how Ziggy came to the conclusion that "fag hag" seemed like a joke she was allowed to make. She still doesn't know what Lex is doing with the Cates but then again, Ziggy has never really understood her one-time friend. Trying to force this confusion into a story makes Ziggy feel slippery; the way her body slid around under those evil, shoulder-baring peasant tops.

If she can finish the semester quietly, Ziggy might be able to return refreshed and revamped for the last two months of the year. At her old school, girls often emerged from summer holidays with a woman's body and some facial piercings and were suddenly popular. Ziggy doesn't think she'll ever enjoy skirts but she could spend October experimenting with hair dyes and chunky rings and possibly still attend the formal. Feeling newly oppressed by heterosexual desires is not a win for Ziggy. It is miserable to be a passive agent in a sexual ecosystem designed to annihilate your essence. Obviously it would be preferable to drink the ayahuasca and transcend social illusions altogether, but she is too afraid to take it alone. Ziggy needs a friend to help her transcend the concept of friendship, and enter a new enlightened stage of life. But nobody at school will even talk to her.

That Wednesday afternoon a flyer appears outside Ziggy's bedroom door. At first she thinks Mother Lode must be some kind of women's workshop and that she is now being spammed by her mother's clients; or worse, Hitler Youth have switched sides. But reading the imperative to join her comrades in "post-*DSM* manic euphoria," Ziggy realizes that this must be Rowena's nonbinary drag show. Ziggy is moved by the gesture, and Rowena's willingness to forgive and accept her for abandoning her grandmother in the mall. Last time she checked Facebook, Tim was schooling someone for making kale jokes about a "Trans Violence" pie chart.

> It is not my job to explain the acronym *TV* to you,
> a white cisgender straight male, unless you want to
> pay me for my emotional toil.

Ziggy found this entirely unreasonable, particularly because the pie chart did look like a pizza and Tim's acronym was obviously versatile. She worries he might be the kind of person who treats vegetables like the new proletariat. But Tessa and Lex really liked him. There is something sweet about Tim. Whatever his preference, Ziggy feels a comfortable sexual incompatibility between the two of them. If Tim tied his hair back and didn't talk about baking, he could make a very presentable formal date.

The drag show is in Kings Cross—the city's red-light district—which despite its proximity to Ziggy's home has always seemed a mysterious underworld of sexual deviance. She knows the tall, shadowy terrace houses on Victoria Street with their ornate iron balconies stacked like many dark, vampiric mouths. Driving past them with her parents, Ziggy has strained to see the women propped in dim doorways, a flash of nipple in the dusky glow. Compared to the main drag, these brotheled blocks of Kings Cross have only a crepuscular eroticism. One street south lies the true heart of sexual darkness: that manic hub of strip clubs and rough pubs and cheap sandwich shops where meth heads dine al fresco on beer schooners and chips. Darling-hurst Road is a place where strippers dominate the pavement, baiting tourists while munching on meat pies; where internet cafés are still democratically plentiful; and the police swagger in fat, sated packs, chuckling at the local hobos piddling into the fountain. Walking from the train station to the drag club, Ziggy is captivated by everything she sees. Backpackers vomiting into the gutter, junkies loudly plotting to rob their own mothers, a white man with dreadlocks playing an electric didgeridoo. She finds the club in a back lane beside a café packed with old Arabic men smoking hookah and younger ones playing chess, passing joints back and forth between them. Ziggy has never been any-where so cosmopolitan. A boundariless place that still has a fully realized self and a terrific sense of humor.

The atmosphere inside the club is drastically different from Dong Dong's. Ziggy takes a long narrow corridor to a back room lit by a snake of green lights strung above the stage. This dance floor is neatly packed: a younger and meticulously an-drogynous audience. Ziggy sees flashes of brilliance all around her: a thin string of pearls dipped into a dark ruff of chest hair, a diamante drop earring that spells the acronym CUNT. She scans the room for Tim in his white pajamas then gets distracted by a blue light blinking in the thick of the crowd. The music is sud-denly loud and synthetic and the bodies ahead shuffle quickly sideways, clearing a space in the center of the room. The two long, overalled people in front of her drift apart, and in their wake Ziggy sees the dancer: a dark-skinned woman, topless and moving with anxious, intricate gestures. Her breasts are dotted with Day-Glo paint, and she wears a traditional indigenous skirt. On her shoulder hangs a Hessian sack with a huge blue *F* on it. Each step sends her bag swinging sideways, and the bounty of fluorescent tube lights shift, throwing sharp blue rays at the ceiling. Ziggy remembers a recent news story about an Aboriginal welcoming ceremony performed for the queen. The dancers had worn traditional body paint over their bare breasts, and their ceremony was later shared on social media. Within hours, Facebook had very insensitively removed these photos, calling their ancient culture "pornographic." Awe and shame swirl inside her as Ziggy realizes that she is witnessing a true cyborgian woman of color; the Haraway essay come magically to life.

At interval Ziggy spots Tim, standing in the back corner, holding a bottle of water. He wears his usual all-white apparel, but on his bracelet hand, instead, she sees a silver mesh glove. She moves toward him through the dense and fascinating crowd. When he sees her, Tim points at the GoPro.

"My mum said you'd started wearing a camera. . . ."

Ziggy nods nervously. "Did she say why?"

"No. Maybe something to do with fashion. Or anti-fashion. She said you and your granny had a fight about it in Zara—"

"I was kind of confused . . ."

"—which I thought was amazing."

"Oh." Ziggy can feel the heat returning to her body. "I just got a bit carried away with the semantics."

"Which ones?"

Ziggy cringes. "It was meant to be transhuman."

"It *is* transhuman."

"But not queer . . . ?"

"It *could* be queer . . ." Tim equivocates, and the yo-yo bounces from his gloved hand. "But I guess it could also be patriarchal."

Which is what she feared. Ziggy tries to move the discussion away from her camera. "What about your yo-yo?" she says. "Is that queer?"

"Well, I use it for stress, but it's an ancient Greek invention, so maybe."

"I thought Western things couldn't be queer?"

"No, they just can't be privileged."

"I think the honey cake kind of threw me," she says hotly. "And whether Sephardic Jews are people of color."

Tim looks pensive as a strobe light winks across his face. "That's a very good point," he says. "And very destabilizing."

"For the region?"

"For my world view."

"Sorry."

"It's okay," he says. "I'm not as orthodox as you probably think." He twinkles the fingers on his silver glove. "Lots of queer people would disapprove of this."

"Because of Michael Jackson?"

"Defending Michael Jackson's aesthetics is really hard to do without offending someone."

Ziggy isn't sure how Sufism and the King of Pop are complementary, but Tim is very cunning. She senses Michael's egregiousness has something to do with Elizabeth Taylor. "You mean because he tried to make himself look like a white woman?" she tries.

"That's one way of seeing it," says Tim, "but I think he was actually trying to transcend *everything*—race, age, gender, species." He glances around cautiously. "You know the 'Black or White' video, where the faces all merge at the end and then the last person turns into a jaguar? And then 'Remember the Time,' where Michael dresses as an Egyptian and steals the queen from Eddie Murphy? You could never dress like an Arab now, even as a black person with a pigmentation disorder."

Ziggy feels lightheaded. Tim seems to be a secret detractor. "It's like Michael was in child drag," she says.

Tim nods. "Yes, exactly." He points at the stage where a man in an evening gown whips a Bentwood chair. "I just find some of this stuff lacks imagination."

"Yep," says Ziggy, a little delirious with vindication. "My GoPro was meant to be about cyborgs but everyone thought it was a penis."

Tim shakes his head. "People literalize everything. It's secular fundamentalism."

Ziggy nods emphatically, though the music is too loud and she isn't sure whether Tim has said fundamentalism or one dimensionalism. Either way. Now he is smiling at her.

"Maybe your camera is like the conscious witness."

Ziggy is vaguely familiar with this concept. And she has often felt the camera creates distance between herself and the rest of the world. "You mean like the silent observer?"

"Who is observing the observer."

"I don't know."

"No," Tim says sensibly, "consciousness is."

"Is what?"

"Observing."

"Consciousness is observing the observer?"

"Yes, who is consciousness."

"I don't know!"

"No, Ziggy! The observer is consciousness!"

She takes a deep breath. "So consciousness is observing consciousness?"

"Yes. Or being observed."

They watch the man on stage whip his chair for a few more moments. Beside Tim, Ziggy can feel her skin tingling. It isn't an erotic thrill—more a sense of spiritual closeness. "So," she yells over the loud distortions of noise music, "you're kind of more into Oneness?"

"Privately." Tim blinks around, appearing both besieged and inwardly tortured. "Some people think Oneness means denying individual pain."

"What's so good about individual pain?"

Tim hasn't heard her. Ziggy tries again, this time attracting the attention of two white women with cropped hair and large bones through their septums. They scowl at her.

"Until we have universal equality," Tim answers sagely, "it's important to point out the different ways that people suffer."

"I totally agree that we need a call-out culture." Ziggy feels herself leaning slyly toward him. "I guess I just prefer it when drag queens do it."

But Tim doesn't like this. "Well, we can't all be drag queens," he says in a prickly voice, "especially not the psychic empaths."

"What's that?"

"It means you can't help feeling other people's pain."

"That must make Oneness really difficult."

His look softens. "My psychotherapist says I'm more open to the concept of 'no separation.' Which is good for universal consciousness, but problematic for people with boundary issues. Anyway, I don't want to offend anyone . . . because it's just not nice."

Ziggy nods, chastised. It's one thing to transcend social illusions as a rich celebrity, and another as a lower-middle-class queer Muslim schoolboy. But it is obvious that Tim desperately wants to. "Have you ever tried psychedelics?"

He shakes his head.

"Because of your religion?"

"No, I'm secular," he says. "I don't take drugs because I'm too porous." In Tim's mouth this word is less annoying than in Ziggy's mother's. "If I take drugs," he continues, "I may never return to reality." Ziggy wants to explain that this is the whole point, but now Tim is nodding back at the stage. "Look," he whispers, "there's Mum."

Rowena stands onstage in a silver space suit, head lolling inside a huge moon-shaped helmet. The song starts and people hush. As she raises the helmet's visor, Rowena lip-syncs the first line: *"Ground Control to Major Tom . . ."* She glides across the stage, zipping and unzipping her pockets and pressing buttons on an imaginary motherboard. From her breast pocket, she withdraws a small bottle marked with the female symbol, and pops a pill. When the countdown commences she drifts back to center stage, beginning, very gradually, to remove her headgear. As the guitar distorts and the strings soar, a full blond wig eclipses the helmet moon. Her curls glint in the light, and Rowena bounces them from side to side. The crowd roars.

As the performance continues, Rowena sheds the pieces of her space suit, revealing a pink cone bra underneath and then the flossy tip of a tutu. Once she is fully female, Rowena floats serenely to the front of the stage. *"And I think my spaceship knows which way to go. . . ."* Ziggy watches with a hot lump in her throat. When Rowena starts to short-circuit, the performance gets slapsticky and Ziggy is relieved to laugh. She glances at Tim and he smiles back.

"At least she was nonbinary until the last part."

When she finishes, Rowena bows, steps off the stage, and heads straight toward them.

"Ziggy!" she trills. "Now I'll have a showreel!"

"That was even better than 'Life on Mars,'" Ziggy gushes.

"Well, it was more upbeat, anyway. Thank you for coming, sweethearts."

Rowena ushers them over to the bar, where they take the corner, hopping onto three sticky stools. Ziggy pops up between mother and son like a stubborn weed.

"I *did* find it amusing at the end," Tim says to Rowena, as if conceding an earlier point. "But also, Mum, you want to be careful about coming across as a malfunctioning robot. That can be an offensive trope to transgender women."

"Yes, Timmy." Rowena's voice drags with irritation. She gives Ziggy a beleaguered look. "Ziggy, you're into blasphemy, what was that thing you said the other day?"

Ziggy is mortified. "I'm sorry, I don't normally call old people sluts."

Rowena giggles. "No, no! Not your grandmother. That thing you were saying about the moral majority within . . ."

Ziggy feels trapped. She doesn't want to get into an argument with Tim. "That's all I really remember."

But Rowena is insistent. "Or what about Shunyata?"

Now Ziggy wants to run outside. "The polarities?" she says, feeling sick.

"That's more her early work," says Rowena. "I mean the stuff on consciousness and humor."

"The Jet Skis?"

"I think Shunyata is also saying that blasphemy can be liberating."

"What, like internet trolls?" sneers Tim.

Rowena's eyes go a glum gray. Ziggy can tell mother and son have covered similar ground before. She can feel Tim's body burning at her side.

"Didn't Shunyata like to compare Hitler to the Catholic saints?" he says gruffly.

Ziggy is aware of the controversial things Shuni has said of almost everyone deemed pious or sacrosanct. She has heard her mother repeat provocations like, "What are shelter dogs now, the new refugees?" But it is exactly this kind of blitzing irreverence that seems, to Ziggy, so culturally gay.

"But isn't humor like that sort of queer?"

"Thank you, Ziggy!" cries Rowena. "It's gay survival strategy!"

Tim flusters. "Your generation was different, Mum! Drag queens were much more offensive back then. They called *themselves* trannies! Which I know was important for fighting the major battles, but now we've moved on to microaggressions."

Rowena smirks. "Which are no laughing matter."

"Jokes don't emancipate people!" Tim is yelling. "They dilute the anger of the oppressed!"

"All right, Timmy. Let's just enjoy the show."

Rowena ruffles his hair and Tim seems to settle. The two of them turn back to the stage, where a performer in military fatigues has appeared before a microphone. Mother and son watch placidly, apparently resigned to their terminal disagreement. Ziggy leans against the bar, sliding into deep disappointment. She can't imagine convincing Tim to be her formal date. Not when the word *corsage* is probably offensive; when the sight of little men in Armani suits will cause him so much suffering; when he won't make fun of the pretty girls. How can he not see the link between Shuni's "cosmic joke" and the one they are watching unfold right now about the buff soldier and the auto-tune transmuting his voice into the angelic soprano of a tween girl? Even in the earnest, listening faces of the audience Ziggy senses a big, benign chuckle. She also wants to laugh, but worries her explanation might be somehow insulting.

WHEN SHE GETS HOME, Ziggy finds the lecture where Shuni talks about the Catholic martyrs. With headings like "Hitler Was a Religious Saint," it is no surprise that these videos have received millions of views. Not from experienced devotees teetering on the brink of spiritual transformation, but rather every kind of ignorant, bigoted, bored layperson. It is the internet that has restyled the guru as a troll. Already, Ziggy feels warmer toward Shunyata. She clicks play.

The guru sits in an armchair on a low stage beneath an epic marquee. The picture is grainy and there is an almost suspicious proliferation of ambient birdcall. *"When you live a life of deprivation, focused on the hereafter, you become a type of Hitler."* The guru gazes at her maroon audience. *"True godliness is about inhabiting the present, not concerning yourself with future or past. That is for the ego. Abstinence is for the ego. Aspiration and holiness are both for the ego. Hitler was a vegetarian. He was never satisfied with the present, always trying to make improvements. Always in the future or the past, always in* Mein Kampfort *zone. You see? The mental struggle is where most people feel at home."*

Normally, Nazi analogies arouse in Ziggy a tough nub of indignation. But not tonight. She finds the guru funny. When Ziggy laughs it has a deep, pacifying quality. Like the beingness she experienced at the bottom of Cate Lansell-Jones's swimming pool. The conscious witness observing consciousness.

"*The self keeps us separate. Equality and identity cannot coexist. Or only to sell Coca-Cola.*" She smiles. "*Coca-Cola would have told Hitler to be himself. A bad artist, a genocidal maniac. Coca-Cola is a Hitler machine.*" The maroon sea agrees in rapturous shimmies. "*If you want to dismantle the system, dismantle the self. Live and love freely but no more identifying. Self-identification is the greatest source of human incarceration.*"

As Ziggy listens, an oozy warmth fills her body. For a few minutes, it seems to nuke all negative thoughts; dissolving them in an orange haze. Only Hitler Youth resist. They argue that the past is real because *look: here it is.* Ziggy tries to stay present, calmly witnessing the Nazis accelerate into a tirade of insults. Some of them make her giggle. When they tell her that listening to Shuni makes Ziggy an anti-Semite, she even guffaws—dispersing the mental tension into a fine mist. Ziggy observes herself observing herself, then something goes wrong and she is suddenly self-conscious. It might *feel* good to be an egoless being but she can imagine how stupid it looks. And if nothing means anything and everything is just concepts disintegrating with the self, what are you supposed to talk about? And more importantly, who is going to want to be your friend? Ziggy understands that all selves are phantoms but she feels too young to be this alienated. Though, Tim also seems tormented by the paradox of being and self-consciousness. Ziggy pastes the URL into a private message.

I'm glad you sent this—it's just standard eastern philosophy. She's simply removed the ideas from their original context.

Ziggy's heart sinks.

You mean appropriated?

Yes, but she's Indian so it's okay.

You don't mind the Coca-Cola Hitler thing?

She's speaking to Westerners so it's only about as offensive as the Chai Latte.

And what about non-identification and how she thinks people shouldn't be themselves because there are no selves to be?

Unity consciousness isn't very practical but if we could end patriarchy and all just wear white I would be gay without the flags.

And so it is confirmed that Tim likes boys. Which comes as a relief. Now Ziggy really wants to take him to the formal. Even though she is at best bisexual, they could still be one another's queer complementary opposite, complete with camera and mesh-glove transcendent transhumanist augmentation. Beyond identity. She ventures a practical question.

Can you be a conscious witness at a year-ten formal?

The three rippling dots of Tim's reply appear and disappear five times before he answers simply:

Probably not.

Ziggy tries to just observe the disappointment spilling through her chest like an icy drink. Fun and being have never really seemed compatible. A moment later, Tim is apologizing for something.

> Forgive me, Ziggy, I didn't mean to compare Shun-yata to chai tea because she's Indian.
>
> I think offensive jokes are part of the emancipation process.
>
> So no sacred cows? Lol. Sorry. Lol.

It seems Tim is at least getting a sense of humor.

ZIGGY WALKS AROUND WITH a tranquil inner atmosphere. As an egoless being, she feels both at ease in the world and pitying of all its denizens. People have suddenly taken on a garish, greedy quality. They hunch over insect-like, egos pouring into their phones or supping from the screen's bluish glow. Everywhere she looks, egos wink out from complex networks of fashion accessories. Girls with facial piercings no longer project the same arcane ferocity. They just look exposed and vulnerable, the silver balls in their skin like plugs for a seeping black pain. Ziggy is letting go of the unreality of other people. It's not very social, but at least the Nazis are quiet.

Being egoless is less easily practiced at school. Ziggy sits on the common room's sectional sofa and tries to let her thoughts flit past with the streaming of girls. But their formal mania proves distracting; the impending eyebrow tints and laser hair removal and self-generated quizzes for "What's Your Limo

Style?" Having renounced her identity, attending the formal seems pointless to Ziggy. And Tim is clearly not the type to stand beside her, laughing like happy Buddhas at all the earthly suffering. There is nothing she could do there to impress her old friends, and besides, good impressions are themselves the devil's hair extensions. Enlightenment should, technically, be more than enough.

Now an even greater challenge to Ziggy's mindfulness appears in the doorway. Cate Lansell-Jones bursts into the room yelling, "This place smells like fat people," and "Stephanides! Out of my recliner!" As the four Cates rush out onto the deck, a deluge of negative emotion crashes through Ziggy's fragile peace. She watches them colonize the outdoor furniture—sunning their cleavage and snapping erotic selfies. Fliss squints anxiously at the neighboring roof garden. "Have you guys ever noticed how poinsettias look like builders in safety vests?" The others mumble their agreement but remain unbuttoned down to their breastbones. Ziggy reminds herself that the girls are suffering. Of course they are. Stuck in Time, deluded by concepts like "formal-appropriate" and "classy tiara." Ziggy's anger settles; her serenity swims back in. She drifts in and out of listening as she watches the white sails switch on the harbor. The broccoli head of Shark Island blobs frumpy and unfazed. If she defocuses her eyes she can almost merge with the sparkling essence of the natural world. For the first time since she came to Kandara, Ziggy enjoys the view with sincere gratitude and thinks, jarringly, that hers is a really good school.

When the bell goes, the Cates groan and drag themselves up. They clutch their iced coffees close to their chests and begin their mournful procession to class. Reaching the door, Kate pauses, and tells Lex to pose against it.

"Wrap your leg around it like a pole," she instructs.

Lex makes a shy hoist of her leg and touches her chest to the glass. Kate snaps a couple of photos and then raises the phone aloft.

"Sending to Lance!" she teases, and Lex tackles her down to the floor with a rough affection that Ziggy finds painful to watch. It takes a moment for any meaning to inhabit the boy's name. Then a cool sweat furs across Ziggy's upper lip. Her eczema feels almost immediate. Since her first sighting that day outside Suze's store, Ziggy has often observed Kate's brother buying face cream or boat shoes at the mall. He has a pristine flop of blond fringe and wears pastel shirts with chinos in impersonation of a cupcake or father figure envisioned by a five-year-old girl. Realizing that Lance Fairfax is in a relationship with Lex Cameron, the two concepts, side by side, have the reality-shattering effect of a koan.

ONCE AGAIN, ZIGGY'S FRIEND has shocked her beyond any hope of compassionate understanding. Lance Fairfax is a one-man social injustice who makes it unthinkable to sit in Lotus as the world passes by. In other words, Ziggy finds it impossible not to spy on the new couple at Bondi Junction. Discreetly, she films the pair parading around the mall. On her phone she can magnify her footage and loosely decode their conversations. When Lex turns down a cold-pressed juice for a milk shake, Lance casually informs her that he would sue any girl who gave him HPV. When Lex assures him she's been vaccinated, Lance rewards her with one of his headphones. "Let's listen to a pod-cast on the fall of Rome," he suggests. Lex's eyes go dewy as she ruffles his floppy fringe and fingers the buttons of his Oxford. Ziggy can see that there is something about Lance. He is both bland and fascinating. Like a film set. Like America.

Ziggy spends her evenings scouring Lance's social media profiles. His Facebook cover photo is a famous marble bust of Caligula, and his posts reveal a philosophical affinity for Nietzsche and Darwin and the racist lesser work of several mid-century American authors. There are photos of the Fairfaxes sitting in lush gardens at long tables cluttered with complicated salads and quiches and many, many bottles of wine. Everyone in white, smiling behind expensive sunglasses, including the golden retrievers. From Instagram, Ziggy learns about Lance's love of watches. His collection includes priceless family heirlooms, classic design pieces, and inexpensive scuba-friendly junk, purchased "in case it falls off in the water or a local rips it from my wrist." Some of the watches are so old, they only keep "metaphorical time." Lance appears to harken from a bygone era when men aspired to empire and owning only tailor-made suits. The young scion may have made it through puberty, but he is not, according to Ziggy, coming of age. Lance is still stuck on monogrammed pocket squares, princesses in towers, and kings whose confidantes are cross-dressing dwarves. He quite seriously wants a castle with a moat. His political leanings suggest that Lance is frightened of boat people—in fact, he fears many aspects of the ocean. Lance claims to have dived fifty meters below sea level, but his Tumblr is a horror reel of gaping great whites and monster waves. And if Lance is scared of the sea, then Woman must be the ocean. Pictures of his voluptuous *Sports Illustrated* cover girls get a "Kit Kat Diet" caption from Lance. Otherness is something it seems he can handle only in neat doses (he sees Lex solely on Wednesday afternoons and Saturday evenings). Lance is the kind of misogynist who kisses his lipsticked mouth in the mirror and doesn't think to worry he's gay. Lance is a Roman. A stunted soul, a runt of history.

The dimple in his left cheek somehow confirms this. Despite herself, Ziggy finds him extremely cute.

It isn't clear to Ziggy why she feels she must monitor the banal movements of her spiritual enemy. Especially when she knows he is suffering, Lex is suffering, and eventually both of them will hurt each other's feelings far more than she ever could. But their mystifying romance calls to her from the tyrannical glamor of that late-November night. Her whole being leans lustily toward it. Or this might just be the weather. The spring days are getting longer and the evening skies are now a warm, flossy pink. Ziggy can feel the future waiting, a bright thing swirling in shadow on the season's other side, in the placid heat of early summer, just after the formal. Ziggy wants to attend. She knows fantasies create suffering, but Ziggy can't help it; she needs something to look forward to after mindfulness meditation. *Being* is boring when your only friend exists either on the internet or the equally uneventful spiritual plane. Ziggy knows something will happen at the formal, something even more transformative than the present moment.

Chapter 12

All November, Ziggy throws herself into disciplehood. On the internet, she reads about the inner workings of Shunyata's old ashram. The fleet of female, Ivy-educated Indian émigrés who managed the cult's geographical expansion: drugging homeless people then busing them in from Mumbai to elect Shuni onto their county's council; women who poisoned water reservoirs to sway the rural opposition; women who armed long-haired Aryan men with assault rifles to stand guard while they rode stallions through a poppy field. Despite the matriarchal structure of the ashram, Shuni talks very little about women. There is nothing in the lectures about Woman being the elemental substance of eternity. In fact, gender barely features at all. Some nights, Ziggy shares her findings with Tim. Some nights, he sends her videos of his own gurus. Shriveled men in white pajamas with liquid, bovine eyes. They all say similar things; Shuni just has the best sense of humor. One night, Ziggy sends Tim a clip where Shunyata instructs an acolyte to stand, burping at the crowd for a full two minutes. Tim *lol*s and then, touchingly, he opens up.

> It's not that I'm necessarily opposed to blasphemy, my whole life is blasphemous . . .

> You mean because you're not a good Muslim?

> I'm a gay Muslim.

Ziggy thinks she understands.

> I hear Nazis telling me I'm bad . . .

> I have an imam in my head and a transgender woman and they argue about everything.

Knowing it is not just cuisine, Ziggy's heart pangs for her friend. She is sure that Shuni's teachings can help him.

> I know it's hard to consider Muslim immigrants or transgender women a moral majority, but I think that's what those voices are.

> What are your Nazis?

> Probably religious Jews.

> So your grandmother is a Holocaust survivor and you still find Jewish jokes funny?

> Only good ones.

Maybe I'm just more identified with my family?

I doubt it.

Sometimes being queer feels like applying for Australian citizenship. 😦

Moved, Ziggy checks the ashram's old website. She has visited before and been disappointed with the offerings. The site has devolved into a virtual noticeboard for Shuni's disciples, advertising seminars allegedly related to the master's teachings—everything from canine meditation to something called LaughterLates. Ziggy has previously found nothing of interest on the site, but now she returns, determined to scan thoroughly for a workshop that might resemble the satsangs she has heard Shuni give on YouTube. But she doesn't have to look far. At the top of the homepage, Ziggy sees the guru's smiling face behind her trademark electric-blue aviators. A speech bubble floats up from her mouth, and inside it Ziggy reads an invitation to join the guru for a constellation workshop this spring. In Sydney, in two weeks' time. Ziggy can't believe it. She knew Shuni now lived in a remote valley in the Blue Mountains but had no idea that she was still a practicing guru. Ziggy is nervous to send Tim the link; she knows how these things can sound. Ziggy has read her mother's pamphlets aloud to a nearly hyperventilating Tessa and Lex. And she has filmed Ruth's workshops then given all the women crocodile jaws for the enjoyment of the Red Pill. Ziggy has replaced their primal screaming pillows with turd emojis and pasted all their feathered effigies inside an animated ring of rising flames. But Ziggy has also witnessed healing in her living room. Even when they are crying, the women speak through their tears with powerful gravitas; they make group eye contact with radiant self-possession; and one of them recently left a sad marriage for her alpha-male personal trainer. Ziggy knows these therapies work, and that Shuni's castrating sense of humor probably eliminates the gendering parts. If Ziggy can get Tim to attend, she is sure the guru's workshop will be transformational.

Ziggy forwards the link and Tim responds right away that he would do it if it weren't two hundred dollars. Ziggy stares prayerfully into Shuni's electric-blue gaze, and then as if the guru has answered her, a haggle springs to mind: maybe her mother can get them a discount. Ziggy tells Tim to wait. She jogs downstairs to where Ruth is sitting at the kitchen table, painting a gourd into a fertility figure. Seeing Ruth slumped over the dried legume, Ziggy wants to laugh. The Magnetic Poles are just another ego-trap, like the formal—that primitive pageant that costs seven hundred dollars per couple. If she doesn't pay the formal's outstanding five hundred and twenty dollars, Ziggy could cover both her and Tim's workshop fees plus lunch and taxis. At last the choice is clear: it's consciousness or a school dance. Ziggy walks resolutely to her mother's side.

"If I don't go to the formal, can I use that money for a spiritual workshop?"

Ruth's eyes stay fixed on the gourd. "Depends on the workshop."

Ziggy considers lying and then decides she can handle her mother's arrogance if the truth will strengthen her case. "It's one of Shuni's."

"Next weekend?"

Her mother's intel is unnerving. "Yes . . ."

Ruth places her paintbrush on the table. "No," she says, smirking. "You can't do that one."

"Why not?"

"Because your dad and I already paid our deposits."

Ziggy's chest squeezes. It suddenly feels like there isn't enough enlightenment to go around. Her mother is sucking up all the beauty and truth in the cosmos. "Since when do you do Shuni's workshops? She hates gender!"

"I thought you were done with all that stuff?"

"With what, the ego?"

Ruth rolls her shoulders back with melodramatic fatigue. "How does Shuni hate gender?"

"She hates identity! The Magnetic Poles are all about identity!"

"The polarities is her idea; I just appropriated it."

"The polarities is nowhere on the internet."

"This may come as a shock to you, but not everything is on the internet."

Ziggy knows her mother is wrong. "How can Woman be the Source when Shuni says there's no such thing as separation?"

Ruth smiles. "It's actually a shame you can't come on Saturday."

"Then let me!"

"I'm sorry, Zigs." Her mother eyes the gourd solemnly. "Your father and I need it more."

Conjuring her loveless marriage, Ruth has dampened Ziggy's indignation. She trudges back upstairs. Ziggy recognizes that the only person who can disabuse her parents of their over-identification with gender, potentially saving their relationship, is Shuni. Her mother's sexy Halloween version of an indigenous tribal elder will not go unconstellated; and she can hear the guru mocking Jeff's sleeveless gym shirt in that cutting Indian singsong. Ziggy imagines her parents' public humiliation and wishes even more desperately to be there.

Back at the computer, she scrolls over the seminar's venue. The Happy Lotus sounds uncannily familiar. She can even picture the sidewalk sign: HAPPY LOTUS, LEVEL 3, with its green arrow pointing left. Now she can visualize the building. It is one of several Lex used to gaze at longingly for its authentic American fire escape. Ziggy imagines herself crouched on the fourth-floor landing, angling her tripod down through the bars above the yoga studio's window. At first it seems crazy, and then Ziggy lets the word *crazy* float detached and fascinating in her mental field of view. Spying on the workshop isn't crazy. Staying home and checking Instagram and trying to "be" somebody is crazy. Not watching the spiritual master annihilate her parents' identities denies every instinct in Ziggy's body.

She lays her plan out to Tim. Aside from her motives, he has many concerns. His first: How will they climb up onto the fire escape? Ziggy has vaguely considered this. She thinks they could probably get a boost-up from one of the local meth-heads or just stack some empty milk crates under the suspended ladder. Tim finds this deeply impractical.

> I think you're romanticizing urban suffering—a pile
> of milk crates will just tip over.

So Ziggy hands the logistics over to him. As expected, Tim shines in this role. Within ten minutes he has devised a plan to get them in through the dance studio on level two, where they can sign up for Hip-Hop Intermediate at ten A.M. From here they hoist the windows for some ventilation, slip out onto the fire escape, and ascend to their observation deck on level four.

When that is settled, Tim asks her again if she is sure she wants to spy on her parents.

> As someone whose mother is Rowena, I have experience with oversharing.

But Ziggy does too. She has seen her mother striptease, watched her father do a misogynistic karaoke drag show. Ziggy knows more about her parents' sex life than anyone's her own age and that Shuni's workshop will destroy Ruth's gender theory and Jeff's weak counterargument.

> I just think it will be funny.

Tim accepts this. Spying is not a bad option. They get to watch Shuni at work, maybe get a little enlightened, and feel affirmed about the spurious gender binary. Shuni's workshop is the Saturday morning before the formal on Sunday evening. Ziggy knows the Future is a mental sickness, but it still feels good to have something to look forward to.

THE MORNING OF THE WORKSHOP, Tim and Ziggy watch her parents ready themselves in frantic hostility all across the house. Ziggy can tell her father is irritated to be spending Saturday with his wife. All the windsurfing and ocean-swimming and life-affirming mateship he is missing out on. He irons a shirt Ruth said looked too tight on him. Then he irons her shirt too.

"Your parents have an interesting dynamic," Tim observes.

"I know," says Ziggy, eyeing her mother's passive-aggressive application of hand cream. "It can be hard to know which one of them is being subordinated."

Now Ruth is yelling from the entrance. "I'm standing at the front door!"

Jeff nods to Tim and Ziggy, then hurries away down the stairs. From the window, they watch her parents seethe and snap their way up to the garage. As the car spins out onto the road, Ziggy is certain she hears the words, "being a serious cunt, Ruth." Her parents' day has begun at a high level of mutual castration, and Ziggy feels optimistic about an explosive workshop. And then she feels afraid. Realizing that this might involve the destruction of more than just their egos.

TIM AND ZIGGY'S INFILTRATION OF the Hip-Hop intermediate dance class goes less smoothly than anticipated. They have to fill out insurance forms and endure the cross-examination of a suspicious female teacher who also makes them remove their shoes. The large olive-skinned woman keeps looking at Tim's crescent-star bracelet. She tugs on a giant hoop earring as she speaks. "So you've never done hip-hop but you wanna take intermediate?"

Tim nods. "Correct. I'm a very fast learner and have a photographic memory."

The woman raises one large, painted slug of eyebrow. "Have you ever taken a dance class before?"

"I once did a workshop with a world-famous Whirling Dervish."

"What's a Whirling Dervish?" The woman chews on the words like she is trying to smear lipstick from her front teeth. Ziggy eyes the clock anxiously. She knows Tim's explanation will be a long circuitous Wikipedia entry, so she answers for him.

"It's a kind of mystical dance that Sufis do."

The woman nods, appeased by the word *mystical*. "I had a Malaysian boy come in once asking about break-dance classes, but you're the first Muslim guy who's ever wanted to do hip-hop."

Tim squints, baffled by the ethnic comparison. The woman rises and makes a posterior adjustment to her booty shorts. Her body is a miracle of ledged curvature accentuated by the sheerest Lycra. What Ziggy's father would describe as calli-pygous.

"It's a shame more of you don't dance," the woman continues. "Where I live, out west, the boys just sit around all day catcall-ing from their shit cars."

Mercifully, the door flies open and three girls come kicking violent choreography into the room. The teacher lowers her voice. "I gotta warn you though—most of the girls here only wear sports bras, and the moves can get pretty *nasty*."

Ziggy cringes, but Tim seems to have recovered and reac-cessed his strong inner core.

"I'm gay," he says pleasantly. "So I stopped being obsessed with breasts at age two. And I would never catcall a woman whether I was inside a car or a dance studio. I actually get cat-called a lot myself."

Ziggy feels a twinge of jealousy. She has yet to be verbally catcalled but looks forward to making up her own mind about it.

"Oh, honey, I'm so glad you're gay," the woman says with magnanimous, maternal warmth. "I teach a super-booby class."

As the teacher signs in her new arrivals, Ziggy watches the girls removing their sweatshirts and tying their hair back into tight, eye-slanting ponytails. She thinks of Tessa at her dance academy with all the public school girls. How insecure she must have felt as a private school virgin trying to be an existentialist cyborg movie star. It does seem just easier to get a boyfriend. Ziggy has noticed both Tessa's and Lex's boyfriended transformations: their fervor now dulled, their bodies soft and blurry in the halls. The girls have lost the hard-ons they once had for themselves. That private, autoerotic drive that Ziggy knows so well.

"You guys coming in?" The teacher pauses in the doorway.

Tim and Ziggy nod and then make awkward gestures toward taking off more of their clothes. The waiting room quickly empties, and from inside the studio a thunderous dance track starts shaking the walls. The two friends pocket their forms, grab their shoes, and hurry to the fire escape.

WHEN THEY REACH THE LEVEL above the Happy Lotus, Ziggy attaches the GoPro to its tripod and maneuvers it down through the bars. She watches the image on her phone as she angles the camera into the top right corner of the studio's tall window. When the GoPro has captured a full, sweeping aerial of the studio, Ziggy secures the tripod to the railing. Now they connect the camera to Jeff's iPad and prop the larger screen against the stairwell's inner pole. Then they sit back along the wall and watch the yoga studio pixelate to life.

In the vast, carpeted room, a wide circle of fit middle-aged people sit in placid-faced silence. There is an audiovisual station where an Aryan yogi with a deft, managerial ponytail adjusts the sound levels on a Hindu chant. A pile of abused pillows slumps against the back wall; a samovar whistles down the front. It takes Ziggy a moment to recognize the guru. She sits among the people, eyes closed, the tip of her nose tracing tiny arabesques in time to the music. She wears her skullcap, no sunglasses, and a loose guayabera shirt with a complicated tangle of microphone equipment curly at her chest. Ziggy spots her parents seated beside each other, staring off around the room.

When the chanting fades, the guru opens her eyes. She looks around the circle, making sincere eye contact with each of the participants. Ziggy watches every single one of them melt under her gaze. Then Shuni begins, disturbingly, with gender.

"Men," she says, "you are suffering terribly. Feminism has hurt your pride and caused you to question your God-given natures." The guru stands and walks across the circle to an older man whose T-shirt is printed with a hyperrealistic illustration of a polar bear. "Why are you wearing this?" she asks the man. "You are sad for the polar bears?"

The man nods. "I am."

"Are you? Are you sad for these creatures with white fur and black skin that live in the snow and would rip your head off if you came anywhere near them?"

The man nods less energetically.

"You are not sad for polar bears. You are sad for yourself. That is obvious to anyone. You are a healthy man who lives in a comfortable house and hardly ever gets out into nature. Who hardly ever screams or shouts or ravishes a woman in unbearable ecstasy. Be sad for yourself. Be sad that you think you are sad for a wild creature because you don't know how to be alive." Shuni shakes her head and walks back to her seat. The man begins diligently taking notes.

"Women," the guru says, warmth returning to her voice, "you are also suffering. Feminism has split the men into women and lumberjacks. Everyone is too sensitive. Even the lumberjacks."

"I guess she *is* an essentialist," Ziggy whispers to Tim. "Sorry."

Tim shrugs diplomatically. "It might get more spiritual."

Shuni points to a white-haired woman sitting beside the man in the polar bear shirt. Her face is youthful and plain and her gray eyes gaze somberly. "Do you also like polar bears?" Shuni asks her.

"Yes," says the white-haired woman. "We both love the Arctic."

"And why is that?"

The woman looks affronted but hides it behind a tepid smile. "Because it's breathtakingly beautiful."

"Isn't it all just white?"

The woman nods. "It's like an alien landscape."

"And it's endangered."

"Very."

"And you like this place, you *love* this beautiful white place that looks like an alien landscape?"

"I do. We do."

Shuni nods and then turns abruptly to the man in the polar bear shirt. "Polar Bear?"

"Yes," the man says sheepishly.

"Does this woman like to make love?"

Polar Bear peeks at his wife and then looks back to Shuni, mortified. "Yes, of course."

"I don't believe you. I think this woman wants to die. She wants to be in the Arctic. She even looks like the Arctic. I would get away from her very fast if I were you. This woman no longer wants to be among the living."

Tim is grinning wildly. "That's so mean," he says. "But it's true: she's overidentified with the Arctic Circle."

The couple sits there, insulted, despairing. Shuni returns to her seat and begins calmly untangling her microphone cords. "You godless liberals, wasting your lives." She shakes her head.

"Always looking for an identity; always seeking meaning in causes; desperately trying to be as separate and distinct as possible before you are swallowed back up by existence."

Shuni squints intensely at her cords and takes a long, focused moment to tease out the knot. "Miracle of miracles." The wires flop back into her lap and she looks up at the group, smiling. "So now we are going to reveal your delusions and dig up your pain and then we are going to hold these things to the blowtorch of pure presence. Equality is just an idea whose only real proof is Oneness."

Ziggy tries to dismiss the intense feeling of identification she is having with this overidentifying godless liberal. Tim is also having an emotional reaction.

"Do you think she means gender is a delusion that Westerners can transmute into dance?"

Ziggy assumes Tim is thinking of the Whirling Dervishes. "I guess dancing is kind of like presence."

Tim sighs in awe. "This is pure Michael Jackson."

The workshop continues in a similar fashion until lunch. Shuni walks around criticizing people's clothing and telling them their thought patterns are insane. She homes in on their likes and dislikes, explaining that all affinities belie a complicated ego identification schema. On an exposed shoulder blade, Shuni sees the sanskrit word for *impermanence* and brings the tattoo's owner to remorseful tears. The guru scolds the proud vegans and tells the PTSD sufferers to loosen up: existence itself is a trauma.

By lunch, Ziggy is anxious: her parents remain ideologically unharmed. She wonders if Shuni is avoiding Ruth because she is a former devotee. "My mother identifies as a premenopausal sex-witch," Ziggy groans. "Why isn't Shuni going after her?"

Unsurprisingly, Tim has no answer for this. "And I thought you said there would be constellations?"

But Ziggy understands the procedure. First you expose everybody's weakness, and then you utilize that data to direct the constellation. "There will be. I'm just worried that Shuni won't constellate my parents if she hasn't humiliated them first."

"She's definitely running out of time."

After lunch, the group dribbles back in slowly—teacups nestled between palms or phones out, already exchanging contact information. The Hindu chanting quiets and Shuni stands and walks around the circle, slowing at Jeff's chair then stopping directly behind Ruth's. She places her hands on Ruth's shoulders.

"Shunya Rutie." Her voice is like a kiss on the crown of Ruth's head. Ziggy feels it too. "Why don't you tell the group why you are wearing those shoes."

Ziggy squints at the screen. Her mother has chosen the red velvet kitten heels inherited from Twinkles's collection. They might be vintage Valentino.

"They go well with these pants?" Ruth tries.

The guru makes a disappointed clicking with her tongue. "Come on, Rutie. You can do better than that. Why those shoes? Who are they for?"

"My husband."

"Good. Now, why?"

"Because I think they look sexy."

"You want to look sexy for your husband. I remember: the Sacred Feminine, the gender polarities, how to keep the sex alive in a long-term relationship. Tell me, is it working?"

Ruth shakes her head.

"There isn't enough sex?"

"No."

"Why not?"

Ruth shoots a lethal look at her husband. "You'll have to ask him."

Tim nudges Ziggy. "Are you sure you can handle this?"

Ziggy nods, though she isn't.

Shuni clicks her tongue again. "You know that's not how this works, Rutie. I'm not going to ask *him* why you're not having enough sex. We don't need to ask your husband what he thinks." The guru tips her nose up and sniffs, as if for a sign of inclement weather. "The person we need to ask," she says ominously, "is your mother."

Shuni points to the white-haired woman and tells her to stand in the middle of the circle. Then she summons four men to rise and form a circle around the Arctic Circle.

"Rutie, what is your mother's name?"

"Twinkles," Ruth says simperingly.

"Twinkles," Shuni addresses the Arctic woman. "How do you feel being surrounded by these men?"

"It's a little claustrophobic," says Twinkles's avatar.

"You are afraid of them?"

"Not afraid. I'd just like them to move a bit farther back."

"Ruth, does this make sense to you?"

Ziggy's mother nods, transfixed by the human tableau. "Yes," she says shakily. "My mother never remarried. For forty-five years she's just had boyfriends. A new one every few months. Even now at seventy-nine."

"Good," says Shuni, smiling elusively. "Very good." She points to the Polar Bear. "Mr. Twinkles, please come and stand next to your wife."

Polar Bear moves dutifully into place beside proxy Twinkles. "How does it feel to stand next to your husband?" Shuni asks her.

The white-haired woman frowns and places a hand to her heart. She frowns harder. "I feel numb."

Polar Bear hangs his head and Ziggy wonders if this is just the chill of the Arctic Circle or else something profound about her own grandparents' marriage. Shuni also seems unsure.

"Rutie, did your parents divorce?"

"My father died," Ruth says without emotion. "When I was two, back in Hungary."

Shuni's nose tilts up, sniffing again. "When did your mother's father die?"

"When she was five." Ruth's voice is small. "They were all in a concentration camp."

The guru places a hand at her own sternum and taps her fingers. Her eyes flutter whitely.

"What's happening?" whispers Tim, captivated.

"She must be intuiting something," says Ziggy, her own fingers digging painfully into her thighs.

Now Shuni freezes and her eyes pop open, crazed with insight. "I want a line," she says. "All the men behind Jeff."

The menfolk shuffle awkwardly into a long, curving line. When they are assembled, Shuni wags her finger at them with slow, implicating deliberation.

"You are all the Jewish Hungarian men."

Tim's jaw drops. "Amazing."

"Twinkles," says Shuni, "how does it feel to look at these men?"

Twinkles's avatar squints at the Jewish Hungarians. She presses a hand again to her heart and stares harder. Then she looks brazenly repulsed. "They seem weak," she spits. "Pathetic, really."

"Fantastic," says Shuni. "Now look at your daughter."

The white-haired woman turns slowly to Ruth. Seeing the younger woman's face—trembling and red-eyed—a violent shudder racks her whole body, coursing up her throat and pouring out in a long, deep wail. Tim clutches Ziggy's wrist so tight, even she can feel his feelings.

The guru squeezes the Arctic woman's shoulder as she speaks to Ruth. "When she was a child, your mother suffered a terrible trauma, and these men couldn't protect her." Shuni glares, recriminating, at the bewildered line of Hungarians. "But she married one anyway, she had a child, and then the man did what all the men in Twinkles's life do—he failed her, he died. So she took you, her child, and left for a distant land where there were new and different men. And Twinkles met these men and she castrated them. Every single one. Now why do you think your mother did that?"

Ruth shakes her head in frantic perplexity.

"To make sure, Rutie, to be absolutely certain that every one of these men were too weak to be loved." She places a hand on Ruth's arm. "So that they would never be allowed to fail her child."

Ruth sobs openly. Tim sniffles. Ziggy waits for the punch line, but everyone is quiet, feeling the emotions, experiencing the universal pain. Slowly, Twinkles moves toward Ruth, and the two of them embrace. Then the Arctic Lady sits back down beside her husband and kisses the top of his head. Shuni smiles and watches with a swollen look of satisfaction. Ziggy worms her hand free of Tim's. The guru's constellation was just like all the other ones: they located the suffering, everyone cried and forgave their parents and now seem ready to move on with their lives. Her mother wasn't even berated for the sexy shoes.

"This is bullshit," she tells Tim. "So we inherit our mother's digestive bacteria? So we already knew that."

Tim nods, collecting himself. "Yes, it definitely seems like your mother is identifying with the pain."

Hitler Youth emerge from the depths to rejoice in Ziggy's misadventure. She just spent her Saturday witnessing the origin story of all her mother's feelings, which everyone—including the renegade guru—has received with open hearts. Everyone except Ziggy, who Hitler Youth maintain has always had a biological problem with empathy. Demoralized, Ziggy looks back at the screen where a peculiar silence has seized the room. Everyone has returned to their seats, and only Shuni remains standing in the center of the circle. The dopey contentment has drained from her eyes; her mouth is screwy and mean.

"But when you castrate your husband," says Shuni, "he becomes a dyke. You become a dyke. You are now two dykes who are still married under law. Well, why should you get special treatment? No same-sex couples can marry in this country. You should stand with your gay allies and get a divorce."

Polar Bear chuckles politely. No one else moves.

"Drop this suffering," Shuni barks at Ruth. "It doesn't even belong to you. Let the man be."

Ziggy's mother is silent. Jeff looks pale. A tickly elation creeps up Ziggy's spine.

"And you." Shuni stares fiercely at Jeff. "You need to stop swimming so much in the ocean. After a certain point it is philandering." The guru clicks at her assistant, and the slick ponytail whips swiftly toward the sound desk.

"All the women, standing inside the circle," Shuni instructs. "Except for Rutie."

The women rise and join the guru. Ziggy observes that all of them are dressed in loose-fitting pants and T-shirts. Their makeup is light or absent, their hair mostly tied back. They look degendered in the way of seasoned bushwalkers. Clearly, the only one of them who came here to be sexy today is Ziggy's mum. Once the women are assembled, an angelic harmony pours forth from the speakers. The sound bursts lush and golden through the room like music spawned from an ocean sunrise.

"Enya," Tim says in an almost spiritual whisper.

Shuni tells the women to dance. At first they are shy and rigid, swaying and bopping with sexless Western reserve. Then Shuni ushers them in around Jeff and they begin to animate. Their bodies loosen, shaking free from the flat gray room— swimming their hips and snaking their arms with elemental sass. Now Shuni summons Ruth to the edge of the group.

"Jeff," says the guru, "you need to put your wife back in the ocean."

Ziggy's father nods obediently.

"Take her hand," Shuni tells him. "And lead her into the water."

Jeff clasps his wife's hand and guides her into the tangle of gyrating female forms. Ziggy watches her father's arms make cobra jabs mid-air while her mother shimmies underneath them; Ruth caresses his face. Their affection is a little nauseating, but it fills Ziggy with sweet nostalgia. And a specific memory of being the beach. The four of them in the water, Ruth on Jeff's back and her and Jake in their dad's arms. Where Ruth's chest met Jeff's shoulder, the temperature of their skin told Ziggy how her parents loved each other. It was different from their love for her and obscured by a dark, adult enigma that made the world seem secure. Ziggy's feelings are interrupted by the thought that Shuni's ocean dance makes her an essentialist. She is about to apologize to Tim again, when the guru steps between Ruth and Jeff, taking their hands in hers.

"Being speaks through us," she says, "but you cannot get attached to the forms it takes." She waggles Ruth's hand. "Rutie's soft essence attracts her husband—not these little red shoes with a pointy heel like the clitoris. This is your delusion, Rutie. That the clitoris is a little shoe or a little handbag or something red and dangerous to empower you. There is no female empowerment in a love relationship. There is only the energetic integration of two physical beings seeking God." She sweeps Jeff's hand up above his head. "The ocean might make you feel like a Viking, but this woman is your key to the divine."

It isn't a total evisceration, but Ziggy feels vindicated. She can see how the polarities might be a useful system for exploring the true human condition of nothingness. If it brings people into a deeper state of being, that can't be bad. She looks at Tim. "I'm sure it works the same for gay couples."

Her friend nods, unfazed. "Even the Koran, read in a certain way, makes it clear who the wife is in a gay marriage."

Ziggy adores Tim. "And were you okay with the dykes thing?"

"Yes, I understood the metaphor and appreciate the solidarity with same-sex couples." He pauses thoughtfully. "But I don't think this should ever appear on the internet."

Ziggy agrees. Some jokes are better left in therapy.

The remaining constellations are performed in the usual way, without the comic epilogue. It seems this is Shuni's preferred mode of working: first make fun of the delusions and then constellate the pain. As she watches, Ziggy begins to understand why. And how she got it wrong. Shuni's jokes might help dissolve some layers of identity, but transcendence only occurs when Polar Bear stares straight ahead, telling them all in a soft, trembling voice how his mother turned him against cuddles. Now Ziggy is moved. And by nothing more than the crying part of a constellation. Polar Bear's pure, surrendered feeling washes through her, stretching Ziggy out into a shimmering expanse of empathy. A field of energy without form, the eternal thrum of the present moment. Tim has a more succinct way of describing it.

"It's like she traumatizes people out of their trauma."

With queasy pride, Ziggy remembers that this is her mother's work. A kind of reverse storytelling; where the Nazis are absolved and the Jews are saved and everybody is subsumed into what feels—even from the chilly fire escape—like the boundless grace of being. In her living room, there is often lots of laughter. Maybe jokes are always part of the traumatic de-traumatization process.

As the workshop wraps up, Ziggy's gaze drifts from the iPad to the bats flying overhead toward the botanical gardens. It is a comforting sight. And strange to think she shares it, daily, with everyone in her city—the sky darkening with that coursing wave of black. Their bodies blink against the vast white like a visual reminder of the cosmic particles that connect us, and when outdoors to always wear a hat.

Buzzing with vicarious workshop vibes, Tim and Ziggy pack up their equipment and take the bus home via Bondi Junction. On Saturday afternoon, the mall is swarming. Ziggy takes Tim to her favorite bench by the Japanese water feature. They gangle over the railing, critiquing the swirling masses below. Tim has a latent talent for pointing out the insidiousness of mainstream trends. Or what some might call a queer eye.

"It's like metrosexual men need shredded T-shirts to prove they have straight sex."

"And that thing women say, 'I don't dress for men, I dress for other women,' does not make you a Buddha."

"They all need to be constellated," Tim agrees.

Then from behind them at the cold-pressed juice counter, Ziggy hears a familiar request.

"Hold the romaine, hold the spinach."

She spots his silky golden flop just as Lance turns back to his friends.

"One thing beta males are good for: they start faggy juiceries and really *care* that you get your nutrients."

Along with the camera, Ziggy directs Tim's gaze to Lance and the other Randalls seniors, enjoying their Saturday afternoon at the mall. Lex is not in attendance—Ziggy imagines she is self-inflicting last-minute hair removal among other female tortures. Lance's clique appears to be unsubtly encircling a group of Kandara seniors. The girls sip smoothies by the fountain. Their full figures cut a primal image against the faux-rock waterfall and surrounding bamboo. Ziggy has often spied on enigmatic Lucinda Chambers and her posse of platinum heiresses. Lucy has de Kooning's demented femme fatale sex-face—that bug-eyed sultry smudge of last night's makeup and shared bodily fluids. The unvirginal senior has the transgressive air of a girl already graduated and is most often seen perched on the low wall by the school gates, sipping a Diet Coke and pining for adult freedom. Ziggy is certain Lucinda and her friends all have boyfriends at university, but still, they are being polite to their male peers. You never know who might grow up to be the next sexist prime minister.

Soon one of the boys is baiting Lucy with questions about her new beau. From his taunts, Tim and Ziggy glean that Lucinda is seeing some British guy who went to Eton with Prince Harry. When Lucy tells the boy that she recently met Harry on a yacht in Greece, he seems to get annoyed.

"What was he like?" the boy demands, eyes slitty with contempt.

Lucinda shrugs. Ziggy is moved by the older girl's urbane world-weariness.

"Come on," presses the boy. "It must have been cool?"

"It was boring," she says. "Harry's a dick."

Now the boy staggers back theatrically. He tells her to *calm down; leave poor Harry alone.* Lucy gives him a tight smile then turns back to her friends. Polite, diplomatic. The boys retreat, laughing at her—specifically at the unblended bronzer on the backs of her calves. As if her very dismissal of them is evidence of some larger female flaw. Ziggy leans in to Tim. "Prince Harry once wore a Nazi uniform to a fancy dress party."

Then a loud sucking sound gurgles from Lance's cup. The other boys turn to face him, falling silent.

"It's a terrible shame," Lance says dryly, "that date rape became so taboo."

His friends giggle and Lance continues.

"Things were much more efficient in the old days. Everyone agreed that women needed liquoring and men needed a yielding corpse, and people just got on with it. Even frigid girls could have a go."

The boys erupt into a hybrid laughter—equal parts aghast

and titillated. They clearly relish their friend's wry, timeless misogyny.

"And now our 'empowered' girlfriends want us to love them hairy and unwashed! Preening is natural—even clown fish understand the rules of attraction! Date rape at least brings back some of the drama to a rigged game."

The thwarted boy glares bitterly at Lucinda's group. "And if we stopped flirting and making eye contact and doing all the things feminists call 'assault,' the human species would die out."

"If they don't want to make eye contact," says a severely acne-faced boy, "Rohypnol's a good option."

"Correct, Mulvaney!" enjoins Lance. "This is where the caliphate has it right." His eyes twinkle with malice. "Women secretly *want* to be slaves."

"Jesus, Fairfax," comes a quiet protest.

Lance looks wolfishly at the handsome Asian boy who has dared to speak up. "It's true, Yee. The lie of equality is only possible in small countries with low immigrant quotas. And when you pretend that all Western wealth is not built off global poverty."

"He's right," says Lucy's harasser. "You think all those Scandinavian feminists would want equal opportunities for every brown person on Earth?"

"Some of my family are brown," says the isolated challenger.

"Feminists," sneers Lance, "would still be chattel without imperialism. Sorry, Yee, but global communism isn't going to work."

"And women prefer to be dominated," smirks the zitty one.

"Yes," says Lance. "But by men who wear Brooks Brothers."

The laughter rekindles, jocular and brotherly. Ziggy's arm has gone numb where Tim is squeezing it. The blood pounds

viciously at her temples, reminding her—with exhilaration—
that the camera is recording. She feels the tiniest tug toward
Lance and his disdain for liberal hypocrisy. But then there is
universal equality, aka Oneness. And the fact that Ziggy is a
woman. She looks at Tim. His face is white.

"That boy needs to be raped," he says in a voice like a dragged
shovel.

Ziggy thinks her friend must be joking. Every day is consent
day. Tim also owns the T-shirt.

"I'm serious," he says. His eyes look glazed, the quick obsid-
ian slurred a murky brown. "He needs a rape trauma."

Ziggy's heart cants toward Tim—deeply and psychically her
friend. "We could drug him?"

"How exactly?"

Now she feels faint. They are going to poison Lance Fairfax.
Then she remembers. "I have one dose of ayahuasca."

"What is that?"

"It's the mother drug." Gerhard's voice drones in her head.
"It brings up mother issues and is meant to be as traumatic as a
constellation."

Tim looks down across the lower food court. He nods, comprehending. "So he'd be traumatized and we wouldn't even
need to touch him?"

"Exactly," Ziggy says, noticing her disappointment.

"He'd be traumatized out of the trauma of patriarchy."

Ziggy's brain offers up the pain pornography of Lance and
Lex regal under strobe lights. Her voice trembles with excitement. "We could spike his drink at the after party?"

"Which after party?"

Ziggy has never even mentioned the formal to Tim. So now
she backtracks. Telling him a much longer story about three

girls who met pressed against a famous action hero's car and then again in line for a punitive HPV vaccine. How the two who were already friends tortured the third into thinking she was a transhuman of color then abandoned her when they decided to be white people. How she misses them and how she hates them. The story goes on and on, and as she tells it, Tim and Ziggy wind all the way down through the mall, out onto the street, and back along the arbored avenues to Ziggy's house. Finally, she asks him. "Do you want to be my formal date?"

Tim nods eagerly; Ziggy wonders if formals are egalitarian at public school.

"The after party is at a nightclub in Double Bay," she warns him.

"Don't they have a golf course there that doesn't allow Jews or Muslims?"

Ziggy nods apologetically.

"I can't wait."

AMPED ON ADRENALINE and all Ruth's sugary new after-school snacks, Tim and Ziggy sit on the Sofa of a Thousand Tears and map out their plan. It should be easy to shadow Lance around the club then tip the wine-colored liquid into his drink. Ziggy thinks his friends will be dipping their pinkies into plastic baggies of MDMA, but she knows from her research that Lance would never harm his body with synthetic chemicals. He likes his liquids cold-pressed or heavy on the antioxidizing poly-phenols. Tim and Ziggy's plotting moves between chilling logistics and giddy hilarity. Soon they become enamored with a vision of Lance on the dance floor ducking from hallucinations.

"Maybe he'll strip naked," Ziggy speculates. "Maybe he'll start apologizing to all the unpopular girls."

Tim giggles up from the rug as Ziggy paces around him, re-
laying bizarre scenarios. Lance's psychic transformation is the
general theme, but Ziggy's story lines sprout weird cinematic
tentacles. Lance swinging from the bathroom stalls like a mon-
key; mermaid-bathing in the urinal; stealing someone's lipstick
to paint a giant blooming vulva on the wall. The room gets fast
around her as Ziggy stomps in demented circles, her head tight
and molten—a mental acuity she associates with bathroom
closets and Method acting.

When she is out of breath, Ziggy collapses onto the floor and
the spell breaks. Now the air cools and the consequences crowd
back into the room. She eyes Tim anxiously.

"So the best and worst thing that could happen is Lance has
a bad trip?"

Tim's voice wavers. "Yes," he says. "I think that's right."

The friends comfort themselves with dark chocolate raisins
and costume ideas. Eventually Tim leaves with the promise of
returning in eighteen hours, dressed and ready for the Kandara
year-ten formal. As Ziggy shuts the door behind him, the night
gets very crisp and loudly silent. The sky in her window has
never been blacker; the light inside is a shocking white. Ziggy
bumps against each moment with the same yawning astonishment. She will be there tomorrow night, with all the other girls.

WHEN SHE WAKES, it is late and to her brother's taunting. He
has found a Pokémon on Ziggy's shoulder and is laughing
hysterically at the top of the stairs.

"That's abusive," Ziggy says, tossing a uterus-shaped pillow
in his direction.

"It's not like I caught it at Auschwitz."

"Someone caught a Pokémon at Auschwitz?"

Jake nods gravely. Ziggy giggles.

"You think that's funny?"

"It's all just ego-identification and concepts of mind, Jake." Ziggy experiences the unfamiliar puff of elder siblinghood. "I can send you some links."

"Why don't you send Twinkles some links?" Jake hurls the pillow hard into Ziggy's knees. "We've got lunch there in an hour."

Ziggy had forgotten. She still hasn't apologized to her grandmother, and will now have to sit in an intimate, aggressively tchotchke'd living room with her parents, Jake, and the slut-shamed septuagenarian. Her grandmother is going to make Ziggy suffer. Everything Ruth knows about emotional manipulation was gleaned from Twinkles's arsenal. Many times, Ziggy has watched her grandmother swan around a room, parading her hurt with the grim ostentation of haute couture.

But remarkably, before she's even gotten the fly screen open, Twinkles forgives her granddaughter's transgression. "Pippi, I love you. We forget the leopard print and have a nice lunch."

Ziggy nods, relief rising in a hot fizz at her eyeballs. She hugs her grandmother, the tears absorbing into Twinkles's poufy shoulder pad.

They sit straight down to eat. Twinkles has made a series of brown, chunky dishes with potatoes. "Last time you ask vegetables, this time I make vegetables."

Ruth scoops a mound of gravy onto her fork. "This would go well with a colonoscopy," she teases her mother.

Mercifully, Twinkles misses the joke. "Sorry, darlink. My VCR broken."

The meal continues pleasantly for a few minutes. Then Jacob

jumps up and lunges toward the glass cabinet, making a swiping gesture with his phone.

"Pippi, what you doing?"

"I caught a Caterpie under the photo of Auntie Magda."

Ziggy scowls at her brother. "We're having lunch with our grandmother."

"What's 'lunch'?" teases Jake. "What's a 'grandmother'?"

"Shut up."

"Isn't everything just ego-identification and concepts of mind?"

Ziggy gives Jake the finger.

"Including Auschwitz?"

Twinkles squints at her granddaughter. "You think Auschwitz just a concept?"

"Isn't everything?" Ziggy asks weakly.

"Who says this?" Her grandmother spits. "Jeff Koons?"

Ziggy giggles and gently corrects her: "The GoPro is actually less about art than Eastern philosophy."

Ruth sighs in mock exasperation. "So all this time the camera was just the third eye?"

"More like the objective observer."

But Twinkles isn't following. "So you become a Buddhist and start denying the Holocaust?"

"I'm not saying the Holocaust didn't happen," Ziggy says carefully. "I'm saying that *Time* is an illusion."

"No *illusions*." Twinkles wrings the word out like a soiled rag. "Look at your auntie Magda." She points to the photo of a middle-aged blond woman in a Guns N' Roses T-shirt. "See her blue eyes?"

Ziggy strains at the photo. "Yes."

"You know why they blue?" Twinkles speaks with aggressive calm. "Because Auntie Magda's grandmother was raped by Magyars."

Jacob is, as usual, first to do the math. His eyes get very round. "Isn't that *your* mother?"

Comprehending, Ziggy feels herself dissolving back into the chair.

Twinkles ignores the question. "You think that just a concept? That *genes*. That DNA."

"Mum," says Ruth, "Ziggy is just experimenting."

"And brown the dominant gene for eye color," Twinkles continues with icy, medical formality. "So there must have been many rapes, going back many, many generations."

Ziggy hangs her head. "I'm sorry," she says to her lunch plate. "I just thought it was funny that they caught a Pokémon at Auschwitz."

But saying it only confirms how unfunny it is. In this room. The gravitational pull of her grandmother's body makes a Holocaust joke feel pesky and void. Maybe because she was physically there while Ziggy is decades removed. Oddly, it is Lance's politics that pop into her mind. Like a wealthy nation, Ziggy's irreverence is built off her grandmother's pain.

"I'm not saying the Holocaust wasn't real," Ziggy tries again.

"Then what you saying? It doesn't matter? Because you learned how to meditate?" Twinkles shakes her head. "You used to be a very sympathetic girl."

"You're right, Mum," says Ruth, "it's all just ideology. But Ziggy is learning. Please . . . don't get offended."

Twinkles leans back exhausted in her chair. Ziggy watches her grandmother. Twinkles *is* right: Ziggy used to be a very sympathetic girl. Which means that, despite her efforts, Ziggy's emotions have always showed. All the stories Twinkles has told her that made Ziggy's heart squeeze like a hot sponge; her grandmother must have seen or known—from the temperature of her skin—exactly what Ziggy was feeling.

"Even the fat little baby eating ice cream, you pity him. I saw it."

Ruth looks alarmed. "Which fat little baby?"

Twinkles waves her daughter away. "It doesn't matter." She looks at Ziggy. "Please. Pippikem. No more adolescence."

Ziggy nods tearfully at her grandmother. "Okay," she says. "No more mean jokes."

The whole room presses in hot and squishy on Ziggy's eyeballs. Ruth starts to clear their plates. Ziggy's mother has a talent for shifting the energy. And casually getting the last word.

"It takes courage to be ignorant," she says.

Twinkles gasps.

"I'm not talking about books, Mum. You can read all the books in the world and still practice ignorance as a form of humility."

"Can I practice ignorance on my biology test?"

Ruth ignores her son. "Ignorance is a type of letting go," she says, balancing five plates on a slender forearm. "There is courage in letting go of your ideas because so many of them come from your pain." Ziggy eyes the trembling crockery. "It's terrifying to drop your suffering, drop your identity, but it's the key to psychic freedom."

Ruth stabilizes her load, squeezes her mother's shoulder and steps safely into the kitchen.

Twinkles shrugs. "My new-age children."

After lunch, Twinkles wants Ruth to see the kaftan they bought that Ziggy is refusing to wear to the formal. While the men loiter out in the hall, Twinkles ushers the women into her boudoir. The walls and carpet and ceiling are all powdery shades of pink. The bed is piled with salmon- and peach-colored throw pillows. It seems harder to breathe in here. And also, it always makes Ziggy feel sleepy. She has spent many hours watching Twinkles tearing through her wardrobe, searching for something that might fit her twiggy granddaughter. In the beginning Ziggy is usually irritated, but she soon succumbs to the pink room's soft, enveloping dermatitis and the hypnotic notes of Bal à Versailles. Twinkles claims this is the fragrance Princess Diana and Elizabeth Taylor and Michael Jackson all wore. What Ziggy thinks of as the deathly notes of celebrity.

While they wait for Twinkles to find the kaftan, Jeff and Jacob lean in curiously from the doorway—making the room seem smaller, smothering, and a little obscene. The boys are strangely reverent in this space, as if bearing witness to something sacred. When the garment is located, Twinkles whips it out with a violent flourish and everybody pretends to like it.

"It's very funky, Mum."

Twinkles nods, breathless with vindication. "She looked really cool."

Ziggy studies the kaftan. She can't possibly wear it. But she can pretend to. "Can you find me some matching shoes?"

In seconds, Twinkles and Ruth are on their knees, foraging among the dense footwear. Her grandmother holds up a pair of suede zebra-striped clogs. She brings them right up to her face and kisses the toe. A faint revulsion seizes Ziggy as she watches Twinkles fawn over the shoes. Behind her grandmother glitters the sequined menagerie of hanging garments; the patterns pulsing under the dim lights. For a moment it seems living, and Ziggy wonders if this is what the animal print is meant to evoke. Not just sex, but a feeling purely physical. A way for Twinkles to confirm the most basic fact for herself—that she is here. A physical being. Still, amazingly, alive.

On the car ride home, Ziggy notices her parents are being affectionate. Their demeanor is newly docile with lovingness. When Jeff spontaneously kisses his wife's hand, the siblings share a fearful glance and, possibly their first, sweeter look of allegiance.

WHEN ZIGGY GETS HOME, Twinkles's words again start to work on her. Traumatizing Lance Fairfax into enlightenment makes Ziggy feel like a very unsympathetic girl. Lance could hurt himself or jump out a window. Ziggy has heard of people scratching their skin off and trying to catch butterflies in busy traffic. She texts Tim and asks if he thinks they should abort the mission. But Tim, ever the pragmatist, has a simple solution. His therapist once gave him a pill prescription for insomnia. Apparently, in their quest to take on all the world's pain, a psychic empath must be well rested. If Lance starts self-harming, they will resort to standard-issue rape drugs.

While she waits for Tim to arrive, Ziggy checks her email. She has ignored all missives from the formal committee, but now she trawls back through them for important logistical information. A message dated two weeks prior has "amaze news" about a special guest who will be appearing at the after party. Girls with gold wristbands will gain access to the VIP room for autograph-signing between eleven and eleven thirty P.M. Ziggy tries to understand how this is possible. Who has bribed the action star and what he or his junior school daughter might have done to deserve such punishment. The eleven-year-old must be under severe threat of expulsion or else her father owes the club owner a favor for unsavory behavior in a toilet stall. Whatever it is, the outcome is an asset to her plan. Now they have a perfect thirty-minute window for the vomiting to occur, unaided, in a bathroom stall. No girls, not even Lex, will be sympathetic to an ailing Lance Fairfax when the midget Earth defender is on-site. The boys, being boys, will be naturally unsympathetic.

Tim arrives in his customary white two-piece. Ziggy was coerced into borrowing her grandmother's cheetah-print shawl, which she is wearing with her mother's black slip and the zebra-striped clogs. With the camera nesting in her curls, she resembles an African safari. Standing beside her, Tim looks like a European colonialist.

"The girls will probably be bitchy," she warns her friend.

"Do we care about that?" Tim asks genuinely.

"Of course not."

Ziggy takes him downstairs into the living room, where she has emptied Ruth's basket of indigenous headwear and accessories. She fits a feathered headdress on over the GoPro.

"I thought we could be shamans."

Tim holds up a stick with a taxidermy bat fixed at the top.

"This feels powerful," he says of probably the stick, possibly the whole endeavor. "But it's also cultural appropriation."

"Can't it be homage?"

"There's no history of homage; there's only a history of oppression."

"I thought we'd stopped subscribing to history?"

Tim holds up the bat staff, staring searchingly into its glass bead eyes. "I just don't see which part of this is funny?"

"You're right." Ziggy begins to remove her headdress. "People might think we go to world music festivals."

"Or take acid in the botanical gardens."

The thought of psychedelics makes her heart quicken. "Did you bring the Temazepam?"

Tim taps his breast pocket affirmatively.

Ziggy is suddenly anxious. Her excitement at being the kind of person who would take spiritual vengeance on Lance Fairfax now rings hollowly for what it is: mere ego-identification. She slips out to her bedroom and the drawer where she keeps potentially incriminating objects hidden from her mother. The shampoo bottle is wedged between a half-empty packet of cigarettes and the DVD of *Irréversible*. Ziggy pulls the bottle out and stares into the cloudy, purple liquid. She hears Gerhard's voice: *Last week I was Tutankhamen*, and imagines Lance walking sideways on the bar top, like an Egyptian. Ziggy's camera isn't just an objective observer. The watching has always felt more like a telling, and Ziggy's deeper wish, she knows, is to tell the story. Lurking in that secret subterranean place where ambition jerks itself off to future goals, Ziggy has wanted to film something good, something paradigm-shattering that also goes viral on YouTube. Something to make her a hundred thousand new friends. She pockets the ayahuasca and walks back out to her accomplice.

Chapter 13

Most of Ziggy's peers are standing in front of the hotel, staging selfies around their limos. Along with the established social categories, Ziggy notices many new subgroups. A tight circle of girls she had previously considered academic boarders now appear to be outing themselves as goths. One subset of smart Asians sport matching semicolon tattoos on their exposed shoulders. Three pretty blond girls Ziggy assumed were B-list Cates have dyed their hair green and pinned political badges to their spaghetti straps. One of the sexy druggie girls has brought a female date. Ziggy is surprised then ashamed to be surprised that the rugby players all have male partners; they stand together, but their outfits are incongruous—united only by broad shoulders and high self-esteem. Ziggy tries to imagine how she and Tim appear to her year group. She managed to convince her friend to wear a belt strung with shells and apple seeds—just for ritualistic flare. Under her mother's silk dress Ziggy's body is slippery and elliptical. But she doesn't feel self-conscious—all around her twitters a peaceful, disinterested coexistence. From their tight insular focus and obvious aesthetic labor it is clear that each group is much more concerned with its own appearance.

Now a pale pink limo pulls into the curb, electronica soaring from the open windows. Cate Lansell-Jones rises from the flung door like a sulfur cloud, a pale nimbus of lemon tulle with bustle and train. But nobody is paying attention. The mood is more tribal—the usual Cate-worship and self-denigration has been swapped for a stubborn sense of earthly belonging. Still, Cate appears intoxicated by her perfect moment, basking in the imagined awe of her peers. Then Cate's date steps out beside her, a cute sandy-haired boy in a slick navy suit. Toby is a senior at Randalls and the proud owner of a website that reviews men's luxury retail. Ziggy has perused it. Toby seems to spend his days penning villanelles about cuff links and posting sexist GIFs from *Caddyshack*.

Kate Fairfax shuffles out next, her face a haunted pale. Kate also wears lemon with tulle roses pinned across her décolletage. Like Cate, her dress has the dreamy, scene-stealing grandeur of a wedding gown, but unlike Cate, Kate doesn't radiate *this is my special day*. She looks like she's been crying. Ziggy can only assume Kate has been chastised for the eerie doppelganger effect. Clearly, a year-ten formal is no place for the uncanny. Kate's date—someone known as Little Matty, a colossal oaf and captain of the senior rugby team—staggers out after her with a Grey Goose bottle tucked under-arm, his slicked quiff floppy with perspiration. Ziggy's attention now flies to Fliss, bounding around from the other door in a more auspicious shade of chartreuse, arms linked with her boyfriend, Declan Yee, another Randalls senior who has modeled men's suits in Bangkok and brags about his ADHD: "All the great artists had it—Kerouac, Bukowski, Bono." It isn't entirely clear what kind of artistry Declan aspires to. Until last year, he was a state skateboarding champion. Now he deejays sweet sixteens.

The six of them step onto the red carpet, laid out especially for this night and specifically for this moment. Bathed in the last crimson grill of sun, they shine like icons inside a moiling sea of apostates.

"Where's Lance?" Tim says anxiously.

Ziggy ushers them closer to the limo. The door is still ajar and she can see two shadowed figures shifting around inside. Their movements are jerky; it looks like a fight. A handbag's gold chain-strap flies out across the seat and then Lex lurches violently from the door. She wears a sleek, black halter-neck with a devastating side-split. Her hair is drawn into a slick bun. She looks so beautiful, a whimper slips up Ziggy's throat.

"Lance," Tim whispers, eyes gleaming.

As he steps onto the red carpet, Ziggy watches Lance puff out his chest and then lean into an unconvincingly macho hip-tilt. His eyes dart around; he blinks too frequently, tugs restively on his cravat. There is an avian alertness shifting his body through these awkward gestures of manhood, the absurd accoutrements trapping him in time and oppressing the primal spirit beneath. Ziggy almost pities him, sensing that their trauma victim might already be in some sort of psychic pain.

TIM AND ZIGGY HAVE BEEN assigned seats in the far west corner of the function room. The formal committee is front and center. On every table sits an arrangement of white calla lilies and a cream-colored gourd. Ziggy recognizes these from Suze's store. On the prix fixe menu she reads that proceeds from the beet salad will go to AIDS. Whatever that means. The running order appears to leave forty-five minutes for thank-you speeches.

Once everyone is inside, the lights dim and a loud dance track begins its synthy ascent. Pink and green strobe lights saber through the dark, and a spotlight chases itself around the room. Finally, it lands on the emergency exit door, at which moment the four formal committee cochairs come bursting through, and the beat drops. The girls jump around in a circle, holding hands, their little orb contracting and expanding. Then the whole grade is bouncing and grinding at their tables. Even the goths. Even Tessa and her high-brow boyfriend.

I feel so close to you right now—

Lance jumps in place with the other boys—arms extended, pumping what looks like the heil in triple time. Ziggy has seen videos for EDM festivals in dark European woods where pastel-colored hordes heil in mindless ecstasy. The way this music unites people through crafted moments of mass emotion feels, to Ziggy, very Third Reich. Tim agrees, giving his ambiguous frowning smile. Even Ziggy is now finding it difficult to know which Nazi jokes are actually funny.

When the song ends, everyone finds their seats. Ziggy and Tim share their table with the dregs of Kandara's society. To Ziggy's right is Cyndi Yang, to her left, Patricia Katsatouris. Vivian Levy, the violin prodigy with the neck hair, sits beside a tiny boy who turtles out of an oversized suit. There are some other plain-faced, bespectacled girls with careful gazes. The Latin electives. These are the girls who always scuttle away from the GoPro, and tonight, Ziggy can tell they are annoyed to be sharing a table with the camera. But now she is on their side. Ziggy doesn't want them to be self-conscious. She wants them to cure AIDS and invent sustainable technologies and find a two-state solution.

"Hey, Patricia," says Ziggy. "Remember when Dr. LeStrange said all Randalls boys were lazy and couldn't spell?"

Patricia giggles. Her date's laughter is booming.

"I'm at Boys Grammar," says the massive, hairy man. He puts out a hand. "Brian."

"Ziggy, and this is Tim."

"I also go to a public school," Tim says proudly.

Everyone at their table is grinning. None of these boys are Randalls. In fact, there's a good chance they are mostly government schooled. Now the tiny boy in the bulky blazer tells them that Randalls's academic ranking has been sliding steadily for years.

"Ever since the rugby rape scandal," he explains, "they lost some funding and couldn't give out as many scholarships."

"I heard it was the new building," says Ziggy. "Apparently the views are very distracting."

Brian nods. "And there was that incident with the female history teacher."

"They had that creepy choirmaster."

Patricia stabs her filet mignon with a heavy fork. "I heard too many boys had started taking *drama*."

Everyone chuckles with what Ziggy finds a touching solidarity. Sure, Patricia has made a gay joke, but it is for a higher cause. Ziggy winks at Tim and he smiles back. Their goal tonight is conscious transformation. If in the process of its attainment, a few private school boys must be conceptually sodomized, so be it. Ziggy looks around at this clever, hairy, mysterious table of girls. If they are not driven to achieve perfect beauty or fame, their inner workings suddenly strike her as much more interesting. She feels foolish for having never bothered to inquire, and then sad that these girls are not her friends. That they are not a tight-knit group devoted to their own mental and spiritual betterment. Watching the girls laugh and chatter, Ziggy zooms in hungrily on their little ecosystem—so bravely poised. Then she remembers the imminent poisoning and their faces seem to recede. A great gap yawns open between Ziggy and her tablemates. From across the cloth's creamy expanse, the girls continue their evening at an infinite remove. Ziggy feels pulled in the wrong direction, inward to a dark, apocalyptic tundra.

"Are you okay?" Tim is tapping her hand.

But Ziggy can't explain this to him. That what she wants more than anything is a girlfriend to go to the bathroom with.

"I'm just nervous about our plan," she says.

Tim looks concerned. "We don't have to do it if you'd rather just be social."

Ziggy had never considered this an option until now. The formal was an evening specifically designed to define your difference, your special inner sense of unique chosenness. This was the night you came out as fundamentally incompatible with everyone else in your grade. The night you expressed your way of being and set about defending it for the rest of your life. But it seems now that the night is more about closeness, though Ziggy has no one to be close to. She has alienated herself from everyone but Tim. She smiles gratefully at her friend.

"It's okay," she says. "I'll just have a shot at the after party."

After dinner, Tim takes a long time returning from the bathroom. Ziggy fears he has run into the ethereal Swedish exchange student. When the progressive Northern European arrived late last semester, Ziggy wondered if she might have a new ally. But on her second day, Kristiana told Ziggy point-blank that her camera was a violation of personal privacy, and when Ziggy cried "transhumanism" (weakly), the girl shook her head with such moral superiority and corn-silk-blond hair that Ziggy felt compelled to make the GoPro an ethnic statement. She told Kristiana that the camera was like a religious head scarf. Or the little black box Hasids wore on the tops of their heads. She explained that Australia was not a secular country, and if Kristiana wanted to be surrounded by godless people with white hair, she should return to Sweden. The girl had backed away from Ziggy as if retreating from a rough beast. She suspects the Scandinavian has been petitioning against her ever since.

But when Ziggy finds Tim, he is holed up outside the men's bathroom, not by the humorless snow angel, but by an enemy much more dangerous. Tessa is pointing to Tim's silver glove, speaking animatedly as Eamon listens in. Ziggy can guess what has happened. Tessa must have charged Tim with pseudo-transhumanism, and when Tim explained that the glove was a tribute to transcendent Michael Jackson, Tessa would have berated him for including a child-molesting, skin-whitening cis-male in the woman-of-color category. But the mood seems too buoyant. The three of them are smiling. Eamon suddenly breaks into a virtuosic moonwalk, which Tim enthusiastically applauds. When Tessa sees Ziggy approaching, she takes a step back from Tim. Though her expression is not entirely unfriendly.

"Nice shoes," says Tessa, grinning at the clogs.

Ziggy detects no sarcasm. "Thanks," she says tentatively, scanning Tessa's outfit for a commensurate response. The thespian is wearing a heavy velvet gown with blinding white neck ruff. Something Ziggy imagines she stole from the school drama department. "I like your frills."

"Thank you." Tessa gives a quick but nontoxic smile.

Ziggy tries to think why her old friend is even talking to her. She looks at Tim. "Did you tell them why Michael Jackson is transcendent?"

Tim nods. "They also love Michael."

"So he liked to share ice cream cones with children?" Tessa shrugs theatrically. "So what?"

Eamon gives an indignant headshake. "He was a genius."

Ziggy doesn't understand what is happening. Why Tessa and Eamon have taken such a strong liking to Tim and everything he stands for. Including Ziggy. Why it feels like they are suddenly some kind of little group. Eamon leans in conspiratorially. "Did you see Lance Fairfax accuse the waiter of stealing his Cosmograph Daytona?"

"What is that?" asks Ziggy.

"A type of Rolex," says Tessa. She clutches Eamon's arm. "Lance bullied him so badly in year nine, he had to see a dietician."

"I used to be tubby."

Ziggy is stunned. She wonders what worked, the bullying or the diet. "We hate Lance too," she tells the thespian couple.

Tim nods. "He thinks women should be slaves."

"Do they still cane boys at Randalls?" Tessa asks hopefully.

Eamon shakes his head. "Plus, if you caned Lance, he'd probably enjoy it."

This is almost a gay joke, but thankfully Tim stays fraternal. "He definitely deserves *some* kind of punishment."

"A serious fucking trauma," agrees Tessa.

It happens in a second or rather a moment outside of time:

Ziggy experiences the full emotional download of their friendship and leans toward Tessa with no instinct for self-preservation.
"We were thinking of inflicting a trauma," she says giddily. "To
make him a better feminist."

"Catcalling trauma?"

"Date-rape trauma."

"How would you do it?" Tessa beams at Ziggy, so keen and
believing, it pangs. *Shark attack, but my friend gouged out its eyes.*

"We've got one dose of ayahuasca," Ziggy says deliriously.
"Which works like the trauma technique I learned from my
mum."

Tessa is suddenly reverent. "The constellations?"

Ziggy nods.

"Wow."

Tim looks panicked at the unplanned disclosure. He taps
manically against a fox tooth hanging from his belt. Ziggy gives
him a bright, reassuring smile.

"So you drug him," Tessa clarifies, "and then let the drugs do
the traumatizing?"

Ziggy nods.

"You guys are really going to do this?" Tessa glances between the two of them.

"Yes," says Ziggy. "Unless you have any better ideas?"

Naturally, Tessa does. And the first one is to go somewhere
more private. The four of them hurry down the hall and out into
the fire stairs. Hunched in urgent congress, they revise Tim and
Ziggy's plan. For Lance to have an authentic experience, Tessa
thinks they will need to dispose of his friends as well.

"How much ayahuasca do you have?" she asks Ziggy.

"One dose, but we've also got sleeping pills."

"Then we could do an actual date rape," says Tessa, fingering her ruff with strange, unconscious prurience. "Once his friends pass out, we can pull their pants down and cover them with dirt and Vaseline!"

Eamon smiles adoringly at his girlfriend. "And maybe bruise them a bit with their own iPhones."

"And choke them a bit with their cravats." The couple's banter feels almost like foreplay.

Tim looks disturbed. "But we can't give them date-rape trauma inside the venue."

"True," says Tessa. "We'd have to get them all the way to the park."

Ziggy's intimacy with the nightclub surprises everyone. "If we can get the three boys down into the basement parking lot, no one will find them there until the next day."

"She's right," says Tessa. "The parking lot will be empty—no one drives themselves to the formal."

Eamon speaks with rhapsodic delight. "And then they'll wake up the next morning in a cold concrete bunker!"

"Like a real date rape," marvels Tessa.

Ziggy's concern for Lance again accosts her. "But someone will need to stay upstairs with Lance while he vomits." By saying it, Ziggy apparently volunteers herself. The others give her cloying looks of gratitude. "Fine," she says. "I'll look after him."

Outside, it sounds like the formal is winding down, so the four of them agree to reconvene in thirty minutes at the after party. As she steps out through the fire door, Ziggy feels Tessa's fingers encircle her wrist.

"This is pure Haraway," says Tessa. "Traumatizing men into empathizing with women is exactly what she meant by feminist socialism."

"I'm going to film it," Ziggy warns her. "But none of us will be recognizable."

"Kitlers over all our faces?" Tessa is grinning.

"I hope this one makes a better video."

"It's going to go viral," Tessa says sweetly. "People *hate* private school boys."

Chapter 14

When they get to the nightclub, there is an enormous doorman propped on a stool at the entrance. He has the sad gaze of a large dog in a small apartment. Tonight he can't check IDs, can't even hand out wristbands. That job has gone to Cate, who sits beside him at a long table ticking names off a list and massaging her chemically tightened jaw. A small pile of the exclusive gold wristbands lie to her left. She doesn't appear to be giving any of them out. Ziggy feels lucky to get even a yellow one.

Inside, already a large group of girls are dancing in various states of formal undress. Some have swapped their floor-length gowns for tube tops. Others remain cumbersomely frocked but now in sparkly Converse or fun-loving fluoro ballet slippers. Ziggy is excited to be here, newly refriended and with thrilling purpose. At the bar, she sees that the cocktails are themed: Pink Pussycats for the girls and Blue Bloods for the boys. Ziggy imagines this is one of Cate's heteronormative flourishes. But she is grateful. The deep blue will nicely disguise the ayahuasca's purple.

Tessa and Eamon find Ziggy at the bar. The four of them squish together, palms open under the countertop. Tim hands out the pills. He assigns each of them a boy, identifying him by his pocket square. The idea is to shadow the victim, waiting for the moment a Blue Blood goes unattended. Lance's friends are all drinking the designated boys' beverage, making it impossible for them to accidentally drug their girlfriends. Although, spotting the Cates, Ziggy sees that the girls aren't even drinking cocktails. They have established a small circle on the dance floor, from where Kate pumps a single, communal water bottle. Their orbiting jaws and buggy eyes make it obvious that they have taken MDMA. Ziggy watches them dance, sprayed waves bouncing in the strobey air. They are having so much tightly curated fun. Even Lex looks utterly blissful—her eyes roll back as she shimmies her shoulders, mouth agape—high, it seems, on the perks of straight, cis-normative friendship.

Now Tessa slinks away toward Little Matty, while Eamon skips off after Declan. Tim is taking Toby, and Ziggy, of course, has treated herself to Lance. Tim squeezes her hand.

"It's going to be hilarious," he promises.

Ziggy is moved by her friend's sentiment. Considering that most of her sexual fantasies are about powerful Aryan men, it is humbling to think she has helped Tim access his queer sense of humor.

Ziggy remains beside the bar. After a few minutes, Lance appears at the opposite end by the register, clicking for the bartender's attention. Ziggy moves quickly toward him, sliding in casually beside his cream blazer. While Lance stares impatiently ahead, Ziggy studies the familiar contours of his profile. She admires his dimple—the perfectly placed indent that makes him seem designed, touched by God's fountain pen. Being this close to Lance sends the blood thumping through her ears. Ziggy isn't sure she can do this. When the bartender passes him his drink, Lance turns and looks straight at her. His eyes hold hers with gleaming interest, and for a moment it seems he might think she's cute. A dense heat roils through her body. Ziggy would absolutely let him finger her in the bathroom like a normal girl. Then she notices that Lance's gaze is askew; he isn't actually looking at Ziggy's face; he's staring at the camera. Checking his hair in the lens's reflection. For a moment, Ziggy disappears. She watches the scene with cool astral detachment as Lance's narcissism continues unabated back on Earth. And then she sees her chance. Ziggy tilts her head up and Lance's eyes follow it. While he watches himself, she slides her hand low along the bar, finds his tumbler, and tips the bottle into the blue froth. Then she turns away, taking Lance's image with her. She doesn't feel even remotely bad.

Ziggy meets her friends back at a booth in the club's front corner. Everyone has been successful, even Tessa, who had to join Little Matty on the dance floor and get gently groped. The four of them sip soda water as they watch their victims drinking in the adjacent booth. Minutes later, there is a demented squealing from the dance floor, and then a sudden ambush of girls to the elevator. The exodus to the VIP room has begun. As anticipated, Lance and his cronies are boycotting the celebrity autograph-signing session, preferring to stay petulantly in their seats. Ziggy and her friends listen in as the four boys mock the action hero's last three sequels and the strange, hemmed puff of his surgically altered face. "He's starting to look like bad origami," quips Lance, and Ziggy almost laughs. His friends find this disproportionately funny; Little Matty yowls and slaps his giant hand on the table, disturbing the drinks and swishing Blue Blood everywhere. At this, Toby and Declan throw their heads back, howling in an unwieldy splay of limbs all across the upholstery.

"The Temazepam is kicking in," whispers Tim.

Tessa and Eamon look distraught. Ziggy feels it too: the boys' degeneration is violent and distressing to watch. She sees Declan's arm slur along the tabletop, and has a trembling need to dissolve into the ether.

"What did the girls give you losers?" Lance teases his friends. "Horse tranquilizers?"

The boys just laugh, hugging and slapping each other in a slow-motion ballet of aggressive mateship. Lance edges away, reviled by their sloppiness.

"Who wants another bottle of aqua?" he says to the masculinity disintegrating all around him. The boys murmur their appreciation and Lance sets off across the room. Ziggy watches him strut, still alarmingly sober. Then just before the bar he stops, blinks up randomly at the ceiling, and continues. Now a second wave of panic eclipses the first, turning Ziggy into an insensate machine of pure action.

"You guys need to go," she says nodding in Lance's direction. Her friends turn to watch as he reaches the bar and becomes deeply fascinated by a jar of lemon slivers. "Get the boys downstairs before Lance starts vomiting."

Tim and Eamon leap up. But Tessa sits frowning at the three sweaty heads lolling back against their seats. The pretext for getting these boys to follow them into the elevator now seems ludicrously flawed. "I don't think they'll care that their girlfriends are downstairs waiting to have sex with them."

"Maybe we just say they're waiting to take them home to sleep?" Tim's suggestion is met with more uncertainty. Then Declan's head hits the table.

"Go!" orders Ziggy, and her friends rally.

While they close in around the boys, Ziggy sets off toward Lance. Approaching him, she can see that Lance is very slightly swaying. His face is pale. His focus is intense and nearsighted, as if he is doing a difficult mental calculation in the air just beyond his nose. He jerks forward, clutching his belly, and then quickly cups a hand to his mouth. It is the sudden mad bulge of his eyes that makes Ziggy regret everything. She imagines a whole Boschian underworld storming up his esophagus, a tiny army installed by her, and she shudders with a powerful, regurgitative reflex. Or maybe she is just about to sympathy vomit. Lance glances down into his palms then starts bolting toward the bathroom.

Ziggy waits outside for several minutes. Other boys hurry out, noses pinched, nauseated and groaning. Ziggy reasons that she must now act not just as Lance's bathroom guard, but as his spiritual guardian. She stands to the side, steeling herself for the role. Despite her remorse, Ziggy still feels the moment's theatrical edge, the plucky rush that might chaperone a girl through her first date. When the bathroom is empty, Ziggy steps in and locks the door. The stench is evil. The sharp vinegar of vomit cuts through the deeper, sodden cling of piss. There is only one closed stall door. Ziggy inhales deeply through her mouth.

"Are you okay in there?"

There is a long, pointy silence followed by a tremulous intake of breath. "I'm scared."

Ziggy's heart swoons with compassion. She leans against the door and speaks to it gently. "What are you scared of?"

"My mind," says Lance. "Something's wrong with it."

"You know," Ziggy says kindly, "all minds are delusional and cause suffering."

Lance groans in psychic pain.

"It's okay, it's okay," she coos. "I'm just saying you don't have to listen to it."

"But I have an HSC exam on Tuesday," Lance whines. "Oh God, what's happening to me?"

"It's just chemicals," says Ziggy. "Aren't you guys all on drugs?"

"They are," Lance whimpers. "But I didn't have any."

"Well, maybe you did. Accidentally."

"Oh God."

"Try not to focus on the thoughts." In her own voice Ziggy starts to hear the soft strains of her mother's. "They just create more negativity."

"Then what should I focus on?"

"Sensations," she says, blushing. "Try to stay focused on your body."

"Okay," Lance says studiously. "I'm focusing on my heart and it's beating really fast."

"That's okay. That just means you're alive. That's good. Stay focused on your heart."

Lance gets quiet. Then Ziggy hears a sniffle.

"What's happening now?"

"I feel sad," says Lance. "So incredibly . . . sad." He sobs.

Ziggy's heart tilts steeply toward him. "Why do you feel so sad?"

"I don't know. I just do." Lance sighs wearily into the toilet bowl. "I think it's because I'm about to graduate." His voice quavers with feeling. "And I'm scared to leave school."

"Of course you are," Ziggy says tenderly. "Your whole identity is there. Now you have to make a new one."

Lance sniffles again. Ziggy has never been so nice to anyone. She didn't know this sweetness lived inside her, that she possessed an EMT's talent for nurture under duress. The world seems neat and small and toylike. Ziggy wants to hold Lance's hand. "Can you open the door?"

There is a pause and then the toilet flushes. Slowly, the door peels open. Lance looks at Ziggy with glassy pink eyes. "Am I in the female restroom?"

"No," she says. "They're gender neutral."

Lance seems relieved. They stare at each other. "Oh God," he says. "I feel so strange."

There is a loud knock at the door. Ziggy has a second to decide whether or not to abandon Lance to the chaos of the after party and join her friends. She takes his hand. "I think you should come downstairs with me," she says. "You'll be safer there."

Lance is obedient. He hooks his arm around hers and allows Ziggy to lead him out through the door and swiftly to the elevator. The club is now mostly drunken boys swaying in small dejected clusters, but Ziggy still bolts, her head hot and imploding as she flees with her charge. In the elevator she can feel Lance leaning into her shoulder, giving her his weight like a sleepy child. Inches from her own, Ziggy can sense the mad, crackling activity of his brain. She can't imagine how they will keep Lance safe for the next several hours, but Ziggy knows that they need to.

She finds the others just behind a large pillar near the ticket machines. Lance's friends have been laid out in a line on the concrete floor. The other three squat busily around them. The boys' peaceful somnolence is jarred by gaping jaws and hands twisted back at unnatural angles. When Lance sees his friends, he screams. "They're dead!"

Tessa spins around. "They're sleeping," she refutes. "The pills they took were smacky." Tim and Eamon stare up anxiously over Tessa's shoulder. The three of them shooting Ziggy looks of horror and betrayal.

"What are you all doing down here?" Lance asks Ziggy's friends, seeming to include the ticket machines.

Tessa lies with impressive fluency. "We came to smoke a joint," she says, "and heard the boys passing out."

"And who *are* you people?" Lance says rudely, scanning from Tim's shamanic belt to Eamon's orange flares and finally settling in grim disgust on Tessa's garish Elizabethan frock. "Where did you come from?"

"Our mothers' vaginas," Tessa spits back.

"Or *one* of our mothers' vaginas," appends Tim.

Lance turns helplessly to Ziggy. She is touched and then quickly torn between this startling new allegiance and the other ones. "Lance isn't feeling well," she tells her friends. "I thought he could join us?"

"Join us while we do *what?*" With her eyebrows, Tessa appears to be communicating the entire history of female oppression.

Ziggy thinks quick. "A sharing circle?"

"Wait," says Tessa. "This is a *date rapist*. I'm not sharing anything with him."

"A date rapist?" Lance scoffs. "Date rape is for betas. A real man enjoys the hunt."

"The hunt?" roars Tessa. "Do you have female heads mounted on your walls?"

Lance flinches in disgust; Ziggy wishes he was still being vulnerable.

"Guys," she says, "I think we should just sit in a circle."

"No," says Tessa, rising and dragging Eamon up violently with her. "Not with *him*."

Ziggy panics. "Lance," she says, "I think we'd better go back upstairs."

The vicious veneer shatters like bones in his face; Lance looks suddenly soft and pudgy and tearful. He blinks desperately. "I need to close my eyes."

"You can close them," Ziggy indulges him.

Lance squeezes shut his eyes then drops to his haunches.

Ziggy goes down after him. "What is it?" she says frantically.

"Patterns . . ." he moans. "I can't make them stop."

"That's okay," she says, glancing up nervously at her friends. Everyone stares back, bewildered.

"What do the patterns look like?" she asks Lance, stroking his head.

"Like waves," he says in a small voice. "Like the ocean."

"That's nice," says Ziggy. "Why don't you just watch the waves rising and falling?"

Lance nods, wiping his nose. His head rises and falls minutely with his gentle inner tide.

"Good," says Ziggy, caressing his arm—ignoring the giddy heat at her fingertips. "Just keep watching the waves and enjoying the sensations. Feel the sun beating down warmly on the crown of your head. . . ."

From Tessa and Eamon, Ziggy hears suppressed snorting. She has never given a guided visualization before but has heard enough of Ruth's to get the basic idea. Part of her is embarrassed by this and another part turns toward Lance with powerful, uterine heat. He seems to be calming down. Ziggy smiles up at Tim, anxiously fingering the cockles on his belt. Then the elevator dings.

"Ziii-gy!" Kate's voice rushes shrilly into the cavernous space. "Laaa-ance!"

Ziggy can hear kitten heels approaching. Someone upstairs must have seen her. She looks up at her friends, the three of them paralyzed in sharp relief against the concrete wall. There is nowhere to hide. Ziggy spins around just as the Cates and Lex come peering around the pillar. The girls emerge in shocked, arm-linked animosity, their hairdos haloed by the industrial fluorescence.

Cate's voice drops straight through Ziggy's stomach. "What. The. Actual. Fuck."

The girls break apart, rushing to inspect their dates.

"Matty!" yells Kate and kicks him lightly in the ribs. Cate shakes her boyfriend's shoulders and whimpers his name. It is hard to know if she is genuinely distressed or just pretending she's in a movie. The MDMA is making Fliss move over Declan with the jerky lyricism of a contemporary dancer. It appears she is trying to wake him with the whipping motion of her hair. Lex watches Lance cross-legged on the floor, swaying and gaping at the ceiling.

Fliss whips her head back, and blinks up at Tessa. "Are they sleeping?" she asks hopefully.

"We think they accidentally roofied themselves," says Tessa, brilliant as ever.

"What?" Kate snaps, her face wizening with deep sarcasm. "Why would they want to date-rape us if we're already having sex with them?"

Kate makes a good point, but Ziggy is sure the Cates are not that naïve. These girls are familiar with the eternal power struggle between heteronormative Man and Woman. Ziggy runs with Tessa's theory.

"They probably put the drugs in the wrong water bottle," Ziggy says. "Weren't you all sharing a bottle of Mount Franklin?"

Kate takes a menacing step toward her. "So what?"

"So, so were the boys—Lance bought them one." Ziggy gives him an affectionate nudge. "Didn't you, Lance?"

"Aqua?" he says serenely. "Yes, please."

Kate eyes her brother anxiously. "Lance, what happened?"

He shrugs. "Smacky pills?"

"What's wrong with my brother?" Kate glares murderously at Ziggy, her jaw rotating at alarming speed.

Now Ziggy falters. "I'm not sure," she says, glancing around for help. She sees Lance lick his cuff link. "Maybe someone put acid in his Blue Blood?"

Kate's "Ha!" cracks across the parking lot like a skimmed stone. "So Lance's drink was spiked and the other three accidentally roofied themselves and you four just happened to be walking past?" Kate's hands meet her hips at the tulle spray of skirt—giving her the look of a furious human pom-pom. In their sheer formal gowns, the other girls rise like vengeful ghosts above their dates. Their euphoric high quickly slips into dippy hysteria.

"What did you *do* to them?" Cate rasps, grabbing Fliss and squeezing her like a teddy.

"Nothing!" Ziggy pleads, inexplicably, with Lex. Her old friend hangs back strangely quiet, chewing on her lip.

"Oh my God!" screams Kate. "The drama freaks were date-raping our boyfriends!"

"Your boyfriends were trying to date-rape you!" Tessa shouts back.

"What part of boyyfriend," slurs Cate, "don't you understand?"

"Rapists!" yells Kate.

Tim looks helplessly at Ziggy as he gnaws on the yo-yo string pulled taut from his pocket. She feels the soft tug of fidelity to Lance, but promptly defeats it.

"Wait!" Ziggy cries, whipping out her phone. "I've got proof!"

She holds the phone up, scrolling frenetically to the clip. The Cates step over their boyfriends and shuffle in toward Ziggy. The video plays, and as Lance's voice comes barking through the speakers, he giggles then lays out flat and absorbed on the floor. The Cates glare at him, gasping and squealing "ohmyfuckinggod" at every pause in the dialogue. "Yielding corpse," Lance recites after himself. "Hairy, unwashed girlfriends," he whispers, enthralled. The rape eulogy is even more offensive than Ziggy remembered. With impressive economy, Lance managed to include sexism, sexual assault, white imperialism, and Islamophobia, and his tart delivery added a nasty classist after-kick. Cate and Fliss shake their heads, grimly comprehending their boyfriends' misogyny, while Lex growls a sickened "white supremacist," then starts typing feverishly into her phone. Now Ziggy feels bad for throwing Lance to these furious, albeit infrequent, feminists. And then, as the clip finishes, Lance again begins to giggle.

"What the fuck is wrong with you?" Kate yells at her brother, hiking her skirt and stomping violently toward him.

Lance ducks away from her. "It was a joke," he says, eyes aglow with mischief. Ziggy almost believes him.

"What kind of fucked-up joke is that?" Lex hurls her corsage at his head. "And 'the caliphate has it right'?"

"That was a character!" Lance says with a deranged smile. "We're all just playing *characters*!"

Ziggy can't help feeling, uneasily, that this is her influence.

"It's not a character," Kate shouts. "You're a sexist!"

"I'm only *playing* a sexist!" Lance cries, gesturing to his fallen comrades. "Just like them." He grins, his eyes rounding. "None of this is even real."

"Whatever, you freak," Kate screeches. "Should I tell everyone how you punched our old nanny in the vagina?"

At this the Cates erupt into hysterical cackling. Kate makes a splashy flick of her skirt, enjoying the attention. "It's true. He used to whinge to Mum: 'Analisa pulls her chair too close to mii-iine.'"

Cate and Fliss collapse together laughing, and even Lex chuckles softly against the pillar. Tessa also seems pleased with the sharp swerve toward their new target.

"What else did he do?" she coaxes the loose-lipped Fairfax sibling.

"Oh, lots of things," says Kate, bunching the organza up around her hips as if preparing to squat over her brother's head. "He spat juice in the maids' faces, but they were so scared of our mother they just laughed and called him 'funny boy.'"

"Our mother," Lance repeats, ". . . is perfect."

Now the laughter is unanimous and mean. Ziggy crouches down beside her baffled confidante.

"What do you mean 'perfect'?" she asks him.

Lance stares straight ahead, breathless at the vision unfolding before him. "She's a hologram," he says, "just an outline of a human being . . . with a little clutch purse . . . a woman."

"Uh, that's called misogyny!" bays Tessa.

Eamon glowers at his former tormentor. "Just because you love your mother doesn't mean you don't hate women."

"He only loves her because our mother is obsessed with him," Kate announces, reclaiming her mantle as primary persecutor. "She's always touching his arms, and telling him how muscly he is."

Ziggy wants to pat poor Lance's shoulder, but manages to restrain herself. "It sounds like mother enmeshment," she says sympathetically.

"What the hell does that mean?" sneers Kate.

"That she treats Lance like her husband."

Kate's eyes go poppy. "Yes!" she squeals. "She texts him all day long, and if there's a spider in the house, she always gets Lance to kill it!"

Ziggy is filled with a strange, maternal warmth for both brother and sister. She knows the family dynamic well. Lance's mother might be perfect but her engulfing love has made him revile the female body.

"Lance," says Ziggy, "is your mother the most beautiful woman in the world?"

He gives a dreamy nod.

"But does her breath also smell funny?"

"Sometimes," he admits.

Kate grins wildly, and then points a fierce, anointing finger. "Ziggy's like a therapist!"

The others agree in similarly shrill tones of delight. It seems they all want Kate to have therapy.

"Tell us more about Lance and my mother," she commands, her jaw struggling to keep pace with her tongue.

Tim has raised his hand. "Sorry to interrupt," he says, "but I don't think you're meant to blame the mother."

"That's right," says Ziggy. "You can only ask the mother how she feels."

Kate rustles her skirts in frustration. "But how can we ask her?"

"Simple," says Lance in a distant, mystical voice. "She's right here." He looks out across the gray expanse of parking lot.

"Where?" says Ziggy gently.

"She's everywhere."

"Ask her if she wants to have sex with her son," teases Kate.

Lance ignores her. He listens. "There," he says. "She's in the dripping."

"The dripping?" Ziggy looks anxiously at Tim.

"There."

Everybody quiets. A soft tinkling at the far wall. Either a leaking pipe or trickling rain. Doubtfully Lance's mum.

"Why don't you get someone to channel Mrs. Fairfax?" Tim suggests.

"What are you two," Kate says, "witches?"

"It's called a constellation," Tessa snaps. "You can ask dead people and Nazis why they were murderers and rapists."

Tim speaks kindly to Kate. "If you want to know why your mum favors Lance over you, Ziggy can just ask her."

"Ask a drip?"

"Ask your ancestors," says Tessa, already arranging Tim and Eamon on either side of her. "Everyone make a circle."

The girls are surprisingly obedient. Kate plops down onto Matty's rump, surrendering to the vague promise of psychic matricide, as well as an intense desire to vigorously massage her own scalp. She scratches luxuriously beside Cate and Fliss's giggly human pretzel. Lex squats on their other side. Tessa quickly scurries around to close up the circle, and Tim sits crosslegged next to Ziggy. Her three friends smile up eagerly. It can't be that hard. You just get a few people to stand inside the circle and talk about their feelings. The game plays itself.

"Come on," says Kate. "I want to know why my mother still cuts Lance's toenails."

"Okay," says Ziggy, buoyed by peer esteem, adrenaline, and the knowledge that her camera is recording. "So who wants to play Mrs. Fairfax?"

Fliss leaps up, disturbing Cate's repose and more grievously, her chignon. "I'll do it!" Fliss squeaks.

"Thank you, Fliss," says Ziggy, her voice suddenly low and remote as if it is coming from her feet. "Mrs. Fairfax, would you please come and stand beside your son."

Fliss swishes over to Lance's side.

"Now close your eyes," Ziggy instructs. "And tell us how you feel."

Fliss squeezes her lids closed and sways on her feet. "I feel love," she says, smiling.

"That's just the drugs," heckles Kate.

"Hang on," says Ziggy. "Lance, how do you feel sitting beside your mum?"

He rolls his head back sensually against her dress. "Like I don't have a body," he says. "Like we share the same skin . . . and everything else is just . . . molecules."

"Good!" Ziggy's neck tingles. "That's your boundary issue."

"Oh my God, gross," says Kate. "Like she's a child molester?"

"No," says Ziggy, "she's just too affectionate, which makes Lance feel engulfed."

"He looks happy," says Kate, grimacing at her brother.

"He said he feels like he doesn't have a body. That's called engulfment."

Tim chimes in softly. "Which is why he says all girls smell fishy."

"It isn't his fault," says Ziggy. The language spurts expertly from her mouth. "Lance is just the Oedipal victor because your mum hates your dad."

Kate puffs up, red and demonic. "I have the best dad in the world!"

"That's because you have father issues."

Kate's friends break into vicious jeers of "Daddy's Girl."

"I'm sorry my dad looks like Harrison Ford, you bitches!"

"Enough," says Ziggy. "We're here to resolve Lance's mother issues. Try to stay focused."

Tim gives her a gentle nudge of approval. The others settle.

"Okay," says Ziggy, regaining her gravitas. "I need someone to play the grandma."

"Me!" squeals Cate, bounding up and into the circle, her dress trailing across Little Matty's face.

Ziggy requests the grandma's maiden name and then tells Mrs. Potts to please stand beside her daughter, Mrs. Fairfax.

"Mrs. Fairfax," Ziggy says to Fliss. "How does it feel being beside your mother?"

It is immediately obvious that Fliss is having a negative feeling, and that she doesn't want to offend their group's punitive leader by sharing it. Ziggy watches Fliss fidget, her forehead gleaming with sweat. Defeated, Fliss mumbles, "I guess I feel stuck."

"What about now?" says Cate and pokes her in the rib.

Fliss dodges sideways, stumbling over onto Lance's crouched back. He wraps his hands around her shins.

"Don't be afraid," Lance says, squeezing. "We're just quarks, dancing in a field."

This instigates riotous laughter, and Cate takes the opportunity to attack the mother-son tableau, poking Fliss and flicking Lance with her tulle train. Ziggy watches, unamused, as her constellation quickly comes apart. Cate has not dropped into the universal grandmother, or else Grandma Potts is a terrible bully. Watching Fliss stand adhesed to her son while fending off the jabbing matriarch, Ziggy is reminded of the heavier women in Ruth's workshops; the ones who use the word "stuck" when describing the bodily sensation that subdues their life force and hinders them from routine exercise. In constellation theory, it seems *stuck* is synonymous with mothers who demand too much and immobilize their daughters with self-loathing. Ziggy has watched these participants return late from lunch and blame the women who bore them. Observing Fliss, Ziggy's brain fizzes with high, cosmic purpose.

"Kate," she says, "is your mum a bit chubby?"

Kate wants to be offended, but she also wants to hate her mother. The maternal bond is, as Ziggy predicted, very weak. "Yes," says Kate. "And so is my grandma."

"Gross," whines Cate. "Can I play one of the cousins?"

"Get her to play the granddad," Tim suggests.

"Why don't you play the granddad, pajama pants?"

Enlightened, Tim ignores Cate. "Ziggy," he says. "I really think you need to start blaming the patriarchy now."

"Uh-oh!" says Cate. "Here comes the feminist dissectionality!"

"No, he's right," says Ziggy. "If all the women are chubby, we probably need to talk to a grandfather."

"Grandfathers!" cries Lance, releasing his mother, and rocking forward in a tight, contemplative ball. "But grandfathers are just vapor," he says, brows knit in astonishment. "And grandmothers are tetrahedrons. Mums and Dads and even my penis has zero reality."

The group laughter bounces around them like a violent hurling of basketballs. Ziggy notices that Lex has doubled over in a fit of giggling, but she barely collects herself before she is once again typing giddily into her phone.

"Who are you texting?" Ziggy says, reaching for curious but falling just short of annoyed.

Lex doesn't look up. "I'm not," she says. "I'm just writing these lyrics before I forget them."

"Our lyrics?"

"My lyrics."

Lex is making fun of them. Ziggy's body feels light, a faint heat burning at the edges. Like a hologram, like Mrs. Fairfax the outline of a human being. Buried within the floating layers is a bright flint of pain.

Now freed from Lance's grip, Fliss pleads with Ziggy. "Can I play Grandpa Potts?"

"No," barks Cate. "None of us are playing an old man."

Lex's voice lobs violently into the air. "Can you please stop being such a diva?"

Cate's face quivers and falls. Ziggy feels a weird glitch of sympathy.

Lex bounces up, unperturbed, onto her feet. "I'll play the old white man," she says, smirking to herself. Then, as Lex steps in beside her proxy wife, Cate flinches.

"What was that?" Ziggy asks her.

"She scared me," Cate says innocently.

"I didn't do anything," says Lex.

"I know," says Cate. "You just *looked* scary."

Ziggy can feel where this is going. The girls don't understand psychic energy. That Grandma Potts was probably afraid of her husband. They are instead going to make this about skin color. Ziggy could start a fight between them. She could expose the Cates, at last, as racist. But she wants the constellation to work. Ziggy wants everyone to be friends.

"You felt fear," she tells Cate, "because Grandma Potts was probably her husband's sexual slave."

Lex squints disbelievingly, but Cate seems intrigued. "So why was the grandma mean to her daughter?"

"Because she's fat," says Kate.

"No," Eamon says gruffly. "Because women have to hurt one another in order to survive within a system of patriarchal oppression."

Tessa kisses her boyfriend's slender bicep, and Ziggy feels happy for them. Eamon really is Tessa's perfect formal partner.

"Fine," says Kate, "but my mother is still a bitch."

"Yes," says Ziggy, "because *her* mother is a bitch."

Kate looks confused. "Hey," she says, "*your* grandmother is a bitch."

"I know!" Ziggy cries triumphantly. "Because the patriarchy made her that way!"

Kate stalls, processing. Then she looks across the circle to Lance. Her eyes are suddenly wet. "Yes!" she screams. "You should never, *ever* tell a girl her farts smell like sulfur!"

Kate bursts into tears, and the other Cates rush to their friend. They huddle in around her, hugging her and stroking her hair. Ziggy hears Fliss consoling Kate: "You don't even fart."

Lance looks genuinely sorry. He rises and wobbles toward his sister. "I'm sorry, Katie," he says. "It's my farts that smell like sulfur, not yours."

But Kate isn't done. "And when I try to tell you some good gossip, you always say you don't care."

"I'm sorry." Lance's eyes are dewey. "You know I care; I love gossip."

The siblings stare at each other intensely. "Fine," says Kate. "But when the drugs wear off, you have to stay nice."

"I promise," says Lance. "But now I really need to be in a small enclosed space." He blinkers his hands at the sides of his face. "Lex," he says, finally noticing his girlfriend. "Where's my car?"

"We took a limo," she says coolly.

Lance shakes his head chaotically, as if to rid himself of this inconvenient fact. When he stops, it seems to have worked. "No," he says, pointing to the lone vehicle parked in the station's far corner. "There it is."

Lex shrugs, and returns to her screen.

"Is it his?" Ziggy asks Kate, watching as Lance rattles the back door handle and slinks inside. She can vaguely recall the car being a blue BMW.

"Looks like it," says Kate, though she is not looking at Lance, but at her supine boyfriend. "And what about these little creeps?"

"They're like Lance," says Tim. "You have to forgive them, too."

"But they tried to rape us," says Cate.

Ziggy flusters. "*Symbolically* maybe."

Lex looks up from her phone. "Just because you have a needy mother," she says, "doesn't mean you get to call other women sluts."

"Exactly," says Tessa. "Even if your mother actually is a slut."

"But the idea is to have empathy for everyone," Ziggy says weakly. "And acknowledge everybody's pain."

"That's very poetic," says Cate. "But they still tried to rape us."

So the constellation was *partially* successful—the girls have love for each other, just not the opposite sex. The next step in Shuni's process would be to make a joke of feminism so that the Cates stop identifying with it so much. But the feeling among their unlikely group is suddenly so intimate, Ziggy really doesn't want them to splinter. She watches Cate pull an eyeliner pencil from her clutch purse as she straddles Toby's prostrate body. Then Ziggy joins the communal cheer as a gigantic penis takes green, glittery shape across his forehead.

Next, Kate rushes to Matty, mounting him and sketching a daisy chain of dicks around his nose; while Fliss gets to work on a detailed bouquet of vaginas across Declan's chest. Ziggy admires her vision, how Fliss unbuttons his shirt to fit the clump of tampon strings tied at the bottom in a bow. Lex stands off typing to the side, immortalizing them all as feminists, or just vengeful girlfriends.

Now Eamon and Tessa step forward and, in a moment of sweet, awkward fraternity, they are invited to join the proceedings. Ziggy sees Tessa smile at Cate and Cate arrange her face into something benevolently neutral. Kate even gives Ziggy a grim nod of thanks. The world feels improved, more matriarchal. New friendships seem possible.

And then the traumatizing recommences. Eamon starts yanking down each of the boys' pants while Tim carefully musses their cravats. Ziggy can tell her friend is conflicted; his eyes dart around and he is clearly holding himself back from their frenzy. She squats down beside him.

"The boys won't remember anything," she says, squeezing his shoulder.

"Like a date rape . . ." Tim's voice is small and haunted.

Ziggy knows she should have sympathy, but she doesn't want to stop. The date rape's traumatic reversal is exactly what Ziggy wanted to capture: the paradigm shift, the punch line. That sweet spot at the center of a joke where both things are true—the good and the uncomfortably amoral—and for one moment, all selves are transcended and all beings unite.

"Tim," she says, "you can't worry so much about other people's feelings. We did a good thing for humanity! Date rapists getting date-raped!" She squeezes his shoulder harder.

"All right," he mutters, returning to his tepid violations. Ziggy considers how she might offer further comfort but is abruptly relieved by Tessa's summons.

"Hey, Ziggy!" Tessa balances Little Matty's vast thigh on her palms. "Help me with this?"

Ziggy dashes over, then shuffles in beside her, and together they haul the gargantuan limb over Toby's slim hips. Then they cup Matty's palms to his friend's exposed bum cheeks. And now everyone starts whipping off belts and ties and cummerbunds, repurposing them as torture instruments. Soon the boy-cluster resembles a homophobic conga line from a classical hellscape. Ziggy rises over it for a sweeping aerial.

She doesn't hear the elevator ding, but Ziggy does feel the air change as someone steps out into the parking station. She cranes her neck and spots him—small, suited, in a hurry. Fliss also glances up, seeing the man and then squinting fiercely at his profile.

"Hey!" she screams. "It's him!"

Everyone looks up at the tiny man now jogging toward the black BMW.

"Lance!" Kate squeals, more as entertainment than as warning to her brother.

They all scramble to their feet, subdued by wicked, shrieking laughter. Eamon lunges toward the man as he shoots past.

"Wait!" he calls after the action hero. "Stop!"

But he doesn't stop. And he is unsurprisingly fast. The man has sprinted from crashing planes and falling skyscrapers without moving a single muscle in his face. He ducks into the car just as his pursuers begin hobbling forward in their frocks.

"It's like that scene in the last movie!" Tessa cries. "Lance is the sexy Serbian journalist!"

But the seasoned escape artist doesn't pause to check the rear seat of his vehicle. The BMW spins back, corrects, and flies away up the ramp. Once more, their little group dissolves into delicious, loopy cackling.

Ziggy turns back to the boy-centerfold, and feels terribly excited to share her footage with the internet. Then she remembers Tim. As the others begin to speculate on the unfolding car ride, Ziggy drags her friend away behind the pillar.

"Don't get mad," she says, "but the camera recorded everything."

Tim's face falls. "I thought it was just part of your outfit?"

Ziggy grins impishly. Tim's yo-yo flies out of his pocket, the red panic of his conscience always jumping between them.

"But if you show people," he says, "the boys will know who drugged them."

"I've done this before," says Ziggy. "I can easily disguise all of our identities."

"But the GoPro films things from inside a fishbowl! Everyone will know it was you!"

"I can do a lens adjustment in postproduction!"

The yo-yo hits the floor and licks sickly across it. "And what if the boys recognize themselves? Won't they feel dehumanized?"

"That was the whole point!"

"Oh dear." Tim stares ahead, squirming with anguish, as if only now realizing what they have done. "I guess I figured they would wake up thinking they'd had a spontaneous gay moment."

A small space in Ziggy's heart cracks open for overture. "I can cover up their faces if you really want me to?"

Tim crosses his arms. "I thought the purpose of the GoPro was just to be an objective witness?"

"That's what making a movie is . . ." Ziggy's voice whittles with insincerity.

"Movies aren't objective," he says bluntly. "And anyway, this is more like a snuff film."

He gives her one final chastising look, and then walks back around the pillar. Ziggy follows glumly behind. Lex is now standing at the ticket machines, mumbling to herself. Ziggy hears snippets. Something about fake white girls and their molly humanity, and rich white boys with their heirloom Rolexes, keeping patriarchal time. She hears her own name, and Tessa's too. Ziggy wonders if Lex is always laughing at her friends. If this is how she tolerates them, and why. Ziggy is suddenly self-conscious; a strange sense of feeling naked in her clothes, both seen and unseen. An outline. She feels a mix of awe and anger toward the aspiring rapper. For having her own mysterious life-world. For dehumanizing all of them, and making Ziggy feel like maybe she really should delete her footage.

Hovering over the boys, the rest of their group now seems restless.

"Should we go back upstairs?" suggests Tessa.

"Totally," says Cate. "It's our year-ten formal; we should be dancing our fucking faces off."

WHEN THEY GET THERE, Ziggy is surprised to see that the dance floor is still packed. Every type of Kandara girl is represented. Goths dance next to rugby jerseys; bare thighs grind beside someone who thought it would be funny to wear a panda suit. It isn't exactly queer, but it is diverse in its details. A charm bracelet jangles in the air, strung with elements from the periodic table; a chubby girl in a tight white onesie body-rolls with abandon like an endless stream of pouring milk. When Ziggy looks over, Eamon is teaching Tim to moonwalk. It seems they are going to be friends, which might mean the same for her and Tessa. Disappointingly, the male date rape doesn't appear to have brought Lex any closer; her wounds must be more profound. Still, something is stopping Ziggy from saying sorry. Some combination of shame, hurt, and a sense of futility. That the sorry will be ongoing, a mantra that defines her forever in Lex's mind. She knows it's a small-hearted response, but that's all the space Ziggy feels she has been given.

As the dancing gets wilder, her peers no longer seem so tribal and exclusive. Their bold body rolls and vivid gyrations make them look both distinct and unified in their chaos. It reminds Ziggy of something the guru once said about teenagers. That they were hyper-present: always on the brink of transformation. Like old people, her mother might say. Teenagers fill themselves up, and old people let themselves go. Like Tessa said: all stories try to solve this inner emptiness. Like Shuni said. Only in the flux, in stupid dance moves and other rare moments beyond self, does Ziggy feel she belongs to the world. In those flashes of presence. That pure, eternal place where Ziggy will one day meet her grandmother in Bondi Junction.

As she dances, Ziggy notices the vast sky through the cube's tall windows. Its deep indigo glows like a notion. An unknown entity beckoning, as if the future itself was there just beyond the glass. Ziggy does a little spin and the GoPro wonks on her head, silly as a loose tooth. She slips it off.

Acknowledgments

Thank you to my agent, Susan Golomb; my editor, Megan Lynch; and her assistant, Emma Dries. Thank you also to my "aunt," Ziva Freiman, whose generosity, support, and friendship made so much of this work possible. Thank you to my New York family, Jonathan and Hannah Katz, and my Australian one. Especially my brother, Paul, and my parents, John and Jutka, for all they have given me; most importantly their love, support, and a sense of humor.

About the Author

Lexi Freiman is a fiction editor and a recent Columbia University MFA grad. She was a Center for Fiction Writing Fellow in 2013 and has published in *The Literary Review*. Before moving to New York, she was an actress with Australia's national Shakespeare company, where she performed roles such as Celia from *As You Like It*, Lady Capulet from *Romeo and Juliet*, and Thaisa from *Pericles*, all at the Sydney Opera House.